THE WORDS OF *CATH*

"One of the great moral crises of my l... ing of my first Communion. I took a dr... ingly, of course, for had it not been drilled into me that the Host must be received fasting, on the penalty of mortal sin?... I went through a ferocious struggle with my conscience, and all the while, I think, I knew the devil was going to prevail: I was going to take Communion, and only God and I would know the real facts."

— Mary McCarthy, *Memories of a Catholic Girlhood*

"The day Ann Cunningham told me the facts of life I decided to become a saint.... I draped myself in white curtains with a rope tied around my waist and practiced looking saintly. The saints I read about died defending their virginity, whatever that was. The dying I could handle but the mechanics of defense eluded me."

— Kay Hogan, "Of Saints and Other Things"

"We stand in the vestibule of St. Andrew's Church, digging into our purses for white lace handkerchiefs and bobby pins. 'Shit,' Karen mutters. 'I can't find it.' 'Here, use a Kleenex. My mother does.' 'This looks really stupid,' Karen says, laying the tissue on top of her teased and sprayed-until-stiff hair. We start to giggle, remember where we are. We've driven twenty miles to make our confessions so that the priest won't recognize our voices."

— Amber Coverdale Sumrall, "Last Confession"

AMBER COVERDALE SUMRALL is co-editor of *Women of the 14th Moon: Writings on Menopause, Touching Fire: Erotic Writings by Women,* and *Sexual Harassment: Women Speak Out.*

PATRICE VECCHIONE is a poet and founder of a Santa Cruz reading series, "In Celebration of the Muse." The editor of three books, including *Fault Lines: Children's Earthquake Poetry,* she teaches poetry to children and conducts writing workshops for women.

Catholic Girls

Edited by
**Amber Coverdale Sumrall
and Patrice Vecchione**

A PLUME BOOK

PLUME
Published by the Penguin Group
Penguin Books USA Inc., 375 Hudson Street,
New York, New York 10014, U.S.A.
Penguin Books Ltd, 27 Wrights Lane, London W8 5TZ, England
Penguin Books Australia Ltd, Ringwood, Victoria, Australia
Penguin Books Canada Ltd, 10 Alcorn Avenue, Toronto, Ontario, Canada M4V 3B2
Penguin Books (N.Z.) Ltd, 182–190 Wairau Road, Auckland 10, New Zealand
Penguin Books Ltd, Registered Offices: Harmondsworth, Middlesex, England

First published by Plume, an imprint of New American Library,
a division of Penguin Books USA Inc.

First Printing, October, 1992
10 9 8 7 6 5 4

Permissions to reprint these stories are listed on page 337.

REGISTERED TRADEMARK—MARCA REGISTRADA

LIBRARY OF CONGRESS CATALOGING IN PUBLICATION DATA:

Catholic girls / edited by Amber Coverdale Sumrall and Patrice Vecchione.
    p.   cm.
  ISBN 0-452-26842-7
  1. Women, Catholic—United States—Literary collections. 2. Catholics—United
States—Literary collections. 3. Girls—United States—Literary collections. 4. American
literature—Catholic authors. 5. American literature—Women authors. 6. American
literature—20th century.   I. Sumrall, Amber Coverdale.   II. Vecchione, Patrice.
PS509.W6C37   1992
810.8′09287′08822—dc20   92-53561
                                                                        CIP

PRINTED IN THE UNITED STATES OF AMERICA
Designed by Eve L. Kirch

PUBLISHER'S NOTE
These are works of fiction. Names, characters, places, and incidents either are
the product of the authors' imagination or are used fictitiously, and any resemblance to actual persons, living or dead, events, or locales is entirely
coincidental.

For our mothers: Mary Vandiver Park
and Peggy McCarthy Vecchione,
our first Catholic girls

Contents

Contents

Acknowledgments

To our agent, Charlotte Cecil Raymond, and our editor, Rosemary Ahern, we wish to express our deepest appreciation.

To our contributors—Catholic girls in thought, word, and deed—we extend our heartfelt thanks.

What would have been the effect upon religion if it had come to us through the minds of women? —Charlotte Perkins Gilman

If you bring forth what is within you, what you bring forth will save you. If you do not bring forth what is within you, what you do not bring forth will destroy you.
—St. Thomas, *The Gnostic Gospels*

It is the creative potential itself in human beings that is the image of God.
—Mary Daly

Introduction

We were at the Grey Whale Bar in the northern California coastal town of Mendocino, putting down a little scotch. It was mid-September; most of the tourists had already left. We had come here for a few days of relaxation before the rush of autumn. Looking out beyond the headlands, we began to reflect upon the years of our friendship, the differences and similarities of our childhoods, our common religious beginnings. We had never before discussed in depth the influence that our Italian Catholic and Irish Catholic backgrounds have had upon our lives, our writing, our love of ritual and ceremony, our rebelliousness. Although we both left the church as teenagers, at least in spirit, years later we are still affected by the intensity of its force. Our Catholic girl selves, like the vigil flame at the altar, live in us always.

We told stories to one another as the sun disappeared into the ocean, leaving the sky streaked with hues of orange and lavender. "Some nights I only pretended to pray, kneeling beside my bed. My way into faith was not through those words, which always seemed empty to me. When I got into bed I slept curled in the corner, leaving room for the Virgin and Baby Jesus, hoping they would keep the nightmares away."

"I always prayed to Mary. I was taught that God could

1

refuse her nothing. I didn't believe that God could be both loving and punishing. How could the God who died for us on the cross also condemn us to hell for sins as minor as eating meat on Friday or missing Mass on Sunday?"

"I think I stopped believing in God when no matter how many Hail Marys I recited my mother still drank her six pack every night, and became as distant and invisible as prayer itself."

"My mother always wanted to sit in a pew close to the altar. The incense was so thick and pungent I had to summon all my willpower to keep from fainting or throwing up. I'd been fasting since dinner the night before so I could receive Holy Communion."

"I remember my First Communion, everyone fussing over me, commenting on how I looked like a little bride. Just before we left for church, my mother, who even then was convinced I'd never marry, touched my hand and said, 'Look in the mirror now. You will never see yourself in a veil again.'"

For those of us who grew up Catholic, religion is at the heart of memory. The tremendous beauty and ritual of Catholicism: the ornate darkness of the church, the statues, the Stations of the Cross, the hushing of conversation upon entering, the sign of the cross at the holy water font, the celebration of Mass, the solo voice of the priest followed by the voices of the congregation, kneeling at the communion rail to receive the Body of Christ, the songs of the choir, all instill in us a reverence for the sacred, an honoring of the mystical. Our highest, most holy selves rise like angels.

"Whenever I smell frankincense burning I remember the church of my childhood at the top of a steep hill in upper Manhattan. I see the dark stained glass windows and I hear the choir's lilting songs. I don't know if I ever believed, but I do know I liked the feeling that entered my body as Mass began, soothing me. That feeling was something larger than just myself; it connected me to my mother, sister, and everyone else in church."

"I used to sneak into Church during recess or after school and light all the votive candles to free the poor souls in Purgatory. I saw them ascending into Heaven, flocks of white birds."

Although the Church demands truth from its faithful, we learn early that the word of God, the priests, and the nuns has more credibility than our own experience. The Church instills in us a belief that we are in essence born scarred and must atone for the Original Sin that we inherited from Eve. We must repent, silence ourselves, submit. For Catholic girls the need to define one's own truth is crucial.

"I never believed that what I did was really a sin. I was good; everyone said I was such a good girl. And I knew they were right; I was a good girl. Even when I touched myself and my mother caught me and tied my arms to the bed, I knew what I had done could not be wrong because it felt so good. But I offered up dozens of ejaculations a day for the poor souls in Purgatory, who, I suspected, hadn't really done anything bad either.

" 'Forgive me Father, for I have sinned. It has been one week since my last confession. These are my sins. I talked back to my mother five times. I yelled at my father, kicked the dog.' I never told the priest about masturbating or wishing my younger sister dead for pinching and hitting me or anything else that was truly awful. I carried my guilt with me. I knew I would always be doing something wrong, something unforgivable. I figured I would eventually end up in hell, unless I could do something really good in my life to redeem myself, to make myself worthy in God's eyes."

"I thought nuns were angels on earth. I wanted to be that way: one of the chosen, a Bride of Christ. I made a secret altar to the Blessed Virgin in my backyard and after school I'd pray for her help in choosing the right order of nuns. I'd sent away for catalogues from every Motherhouse I could think of and planned to travel the country to see each one, hoping I would find the place where I belonged. My hope for

a vocation, however, was later replaced by hope for the perfect marriage."

"During the late summer—before I entered Mother Cabrini School as a first grader—the principal, Mother George, showed my mother and me around the school. Mother George was very tall and skinny and old and she didn't smile, not even at my mother. It looked to me as though the wrinkles on her face had formed in such a way that she was no longer able to smile. Her voice was stern and steely. She made it clear that tardiness would not be tolerated, nor would an even slightly wrinkled uniform. She was scary; even my mother thought so. When she led us into the chapel I was startled by the casket at the foot of the altar. As we got closer she told us it was the body of Mother Cabrini herself. And sure enough, there she was, a tiny nun, her face smooth and beautiful. But she frightened me; I didn't like knowing I would come to daily Mass and have to see her there. A dead person ought to be in the ground, I thought."

Catholicism provides girls with only one narrow concept of womanhood: the Virgin—who is emblematic of modesty, purity, passivity, submission—the silent one who obeys God and yet is the mother of God, the one who has value not by virtue of her selfhood, but by virtue of her function. To actually be like Mary—a virgin before, during, and after giving birth—is, of course, impossible. Yet she is the one held up to us as an example of supreme womanhood; the one we are taught to aspire to.

Eve, on the other hand, is the fallen woman, the one who destroyed paradise on earth, the temptress, the one with knowledge and the desire for knowledge, the bad woman. Although we know the role of Eve is forbidden, her position is one of knowledge, choice, sexuality, and power.

We discovered sex young and furtively, as did many other Catholic girls. Rebellion took hold in us early. At thirteen we were both challenging family and church in numerous ways, there being so much to rebel against. We questioned author-

ity, talked back, were accused of "being sassy." We took pleasure in our emerging sexuality and in our new bodies.

"The blond boy I loved the summer I turned thirteen
would meet me after Mass and we'd walk to the field behind
Holy Cross, lie down in the tall grass and kiss each other for
hours, taking sips from the hip flask he'd hidden in his
pocket, filled with a bitter mixture from his parents' liquor
cabinet."

*"At a high school dance I was suspended for kissing my
boyfriend in a way that wasn't the way I would kiss my
brother. Nothing, not even the Church could stop me from
such pleasure. Our mouths open, tongues touching."*

"When I was in Catechism to prepare for Confirmation I
argued with the priest teaching the class. I wanted him to
justify the Church's stand on abortion and birth control.
When my mother began taking the Pill, she stopped receiving
communion; she was no longer entitled to receive the sacraments and she was bitterly angry about this. No matter what
explanation the priest gave, it never made sense to me, was
never satisfactory."

*"I remember going into Church with my head uncovered
rather than bobby-pin a tissue to it. It was exhilarating to
break a rule, a rule that applied only to girls and women,
a restriction meant to shame us, another reminder that we
weren't worthy to be in the presence of God without humbling
ourselves."*

Our mothers were not happy women. They considered this
life a painful existence, in which they were perpetual martyrs,
waiting for the next life. They sacrificed themselves for their
husbands and families in order to be the subservient women
they were expected to be. They clearly did not want to experience pleasure, which would remind them of all they had
given up. The true pleasure for us, as their daughters, would
have been the unequivical pleasure of their attention, but our
mothers each had one foot in the next life, the rewards of
Heaven. "At a very young age I was taught that happiness was

not important; what was important was to save my soul" writes Mary Gordon.

During our stay in Mendocino we wondered about the stories other Catholic girls had never told anyone. We wanted to create this book in order that Catholic girlhood could be more fully understood, to see what women remember when they look back upon their childhoods. We wanted to share these stories and to see what collective story exists about growing up Catholic. Until now, no collection has been published that bears witness to Catholic girlhood.

Our process in obtaining this work began when we contacted writers we knew who had grown up Catholic, asking them to contribute stories and poems. We placed calls for materials in many feminist publications and writers' magazines. The response was impressive; we received over five hundred manuscripts, some from as far away as Italy, Ireland, and Japan. Although we collected enough fine work for several volumes, we made a decision to include only the work of North American women and set about the difficult task of making the final selection of fifty-two stories, poems, and memoirs.

Catholic Girls is divided into three sections. The first, "The Company of Angels," reflects the spirit and innocence of early girlhood, and includes work by Mary McCarthy, Audre Lorde, and Mary Gordon. "Falling Away," the second section, examines the concept of faith from various perspectives. Here you will find the work of Valerie Miner, Ana Castillo, and Maureen Brady. The third section, "A Temple of the Holy Ghost," explores the emergence of sexuality and the loss of innocence.

In each of the pieces in *Catholic Girls* the girl's or woman's voice is one of strength and integrity. There is humor, pathos, devotion, fear, playfulness, and *such* spirit.

Even now, the church is still threatened by our voices. In 1989, Pope John Paul II and thirty-five American archbishops met at the Vatican in an underground chamber, the Room of the Broken Heads. They issued dire warnings, branding women who refused to honor the Church's authority as "radical feminists."

In this book you will find girls who didn't acquiesce to prescribed roles, but asked questions and demanded answers in order to overcome the invalidation of women's experience. What power do the Church fathers hear in our voices that they want them silenced? Here is what happens when we speak out loud in poem and story and say, "Listen, this is my girlhood, this is the sound of my voice, its timbre and pitch. This is what I have been told should always be hidden, should not be spoken."

PART ONE

The Company of Angels

For each of us as women, there is a dark place within where hidden and growing our true spirit rises. —Audre Lorde

Mary McCarthy

Excerpt from
Memories of a
Catholic Girlhood

Looking back, I see that it was religion that saved me. Our ugly church and parochial school provided me with my only aesthetic outlet, in the words of the Mass and the litanies and the old Latin hymns, in the Easter lilies around the altar, rosaries, ornamented prayer books, votive lamps, holy cards stamped in gold and decorated with flower wreaths and a saint's picture. This side of Catholicism, much of it cheapened and debased by mass production, was for me, nevertheless, the equivalent of Gothic cathedrals and illuminated manuscripts and mystery plays. I threw myself into it with ardor, this sensuous life, and when I was not dreaming that I was going to grow up to marry the pretender to the throne of France and win back his crown with him, I was dreaming of being a Carmelite nun, cloistered and penitential; I was also much attracted by an order for fallen women called the Magdalens. A desire to excel governed all my thoughts, and this was quickened, if possible, by the parochial-school methods of education, which were based on the competitive principle. Everything was a contest; our schoolroom was divided into teams, with captains, for spelling bees and other feats of learning, and on the playground we organized ourselves in the same fashion. To win, to skip a grade, to get ahead—the nuns' methods were well adapted to the place and time, for most of the little Catholics of our neighborhood were children of poor immigrants, bent on bettering themselves and also on surpassing the Protestants, whose children went to Whittier, the public school. There was no idea of equality in the parochial school, and such an idea would have been abhorent to me, if it had existed; equality, a sort of brutal cutting down to size, was what I was treated to at home. Equality was a species of unfairness which the good sisters of St. Joseph would not have tolerated.

I stood at the head of my class and I was also the best runner and performer on the turning poles in the schoolyard; I was the best actress and elocutionist and the second-most devout, being surpassed in this by a blonde boy with a face like a saint, who sat in front of me and whom I loved; his name was John Klosick. No doubt, the standards of the school were not very high, and they gave me a false idea of myself; I have never excelled at athletics elsewhere. Nor have I ever been devout again. When I left the competitive atmosphere of the parochial school, my religion withered on the stalk.

But in St. Stephen's School, I was not devout just to show off; I felt my religion very intensely and longed to serve God better than anyone else. This, I thought, was what He asked of me. I lived in fear of making a poor confession or of not getting my tongue flat enough to receive the Host reverently. One of the great moral crises of my life occurred on the morning of my first Communion. I took a drink of water. Unthinkingly, of course, for had it not been drilled into me that the Host must be received fasting, on the penalty of mortal sin? It was only a sip, but that made no difference, I knew. A sip was as bad as a gallon; I could not take Communion. And yet I had to. My Communion dress and veil and prayer book were laid out for me, and I was supposed to lead the girls' procession; John Klosick, in a white suit, would be leading the boys. It seemed to me that I would be failing the school and my class, if, after all the rehearsals, I had to confess what I had done and drop out. The sisters would be angry; my guardians would be angry, having paid for the dress and veil. I thought of the procession without me in it, and I could not bear it. To make my first Communion later, in ordinary clothes, would not be the same. On the other hand, if I took my first Communion in a state of mortal sin, God would never forgive me; it would be a fatal beginning. I went through a ferocious struggle with my conscience, and all the while, I think, I knew the devil was going to prevail: I was going to take Communion, and only God and I would know the real facts. So it came about: I received my first Communion in a state of outward holiness and inward horror, believing I was damned, for I could not imagine that I could make a true repentance. The time to repent was now, before committing the sacrilege; afterward, I could not be really sorry for I would have achieved what I had wanted.

I supposed I must have confessed this at my next confession, scarcely daring to breathe it, and the priest must have treated it lightly: my sins, as I slowly discovered, weighed heavier on me than they did on my confessors. Actually, it is quite common for children making their first Communion to have just such a mishap as mine: they are so excited on that long-awaited morning that they hardly know what they are doing, or possibly the very taboo on food and water and the importance of the occasion drive them into an unconscious resistance. I heard a story almost identical with mine from Ignazio Silone. Yet the despair I felt that summer morning (I think it was Corpus Christi Day) was in a certain sense fully justified: I knew myself, how I was and would be forever; such dry self-knowledge is terrible. Every subsequent moral crisis of my life, moreover, has had precisely the pattern of this struggle over the first Communion; I have battled, usually without avail, against a temptation to do something which only I knew was bad, being swept on by a need to preserve outward appearances and to live up to other people's expectations of me. The heroine of one of my novels, who finds herself pregnant, possibly as the result of an infidelity, and is tempted to have the baby and say nothing to her husband, is in the same fix, morally, as I was at eight years old, with that drink of water inside me that only I knew was there. When I supposed I was damned, I was right—damned, that is, to a repetition or endless reenactment of that conflict between excited scruples and inertia of will.

First Communion

I have been in this photograph for seventeen years;
dressed like a miniature bride,
holding a bouquet with both hands,
white and yellow flowers,
"Look at yourself in the mirror, now," my mother says.
"You will never see yourself in a veil again."
I am eight years old.

Her white hands pull at the folds
of my white dress, hands bigger than mine.
What the photograph does not show
is what the photographer refuses to see.
My father has gone to a new city.
He mistakes those hands pulling at his tie for love.
She says he has made too many mistakes.

I lose my voice in what I say.
Borrow the girl for the photograph.
Tell her you love her this way, she is certainly pretty enough.
The kitchen table was so clean after dinner.
We sat down with everything spread open
this way. And oh, the little girl was clean, too.

At night they leave the lights on. I draw pictures in the air.
I make tunnels. I crawl down into the blankets

and get lost burying myself,
until the angry man hears me crying
and he comes in, smiling.

A hundred other little girls walk down the aisle
of the church. We had practiced the walk.
We had invented sins to tell the hidden priest.
I could never tell the wooden man what I'd really done.
We are as complacent and quiet as dolls.

There isn't actually a first memory.
Rather, there exists a collection of things
all happening at the same time. I can't distinguish
anyone in the picture, except for myself
and a series of formless shadows
behind the trees.

School wouldn't be so bad, except for all the other girls
who don't want to play with me and who I don't really
want to play with.

In first grade our teachers are the women
who cover themselves in black gowns;
their words are polite and compressed.
I do not like looking like everyone else, even at seven,
a school of children dressed like military men.
My braids are especially long, tightly woven.

I make my gums bleed at the back of my mouth,
cutting the skin there with short fingernails,
anything to be let out of the classroom for a little while,
a drink of water to stop the blood.
If only for some untampered air,
something to remind me of myself.

After school I like to walk down the hill
ahead of all the other girls.
Their voices follow me like a choir.
As I walk slowly home my thighs rub together,
sticking. I do not think of myself as being fat.

"This is the way to hold your hands, like a sign toward God."
I mouth the prayers, refusing to memorize
what I do not understand.
After awhile of watching the really fat girl
sway back and forth as she prays,
I learn the words. It is easier this way.

My family will move to Chicago. What is Chicago?
I like surprises. An airplane is like a boat that flies.
Before leaving our apartment
I take a lipstick from Mommy's purse,
the reddest one. I write up and down on the closet walls
of my empty bedroom. An echo falls all over me.
I write words I have learned: going, away, goodbye,
and I write the secret words I have invented:
wide, looping letters, long scribbled red words.
I want the next people who live here
to know a child who once was.

Trudy Riley

Digger and Margaret Mary

Margaret Mary felt a shiver go through her eight-year-old body the minute Sister Benedict got that weird look in her eyes and started talking about the lepers. Every morning she stood by the blackboard, stared at Margaret Mary, and told stories about how terrible it was to be a leper. It scared Digger so much he would curl up in Margaret Mary's lap and hang onto her thumb real tight.

When Sister really got warmed up she would tell how their bodies got rotten and their noses dropped off and how the priest who tried to help them got sick, too. By this time Digger's grip was so tight Margaret Mary couldn't feel her thumb at all.

The rest of the day all she could think about was how it would feel if an arm or a leg dropped off her body, so when Sister ended her talk with how bad the Church needed money to build hospitals for the lepers, Margaret Mary got her thumb loose from Digger, untied the knot in her hand-kerchief, and took out half her lunch money. Her hand got sweaty, so she was happy when the recess bell rang and she could run up to Sister's desk and drop it in the leper box.

She got pretty hungry. Her stomach growled and her head felt funny. She told herself it didn't matter because Sister had told her when things felt bad they were called sacrifices and she could send them up to God to trade for a big favor.

She had been doing that the day they took the school picture. She had just finished asking God to "Please help Daddy" when Sister Clarita told them all to line up. "C'mon Digger," she said, reaching under the desk where he was taking a snooze. "Let's go."

"No," he said, staring at her with eyes that looked like a pair of cat's-eye marbles. She knew this meant trouble 'cause Digger's eyes changed with his mood. When he was mad they turned frosty and when he was happy they were the kind of blue that made her think of diving in and swimming around.

"Aw c'mon," she pleaded, thinking how great he would look in the picture. Here would be all these grammar school kids and there would be Digger looking like a monkey except for his rose-colored skin and big blue eyes.

While she was staring down at her desk, worrying about how she was going to get Digger into the picture, he disappeared.

When she got outside, Sister Clarita put her in the first row and asked everyone to stand close together. Just then, Digger came skipping by. She grabbed him and asked Rosella to move over and make room. Rosella stood firm and said, "You're dumb. We all know there's nobody there."

"There is, too," Margaret Mary yelled, and punched her. Rosella began to cry and Sister Clarita ran over and put her face so close to Margaret Mary's the mole on Sister's nose stood out real clear.

"Move over," she ordered.

"No, I might squash him!"

In a very angry voice Sister Clarita told the other kids to stop giggling. When it was quiet she said, "Margaret Mary, your mother's going to hear about this."

Margaret Mary sat at her desk and worried all afternoon about what Sister had said because her mom got so upset every time she caught her talking to Digger.

The first time it had happened was the day after he moved in and Margaret Mary was teaching him about all the wonderful things they could do together, like listen to good radio programs. Edgar Bergen and Charlie McCarthy was her favorite. She had just told Digger that she bet if he ever met Charlie the two of them would get along swell because they were both so smart, when she looked up and there was her mom.

"As if I don't have enough with your father, I've got to watch you talking to yourself? Her mom plopped down on the bed and asked, "What am I doing wrong?"

Margaret Mary ran over and hugged her, making sure not to mess her hair because she was on her way to work. She told her mom she loved her, but she was pretty sure it hadn't helped. And here it was a month later and Sister Clarita was going to get her mom worried all over again.

Margaret Mary knew Digger felt bad, too, because when they got home from school he kept swinging on the bedroom door and didn't settle down until she promised to read him the end of *The Wizard of Oz*. The minute she opened the book he jumped into her lap and curled up. He was calming down until she got to the part where the good witch asks Dorothy what she wants most in the world and Dorothy says, "I want to go back to Kansas."

At that, Digger sat up, turned angry purple, and howled, "Kansas! How can she leave Oz for Kansas!"

"I don't know. If I were her I'd stay in Oz forever."

"Stop talking to that creature," her mother said, charging into her room. "That nun called me today and told me you held up the whole school picture talking to that miserable thing you imagine follows you around. It's got to stop. Look, there's no one here." She started hitting the air. Digger ducked just in time and slid under the bed.

Her mom stopped talking and sat down next to her. There were tears in the corners of her eyes. "I didn't mean to scare you, but I'm so upset."

Margaret Mary stared at the bumps in her blue, chenille bedspread. Her mother put her arm around Margaret Mary's shoulder and held her close. "My God, Honey, what's happening to you?" Her mom began to cry. Margaret Mary felt terrible.

*   *   *

That very morning she had gotten on her knees and prayed, "Please make Mommie happy." Digger was there. He was moving his lips but not really praying. He was hiccuping and practicing color changes. She tried to ignore him because she wanted to ask God to do a lot of work, but Digger got so restless she had to say a quick Amen.

After that day she and Digger started to go way back in the closet when they wanted to talk. It was hot and stuffy but it was worth it because they could have lots of fun telling each other jokes and stories.

Digger always wanted to hear the exact same story. He reminded Margaret Mary of herself when she used to ask her mom to read the same Golden Book over and over again. Her mom had tried a couple of times, but one day she put the book down and said, "Mommy's too restless for this crap," and hugged Margaret Mary close to make it all right.

Margaret Mary wasn't like her mom. She told Digger his favorite story every time he wanted to hear it. It was the one about how he got born.

"Once upon a time," she'd say, letting Digger curl up in her lap, "it was Daddy's birthday and Mom and me were decorating the kitchen with pretty red and white crepe paper. Mom was standing on a kitchen chair humming and asking me if she was sticking the crepe paper in the right places. I was so happy keeping track of the scissors and tape and handing her things the minute she wanted them. When we were through we sat down and waited for Daddy to come home so we could say, 'Surprise!'

"We stayed there a long time because it started to get dark. Mom began to pick at her nail polish like she does when she gets nervous. I started talking about how pretty the kitchen looked.

"She didn't seem to hear me 'cause she got up real fast and went into the hall to the telephone. I knew she was calling Aunt Ethel. She did that when Daddy was late. Her voice was so loud I could hear every word and I was scared because she said she was going out of her mind with worry because Daddy had been going to night school to learn to be an 'countant and hadn't had a drink in over a month and now he was late and she was pretty sure he'd started up again. Ethel must have asked Mom a long question because it got quiet; then Mom said, 'No,' that Dad didn't seem to be enjoying himself at all. 'Not even in the love department.' "

"What's love department?"

"You ask me that every time, Digger. I think it's like smooching a lot."

Digger sat up, rolled his eyes, and pretended to faint. "Silly," Margaret Mary said and gathered him to her. "After that, Mom yelled at Ethel that she'd called up for some help but all Ethel could think about was whether her string beans were going to burn. Mom didn't even say goodbye, just, 'Go take care of your damn beans.'

"I could hear her crying in the hall so I tried a different kind of praying. I started counting the squares in the linoleum real slow. I asked God to make Daddy come home before I reached number fifty-five. When he didn't come I'd start again. I did that 'til it was too dark to see."

She felt Digger begin to squirm. "Hold on Digger, the good part is coming right now." He became still and she continued. "When Daddy got home his face was red and his hat was on crooked. Instead of showing surprise my mom said, 'Where the hell have you been?'

" 'None of your business.' He sat down at the table without even taking off his hat or coat. Mom started to cry. Daddy began to tear the decorations down. A piece of crepe paper landed on my plate and was soaking in the meat gravy."

"Yuk," Digger groaned and buried his head deeper into Margaret Mary's blue, pleated skirt.

"I tried to sneak away but Daddy said, 'Stay there and eat your dinner.' I took big bites even though it tasted terrible. I prayed Mommy and Daddy would notice how good I was being and stop fighting. Instead, things got worse. Daddy's hand came out of nowhere and hit my mom.

"Everything got quiet. I thought I was hearing my heartbeat. But it wasn't my heart. It was a little tapping under my chair. I looked down and the first thing I saw was a pair of blue eyes looking kind and soft. Then I felt your hand patting me. In a voice like I'd never heard before you were trying to tell me something. I stopped shaking and listened real hard. That's when you half whispered and half croaked, 'My name is Digger and I want to be your friend.'

"When my Dad went running out to get his coat and leave and my Mom ran after him, we snuck up to my bedroom. I was so happy you were there I turned on the radio so that you could have nice music. I got out my old stuffed animals in case you wanted to play. I made you just as comfortable as I could before we fell asleep all curled up together."

"So that's the whole story," Margaret Mary said, happy that Digger didn't want to hear it again. She had other things to talk to him about. The first subject was Sister Benedict and the lepers. She planned to talk Digger into doing some serious praying because she didn't want to hear about one more leper.

The next morning, when Sister Dominica was standing in Sister Benedict's usual spot, Margaret Mary whispered, "Look, Digger, we made a miracle!"

The first thing Sister said was, "Sister Benedict is in the hospital, so we need to remember her in our prayers."

For a minute Margaret Mary was afraid Sister Benedict had leprosy, but Sister Dominica said it wasn't a bad sickness or operation. Sister Benedict had just needed "a long rest."

Other good things were happening, too. Her dad was coming home every night and her mom was beginning to smile more. She was sure her troubles were over until the night she brought home the school picture.

Margaret Mary's mom had just come home from the beauty salon, where they gave her a whole bunch of waves and curls. She was smoking through a cigarette holder. Dad was reading the paper. A clump of hair had come down on his forehead like it did when he was thinking hard.

"You Must Have Been a Beautiful Baby," was playing on the radio. Her mom began to sing and dance around the kitchen while she fixed dinner. She kept looking to see if her daddy was watching her. He wasn't. "You going to read that silly old paper all night?" Mom said in a teasy voice.

Margaret Mary felt bad when her daddy didn't even look up, so she ran to her room and came back with a sealed brown envelope. She handed it to her mom who took it and tossed it over the paper wall.

Her dad sighed and put down the paper.

The school picture was awful. Her eyes were squinty and her clothes looked crooked. Even Digger shook his head, and he thought she was beautiful, no matter what.

"Good Lord, Charlie," her mother said, "you know how I feel about booze, but I have to admit, I've never seen a kid who looked more like she needed a stiff drink."

Her father said, "Hmm," in a voice that sounded like he didn't use it much.

"I thought that imaginary playmate stuff was bad enough, but do you know what she's doing now?"

Her dad didn't look the least bit curious.

"She's losing weight and hiding in her closet. That's what. I really think we need to take her to the doctor again."

"We don't have that kind of money, Liz, and you know it."

When Digger heard the word money he jumped up on the light fixture and started bouncing up and down. Margaret Mary knew he was doing this because the word money meant a fight. She was so afraid he would fall on the floor she prayed, "Please God, make Digger follow me," as she tiptoed out of the kitchen.

When they got to her room they went into the closet, where they couldn't hear the yelling. Margaret Mary was so tired she fell asleep right away.

When she woke up she was scared because she couldn't find Digger. Feeling around in the dark, she finally found him curled up on her Sunday shoes. "Digger," she whispered, "I had the most awful dream that a whole bunch of lepers were chasing me. Their arms and legs were purple and they were dropping off as they ran."

Digger was drowsy but promised to protect her from the leopards.

"No, Digger, the *lepers*," she said, but Digger was already snoring. She closed her eyes, telling herself that if Digger could protect her from leopards, a few lepers weren't going to bother him at all.

The next morning Digger dawdled on the way to school. "C'mon Digger."

He didn't pay any attention, just kept skipping backwards.

She imitated Sister Virginia, the strictest nun she knew. "Digger, what *is* your problem?"

"I want to play hookey."

She pretended to be shocked. "You mean you want to fool around all day," she asked, feeling the beginnings of relief soothing her tummy. "But what will we do?"

Digger didn't answer. He took her hand and led her across Fair Oaks Street.

It took forever for Gramma to answer the door. When she did she said, "Fay," looking pleased.

"No Gramma, it's Margaret Mary." She felt bad 'cause Gramma's daughter Fay had been dead a lot of years.

"Oh," her Gramma said, and asked if Margaret Mary's mom and dad were coming, too.

"No, Gramma, they're at work."

Digger was so pleased to be at Gramma's he was jumping up and down. His cheeks were getting rosy because, even though it was a hot day, Gramma had all the heaters on.

Gramma started to make pancakes. She walked back and forth from the cupboard to the stove in her soft slippers. Hair straggled from the bun at the back of her neck. Margaret Mary's mom told her Aunt Lorraine came every day to help Gramma fix up, but it looked like she hadn't been there in a long time.

"This is Digger," Margaret Mary said, pointing.

"Oh yes," Gramma said, like he was someone she knew.

Her pancakes were pretty burned, but Margaret Mary put lots of syrup on them and ate them anyway.

Gramma poured tea for all of them. Margaret Mary drank hers fast and scrunched up close to her grandmother to have her fortune told from the leaves. Gramma seemed to forget what she was doing for a minute, but then she remembered and placed the cup upside down on the saucer. She turned it slowly three times and then brought it close to her face. "I see a beautiful actress who lives in Paris."

"No, Gramma, I was an actress last time."

"Oh," she said, looking closer. "It's not an actress at all but a world-famous dancer who lives in Santa Cruz."

"Santa Cruz!" Margaret Mary wasn't crazy about Santa Cruz but then she remembered that Gramma had spent all her summers there when she was a girl and thought it was a wonderful place.

The minute Margaret Mary opened the front door her mother ran into the hall. "The nuns called me at work. How *could* you skip school! Your father's going to hear about this."

Right after dinner she kept her promise. Margaret Mary's dad was gathering the books he used for his night class when her mom said, "Margaret Mary played hookey today."

Her dad acted like he hadn't heard and stared at Margaret Mary like he didn't know her.

"Charlie, you've got to punish her. You're her father." Her mother said this in the voice Margaret Mary knew her father hated. It was the one that meant her mother was going to cry. It woke her father up.

"Get in the bedroom," he said, getting up from his chair.

She and Digger ran to her parents' room. When they got there, Margaret Mary sat on the bed. Digger slid under a chair and hid his eyes. While her dad was looking for a coat hanger, she leaned down and whispered, "It's ok. It doesn't hurt much."

She guessed that Digger didn't believe her because his eyes stayed closed and he was getting pale. Margaret Mary knew she had to do something so she told him, "Don't think about what's happening right now. Think about going back to Gramma's tomorrow and having a good time."

It didn't work. Digger stayed under the chair, shaking. Margaret Mary was getting nervous, too, because she knew her daddy was taking all this time because he was trying to find the biggest wooden coat hanger he could. Last time, he found the one he used for his heavy winter coat and it had made her hurt all over.

The time before had been better because she had been able to think about a whole bunch of other things while he was hitting her. She had used what Sister Anne called her "majinashon," dreaming she was in the Land of Oz, walking down a street in the Emerald City on her way to have chocolate cupcakes with the Wizard and the good witch Glinda.

When she looked up, her dad was standing over her. He was holding the coat hanger so tight his knuckles had turned white.

"It hurt so much this time," Margaret Mary said, looking around the closet for an old sock so she could blow her nose. She took a deep, shuddery breath. "How come my majinashon didn't work? C'mon, Digger, tell me."

She tried to quiet her ragged breath so Digger could concentrate. He was turning the color of a young fern. It was the color he used when he was trying to figure something out. After a few minutes he looked pleased with himself and said, "I think it's because the more you get hit the more the pretty things in the world disappear."

It was so quiet and dark when Digger woke Margaret Mary that their whispers sounded loud enough to wake her mom and dad. As if that wasn't bad enough, Digger kept bumping into things.

"Can't you see in the dark," she asked when she heard him hit the wall for the third time.

"What do you think I am, a cat?"

"I was just wondering."

"Cats may be able to see in the dark, but I can make plans, and I have a terrific one. Let's go down to the kitchen."

"Golly, Digger, it's three o'clock in the morning," she said, shining the flashlight on the stove clock.

"Turn the light back this way," Digger whispered from the kitchen counter.

"My feet are freezing." Margaret Mary hopped from one foot to the other on the cold linoleum.

Digger didn't pay any attention. He just kept putting sandwiches in a paper bag. "That's it," he said, adding two apples and wrapping it into a tight bundle. "Now we go back to the closet and wait."

"I don't think this plan is going to work."

"You doubt the great Digger?" he asked, hanging upside down from the cabinet door.

"It's not that. It's that Dorothy lived in Kansas. They have tornadoes *there*. We don't have them in California."

"Says who?"

As Margaret Mary and Digger lay curled up in the corner of the closet, she thought she heard music. Moments later she and Digger were dancing in a room full of flowers. It was so beautiful it gave her goose bumps. Digger was in a golden suit and she was in a sparkling, silver dress. Every time they made a turn the hundreds of people watching clapped and shouted, "We love you, Margaret Mary!" She was so happy she hardly noticed they were twirling faster and faster. It wasn't until Digger told her to look down that she realized their feet had left the ground.

Rita Williams

Relief

Fatima Simms sits under the plaque of the prayer of Saint Francis. It is seared into the varnished pine by an acetylene torch. Her gaze reminds me of the sad, sweet Virgin Mary with the chipped nose, who stands on the world globe with dusty toes peeking out beneath her blue robe.

She has shoes, though—brown support ones. Her pity feels benign, at first, like a niche of tenderness carved out especially for me. But as the morning yields itself to midday, her look starts to sting like nettles that at first feel soft as Scarlet O'Hara's velvet but then turn nasty. My skin feels stained by Mrs. Simms's scrutiny and I start furtively scratching myself in the way that makes my aunt Willa Mae tie my hands at night.

A black fly, confused by the freedom it sees outside the window, slams itself against the pane next to Fatima. From that numinous, magical island called White, she winces in distaste. Willa Mae, meanwhile, is scurrying around like an ant on a stove. Later she will punish me for witnessing this.

On Saturdays, when Willa Mae cleans toilets at Our Lady Queen of Martyrs, I go to the library and read the Superman comics. If I could only get Fatima to the library maybe I could have Superman scan her with his X-ray vision and tell me how she got to be a "Mrs." Wonder Woman will rescue me from both, Willa Mae and Fatima.

If I could only smell this white woman. Part her hair. Make her say "aahhh" and look down her throat. Put on her funny shoes. Dump her pocketbook on the table and count the quarters. Feel the lining inside her bag. Click and unclick her pen. I want to see her underpants. Undress her. See if she has a down there, down there. I am pretty sure she doesn't. She's probably like my Janie B. doll, with a mound as smooth and closed as a shoulder. Still, I would like to see.

She has this bosom, rather than breasts. They seem exhausted, like old cushions, encased in pillow ticking the color of milk gravy with brown flowers floating like chips of gizzard. I remember seeing the gray scalloping around the Peter Pan collar in the Spring Jamboree section of the Montgomery Ward catalogue. It seems to me her body aches to leave.

Her glasses magnify irises the color of iced steel. When she tries to smile at me, nothing in them warms. I realize she doesn't know I can see her as well as she can see me.

Already I did it wrong. When she came in the door, I was supposed to kiss her powdery cheek with the little hairs. Willa Mae said she might give us extra beans and tinned beef again, like she did last month. Instead, when I heard her coming up the stairs, I hid in the back. But Willa Mae dragged me out, with my cartoon-stiff braids laced up in peppermint-stripe ribbons.

We are the only black family in Cedar Springs, and I sit next to her son, Roger, in science class. He is really dumb. I see her pick him up after school when I am waiting for the bus.

Mrs. Simms comes once a month to make sure we are still bad enough off to need what Willa Mae calls "reelief." She studies her clipboard and prepares to begin. Her legs are crossed carefully at the ankle—in a manner the nuns would approve—not at the knee, which is considered common.

Since Willa Mae is busy managing her strategy, she does not notice the delicate curl of Mrs. Simms's lip. With a flourish, Willa Mae shoves a pile of junk to the back of the table to make space to serve her raspberry conserve and fresh biscuits.

"This was made from the grade As. Them's the best. You

can believe that, too," she declares, her dentures clicking like beetle feet on cool tile.

Mrs. Simms tries to smile, but it's clear she's trying to figure out how she can avoid eating anything that comes out of such perfect filth.

"Sweet Blessed Jesus, just look at that fly," Willa Mae says, jumping up from the chair she has just sat down in. She grabs a fly swatter from the buffet and cleanly swats the fly before it escapes the windowsill.

Mrs. Simms starts to cry out, but thinks better of it and her mouth settles into an evil little line.

"I just can't keep on top of everything," Willa Mae says, as the expiring fly flexes its legs. "I try to keep this place clean, but . . ."

Willa Mae's idea of clean is that her garden, which is the most glorious in the county, is always meticulously weeded. Her one concession to the Welfare Lady's visit has been to scrub the floor and part of the table.

I look at our home as Mrs. Simms surveys it.

There is nothing pretty here. There are a couple of books; one on anatomy and another on the life of the Apache Geronimo. But no pictures, googaws, or decorations. This is a place in which to cache food and supplies, a structure affording protection from the elements. Willa Mae is as basic as an old sheepherder, with a wad of dough kept for starter to sour each day in a Dutch oven by the stove. She reboils her coffee grounds to make them stretch, and only goes to town once a month to buy flour and lard.

The house looks like a tool shed that only incidentally shares space with a jumble of household furniture.

On the edge of the buffet Willa Mae keeps a loaded .22 rifle for killing magpies, and a photograph laced in coal dust of John Kennedy in front of the American flag. Next to the red glass candle of the Virgin of Guadalupe is an open tin of Bag Balm. Strewn in either direction are mud-caked garden kneepads, the fresh brown eggs from the Rhode Island Reds, fifty-three berry baskets, a chipped crystal bowl of buttons, paperclips, bills, pain killers, bobby pins, a cracked black rosary, and the leather bucket strap for picking berries, which doubles as a whip for me.

The buffet is peerless mahogany, over a hundred years old. One day Willa Mae started sawing the legs off because she thought it stood too high. Then it rocked because she could never get all four legs to be the same length. Now the amputated back leg has a prosthesis made from a Wayside Gardens catalogue. The top layer of veneer has slowly levitated because she dumps any leftover coffee into the geraniums, and the warm water dribbles out of the pot liners, soaking everything.

Next to the window is the round oak table with the claw feet. Willa Mae watches vigilantly to make sure that I never put my feet on the claws because the table is valuable. She swears she has been offered ten thousand dollars for it. Every evening after supper, she pours bleach on it and scrubs it with cleanser. She only scrubs the part of the table that is used for meals, so that over the years the table has been worn down on three sides but remains thick at the back, where she stashes seed and poultry catalogues. Perched precariously on the most recent copy of *Poultry Today* is the white sugar pitcher with the twelve Sorrowful Mysteries.

Brawling for space on the windowsill are three pots of flourishing, flowering geraniums. Every morning she tenderly sticks a finger into the pot to test the soil, and prunes the drying leaves and absently crumbles them next to the sugar. Sometimes bits of leaf fall onto the butter, which sits out all the time. In warm weather the mitered edges of the cube degenerate and remnants of burned toast, currant jelly, and geranium bathe together in the basin of the dish.

Mrs. Simms glances furtively at the fly in rictus, not a foot from her shoulder.

"Joy, what is your favorite subject in school," she suddenly asks.

I know I am supposed to say arithmetic, but I can see this is hopeless. Why doesn't Willa Mae see it's hopeless? All I want to do is study Fatima Simms. I wonder if I can send off for a golden rope like Wonder Woman's to tie her up so I can see inside her skull.

There is a little crucifix with Jesus's feet crossed modestly at the ankles. He is dangling from a gold chain submerged in a fold of skin next to her collar. They are both staring at me. When I realize they expect me to speak, I jump.

"Joy Wayne, cat got your tongue?" Willa Mae is trying to make my muteness into a joke. I know she is furious. She only calls me Joy Wayne when her hand is itching to slam me into the middle of next month. Wayne, my father, is a man she still hates, and he has been dead three years. She is afraid I am a retard.

"I like drawing," I say. I have no idea where that comes from.

"Oh, isn't that nice," says Mrs. Simms.

"What do you like to draw?" she asks me.

I don't know what to say. I am really scared now because I didn't say arithmetic and I shift from one foot to the other trying to figure out what to do. Nothing comes.

"Her best subject is arithmetic," says Willa Mae. "Do your multiplication tables, Joy Wayne," she says, with the kind of edge in her voice like she drank too much coffee.

"Five times one is seven. Seven times seven is five. Five times five is fifty-three." I blurt this out because I know I have to say something that has numbers in it.

"Young Lady, will you please go now and play the piano for Mrs. Simms?" As she says this, Willa Mae is studying the floor.

I know I am really, really, really in trouble now. I was supposed to do so many things to prove I wasn't a dumb nigger. Now the list of what I missed overwhelms me. There is no room to think of anything else. I struggle through dread so deep it's like wading through banks of snow. I open the piano lid and look at the pile of music. I can't think of anything I can play. My feet are too short to reach the pedals and the keys stretch for miles in both directions.

"I bought her that piano so when she grows up she can play for the Church. Play 'Chapel Chimes' Joy Wayne," Willa Mae says.

I hate "Chapel Chimes," but I find the music anyway. When I open it up, the notes have rearranged themselves in the night and I recognize nothing. When I look at my hands, they have become frail as mice paws, and cannot possibly reach an octave.

I can't decide what to do. If I try to play it as it is written, I will play bad notes. If I try to figure it out as I go along, I will get lost. So, I just sit there.

"Perhaps she needs a little more light," ventures Fatima. This little note of kindness is so much worse than a blow that I start to crack and ancient tears erupt out of my eyes, blinding me.

I thought Fatima Simms was a bad person. Now I am confused.

If they see me crying, I know Willa Mae will kill me. I swallow the sobs and pray that if I sit there long enough they will start doing grownup talk. They don't.

Somehow my hands, completely independent of any help on my part, find the chords. I watch them move up the keys, as if small brown birds have flown from inside the piano to rescue me. I make some mistakes, which I know I will hear about later, but the piece unrolls like a player piano until it is finally over. I carefully turn my face away from them and wipe my eyes on my sleeve.

"Well, isn't that just lovely?" says Mrs. Simms, standing up.

I yearn to go home with her. But when I turn back around, neither of them is looking at me. They are both moving toward the door, watching only each other like chess queens, the Black and the White.

"Well, Willa Mae, why don't I just take these biscuits and jam home with me. I had such a big breakfast, I'm just as full as a seed tick."

Willa Mae follows her to the door, laughing far too loud. "Fatima, can you tell me if you're going to let us have some help this month? Joy needs . . ."

"I can't say, Willa Mae," Fatima says. Then she stops. "You haven't been having relations with that man that is known to have been hanging around here in the last month have you?"

Willa Mae closes the door in her face and leans against it with her eyes closed for a really long time.

Ellen Treen

Company of Angels

Ruthie wonders if the May procession will ever start. She wants it to be over so that she can get out of her blue angel gown and back into her regular clothes before something goes wrong. Holding her dress above the damp grass, she moves a few steps away from the three other angels, deeper into the shade of the elms, and looks down the long yard connecting church and school, where the procession is form-ing. On one side, girls in frothy veils and dripping bouquets are finding their places. On the other side, columns of starched white shirts and scrubbed faces reflect the sun. The boys' ears, exposed by harsh new haircuts, emerge like fresh carvings as raw as the letters freshly chiseled into the school cornerstone: Saint Catherine. 1939. Shivering, Ruthie bites her lip and watches; she longs to be in the sunnier school-yard with her own friends.

Black-veiled nuns swoop through the ranks, pushing late-comers into place, scolding, nudging, threatening, rearrang-ing bouquets, snapping out faded flowers. The yard is filled with commotion and excitement. Even the youngest child has glimpsed the vision that urges them on: immaculate children with hands pointed to heaven, eyes cast down, moving for-ward to the celestial music of their own voices. A procession of innocents, led by angels.

Near the angels, but apart from them, a half dozen altar boys in black cassocks and white surplices shuffle around a brass standard. From it swings the masthead of the procession, a gold-fringed satin banner of the Virgin Mary ascending through the clouds to heaven. Ruthie keeps her distance from both groups, and from Jackie Hancock especially. A small boy with a round tanned face, he used to be her friend, but the last time they played together was a year ago, when Jackie first became an altar boy. They had climbed to the top of the apple tree, where Jackie told Ruthie he was going to be a priest, and pointed out that not only could girls never be priests, they could never receive all seven sacraments. After that, things were different. Now he picks on her every chance he gets.

The other angels wait with the calm of the single lily they each hold. Even when she is silent, Ruthie feels boisterous and loud, as if the effort to be quiet were noisy in itself. Often Sister Martha Ann keeps her after school, lecturing her for impulsive behavior.

"You must learn to control yourself, Ruthie," she says. "Calm your spirit; make it acceptable in the sight of God."

Ruthie is more concerned about being acceptable to the other kids. From the first she knew they would laugh at her.

"Not me! I'm no angel!" she declared, rushing to say it first, hoping to stop the laughter before it started. "I'm not going to wear those dumb wings."

"Don't worry." Sister Martha Ann's bright young face shone with amusement. "No one thinks that. We simply want you to act like one for an hour or so."

A scratchy silver ribbon holds the wings in place, crisscrossing her chest and making her itch. She can hardly wait for it all to be over; her mother has promised that if everything goes well she will take her and her sisters to the movies afterward. Somewhere in all of those white veils two of her sisters are lined up with the smaller girls, their arms filled with pink carnations. Her big sister, Kate, will come last, helping to carry the statue of the Blessed Virgin into the church to be crowned with a wreath of tiny pink rosebuds. Softly,

Ruthie sings the hymn they have been practicing in preparation for that climactic moment: "Oh, Mary, we crown thee
with blossoms, today. Queen of the Angels! Queen of the
May!"

"Look who thinks she's one of the angels!"

Spinning around, Ruthie faces Jackie and his pointing finger. Ruthie points back. "Shut up and mind your own business," she snaps.

"You gonna fly away to heaven on those wings?" he asks,
flapping his elbows. He waits for the other boys to laugh,
then joins them.

If she dared, Ruthie would tell him how funny he looks in
long skirts, but making fun of an altar boy is as bad as making
fun of a priest—a mortal sin, or worse. It's okay to laugh at
nuns, but not priests.

"Look who's talking." Ruthie's voice is heavy with insinua-
tion. Jackie is in trouble more frequently than she.

"Yeah? Well, I'm not pretending to be an angel, either."

"Good thing. You couldn't get off the ground wearing
those." Ruthie stares pointedly at the glimmer of copper-toed
boots showing under Jackie's cassock. "Wait till Sister sees
those hightops!"

Watching Jackie take a step backward into thicker grass,
Ruthie holds her lily high and smiles. It would take knee-
high weeds to hide the thick soles and long lacings of those
tall leather boots. Hightops are despised by the nuns, and
forbidden at Church functions. Ruthie has always been intrigued by the sight of heavy shoes under the long priestly
vestments, particularly the muddy soles turned up when they
kneel. She used to think that was what "feet of clay" were. It
was a disappointing surprise to learn that the priests wore
regular clothes under their robes. If the boys were angels,
she wonders, would they wear corduroys and sweaters under
their gowns instead of a slip?

"You'd look better in a coffin with that lily," says Jackie.
"If you did croak they'd probably bury you with your bat
instead of flowers."

Ruthie's enthusiasm for softball has given her a reputation

as a tomboy, but she could never get in the game until her dad bought her a glove and a bat, and she watches them carefully. Without them she will be back on the sidelines.

"I'd rather have my bat. Then I could rise up from the dead, like Lazarus, and strike you down!" She takes a swing at him with her lily, but before she can complete it, her arm is caught in a painful grip and she is jerked around to confront a shouting Sister Martha Ann.

"Ruth Eileen! Stop that at once!" Plucking the lily from Ruthie's hand, Sister inspects it. "A procession to honor our Blessed Mother is hardly the time for her children to be fighting." Sister's dark eyes shine through her polished glasses, into Ruthie's blue ones, holding them, unblinking. "You must control yourself."

"Yes, Sister," Ruthie says, looking sideways at her arm until it is released, pinched and sore. What about Jackie, she thinks. He started it.

Her veil swirling like a curl of black dust, Sister Martha Ann turns to the boys. "Line up behind the banner," she orders, "and march!"

"Except for you, John Ellery Hancock!" she adds, pulling him back. "What kind of behavior is this for a young man aspiring to the priesthood?"

With a face as red as a fresh burn, Jackie stares ahead, erasing every trace of intelligent thought from his expression. He says nothing.

"I'll see you both in the office after the procession," Sister says.

A hot flame of fury rises in Ruthie; now there will be no movies. Instead, they will have to sit on the straight-backed chairs in the school office, listening, for as long as Sister wants to keep them. It's all Jackie's fault.

"Do you understand?" Sister asks, waiting for the automatic nods.

"No, Sister, I don't," Ruthie says in a loud voice.

"This is no time for nonsense, Ruthie. What don't you understand?"

"I don't understand why I'm here, why girls are angels.

Didn't you say the messengers of God are all men? The real angels are Gabriel and Michael and Raphael. Even Lucifer was an angel before he was the devil. It seems like boys should be leading the procession."

"Oh, Ruthie!" Gently, Sister Martha Ann shakes the lily. Her glasses flash in the sun as she looks toward the bits of blue sky filtering through the unfolding elm leaves. She is quiet, as though she might be in prayer. When she looks back at Ruthie, her lips are sucked into one straight line. Solemnly, she bends down to pat Ruthie's head, smooth her straight hair.

"I think I understand what you mean," she says. "It's a good thought—very good. It's too late to change now, but we'll think about it for next year." Smiling her big smile, she nods at Jackie. "Yes, indeed, we'll think about it, for next year, but right now I want the angels to take their places. You, too, Jackie, get in line with the other altar boys."

Firmly, she puts the lily back in Ruthie's hands, and points to the other angels. Following the banner and the altar boys, they are leading the procession in its slow start; the singing has begun.

"Yes, Sister." Ruthie clasps the lily and gazes at Jackie, noting white lines around his mouth. She wonders if he might be going to throw up; someone always does during a procession. Shrugging her shoulders, she feels the wings rise and fall on her back. Maybe she only imagined it—maybe it was the sun on her glasses—but Sister Martha Ann might have winked. There is no way to be sure—any more than she can be sure who will wear the angel gowns next year. Just the thought of it—of angels with feet of clay—calms her spirit. Together, Ruthie and Jackie hurry across to the grass to take their places at the front of the procession. Before they part company, Ruthie waves her lily under his nose.

"Hey, Hancock," she hisses, "want me to save you my wings for next year?"

Normal

My father is missing a leg. My mother is missing a breast. "You are normal," my mother tells me. She smiles and rubs my arms, but I'm not sure what she means.

I love to sit in my bedroom and stare at my toes and tell myself stories. The shades are drawn for my nap, but the summer sun streams in anyway and casts an unreal glow upon the furniture in my room and upon my flesh. Ten toes. Ten fingers. Two arms. Two legs. Two titties. One head. One heart.

Once a week, my mother washes my sheets and even my bedspread and curtains. She uses bleach and hangs everything on the clothesline—the sheets draped and folded just so and clamped with wooden clothespins. It is hard for her to lift her arm. The clothespins are in a bag that hangs on the line. Once, a mother blackbird made a nest there, and when my mother reached for a clothespin, a bird soared down from the sky and pecked my mother's cheek. The story confuses me, and sometimes I think of the nursery rhyme she reads me before I go to sleep, and sometimes I think it is the blackbird who has stolen her breast.

Auntie's dog Midge has had puppies. Auntie lives in California. She sends us a picture and an announcement. Midge is a Chihuahua. The puppies are one girl and two boys. Their names are Elizabeth, Ralph, and Tom. I stare and stare at the photograph. "Can't she do better than that?" my mother asks. "No husband. No kids." At night I dream it is me who has had the puppies. My mother is mad at me. She looks at me in complete disgust. "Can't you do better than that?" she asks.

It is fall. My mother has changed my bedroom curtains to red drapes and has put a red bedspread to match on my bed. Now the golden glow has disappeared, but in its place is a quivering red flame that burns the furniture and sets my flesh on fire. It is time for me to start school. My mother has braided my hair with ribbons. She has bought me a blue uniform with pockets, and a lunch basket, and saddle shoes. She puts five marbles and a quarter into my pocket—a blue puree, a red puree, an orange cat's-eye, a yellow tabby, and a baby-blue solid. As I wait for the bus that will take me to school, I touch the marbles and look at them. I try to decide which is my favorite. Sometimes I choose the red puree, sometimes the baby-blue solid. I cannot make up my mind. My mother has given me the marbles, so that I will play with the other children.

The first grade teacher is Sister Angelica. The second grade teacher is Sister Charlotte. Sister Angelica is sweet, but Sister Charlotte is strict. She hits children with a yardstick. She makes them stand in front of the room and does not care if they cry. She makes the whole class stare at the crucifix and sing, "Jesus died upon the cross just because He loves me."

I am in the first grade. I have Sister Angelica, so I am safe for a while. In second grade you learn to write cursive and everything changes.

Marvin has webbed fingers and feet like a duck. Lois is big with glasses. She is in the sixth grade. Sister Immaculata's room. Her right arm is like a baby's. It never grew and it never will grow. My mother says, "You must play with the other children." But the other children do not want to play with me. They know one another from kindergarten. The girls play Witches and Statuemaker, games that I do not know. I sit on the steps and count my five marbles. I am happy because the sun is warm and bright and it makes my marbles shine. I watch Lois, who also is alone. She walks back and forth across the gravel lot next to the school. I make up a story about her. In my story the Archangel Gabriel comes from heaven to give her a normal arm so that she can fold her hands in church and pray like the rest of us. My mother says, "I drove past the school today at recess time and saw you sitting on the steps alone again."

My father comes to talk to Sister Angelica at recess time. I feel guilty when I see him coming because he limps with his artificial leg. It is because of me that he is coming. My mother is worried because I do not play with the other children. Not only does he limp, but he is not Catholic. I wait with Sister Angelica at the side door as he slowly moves across the gravel lot toward us. I am afraid that Sister will say something because he has never attended mass. My parents have a mixed marriage. But Sister Angelica smiles sweetly at him. "You are one of our war heroes," she tells him. She says, "Do not worry about Bernadette. She is just a bit shy." But my mother continues to ask me every afternoon after school, as I polish my saddle shoes, "Did you play with the kids at recess time? You know I might go by tomorrow in the car to check on you."

It is First Friday. I like First Friday because after mass we get to have hot chocolate and sweet rolls in the school basement. But this First Friday I am crying because my mother has forgotten to make me wear my hat. I cannot go to mass without my hat. I am standing on the sidewalk in front of the church, crying. It is 7:30 in the morning. My father has dropped me off early on his way to work at the VFW. I've never been so scared in my life. If I go to church without my hat, everyone will notice. They will whisper. I'm not sure if it would be a mortal sin or not. It is my fear that leads me to do something almost as scary as entering the church without a hat: to knock on the rectory door. Father Murphy answers the door. He is dressed in black. Next year, when I'm in second grade, I will have to tell him all my sins. He stares at me and waits for me to speak. "I've forgotten my hat and

I want to call home," I shout at him, almost crying. He shows me to the phone. I dial my home telephone number, which my mother made me learn by heart. The telephone rings and rings, but my mother does not answer. Then I remember that on Fridays she goes to physical therapy. "You can wear a doily," Father Murphy says. He gives me a frilly white cloth. I put it on my head and look at myself in the hall mirror. "I'll call my father," I tell him, once again in tears.

My father comes. I wait for him on the sidewalk in front of the church. My father does not drive because of his leg. He always takes a taxicab. He has taken the taxicab home from work to get my wide-brimmed Sunday hat with the elastic band and then to church to give it to me. When he gets out of the cab to bring it to me, I no longer feel afraid, but I feel ashamed. I run toward him, so he does not have to limp so far to reach me.

In second grade, I am one of Sister Charlotte's favorite students. I write in beautiful cursive. She never hits me with the yardstick, but when she smiles in her black habit, I can't help but think of a witch. I also think of the blackbird that stole my mother's breast. She lets me water her plants in the morning. She makes all of us stare at the crucifix and sing, "Jesus died upon the cross just because He loves me." It's a sad song, one that I will remember all my life.

I begin to play with Judith, to go home with her after school or bring her home with me. She is not really my friend, but I play with her to please my mother. I play with her for one month. I play with her even after she takes my five marbles. Then one day my mother says I should not go to Judith's house anymore because her mother works and does not take care of the house or kids. Her father has not planted grass, and their yard is all dirt. Her little sisters don't wear underpants. I am glad when my mother says this. I come home after school alone. I go to my room and read library books about Albert Schweitzer.

*   *   *

In second grade, I make my First Confession and my First Communion. My mother buys me a beautiful white communion dress and a veil months before time. They hang in my closet, and every day I take a look at them. When I sit in my room in the late afternoon or at night, I tell myself a new story. In it, I am an army nurse. I wear my white communion dress and veil. I go into a battlefield and take care of my father, who's been shot.

One day Bulah and my mother go shopping. Bulah has offered to help my mother buy a new breast. Bulah has said that my mother has gotten cancer because she sun bathes. Every summer my mother lies in the sun for hours. She gets a deep and even tan. Many people think my mother is beautiful. I do, too, especially when she wears pink lipstick and pink summer dresses and pink high-heeled shoes. "That's ridiculous," my mother tells my father. "The sun doesn't give you breast cancer. She's just jealous."

I'm supposed to go over to Minny's if I need anything while my mother is shopping with Bulah. Minny is Larry's mom. When I was only four, Larry punched me in the stomach so hard I couldn't breathe. That's when I learned that punching a girl in the stomach was the worst thing a boy could do to you.

Larry urinates outdoors. He calls it pee, but my parents have taught me to call things by their right names. They are very strict about it. Larry goes to public school, because Saint Irene's got rid of him. He comes over while my mother is shopping with Bulah and wants to play war. "Okay," I say slowly. "But not the war where we chase each other." I bring him into my bedroom and show him my communion dress. I put it on in front of him. I put the veil on, too. The idea is that he has been shot in battle against the Germans. I must take care of him. We go to the field with chokecherry trees across the street. He lies on the ground. I feel his arms and legs. I look into his mouth, his nose, his ears. I listen to his heart. Then, suddenly, I am the one who is lying on the ground, my arms pinned to my side, his freckled face so close to my own that I must close my eyes.

The dress is dirty. The veil is torn. My mother finally discovers them a week later in the closet. She slams the bedroom door so hard against the wall that the knob leaves a dent in the wall. She slams it again and again. Then she begins to cry. She cries for over an hour about many things: because my father cannot dance with her; because he forgot to buy goldfish food when she asked him to; because she has only one breast; because I am disobedient and do not have nice friends; because I will grow up to be a lonely old woman, maybe a nun, maybe an evil woman like Cecil, who allows men other than her husband to kiss her.

Outside I hear imaginary children yelling, "Your father has one leg. Your mother has one boob." There is nothing I can do now to save myself from them. I sit on my bed and listen to my mother's anger. I must hug her, tell her I'm sorry. I cannot, my mother tells me through her tears, stay alone in my room for the rest of my life and make up stories.

Audre Lorde

Excerpt from
Zami: A New Spelling of My Name

As a child, the most horrible condition I could contemplate was being wrong and being discovered. Mistakes could mean exposure, maybe even annihilation. In my mother's house, there was no room in which to make errors, no room to be wrong.

I grew Black as my need for life, for affirmation, for love, for sharing—copying from my mother what was in her, unfulfilled. I grew Black as *Seboulisa*, who I was to find in the cool mud halls of Abomey several lifetimes later—and, as alone. My mother's words teaching me all manner of wily and diversionary defenses learned from the white man's tongue, from out of the mouth of her father. She had had to use these defenses, and had survived by them, and had also died by them a little, at the same time. All the colors change and become each other, merge and separate, flow into rainbows and nooses.

I lie beside my sisters in the darkness, who pass me in the street unacknowledged and unadmitted. How much of this is the pretense of self-rejection that became an immovable protective mask, how much the programmed hate that we were fed to keep ourselves a part, apart?

One day (I remember I was still in the second grade) my mother was out marketing, and my sisters were talking about someone being *Colored*. In my six-year-old way, I jumped at this chance to find out what it was all about.

"What does *Colored* mean?" I asked. To my amazement, neither one of my sisters was quite sure.

"Well," Phyllis said. "The nuns are white, and the Short-Neck Store-Man is white, and Father Mulvoy is white and we're Colored."

"And what's Mommy? Is she white or Colored?"

"I don't know," answered Phyllis impatiently.

"Well," I said, "if anybody asks me what I am, I'm going to tell them I'm white same as Mommy."

"Ohhhhhhhhhh, girl, you better not do that," they both chorused in horror.

"Why not?" I asked, more confused than ever. But neither of them could tell me why.

That was the first and only time my sisters and I discussed race as a reality in my house, or at any rate as it applied to ourselves.

Our new apartment was on 152nd Street between Amsterdam Avenue and Broadway in what was called Washington Heights, and already known as a "changing" neighborhood, meaning one where Black people could begin to find over-priced apartments out of the depressed and decaying core of Harlem.

The apartment house that we moved into was owned by a small landlord. We moved at the end of the summer, and I began school that year in a new catholic school which was right across the street from our house.

Two weeks after we moved into the new apartment, our landlord hanged himself in the basement. The *Daily News* reported that the suicide was caused by his despondency over the fact that he finally had to rent to Negroes. I was the first Black student in St. Catherine's School, and all the white kids in my sixth grade class knew about the landlord who had hanged himself in the basement because of me and my family. He had been Jewish; I was Black. That made us both fair game for the cruel curiosity of my pre-adolescent classmates.

Ann Archdeacon, red-headed darling of the nuns and of Monsignor Brady, was the first one to ask me what I knew about the landlord's death. As usual, my parents had discussed the whole matter in patois, and I only read the comics in the daily paper.

"I don't know anything about it," I said, standing in the schoolyard at lunchtime, twisting my front braids and looking around for some friendly face. Ann Archdeacon snickered, and the rest of the group that had gathered around us to hear roared with laughter, until Sister Blanche waddled over to see what was going on.

If the Sisters of the Blessed Sacrament at St. Mark's School had been patronizing, at least their racism was couched in the terms of their mission. At St. Catherine's School, the Sisters of Charity were downright hostile. Their racism was unadorned, unexcused, and particularly painful because I was unprepared for it. I got no help at home. The children in my class made fun of my braids, so Sister Victoire, the principal, sent a note home to my mother asking her to comb my hair in a more "becoming" fashion, since I was too old, she said, to wear "pigtails."

All the girls wore blue gabardine uniforms that by springtime were a little musty, despite frequent drycleanings. I would come in from recess to find notes in my desk saying "You Stink." I showed them to Sister Blanche. She told me that she felt it was her christian duty to tell me that Colored people *did* smell different from white people, but it was cruel of the children to write nasty notes because I couldn't help it, and if I would remain out in the yard the next day after the rest of the class came in after lunchtime, she would talk to them about being nicer to me!

The head of the parish and the school was Monsignor John J. Brady, who told my mother when she registered me that he had never expected to have to take Colored kids into his school. His favorite pastime was holding Ann Archdeacon or Ilene Crimmons on his lap, while he played with their blonde and red curls with one hand, and slid the other hand up the back of their blue gabardine uniforms. I did not care about his lechery, but I did care that he kept me in every Wednesday afternoon after school to memorize latin nouns.

The other children in my class were given a cursory quiz to test their general acquaintance with the words, and then let go early, since it was the early release day for religious instruction.

I came to loathe Wednesday afternoons, sitting by myself in the classroom trying to memorize the singular and plural of a long list of latin nouns, and their genders. Every half-hour or so, Father Brady would look in from the rectory, and ask to hear the words. If I so much as hesitated over any word or its plural, or its gender, or said it out of place on the list, he would spin on his black-robed heel and disappear for another half-hour or so. Although early dismissal was at 2:00 P.M., some Wednesdays I didn't get home until after four o'clock. Sometimes on Wednesday nights I would dream of the white, acrid-smelling mimeograph sheet: *agricola*, *agricolae*, fem., farmer. Three years later when I began Hunter High School and had to take latin in earnest, I had built up such a block to everything about it that I failed my first two terms of it.

When I complained at home about my treatment at school, my mother would get angry with me.

"What do you care what they say about you, anyway? Do they put bread on your plate? You go to school to learn, so learn and leave the rest alone. You don't need friends." I did not see her helplessness, nor her pain.

I was the smartest girl in the class, which did nothing to contribute to my popularity. But the Sisters of the Blessed Sacrament had taught me well, and I was way ahead in math and mental arithmetic.

In the spring of the sixth grade, Sister Blanche announced that we were going to hold elections for two class presidents, one boy and one girl. Anyone could run, she said, and we would vote on Friday of that week. The voting should be according to merit and effort and class spirit, she added, but the most important thing would be marks.

Of course, Ann Archdeacon was nominated immediately. She was not only the most popular girl in the school, she was the prettiest. Ilene Crimmons was also nominated, her blonde curls and favored status with the Monsignor guaranteed that.

I lent Jim Moriarty ten cents, stolen from my father's pocket at lunchtime, so Jim nominated me. A titter went through the class, but I ignored it. I was in seventh heaven. I knew I was the smartest girl in the class. I had to win.

That afternoon when my mother came home from the office, I told her about the election, and how I was going to run, and win. She was furious.

"What in hell are you doing getting yourself involved with so much foolishness? You don't have better sense in your head than that? What-the-france do you need with election? We send you to school to work, not to prance about with president-this election-that. Get down the rice, girl, and stop talking your foolishness." We started preparing the food.

"But I just might win, Mommy. Sister Blanche said it should go to the smartest girl in the class." I wanted her to see how important it was to me.

"Don't bother me with that nonsense. I don't want to hear any more about it. And don't come in here on Friday with a long face, and any 'I didn't win, Mommy,' because I don't want to hear that, either. Your father and I have enough trouble to keep among you in school, never mind election."

I dropped the subject.

The week was a very long and exciting one for me. The only way I could get attention from my classmates in the sixth grade was by having money, and thanks to carefully planned forays into my father's pants pockets every night that week, I made sure I had plenty. Every day at noon, I dashed across the street, gobbled down whatever food my mother had left for my lunch, and headed for the schoolyard.

Sometimes when I came home for lunch my father was asleep in my parents' bedroom before he returned to work.

I now had my very own room, and my two sisters shared another. The day before the election, I tiptoed through the house to the closed french doors of my parents' bedroom, and through a crack in the portières peeked in upon my sleeping father. The doors seemed to shake with his heavy snoring. I watched his mouth open and close a little with each snore, stentorian rattles erupting below his nuzzled moustache. The covers thrown partially back, to reveal his hands in sleep tucked into the top of his drawstring pajamas. He was lying on his side toward me, and the front of his pajama pants had fallen open. I could see only shadows of the vulnerable secrets shading the gap in his clothing, but I was suddenly shaken by this so-human image of him, and the idea that I could spy upon him and he not be aware of it, even in his sleep. I stepped back and closed the door quickly, embarrassed and ashamed of my own curiosity, but wishing his pajamas had gapped more so that I could finally know what exactly was the mysterious secret men carried between their legs.

When I was ten, a little boy on the rooftop had taken off my glasses, and so seeing little, all I could remember of that encounter, when I remembered it at all, was a long thin pencil-like thing that I knew couldn't have any relationship to my father.

Before I closed the door, though, I slipped my hand around the door-curtains to where Daddy's suit hung. I separated a dollar bill from the thin roll which he carried in his pants pocket. Then I retreated back into the kitchen, washed my plate and glass, and hurried back to school. I had electioneering to do.

I knew better than to say another word to my mother about the presidency, but that week was filled with fantasies of how I would break the news to her on Friday when she came home.

"Oh, Mommy, by the way, can I stay later at school on Monday for a presidents' meeting?" Or "Mother, would you please sign this note saying it is all right for me to accept the presidency?" Or maybe even, "Mother, could I have a little get-together here to celebrate the election?"

On Friday, I tied a ribbon around the steel barrette that held my unruly mass of hair tightly at the nape of my neck. Elections were to be held in the afternoon, and when I got home for lunch, for the first time in my life, I was too excited to eat. I buried the can of Campbell's soup that my mother had left out for me way behind the other cans in the pantry and hoped she had not counted how many were left.

We filed out of the schoolyard and up the stairs to the sixth grade room. The walls were still lined with bits of green from the recent St. Patrick's Day decorations. Sister Blanche passed out little pieces of blank paper for our ballots.

The first rude awakening came when she announced that the boy chosen would be president, but the girl would only be vice-president. I thought this was monstrously unfair. Why not the other way around? Since we could not, as she explained, have two presidents, why not a girl president and a boy vice-president? It doesn't really matter, I said to myself. I can live with being vice-president.

I voted for myself. The ballots were collected and passed to the front of the room and duly counted. James O'Connor won for the boys. Ann Archdeacon won for the girls. Ilene Crimmons came in second. I got four votes, one of which was mine. I was in shock. We all clapped for the winners, and Ann Archdeacon turned around in her seat and smiled her shit-eating smile at me. "Too bad you lost." I smiled back. I wanted to break her face off.

I was too much my mother's daughter to let anyone think it mattered. But I felt I had been destroyed. How could this have happened? I was the smartest girl in the class. I had not been elected vice-president. It was as simple as that. But something was escaping me. Something was terribly wrong. It wasn't fair.

A sweet little girl named Helen Ramsey had decided it was her christian duty to befriend me, and she had once lent me her sled during the winter. She lived next to the church, and after school, that day, she invited me to her house for a cup of cocoa. I ran away without answering, dashing across the street and into the safety of my house. I ran up the stairs, my bookbag banging against my legs. I pulled out the key pinned to my uniform pocket and unlocked the door to our apartment. The house was warm and dark and empty and quiet. I did not stop running until I got to my room at the front of the house, where I flung my books and my coat in a corner and collapsed upon my convertible couch-bed, shrieking with fury and disappointment. Finally, in the privacy of my room, I could shed the tears that had been burning my eyes for two hours, and I wept and wept.

I had wanted other things before that I had not gotten. So much so, that I had come to believe if I really wanted something badly enough, the very act of my wanting it was an assurance that I would not get it. Was this what had happened with the election? Had I wanted it too much? Was this what my mother was always talking about? Why she had been so angry? Because wanting meant I would not get? But somehow this felt different. This was the first time that I had wanted something so badly, the getting of which I was sure I could control. The election was supposed to have gone to the smartest girl in the class, and I was clearly the smartest. That was something I had done, on my own, that should have guaranteed me the election. The smartest, not the most popular. That was me. But it hadn't happened. My mother had been right. I hadn't won the election. My mother had been right.

This thought hurt me almost as much as the loss of the election, and when I felt it fully I shrieked with renewed vigor. I luxuriated in my grief in the empty house in a way I could never have done if anyone were home.

All the way up front and buried in my tears, kneeling with my face in the cushions of my couch, I did not hear the key in the lock, nor the main door open. The first thing I knew, there was my mother standing in the doorway of my room, a frown of concern in her voice.

"What happened, what happened? What's wrong with you? What's this racket going on here?"

I turned my wet face up to her from the couch. I wanted a little comfort in my pain, and getting up, I started moving toward her.

"I lost the election, Mommy," I cried, forgetting her warnings. "I'm the smartest girl in class, Sister Blanche says so, and they chose Ann Archdeacon instead!" The unfairness of it all flooded over me again and my voice cracked into fresh sobs.

Through my tears, I saw my mother's face stiffen with rage. Her eyebrows drew together as her hand came up, still holding her handbag. I stopped in my tracks as her first blow caught me full on the side of my head. My mother was no weakling, and I backed away, my ears ringing. The whole world seemed to be going insane. It was only then I remembered our earlier conversations.

"See, the bird forgets, but the trap doesn't! I warned you! What you think you doing coming into this house wailing about election? If I told you once I have told you a hundred times, don't chase yourself behind these people, haven't I? What kind of ninny raise up here to think those good-for-nothing white piss-jets would pass over some little jacabat girl to elect you anything?" Smack! "What did I say to you just now?" She cuffed me again, this time on my shoulders, as I huddled to escape her rain of furious blows, and the edges of her pocketbook.

"Sure enough, didn't I tell you not to come in here bringing down tears over some worthless fool election?" Smack! "What the hell you think we send you to school for?" Smack! "Don't run yourself behind other people's business, you'll do better. Dry up, now, dry up!" Smack! She pulled me to my feet from where I had sunk back onto the couch.

"Is cry you want to cry? I'll give you something hard to cry on!" And she cuffed me again, this time more lightly. "Now get yourself up from there and stop acting like some stupid fool, worrying yourself about these people's business that doesn't concern you. Get-the-france out of here and wipe up your face. Start acting like a human being!"

Pushing me ahead of her, my mother marched back

through the parlor and into the kitchen. "I come in here tired from the street and here you, acting like the world is ending. I thought sure enough some terrible thing happened to you, come to find out it's only election. Now help me put away this foodstuff."

I was relieved to hear her tone mollify, as I wiped my eyes. But I still gave her heavy hands a wide berth.

"It's just that it's not fair, Mother. That's all I was crying about," I said, opening the brown paper bags on the table. To admit I had been hurt would somehow put me in the wrong for feeling pain. "It wasn't the election I cared about so much really, just that it was all so unfair."

"Fair, fair, what's fair, you think? Is fair you want, look in god's face." My mother was busily dropping onions into the bin. She paused, and turning around, held my puffy face up, her hand beneath my chin. Her eyes so sharp and furious before, now just looked tired and sad.

"Child, why you worry your head so much over fair or not fair? Just do what is for you to do and let the rest take care of themselves." She smoothed straggles of hair back from my face, and I felt the anger gone from her fingers. "Look, you hair all mess-up behind from rolling around with foolishness. Go wash your face and hands and come help me dress this fish for supper."

Melissa Anderson Lowry

Doubting the Reality
of God

I am standing in my mother's kitchen, waiting for the business of baking cookies to resume. Our Saturday morning ritual had been rudely interrupted by my older sister, who has chosen this cozy family moment to renew her threat to become a nun.

"You can't be a nun," I tell her. "You have to have a vocation. You have to—" My mother tells me to be quiet, and my sister sticks her tongue out at me. Some nun. Sister Smartass.

A battle of wits and wills has raged throughout our home for most of the winter: my sister has dropped out of college and is working at Boeing, earning her running-away money. My parents have been giving a series of lectures entitled: "You're Too Young to Know What You Want," "Think of What You're Throwing Away," and "Over My Dead Body." The local parish nuns smell victory and have been circling the house like seagulls over a plate of French fries.

We are not a particularly religious family (my father refuses to attend any weekly gathering not held in a bowling alley or on a golf course), but my mother has always taken my sister and me to St. Edward's Catholic Church for Sunday Mass, confession, rosary hours, feast days, arcane holy days of obligation and other religious pit stops.

I do not, however, attend Catholic school. In some neighborhoods going to Catholic school is almost as prestigious as going to "private" (i.e., nonsectarian but vaguely Protestant, suburban prep) school. But in our middle-class, white-bread-eating neighborhood, going to Catholic school means belonging to a large family with enough brothers and sisters to keep the uniforms in circulation for years, as well as to assure a quantity discount on tuition.

Sometimes while I'm hanging around the drugstore after school, I see these unfortunate parochial prisoners trudging homeward in their blue tartan skirts, salt-and-pepper cords, and inevitable white shirts, lugging the suitcase-sized book satchel that is as much a part of the uniform as brown lace-up oxfords or the B.V.M. medal. If you are a St. Edward's kid, you are forbidden to carry books balanced against the stomach, clasped to the chest, or hanging down at the end of the arm, bumping negligently against the thigh: the nuns revile this as "inappropriate behavior" (the official term for everything from chewing gum to swearing to playing in the holy water font). The ponderous satchel is supposed to be a safeguard against leaving your books somewhere by accident, although you are not allowed to stop off anywhere between school and home. God forbid the nuns should catch you loitering in the drugstore.

I am quite familiar with the nuns and their numerous edicts. I take piano lessons from Sister Mary Ita in the convent parlor every Wednesday afternoon, and the nuns all find excuses to troop in while I'm working over "Carry Me Back to Old Virginny" and hitting clinkers. I'm convinced they think they're going to hook me the way they hooked my sister during *her* piano lessons: lots of attention and flattery, a lifetime supply of holy cards, and a chance to be heroic in the Belgian Congo (my sister has dragged all of us to see "The Nun's Story" at least twice). They pet me and let me wear their rosaries and other fashion accessories, and I have amassed a large collection of holy cards inscribed with religious messages, but I am not so easily swayed. Plus there is no way I'd ever stand still for having my head shaved.

My mother and my sister are talking a little louder and

faster now, and I take this opportunity to eat some raw cookie dough. My mother is going to tell me for the millionth time that raw cookie dough gives you worms. My sister is all set to be locked up in some nun-jail where we'll get to talk to her through the chicken wire about once every seven years ... and my mother's worried about worms?

Besides, my sister can't be a nun if she doesn't have a vocation. I know all about vocations because Sister Mary Ita gave me a little book to read one day when I was early for my lesson. There was a picture of Saint Theresa walking on roses in her bare feet, and I guessed that she had a vocation because it didn't hurt her to step on the thorns (I didn't have time to read that part very well). Anyway, my sister, who is the world's biggest baby when it comes to getting a sliver out of her finger, is obviously not brave enough to be a nun and go to the Belgian Congo and be attacked by cannibals. And she can't be terribly interested in being holy because she still has all her cheerleader pom-poms and stuffed animals and tropical fish up in her room. If she wanted to be a really good nun she'd be sleeping on the floor and wouldn't leave her church hat parked on her Saint Theresa statue.

My sister slams out of the kitchen. Something in the cupboard falls down with a crash, but my mother just shakes her head and starts putting more chocolate chips in the cookie dough.

"Mom, now will I *have* to go to St. Edward's school?" My real fear is that this may turn out to be some kind of package deal, with me thrown in as a plenary indulgence. "It's okay with me if she wants to be a nun, but why should I have to suffer?"

"She's not going to be a nun, so you have nothing to worry about," Mom says. "And stop eating that dough. You'll get worms."

Somewhat cheered up, I take my sister some cookies as a sign of solidarity. I really don't care if she wants to be a nun—just as long as she keeps me out of it and I get to move into her room and adopt her fish. Maybe she'll let me have her pom-poms. But all she gives me is her sappy nun-smile (the one she's been practicing in the bathroom mirror) and says she can't eat cookies because she gave them up for Lent. She also says she wants to be alone now and will I please beat it? I notice that since she wants to be a nun she's saying "please" a little more often.

Easter comes, and no one has budged an inch. But I know my sister will get her way because my parents are now saying things like She Has to Find Out for Herself and We Wouldn't Forbid Her. My mother is still hedging her bets, but for every summer-school brochure she plants around the house, my sister gets out another list of things she's supposed to bring with her to the convent. My father says he guesses the poverty part doesn't start until she gets there.

On the Monday morning after Easter I sit on the edge of my sister's bed, watching her pack her suitcase (her big trunk is already down in the car). This is kind of like watching her pack for summer camp, although instead of T-shirts and shorts, everything she is folding up is black: black shoes, black stockings, long black skirts. I ask her if she's taking along black pajamas, but she doesn't answer me. So I just sit there eating the ears off a chocolate bunny and thinking about the postcards she used to send me from Camp Kla-how-ya. I bet I won't be getting any postcards from nun-camp.

Then one Saturday morning I am told to put on a dress and go get in the car. My father (who has parked his golf clubs very pointedly by the front door) is driving us over to the convent to visit my sister, who has made good her escape and become something mysterious called a *postulant*. We haven't seen her for six weeks—who knows what she's turned into by now?

She comes walking across the convent lawn (accompanied by a *real* nun), pretending to smile. She is wearing a black dress with a sliver of white collar, and a short black veil that allows a crescent of hair to show on her forehead (maybe they save the head-shaving until last). I am not sure whether she's glad to see us.

We are allowed to stand around in a nasty medicinal-smelling parlor with waxed gray linoleum floors and talk to her. We don't talk about anything very important, being rather intimidated by her bodyguard with the caterpillar eyebrows and the faint mustache. She's there to keep my sister in line and prevent her from telling us all those deep dark secrets of the convent (like what they eat for dinner and what kind of underwear they have).

Soon it's past my lunchtime and I am really hungry. I know Dad will stop at a drive-in on the way home and buy us hamburgers and Green Rivers, but I want something to eat *right now*, so I begin whining. This time-tested tactic works as always: my now saintly sister volunteers to try to find me some morsel.

She brings me a soft and stale store-bought cookie which I wolf down and then immediately regret: she smiles her sickly smile and says, "Of course, I'll have to confess taking that cookie for you. We're not allowed anything between meals—it's a venial sin."

The wretched cookie turns to lead in my gut: I have just condemned my sister to hell (or at least uncounted centuries in the waiting room of purgatory) because I couldn't rise above the deadly sin of gluttony.

Another Saturday morning. Another batch of chocolate chip cookies. Another argument. After a tearful midnight telephone call, after a rescue mission by my father ... my sister is back home, working at Boeing, saving up her running-away money and telling everyone she's going to be an actress. My mother is renewing her lecture series. I turn up the radio so I won't have to listen to them argue. I sing along with "Standing on the Corner Watching All the Girls Go By" and eat cookie dough.

Kay Hogan

Of Saints and Other Things

The day Ann Cunningham told me the facts of life I decided to become a saint. I had read numerous books on the saints, and the white-robed girls with neon hearts called to me. Why not a saint from the Bronx? Why not, I thought, and the notion of a statue, a medal, and holy cards in my image spurred me on.

I watched her forehead wrinkle with expression as Ann went into gory detail. As a diversion, I chewed my gum loudly and counted her pimples. She just smiled when I said, "Not mine. I just know my mother wouldn't do anything like that."

"Go ask her," she said, and that slippery smile spread across her face again. I knew our friendship would never be the same. No more sharing comic books in the hallway or swapping sins for Saturday confessions. I knew I would never ask my mother anything, especially after last month's gathering. Ever since that meeting, I had felt disconnected, and a strangeness hovered between us.

Having been billed as a "women talk," meeting, I felt awkward and out of place amidst my aunts, Bridie and Margaret, and my mother. Of course, the Blessed Mother was in attendance, if not by sight, certainly by acclamation. I considered the Blessed Mother an invisible relative as she filtered through our daily lives in decision-making, direction, cures, sadness, blessings, and warnings. The formalities behind them, they began to stammer, passing phrases, whispering, letting them go quickly, like a cup of very hot tea.

"And anyway," my mother concluded before I thought she had really started, "no sense worrying now that you've become a woman. The Blessed Mother invented the whole thing."

I wanted to stifle her words and also bury the images that Ann had created for me. I fled to Saint Luke's Church, to the comforting quiet, to the cool marble walls that caressed me. I thought of all the masses I had attended, the monstrance that held the sacred host, the smell of incense that clung like veils, making me feel special—ghostlike. Now, all of it was jarred loose, splayed about, and I needed a plan. Sainthood. With my destiny assured, I didn't have to think about Ann Cunningham or my mother's words.

I draped myself in white curtains, with a rope tied around my waist, and practiced looking saintly. The saints I read about died defending their virginity, whatever that was. The dying I could handle, but the mechanics of defense eluded me. Growing up was becoming confusing. As I looked into the mirror, there were no beams of light, nor flashing heart. Only a girl, quite plain and ordinary.

For a while I tried increasing the novenas, the prayers and ejaculations. Over and over, in rhythmic chants, whenever there was silence, I repeated the words.

"Immaculate heart of Mary, pray for us," or "Jesus, Mary, and Joseph." My neck turned green, but I refused to take my miraculous medal off. That counted, too, in my accumulation of indulgences. I had been adding, "365 days in heaven for those who attend the first Friday of each month for nine consecutive Fridays," busily counting and chanting, when it dawned on me: surely God was more than a warden with a degree in math. Then I remembered a Gospel that spoke about God promising the big reward if you saved a soul. My convert quest began.

Maxie Marx lived next door and was the only Jewish person I had ever seen up close. Every day, after school, my brothers would capture him and hold him down while I read chapters from the Baltimore Catechism. We would pray over him and douse him with holy water. I thought I was making great progress, even though Maxie kept giggling throughout the ceremonies, until his mother came after us one day. She screamed, "Who speaks to my Maxie of Virgin birth?" and we scattered, like birds, to the black-tarred rooftops.

Undaunted, I went after Peggy Bailey, who could have been your ordinary Irishman, except she was Protestant. I often stared at her, trying to find out if her religion showed. I knew that Protestants took the summer off from religion. One day, pen in hand, I showed her the statistics on Catholics, pointing out that in the event she made it to heaven there would always be more of us than them.

"Just look around," I told her. "And count the Catholic kids in the neighborhood, plus all the ones waiting to be born. You'll be outnumbered," I said.

I also noted that we had more sacramental marks than she did. She just cried. Jealous, I guess, but she wouldn't sign up.

I looked everywhere for recruiting possibilities, but the neighborhood and my world were limited. Bearing gifts of Irish soda bread, my mother made me apologize to Maxie and Peggy. Still, I persisted. There must be someone in need of conversion; someone who lived without rosaries and medals, whose life was not scheduled in blocks of time called Lent and Advent. Someone far away.

My missionary plan was employed. Visions of a nun, with a suitcaseful of faith, sailing into some obscure African township, drove me on. I could see the converts now, thousands of them. I would announce my plans as soon as my vacation was over, or perhaps after the big dance. I started to clean out my closet and wondered why nuns came in black and white. An ache rose up in me. I would miss color, and I would miss Johnny Keenan.

We had started out as friends, playing kickball and "Ring-a-Lievio" in the streets, and card games, like "knucks," in the hallways. Together, every Sunday after mass, we checked the lists for forbidden movies and, for a while, Johnny talked about having a vocation. We played pretend and I was Batgirl; he was Batman, and one day I put my pretend-saint curtain on and everything changed.

"You look beautiful," he said, and a rush of warmth filled me as he touched my hand. I knew that if I looked in the mirror I would glow with radiance, not like the saints in the books or the pictures of the Sacred Heart and Blessed Mother that lined the wall, but from something more mysterious.

The religion and saintliness, the touching and feelings were all mixed up and, somehow, I knew they always would be.

Kathleen Guillaume

Poem of Childhood

Winter comes early here.
The sun sets by four-thirty,
by dinner it is dark . . .

I am in first grade.
My brother, Mike, is only three.

I like my new uniform.
It keeps me warm.
I can dress myself,
put on my own undershirt,
my garter belt,
long black wool stockings,
my black princess dress,
wool bloomers.

Mother scrubs my face and hands,
helps me attach the starched
white collar and cuffs.

In school after prayers
we sit at our desks,
our eyes down, spread our hands
across the wooden tops.
Sister Mary Alacoque

walks up each aisle.
You can hear her coming,
the rustle of her robe,
feel her eyes inspect each finger.

Our nails must be clean, or
we are sent to the bathrooms,
where there is no heat
and the water is cold and stings.
Ice crusts on the edge of the toilet.

My nails are always clean, so
I can pick up my pen, dip it
into the inkwell and begin my day.

I am good at penmanship.
My letters are round and open.
My papers . . . spotless.
I am proud of my neatness.
I get gold stars.
I am a good girl,
Sister Mary Alacoque
told me so.

We practice First Confession—
close our eyes,
name our sins to ourselves.
"Mea culpa, mea culpa,
mea maxima culpa."

I am reaching the age of culpability.
Sister Mary Alacoque explains
"culpable"; it means responsible.
You can't say, "I didn't know better."
It means you are supposed to know.

First Communion is in May,
the month of Mary.
I want to be a child of God,
a bride of Christ.
I will be a tabernacle

when He enters my body.
I know. Sister Mary Alacoque
told me so.

Mother loves me.
She is making
the most beautiful white gown.
I already have my veil.
I practice walking in it,
hold my head up high
so it hardly touches my shoulders.

Winter comes early here.
The sun sets by four-thirty,
by dinner it is dark.

After dinner Mike and I
are bathed and scrubbed for bed.
We run . . .
turn off the lights,
pull the covers up to our noses,
try to fall asleep
before we can count to ten.

It never works.

I hear her coming,
hear her walk into our room.
She turns on the light.
I try to remember
people in movies
who are sleeping—
try to make my face like that.

It never works.

She sits on the edge of my bed
with her towel;
pulls down the blanket;
lifts my flannel gown.
"Be a good girl," she says.

"Mommy has to do this."
I have not learned yet to ask why.
I am a good girl.

There is this place
on the ceiling.
You can only see it
when the light is on.
It looks like a big wide tree.
I hide in its branches.
I do not move.
I do not breathe.
Her hairpin scoops into me,
scrapes me clean.

I am a good girl.
I do not cry.
I hold onto the branches
of my tree.

Soon it will be May,
the month of Mary.
I will be the bride of Christ.
I will be a tabernacle,
my soul as white as the snow.
I know. Sister Mary Alacoque
told me so.

Anita Roberts

The Last Chance

Anna and her sisters lived in the back of the Last Chance Cafe. A cafe, general store, and gas station that was fifty miles south of the next small town on the highway. Last chance to eat and gas up before heading north. Last chance to have a happy childhood.

The house was just a couple of rooms built onto the back of the store. Anna slept with her five sisters in a long room, the narrow cast iron beds all side by side, like in a hospital. Six girls, no boys. Anna was the third girl not born a boy.

Anna usually woke up Sunday mornings with a little bird of anxiety stirring in her tummy. Church day. It wasn't that Anna didn't like church. She liked the singing and the Latin phrases she had memorized until she knew them all by heart. "Agnus De-e-i, Quitolispecota mundi, Miserari No-o-bis." She had no idea what the phrases meant, but that didn't matter. They were like one big long exotic word to her.

The little bird whispered "Get up! Get up!" Anna sat up in bed and looked over at the mound on the other bed that was her oldest sister, Theresa. Theresa had chosen Anna as her roommate after the partition had gone up. Now that there were two rooms, Theresa and Anna were sharing the smaller one. It meant Anna was "in" right now. She didn't recall doing anything to deserve this special privilege but she knew it made her other sisters envious and that was definitely a plus.

The bird flexed its wings and stretched its neck nervously. Anna started getting dressed for church. She rummaged through the pile of clothes on the floor near her bed and came up with a cotton dress that wasn't too badly wrinkled. It wasn't cotton dress weather, but that wasn't something anyone in her family ever thought of.

She walked sleepily into the other room and started digging through the socks and underwear drawers for a matching pair of something. Most of their clothes were kept in an enormous nine-drawer dresser in the big room that her four other sisters shared. The dresser always had its nine drawers open. Enormous mouths regurgitating articles of clothing; spewing out underwear and socks that dribbled in bits and holey pieces onto the floor. Inevitably, a stray would be kicked under a bed, where it would be lost among the clouds of dust collected there. A matched pair of anything was a rare find.

This particular morning Anna did find two white bobby socks that looked enough like a pair. The hole in the heel wouldn't show if she scrunched the sock down far enough under her foot. This caused an uncomfortable bulge, but she decided it wouldn't be too bad because she knew she would spend a lot of the time in church on her knees.

As she observed the unmoving lumps of blankets on her sisters' beds, the little bird fluttered in her chest again. "C'mon you guys . . . get up!" she said between her teeth.

Toni sat up and Anna could hear Theresa stretching and yawning languorously in the other room. Lou just pulled the covers over her head. She hated to get out of bed in the morning.

"You're gonna get it," Anna warned, and then she heard her father's footsteps approaching the door. A wild flapping started in that little space just in between her ribs, that little triangle spot that makes you feel sick if you press it too hard. Anna ran quickly into the bathroom and locked the door. She stood in front of the mirror and stared at her face. Soft brown eyes, soft brown hair waving down to her shoulders, soft brown freckles sprinkled over her nose. She stood very, very still; she was listening with her entire body.

"What? Not up yet, eh?" Her dad's voice. The cold steel one. Then a crying out and Anna could see, as though reflected in the mirror before her, Lou desperately hanging onto the covers in a futile attempt to protect her brand new breasts from his hungry eyes. Anna cringed with the shame that she knew Lou felt. "Dad, please ... no ... Dad, please don't!" Her pathetic cries pierced Anna's skin. Anna closed her eyes tight and clenched her fists.

"Get up you lazy bum!"

Anna's cheeks flushed hot as she heard the loud smack and Lou's ensuing howl. "Oh no," she prayed, "don't scream like that—he'll only hit you more! Oh God, please make Lou stop screaming." But she knew it was no use. She sat down on the toilet lid and stared at the floor.

"Stop your bloody screaming you big baby! You think you have something to scream about? I'll give you something to scream about! Shut up, you little bitch ... I said *shut up!*"

"*Ow, ow, ow*, my hair, my hair! Dad, it *hurts!*"

Anna's scalp tingled and Lou's screams got louder. They were edged with panic now.

"Hysterical little bitch! Shut up right now or you'll be really sorry ... I said *now!*"

The screaming stopped suddenly and was replaced by choking and gagging sounds. Desperate sounds that washed over Anna as she sat, slumped over, her knees apart and her hands lying numbly in her lap.

A hiccuping sob came from the other room. She stepped softly to the bathroom door to listen. He was gone.

Lou was two years older, but Anna didn't follow her example when it came to how to deal with her dad. Lou was always getting it. The same went for Theresa. Anna watched carefully and knew exactly what not to do. She thought they must be stupid. It seemed like they were almost asking for it. Couldn't they see?

*   *   *

Anna emerged from the bathroom with both hands cupped over her abdomen to still the fluttering that had started up there again. She didn't look at Lou as she walked by to get her shoes. She strapped them on. They were hand-me-down Mary Janes and they were too small. This, like the sock, didn't matter. She was just glad they weren't brown Oxfords like her dad had just bought Lou and Theresa. Boys' shoes. She rubbed her palm over the shiny black surfaces and, pressing firmly with her index finger, stuck down a piece of the vinyl that had begun to peel up.

To get to the laundry room to find a cardigan she must once more walk by Lou, and this time she glanced sidelong and saw that Lou had begun getting dressed. Relief. Lou was pulling on a corduroy jumper, all the while gulping in air in short spasms through her mouth, causing her bottom lip to suck in over her teeth. Feeling-sorry-for-yourself sounds, thought Anna.

In the laundry room she ploughed through a mountain of clothes (the clean pile) and pulled out a sweater. It was missing a button and two of the others were dangling by threads, but the blue color matched her dress so she put it on. The sock with the hole had wriggled its way under her heel and when she bent down to pull it up she saw two chubby feet in the open crack of the cupboard door. One small foot was folded protectively over the other and the toes were scrunched up tight.

"Suzie?" Anna slid the door open and saw her four-year-old sister sitting curled up, her arms wrapped around her knees. Suzie looked up at her big sister with round eyes.

"Hey silly! What are you doing in there? C'mon, you have to get dressed for church!"

Suzie was quiet, but allowed Anna to help her out of the cupboard. She was quiet when Anna handed her an assortment of clothes to put on. Suzie was always the quiet one. "I was practicing being invisible," she said.

Anna made her way through the back door onto the boardwalk that ran between the "house" and the store and through another door into the back room. The back room was a small storage room that nestled between the kitchen of the cafe and Anna's parents' room. She could hear muffled arguing noises coming from their door as she slipped silently by.

Anna lingered for a moment, smelling the kitchen smells of French fries and cold hamburger grease and feeling her hunger, which was somehow always more intense on Sunday mornings. She knew better than to eat before Church, though, and resisted even the small temptation of dipping her finger in the big tub of butter as she walked by. The clean-scraped grill and the thought of the porous cleaning stone sliding over it gave her a nails-on-the-blackboard kind of shiver.

She wove her way around to the front of the store, past the long coffee counter and then the candy bar stand. She inhaled deeply the amalgam of wax paper and chocolate. Sweet Marie and Oh Henry. She imagined them as lovers. Turkish Delight. The exotic name appealed, but she didn't like the firm red jelly or its perfumey smell. Kit Kats were lovely crisp sticks that snapped apart with a nice clean snap. The jaw breakers and spongy yellow bananas called to her, and the shoestring licorice coiled seductively in its long narrow boxes. She sniffed longingly at the Double Bubble box, itching for the promise of the miniature comic that each cube held. The sugar-pink smell stayed with her all the way to the cigarette counter, where it was overwhelmed by the wicked and enticing odor of tobacco.

Next to the cigarettes was the till. She loved the ting-ting-ring as she pulled the handle, and the satisfying ching as the neatly partitioned drawer popped out. She didn't dare pull the handle today, though, and moved quickly around the end of the cash counter into the front of the store.

Minding the front was what they called it when they worked in that part of the store. Ever since Anna had been eight years old she had served coffee and sold cigarettes, and by the time she was ten she was "working the back," as well. She didn't mind making hamburgers and chips. The French fry machine was neat. A red metal contraption bolted to the kitchen counter. It had a big heavy handle for pressing the potatoes through. She would hang on it with all her weight and delight to see the tidy white rectangles emerge. Peeling the potatoes wasn't fun, though, and neither was doing so many dishes.

Doing dishes was often used as punishment. Anna would have to stand for what seemed like forever with hands immersed in greasy dishwater, shifting from tired foot to tired foot. The long counter stretched out beside her, with stacks and stacks of thick white plates, cups, and saucers. Dish duty it was called, and it would last as long as it would take for her dad to remember that she was still there. If she dared to ask "Can I stop now, Dad?" as he rushed past on his way to answer the ding-ding of the gas bell, he would usually say, "So you think you're working too hard, eh? You don't know what hard work is!" And then he would dole out another hour as if it was just another Hail Mary. She hated dish duty, but she did prefer it to being hit, and suffered in trapped silence.

Crossing the red-and-white tile floor in the front of the store, Anna passed the juke box and paused to look at the titles typed in rows: "North to Alaska," "Yellow Polka Dot Bikini," "Blue Navy" (this was her favorite because of its "walky-talky wind-up doll from Toky-oh," which she wished for with all her heart), and "I Will Follow Him," her older sisters' favorite. They would sing it incessantly: "I love him, I love him, I love him ... and where he goes I'll follow, I'll follow, I'll follow ... he'll always be my true love, my true love, my true love ..." until their mother would clamp her hands over her ears and shout "Enough!" at which point they would begin again with even more fervor and Anna would join in shrilly, enjoying the harassed look on her mother's face. Power. They took it where they could get it.

She left the juke box and sat down in one of the booths near the front door to wait. She kept looking at herself to make sure she was ready, to make sure she had everything, as though a piece of her could suddenly be missing.

One by one her sisters came out in their haphazard Sunday attire. They snipped and snapped at one another and growled in undertones like grumpy puppies. Everyone was in a foul mood. It was always like that on Sunday mornings. Anna's mom kept making shushing noises and jiggling her hip to quiet the baby, who was crying irritably.

"Okay, let's go! Are you all ready? Well, I don't believe it. Bunch of lazy bums, why can't you ever be ready on time? Never learn, will you?" Anna couldn't understand why he was carrying on like that. Everyone was there. They were all ready.

"Come on, get in the car. Hurry up, we're late! What's the matter with you? Come on, let's go. Let's *go!*"

"Calm down, Leo." Anna's mother admonished him anxiously. Then she turned to Anna, who was just getting in the car, and whispered, "Anna, where's your hat?"

Anna could feel her face turn pale and the wild flapping started up again, taking her breath away. "I ... forgot," she said in a thin voice.

Her father's enraged face turned on her and he shouted, "Well, for Christ's sake, don't just stand there, go find something, and hurry up or you'll really get it!" His voice was full of hitting, now, and Anna ran to look for a scarf. She ploughed through the drawers, throwing things out of her way, wiping away her tears, but everything was a blur.

Her mother came in and saw that there was no hope of finding another kerchief in time. She took Anna by the arm and pulled her into the cafe. She handed her a paper doily and a bobby pin and said, "Here, this will have to do. Hurry now, Dad's at the end of his rope!"

Anna got into the car. She didn't dare look up. She stared at the white paper circle with the scalloped edges and thought she would die of shame. Everyone would know this was one of those things you put under milkshakes and pies and stuff. Everyone would think she was too poor to own a hat. She knew she had to wear a hat in church, and she knew there was no getting out of going, so she pinned it to the top of her head and steeled herself for the humiliation. She cried as quietly as she could. She knew what her father would say if he heard her crying. "You think you have something to cry about? Here, I'll give you something to cry about." And then he would.

In the seat next to her, seven-year-old Toni scrunched up her face and covered her mouth with one hand to hide her snicker. She pointed at Anna and hunched her shoulders, shaking them up and down in an exaggerated gesture of mirth. Quick as a snake, Anna grabbed Toni's extended finger and hissed "Shut up!" Toni's impish face dissolved. She pulled away. She was afraid of Anna. Anna was three years older and she was strong.

In church Anna managed to forget about the paper doily. She sang the Latin songs and kneeled and stood at all the right times. Her bony knees ached and got all purply and bruisy-feeling from the hard wooden benches, but she didn't mind so much. It was somehow different from having to kneel at home when she was being punished by her father— those long humiliating times in the corners with the other kids walking by, sometimes with their friends. When that happened, she would try to pretend she was looking for something on the floor.

Going to communion was always interesting. Anna knew she was supposed to have holy thoughts but she usually found herself trying to get a look at other peoples' tongues. Some of them hung out, quivering for a long time, and some of them just shyly darted out and back in with their prize. Anna preferred not to leave hers out for too long. It felt cold and vulnerable and wanted to be tucked back in behind her teeth, where it could curl up happily, savoring the elusive flavor of the body of Christ. She often felt guilty about wanting another wafer or wishing that they at least be a bit bigger. She knew she was missing the point.

After church, something was wrong. She could feel it in the car on the way home. Everyone was too quiet.

When they pulled up in front of the store, the doors sprang open and everyone started piling out. There was this feeling that she had to get away from the car as fast as possible— like there was a bomb planted in it and it was going to go off any minute.

"Hold it!" Her dad's voice. "Don't you move." The words sliced through Anna and she froze. Only she and Theresa were left sitting in the backseat. In the front seat, the baby on her mother's lap began to wail. Anna looked up and saw her father's finger pointing like the end of a gun into her big sister's face. She felt relief wash over her and then immediately guilt prickled in her gut.

Her dad came around the car and grabbed Theresa by the hair, and the next thing Anna knew, he had Theresa over by the garage and was banging her head against the wall. Her mother looked frantically at Anna and said, "What did she do? Oh, God, what did she do?"

Anna didn't look at her mother. She continued to stare out the window, and said, flatly, "Nothing."

Her mother got out of the car then and started pleading. "Leo, stop ... Oh, God, stop ... she didn't do anything ... stop it, what did she do ... Leo, please ..."

He stopped and stormed off. It was always like that. Suddenly he'd start, and suddenly he'd stop—like he was finished, spent. An ejaculation of rage.

Anna's father had been in the Catholic priesthood before he quit to marry her mother, and so he had his ideas about sex and sin.

Seven-year-old Anna and nine-year-old Lou were playing in the new shower stall one day. The water wasn't hooked up yet, and the stall made a nice private house with the curtain pulled closed. They were sitting side by side, with their panties down around their ankles and a doll blanket over their legs. They were "playing dirty."

When they heard their father calling them, they froze, but not before Anna managed to wiggle her panties up. Then there he was, whipping the shower curtain open and pulling the blanket off their legs. Exposed. Caught. Anna can remember the feeling of shame and some of the words: little pigs, dirty, sin, mortal sin, going to hell. Things like that. There was something else, too, something about the intensity of it and the way he kept smacking and smacking Lou's bare bottom with his bare hand until it was beet red. Anna wasn't caught pants down and that seemed to make a difference. She didn't get a licking that time. The word licking gave Anna the creeps.

The thing he said about going to hell scared her. What did he mean by that? She knew that if you died with a mortal sin on your soul you would go to hell, but she thought kids couldn't do mortal sins. She thought they were the ones in the ten commandments about killing and something about your neighbor's wife. Of course, she would never kill anyone, and she wasn't sure what the other one meant, but she was pretty sure she wouldn't do it either.

She decided to ask her mother about the mortal sin thing, just to be sure.

Her mother was ironing. "Mom, is playing dirty a venial sin or a mortal sin, and will I go to hell if I die with it on my soul?" Anna's mother paused and looked intently at Anna before resuming ironing and replying in a calm voice, "Yes, Anna, it's a mortal sin, but you don't have to stop doing it. Just be sure to confess it." There was a funny look on her mother's face, as though she was secretly pleased about something.

It was clear to Anna in that moment that her mother had some kind of in with God to be able to bend the rules like that. What she'd said hadn't really made sense, but it seemed right somehow.

"But what do I call it?" Surely she couldn't say "playing dirty" to the priest!

"You call it a sin of immodesty," her mother replied without a break in the rhythm of the iron. Anna watched for a moment, wondering how her mother managed to get her fingers out of the way so perfectly each time. They flew lightly over the garment, smoothing out corners and holding down pleats with the steel point of the iron in hot pursuit.

"Sin of immodesty, sin of immodesty, sin of immodesty." Anna repeated this exciting grown-up phrase. Three times on the out-breath and three more times on the in-breath, until she knew she wouldn't forget it. It pleased her, and with the chanting she felt the shame melt away from her, leaving this feeling of certainty about the whole thing. She would add them up carefully, her sins of immodesty, and then, just to be sure she never got caught with one on her soul (it was always possible to be hit by a car on the way to church), she would add ten to the total. So, three this week, plus ten, that's thirteen. She felt very clever.

"Bless me, father, for I have sinned, and it has been one week since my last confession and these are my sins: I took a chocolate bar from the store without asking, I lied to my mom about it, I committed thirteen sins of immodesty, I said a swear word, and that's all, father."

She usually tried to slip it in casually somewhere in the middle like that so it wouldn't stand out too much. The priest didn't seem to notice, and just gave her the usual few Hail Marys and the occasional Our Father, so after a few weeks she wasn't even nervous about confession any more. She continued to do it this way for years—until she was twelve—until the time with the new priest. That awful time when Father Lehane was sick. Anna was used to Father Lehane and didn't like the idea of a stranger-priest at all. Very reluctantly, when her turn came, she stepped into the little closet and knelt down. She went through her confession in her usual way until she got to the part about the sins of immodesty.

"What was that, dear?"

Anna froze.

"Did you say twelve sins of immodesty, dear?"

"Yes, father."

"Were you by yourself when you committed these sins?"

"Yes, father."

"What were you wearing, dear? Did you have your clothes off?"

"Well, sort of . . . uh, some of them." Anna felt trapped; she felt she had to answer his questions, but she couldn't explain to him that ten of them had never happened, and she couldn't just make up stuff. She felt all hot and sweaty and like she couldn't breathe.

"Now, tell me exactly what it was that you did, dear. What was that? Say that again, dear, I can't quite hear you."

Anna wanted to die. He made her repeat her answers over and over until finally she started to cry.

"You can go now," he said in a strange and breathy voice. He didn't even give her any penance.

Anna burst out of the dark closet and ran out of the church. She was supposed to go back to her catechism class but she felt exposed, like the other kids would be able to see her sins hanging out of her in some obscene way. She felt covered in hot sticky shame and ran and ran until she was almost home. By the time she had slowed down to a walk, the thoughts and feelings swirling around inside her had turned into a gray mist, which got thinner and thinner until it fragmented and finally trailed in diaphanous wisps into a dark corner of herself. A place that she never went. Lots of things that happened to Anna in those days went into that dark place and didn't come out again until much later.

Yvonne

Receive This White Garment

sit down
all-American oak
double desks single desks
nailed down in rows
before heavy huge infallible desk
before immutable black veil
black gown against black chalkboard
crucifix nailed above
stand and pray   stand and pledge
sit down
hear listen see believe question answer
memorizememorizememorize
boys in front (cannot be trusted)
girls in back (must not tempt)
and in places of honor
last desk every row
you (always the only "only")
and other really smart girls
sit down
you you really smart girls

hope to be correct to be asked
what do you know what do you remember?
hope to please and be suitable
(competere, in Latin: to come together
to agree, to be suitable
in English: to compete, to vie
as if for a prize) you you
really smart girl with five talents
(give back ten) with ten talents
(give back twenty) only one talent?
what do you mean? retarded? are you poor?
pagan baby in Asia? colored girl in the South?
how dare you hide behind desks in front
stand up   clap erasers   wash boards   hand out
papers scissors   writewritewrite
your hands fall off   thisisatest   grade tests
police when the nun leaves the room
or be cast out into utter darkness   yes
yes   *Evangeline you are colored and a credit*
stand up   in the footsteps of Eve

who wants to do something special for Our Lady?
Sister had an oval almost young rosy face
with eyes obscured by the sun
caught on the surface of her silver spectacles
like two automobile headlights
your right arm shot up above your head
perhaps a bit higher than the others
out of zeal? yours were longer thinner
arms somewhat like a Balinese dancer
a deeper gold among the others
you were the first girl to be chosen
and then another quite short
(you remember she was a mouse) unpopular
with her starchiest collar and cuffs
she confided her father sold insurance
you are my special girls come with me
Sister led you down the long humid waxed linoleum corridor

past the principal's office and the visitors' chapel
and down the front stairs to the great heavy doors
forbidden to the children
you count fourteen linoleum steps to the first landing
where a stained-glass window mottles the light
and another fourteen to the first floor
where a figure of Our Lady stood
like a miraculous medal almost alive
Sister paused before the statue
you know our school is dedicated to the Immaculate
Conception and these are her stairs
then she led you down another fourteen steps
to the locked basement door   but nearby
hidden in the shadows was a narrower door
like a confessional   Sister opened without a key
and handed you both
what would seem all the long autumn winter and spring
like the sacrament of Penance:
a dustpan and small handbroom
every morning without fail
sweep these stairs before the first bell
then Sister smiled a small and perfect smile
begin now

Gretchen Sentry

Academie Sainte-Anne

I first heard of Sainte-Anne's Academie the summer I was five. My parents took me to a small room at the back of a church, where a bald man in long black robes sprinkled water on my head and chanted magical-sounding words. As we left he gave me a white flower and pressed his hands firmly onto my head. The French-Canadian order of nuns who ran Sainte-Anne's Academie accepted only good Catholic girls and, as I would spend the next three years there, this baptism ritual met one of the requirements.

When summer ended, my mother and father drove me to Marlboro, Massachusetts, turning into the long oval driveway in front of the three-story red brick building. On a grassy knoll, a huge Sainte-Anne dressed in concrete robes stood on a stone pedestal, her outstretched arms raised in a benev- olent gesture. We entered the boarding school through tall double doors with etched glass panels and polished brass handles and were ushered into a side room. Papers were filled out and signed; then I was led away into the hushed interior of the school. It was all washed in a golden glow and smelled of lemon oil and wet wood. Undraped windows let light shine on sturdy oak furniture and precise rows of desks and benches. Bare floors and woodwork glistened under layers of varnish. The only sounds and shadows were murmuring nuns and little girls dressed in black moving single file through the hallways.

My instruction started immediately. The fat woman in black was to be called Mother Superior, and all the others, Sister. I would learn a new language; speak only French, except in English grammar class. I would learn to walk slowly in a straight line with the other students; remember that one click of the Sister's hinged wooden clappers meant go, and two clicks meant stop. I would learn prayers and how to say them in this new language; to speak when spoken to and eat whatever was put in front of me, and I would have to remember to thank God for all of this. As it turned out, it was the Sisters who prayed to God; for me, about me, and because of me.

I was resistant to discipline. My mother said I was a handful. While both she and my father worked trying to overcome the shortages of the Depression, I was left in the care of a series of sisters. Some were paid strangers, some were neighbors or relatives, and all declined to be more or less permanent. The last one, a skinny woman named Stella, who was always at me to wash my hands, left in tears when I called her a pickle-faced fuck. The Sisters of Sainte-Anne responded to such language with large bars of Fels Naptha soap. I sputtered, wiggled, splashed, and flailed, but still they managed to clean my mouth; on Saturday nights they scrubbed my entire body raw in hopes of getting me closer to Godliness.

As an only child, I was not practiced in the art of sharing. I expected to have toys, treats, entertainments, and attentions all to myself. My friends were mostly stuffed or imaginary or on a movie screen. Now I was expected to share everything with other girls, most of whom, I suspect, were kindred handfuls. It was a tall order for any small child, impossible for me. As an outlet, I took to pinching a fat Canadian girl named Yvette, who I found deserving of my frustrations. She probably grew up to be a saint because she never once winced or snitched.

Because my mother was thrifty and talented, I had always worn handmade Heidi dresses or high-style outfits bought at Filene's Basement. When I wasn't dressing up, I was stripping down to bare bottom and marching down the neighbor's driveway. By comparison, the Academie clothing was boring and restrictive, two no-nos in my view. Every day we wore the same black uniform with a white stiff collar and clip-on black leatherette bow tie. Black serge bloomers covered white cotton panties, and a vest with attached garters held up long black cotton stockings. We even had black serge aprons to keep us clean. This unnatural attire cost twelve dollars for two complete sets, with the apron extra at a dollar twenty-five. My attempts at distinctive trim were always thwarted. The Sisters confiscated my dandelion chains and buttercup bracelets and made me scrub clean the crayon embroidery on my celluloid cuffs.

While the Sisters of Sainte-Anne practiced their silent gliding in the hallways, praying to instill in us a ladylike decorum, the bare wood floors and open spaces irresistibly called to my preference for slips and slides, whoops and gallops, and my time-step rendition of "East Side, West Side, all around the town." Single file was not my style and so the nuns, armed with the dreaded wooden clappers, flicked them open like switchblades, stinging me, and other small giggling perpetrators, on the rim of an ear or the back of a hand. While I was there, the nuns had many opportunities to develop expertise in the handling of this swift and demoralizing weapon.

Every day we marched from dormitory to classroom, day-room to playground to dining hall and back, and every day we attended early Mass. Monday through Saturday we wore black veils with grosgrain borders and on Sunday we wore white veils with satin ribbons. I liked the veils and I liked the chapel, with its stained-glass windows and banks of candles flickering in red glass holders. Every Friday we took our turn in the small confessional, recounting our every deed and thought that might qualify as a sin. Being a sinner was a responsibility that I took seriously. I took stock and, knowing what was expected of me, padded the list just a little to impress the priest. He was the reason we looked forward to being sinners. He was young and handsome, bearing a striking resemblance to Walt Disney's Prince Charming. His shiny black hair formed one perfect curl that draped romantically over his forehead. It was thrilling to hear his deep baritone voice assigning twenty Hail Marys, ten Our Fathers, and a good Act of Contrition. According to the Sisters, I had a natural ability to sin and just my daily trespassses rated lengthy visits with "Father Charming." I was the envy of my classmates.

One of the many rules I persistently broke was the one about eating all of the food placed before you. We ate at long refectory tables, with nuns strategically placed to serve us from large beige bowls and aluminum platters and to drill us in basic table manners. They did not tolerate finicky eaters, nose pickers, milk spillers, or those of us who wanted food that was a hearty color, of chewable consistency, and separated from other food on the plate. It was at Sainte-Anne's that I developed a lifelong aversion to boiled oatmeal, split pea soup, and prune whip. The sight of any one of them served in those brown bowls inspired tight-lipped rebellion. They each showed up at least once a week, and that would make three more admissions of sin to share with Father Charming.

One of my most creative sins was also my most artistic. I decorated the flyleaf of my catechism book with a drawing that caused the nuns to turn a delicate pink. It was my version of a naked man. My knowledge of male anatomy came from another student, who's older brother forgot to lock the bathroom door, and from my own suspicions that boys had something I didn't have, and whatever it was, was hairy. I stammered through my most convincing denial, but the Sister did not believe that my drawing was of a teddy bear and, given a little more time, that I would have drawn hair over it's entire body. My punishment was to erase the offending artwork and kneel in the hall for one hour. I cursed each of the knitted ribs in my stockings engraving themselves into my bony knees as I knelt on the hardwood floor. I reported my silent curses to Father Charming, but deleted the part about the anatomical artwork.

The dormitory was at the end of a long hall on the second floor. Wide double doors opened into a large room that housed all of the thirty or so live-in students. There were four rows of white iron bedsteads. Each bed was separated from another by a small wooden washstand and dresser. The youngest students slept in the first row; the older girls in the last row by the windows. In that row, in the corner, slept one nun, shielded by a starched white curtain hung from a brass rod. Except for Saturday night baths in the oval porcelain tubs wedged into marble cubicles, we washed at a basin by our bed. When dressed, we made our beds and stood for inspection before going off to chapel and then to breakfast. Thanks to my vivid imagination and stories told by the fervent Sisters, the nighttime hours terrified me. Comparing sunshine and God's love to the darkness and roaming demons, I envisioned myriad monsters residing in the bathroom. When the sun went down, they rose from deep netherworlds through copper pipes and iron drains and escaped in gaseous burps from sink holes and toilet bowls, then hid in the marble stalls waiting to pounce on my soiled and mortal soul. No amount of pressure on my young bladder could convince me to leave my bed and walk into the bathrooms from the dark of the dormitory. Often, my bed stood out as the only one not made in the morning. My mattress, with its yellow circular stains would be left exposed to the air and the sunshine that arrived most mornings to save us from the creatures of the night. Eventually, I was moved up to the second row of longer iron beds, but my shorter first-year mattress moved right along with me.

My two biggest sins were, in part, committed by my mother. Both happened in my third and final year. That fall my mother was allowed to take me on an outing in the middle of the week to celebrate my birthday. We went into Boston to see the new Walt Disney film *Fantasia*. I was enchanted by most of it and spent only a little time hiding under the seat during the scary parts. We ate at a Chinese restaurant, then went home to open gifts and blow out seven candles on my cake before Dad drove me back to Sainte-

Anne's in the early evening. I brought my favorite gifts with me: A Mme. Alexander doll, with several outfits, including an authentic nun's habit, and a *Fantasia* coloring book bought in the theater lobby. The doll was sent back home with my parents but, without careful scrutiny, the coloring book was allowed to be kept in my locker until recreation time on future stormy days.

That fall, I colored in my *Fantasia* book, doing all of the pretty pictures first: the waltzing flowers, the sprites and fairies, and the dancing hippopotami, until nothing was left to color but the scary parts, the ones that had sent me scurrying under the theater seat. It was then that my sin was discovered. Satan's image came alive through my choice of red and yellow and orange crayons. I added pink and maroon to the color scheme and the flames seemed to leap from the page. When the novice nun came around to check on our activities and looked over my shoulder, I heard her draw in air with a strange whistling sound. "Mon Dieu," she whispered. She snatched the book and closed it immediately. Holding my arm in a frightening grip, she lifted me out of my chair. She half dragged, half pushed me out the door of the dayroom and down the varnished hall to the Mother Superior's paneled office. She left me standing in the hallway while she took the book inside, holding it with only two fingers high and away from her body. After a short while, she dragged me back again to the dayroom. I was made to kneel in the center of the room. The other children were instructed to form a circle around me, and led by the zealous young nun, they all prayed earnestly for my soul. I was impressed with the enormity of this particular sin, even though I wasn't too sure what it was. Sister produced a small box of wooden matches from some mysterious fold of her habit, struck one, and held it to the closed book. As it began to burn, the pages curled open and the flaming book was dropped into a metal waste basket. The fire consumed the pretty flowers, the sprites and fairies, the oversized ballerinas in Crayola'd tutus, and finally, the waxed colors of the flames that surrounded

Satan melted and ran into the real fire. He had, most righteously, been sent back to where he belonged.

In late spring we prepared to make our first communion. It had been a long struggle, accepting without question and by rote all that we were taught in catechism. In spite of my sins, God was ready to accept me into the fold. I looked forward to the day I, all dressed in white, would walk down the center aisle of the chapel to receive the round wafer that melted mysteriously on the tongue like a snowflake. I felt important. My mother promised to make me a special dress. The other girls bragged about the ruffles and lace and layers of petticoats they would have, bought from a real store that didn't have a basement or a mark-down rack. I assured them that mine would be better, whiter, lacier, flouncier, and that God would like mine better.

My mother finished my dress and brought it to school the day before the ceremony. It was a subdued white eyelet, covered over with dainty embroidery and openwork flowers. A taffeta sash around the waist tied in a bow at the back, the ends trailing to the hem. It was the hem that caused a problem. The dress barely covered my bloomers. My mother must have had visions of Shirley Temple tap dancing down the aisle, but the Sisters of Sainte-Anne had quite something else in mind. They insisted that when I knelt the dress must touch the polished floor. My mother reluctantly agreed to take it home and make it longer.

I had other things to think about. I decided that such a special day called for curls. Again, Shirley Temple exerted her influence. The nuns were satisfied that pigtails were not only proper but entirely adequate for receiving the Lord's blessing, so I decided to keep my plans a secret. For weeks I had been making a collection of bobby pins I found on the playground. None were too rusted or bent for my purpose. The day before first communion, I made one last survey of the grounds. That night, just before "lights out," I transferred my treasures from my marbles pouch to my pillowcase and waited for everyone to fall asleep. Under the blanket, unseen by nuns and the beasts in the bathroom, I began to create

the curls. Tiny bits of hair were wound around each pin,
then pushed through the hair at the scalp to hold the curl
in place. It took a very long time to make the hundreds of
tiny twists clamped to my head with crooked, rusty pins. I
slept and dreamed of Father Charming, Buddy Ebsen, and
Little Miss Marker leading hundreds of dancing, curly-haired
penitents up the center aisle of the chapel.

In the morning, still hiding under the blankets, I attempted
to remove the makeshift curlers. No matter how I yanked
and pulled, the curls would not unroll. They twisted and
knotted themselves together and refused to come undone. I
finally found the courage to come out from under the covers.
Sister took one look at me, made the sign of the cross, and
rolled her eyes toward heaven. Then she began to laugh.
There had been many times during my stay at Sainte-Anne's
Academie that laughter would have been a kind response.
Now it only prompted tears of moist humiliation. I was hurried into my underpants and petticoat, and the long white
stockings were hooked to my garter vest. Three older students were assigned the task of untying my knotted hair. It
went slowly and painfully, especially when they tried to tame
it with comb and brush. When I was allowed to look in the
mirror, I saw the frizzled hair bushed out around my teary
face. Rusty stripes banded the blonde fuzz at regular intervals.
Even yards of white veiling would never hide it all. Sister
made the decision to tame the kinky curls by braiding, and
I silently let them do what had to be done. The other girls
lined up at the dormitory doors, like Christmas angels, in
their white lacy dresses. Each carried a white prayer book, a
gift from the Sisters of Sainte-Anne, and a white carnation
beribboned with white streamers. All except me. In all the
commotion about my hair, no one realized that my mother
had not yet arrived with my lengthened dress.

The doors to the hall were opened, and with one click of
the wooden clappers the angels moved silently and single
file down the long hall. I stood in my underwear and pigtails
holding back a new set of tears as my classmates rounded
the corner and disappeared. In the great silence the tears

began to flow. Then I heard her footsteps before I saw her running down the hall, the white dress held high. Quickly, she unzipped it and dropped it over my head. It seemed to take a long time to zip it up and tie the big taffeta bow. She turned me around, and bent over and kissed me. I flew down the hall to catch up with the others.

Beverly Sheresh

Sister Mary Sebastian

Rachel hurried along the path in the woods, as quietly as a forest nymph, her steps cushioned by pine needles and moss. Maple leaves, still wet from a spring shower, dripped one upon another. She felt the moist breath of the forest on her face and decided she belonged in this place and could stay here forever. Her mother's anger, her coldness ... here she could forget all of that.

The wind sighed in the pines, and ahead, faintly in the distance, Rachel heard the falls. There was a special place hollowed out of the trees, where silver-streaked water gushed from the rocks and cascaded into a small pool below. The stream continued in a gully next to the path for a short distance, then disappeared into the earth. Rachel had asked her grandfather about it.

He'd shrugged. "No one knows where it comes from or where it goes," he said. He considered her question seriously, as he always did.

It was her grandfather who'd built a crude pine bench so that she could sit by the falls and stay as long as she liked. She'd watched him build it, the nails lined up in his mouth, plucking them out one at the time and pounding them into place. He grunted as he worked and smiled at her with the sweat freckling his face and soaking through the back of his shirt. Rachel didn't remember her father. He'd run away when she was a baby, almost fourteen years ago. It was like he'd never existed. But Rachel didn't need him . . . she had her grandfather.

She was almost there, and ran the rest of the way, slowing as the path rose and then leveled off. Through an archway of birches, she saw the falls. She felt exhilarated, ready to fling herself on the seat, when she stopped quickly, staring at a dark figure on the bench . . . *her* bench. Black robes shuddered with the breeze, the white bib startling in the shadows. A nun. She cradled a small black book in her lap and her lips moved as she read. She wore the old type of habit, the kind Rachel had been used to seeing when she'd gone to Sunday school and when she'd made her first communion.

Fright was the first thing Rachel felt, but only for a moment. Then surprise. She'd never seen anyone here before . . . at this place. And she'd been here often . . . when she stayed with her grandfather, when her mother could no longer deal with her. So she'd been caught shoplifting—the one, and only, time. At least it got her mother's attention.

The nun raised her head and smiled faintly. Her glasses reflected the trees and the sun that filtered through the canopy. She closed her book and moved gently to one side to make room.

Rachel shifted on her feet and brushed her hair back from her face. She didn't want to sit down . . . not now.

"I am Sister Mary Sebastian," the nun said in a voice that rose above the sound of the falls . . . resonant, yet soft. She watched Rachel, fingering a silver crucifix that hung at her breast.

Rachel looked away, feeling a faint pressure, not wanting to speak. But it was as though the nun had placed a soft hand on her shoulder.

"Rachel," she said softly. . . . "My name is Rachel."

Sister Mary Sebastian nodded. With trembling hands, she reached up to draw her wimple back from her face. A silver ring flashed on her right hand. Her habit was faded and worn, and the fingers that gripped her breviary were white

with ragged nails. An air of melancholy seemed to drift from
the blackness of those robes and she looked so forlorn that
Rachel felt a flash of pity. But, she clung to her dislike of this
intruder and she wished she would go ... back to wherever
she came from.

"Where are you from?" Rachel asked, and added, boldly,
"Why are you here?"

"I am from the Sisters of the Good Shepherd." She looked
up at Rachel, the trees dancing in her glasses. "I'm here,"
she continued, "for the same reason you're here." She raised
her head and the white bib quivered. Rachel could see small
blue veins in grayish skin.

"This is a magic place," she continued. "Don't you think?
Don't you feel it?" She spread her arms. "Here you can enjoy
everything—need nothing—own everything."

Rachel had never heard anyone talk like that. It was as if
this nun knew Rachel's thoughts. Words that she'd never spoken out loud, but carried within herself ... a private thing.

The nun seemed to be waiting for Rachel's answer, and
when Rachel was silent, she continued. "Don't mind me....
I am filled with words. Please forgive me." She spoke slowly,
pausing between words in a breathless, hesitant manner.

Although Rachel was drawn to this stranger in a way she
could not understand, she felt uncomfortable. "I've got to
go," she said quickly, and turning, stumbled down the path
with Sister Mary Sebastian's voice calling after her, ringing
through the woods.... "Rachel, let's be friends.... Rachel."

At supper that night Rachel told her grandfather about the
nun. He'd just finished a plate of baked beans and was mop-
ping up the juice with brown bread.

"A nun?"

"Yes."

He shook his head. "No nuns out here. There's Saint Hya-
cinth's in Machias, but that's twenty miles away."

He waited for his sister, Nell, to give him a second helping.
She'd lived with him over ten years, since Rachel's grandmother had died. Her manner was faintly obsequious. Frail,
bent with arthritis, she cared for Rachel's grandfather, grateful

for the home he provided. She was like a shadow moving about the house, occasionally singing a French song, as harmless as a butterfly. Rachel liked her.

"Sisters of the Good Shepherd? Maybe, years ago . . . I don't know. Maybe she's visiting one of our neighbors. . . . Did you ask?"

"No. . . . I don't like her."

"So, what has she done to you?"

Rachel didn't answer. She felt a vague guilt, knowing she'd been selfish, but the resentment was still there and she hoped her grandfather wouldn't ask any more questions. He didn't.

"I'm going for a walk . . . down by the potato fields," Rachel said the next day. She'd decided she wouldn't go to the falls, not today . . . perhaps never again.

"Might rain," her grandfather said, peering at the slate-colored sky. He looked at her over his glasses, rubbing the bristly stubble on his chin. (He shaved only once a week, on Sunday morning, before church.) "And the chickens?"

"When I get back . . . okay?"

After a moment, he nodded, turning toward the barn. "Don't go too far."

Although she felt it wasn't necessary, his concern made Rachel feel good. "I won't."

Along the road, the maples and elms stood quietly, as though waiting for the rain. She breathed in the scent of wild lilac and picked a buttercup, that, Midas-like, had turned to gold. Symmetrical rows of young corn, bright green, stretched out of sight, and to her left, potato plants, a darker green.

She had almost decided to turn back when she saw several men digging in a clearing in the field. A pickup was parked nearby. The foundation of some old house, Rachel thought. A jagged fieldstone fireplace was partially torn down and the truck was almost filled with rock and debris. A huge oak tree spread its branches over the scene, dominating . . . powerful . . . as though it owned all that lay beneath it. Goosebumps traveled up Rachel's arms and she rubbed them with her hands, although she didn't feel cold. A strange sadness she couldn't explain seemed to sink into her body, tightening her stomach.

When it started to rain, she turned toward home, running when the farm was in sight. In the chicken house, she ladled the mash into the feeders, watching with satisfaction as the chickens pecked furiously, looking for bits of corn. And when she gathered the eggs, some were still warm from the hens' bodies.

She found her grandfather in the kitchen, standing with his hands in his pockets, watching the rain. He seemed restless . . . to be idle was not his way.

"Can't do much for a while," he said. "But, we need the rain."

Rachel asked him about the men she'd seen in the field.

"Ahhhhh, the Guimond brothers . . . finally digging up those old ruins."

"Was it an old house or something?"

He sat down at the kitchen table and the chair creaked under his body. "No," he said. "An old school building, I think. . . . I'm not sure."

He stuck a toothpick in his mouth and chewed on it. "Even though I was just a little boy, I remember the night it caught fire. . . . Old wood. . . . Burned to the ground."

Chill air raised the kitchen curtain and Rachel reached over to close the window.

The next morning, she crossed the field, toward the forest. Maybe it was a territorial thing, like a bird defending its nest, but she decided to claim what she felt was hers.

She had barely stepped into the cool dampness of the woods when she heard, rising above the roar of the pines, the sound of singing, a single, clear voice.

As she moved along the path, she could make out words . . . but not English . . . Latin, she thought. The notes rose and fell, wavered, then rose again. Rachel stopped to listen. She'd heard singing like that before at High Mass, but this was infinitely more beautiful. The tones were clean and vibrant and filled with a kind of despair, Rachel thought. Sister Mary Sebastian?

She started up the path once more, no longer sure of her feelings.

The bench stood empty, and for a moment, Rachel stared in surprise. But standing next to a young oak and blending with the shadows of the grotto stood Sister Mary Sebastian. She was shorter than Rachel had expected, and heavier, her cheeks plumped up by the white bib.

Rachel sat on the end of the bench, waiting, but the nun didn't speak.

"Was that you singing?" Rachel asked.

"Yes."

She looked strangely one-dimensional and grainy, like an old photograph that might have been stored in someone's attic. And when she moved toward the bench, Rachel stiffened. The nun hesitated.

"What kind of a song was that?" Suddenly she wanted to hear the nun's voice ... to hear her speak.

"It's a Gregorian chant."

"Why is it so sad?"

"It isn't sad, it's a musical prayer. The sadness is within us ... you and me."

Turning away, Rachel reached down to touch the water that coursed by. There was something curiously unreal about what was happening and she needed reassurance. When her fingers numbed, she quickly withdrew her hand and faced the nun with new strength.

Sister Mary Sebastian moved closer.

"May I sit?"

Rachel didn't answer but moved to the end of the bench.

The nun settled next to her and when her robes brushed Rachel's arm, the young girl shivered. Somehow, she'd expected the odor of incense and would not have been surprised if the nun had drawn a battered catechism, the little gray book, from her robes, much like the one she'd carried around in her jacket pocket when she was a little girl. She could still remember its first question and answer: Who made the world? ... God made the world. But the sister made no move toward her, and smelled of fresh air and something else ... charred wood? Rachel wasn't sure. The nun sat quietly and the silence magnified the flow of sound from the rippling pool and the rustling leaves.

"They have driven me away, you know," she said suddenly. Her head was bowed and Rachel couldn't see her face, only her billowing habit and her restless hands.

"Who?" Rachel asked.

But the sister didn't answer. She sat motionless and Rachel felt no warmth from the body that pressed close to her.

The figure stirred. "I miss my oak tree," the sister said. Her voice trembled. "And the sound of the wind over the fields."

The air felt at once cold, as though from a breath of winter.

She turned. "But I have you, Rachel. . . . God has given me you."

The nun's words touched her. Astonished, she realized that she wanted to comfort the woman, even embrace her, but could not bring herself to do so. The nun made her feel vulnerable. She didn't want that. And yet, there stirred within her a gentle movement ... insistent. She need only release it.

The branches of a birch tree drooped over the pool, and Rachel reached up to pluck a leaf. It was soft and pliant and she pressed it to her cheek.

The nun spoke again. "I would like to stay here ... in this place."

She turned. Now, sitting close to her, Rachel saw the eyes of Sister Mary Sebastian ... green, deep-set and somehow familiar. They were startling, with a tenderness and love so powerful that Rachel turned away, her throat tightening. She suddenly realized she couldn't remember the last time she'd really looked into her mother's eyes.

The nun's shoulders slumped and she sighed. "I am so tired," she said. "I would like to rest here. Yet, I can feel myself drifting away again." She rose and glided over toward the young oak.

Rachel trembled. She recalled her grandfather's words:

". . . a school, something to do with the church?" Maybe she'd suspected all along.

She pushed herself up from the bench and stood on shaking legs. She was frightened. Yet, she felt light-headed, filled with a longing to embrace the world.

"Are you a spirit?" she asked, in a small voice.

The figure stood motionless in a forest that seemed mystic . . . so still and so silent.

It was as though time had paused, waiting for some magic touch to resume. The nun stirred. "I am what you see." She lifted her head skyward as though listening for something, then fixed her gaze once more on the young girl. "Rachel, will you share your grotto with me?"

The young girl nodded but couldn't speak. She moved forward, stumbling over tree roots that seemed to move under her feet. She gasped, pulling the air into her lungs. For a moment, she hesitated . . . then walked into the nun's outstretched arms.

A soft sigh shuddered through the sister's figure and now Rachel could smell the aromatic incense. The forest seemed to awaken as the trees overhead swung and shook in a whirl of wind. Then, like mist under the sun, the nun was gone.

Later, in the barn where her grandfather had built her bench, Rachel searched for special pieces of pine, with swirling grain and good color. She made a simple cross, writing on it with black crayon, Sister Mary Sebastian.

Next to the falls, in the grotto, she pushed the cross down through moss and damp earth close to a cluster of snowflakes.

She sat on the bench for a long time, feeling the nun's presence, comforting, mysterious . . . like a touch on the face, a whisper in the shadows. But, when the light began to fade in the grotto, Rachel knew that she must go.

She'd almost reached the clearing when she stopped suddenly. A familiar sound . . . rising and falling, floating above the canopy . . . the voice of Sister Mary Sebastian.

She was singing.

Rita Signorelli-Pappas

The Nuns of Alba

We had so much love for her,
more than the sisters of Ávila.
We waited so long, but soon
our need to see her just once more
stilled our song at Matins,
spilled through our sleep. We knew
this convent was our tomb,
that we were corpses
as much as she. And always
that strong, sweet scent:
water of angels sprinkled
like perfume over our beds,
the same fragrance that kept
rising from her tomb,
a profusion of wild jasmine
that bloomed suddenly everywhere,
even deep inside the almonry.

We thought we could wait
forever, but without her we
were no more than live fish
lifted from the water:
we could not breathe.

So once more we entered the nave.
One by one we unfastened
glazed bricks. It took all night
to open the limestone wound.
We lifted her coffin's lid
and found there only
a cold, elegant marionette
stamped with cabochons of earth,
and that mysterious fragrance
present still. We washed
the damp, delicate remains
with a light-headed pride,
we looked and looked at her,
biting back our tender sighs
of hunger.

We had so much love for her.
For months after, we were as calm
as stunned puppets
locked inside the best dream
of our lives.

Mary Gordon

Getting Here from There

My mother is the daughter of very simple Irish and Italian Catholics. I think she embodied for my father a kind of peasant Catholicism that he romanticized. But both of them could say with truthfulness that their faith was the most important thing in the world to them.

From an early age I had to take the measure of myself against their devotedness, and I always found myself wanting. Throughout my childhood I prayed to be spared martyrdom. But then I always felt guilty for the prayer. I was no little Teresa of Ávila setting out in the desert, hoping to convert the Moors; the priests in China having bamboo shoved under their fingernails and Cardinal Mindszenty imprisoned in his upper room terrified me. I didn't want that for my fate, but I was told that it was the highest fate. So as a child I had always to be consciously choosing an inferior fate. It was a real burden.

But I do remember that although I didn't want to be a martyr I did want to be a nun. I remember being taken by my parents to the Convent of Mary Reparatrix on Twenty-ninth Street in New York. It's a semicloistered convent—the nuns weren't allowed out, but people could talk to them. And I remember going into the chapel with my parents and a very old nun. I saw a young nun kneeling in a pool of light.

I saw her from the back only. The habits of the Sisters of Mary Reparatrix were sky blue. I've never seen a color like that in a nun's habit, and I'm quite sure I didn't invent it. But if I had wanted to invent it, it would have been perfect, because it was a color dreamed up for movie stars. It was the color of Sleeping Beauty's ball gown, and that was what I wanted for myself. I wanted to be beautifully kneeling in light, my young, straight back clothed in the magic garment of the anointed. I knew that was what I wanted, but I knew I didn't want to drink filthy water or walk barefoot in the snow. A few times, though, I did try some local free-lance missionary work.

Once, for instance, I had just finished reading the life of Saint Dominic Savio, who was a Neapolitan orphan. I was six or seven. Saint Dominic walked into a playground and heard his rough playmates—nobody uses the phrase "rough playmates" anymore—using blasphemous language. And he didn't skip a beat. He held up a crucifix, and he said to those boys, "Say it in front of Him." And the boys fell silent. Inspired, I tried the same thing in my neighborhood. I walked into the crowd of boys with my crucifix aloft, and I said, "Say it in front of Him." And they were glad to.

The comedy of Catholic life. It comes, of course, like all other comedy, from the gap between the ideal and the real. In my case the ideal was so high and the real was so real that the collision was bound to be risible. I tried walking with thorns in my shoes for penance, but then I found out that it hurt. So I walked around on the heels of my shoes and put the thorns in the toes, so I could have them in my shoes but not feel them. My heroisms were always compromised and always unsuccessful. I tried to talk the man in our gas station into taking the nude calendar off his wall. He told me never to come into the office again. I tried to make the candy store man, whom I genuinely liked, stop selling dirty magazines. He stopped giving me free egg creams, and our friendship ended. But he went right on selling dirty magazines.

I always tried. The serious part of the ideals that shaped

my early life was that they did teach me that life was serious. I think all children believe that. I think parents cheat children by refusing to understand that everything is serious to them and that it is the modulations of the adult world that cause them such confused grief. At a very early age I was taught that happiness was not important; what was important was to save my soul. I was not supposed to be only a good girl or even a lady, although I was supposed to begin there. I was not supposed to even strive to be popular, successful, beloved, or valued by the world. I was supposed to be a saint. The cautionary and inspirational tales of my youth were the lives of the saints.

PART TWO

*F*alling *A*way

*The more one demands complete submission
of her, the more surely one will advance her
along the road of salvation.*
                                        —Simone de Beauvoir

Carolyn Banks

The Virgin of Polish Hill

The section of the city was called Polish Hill. It consisted of narrow streets and row houses, brick pavements gradually being replaced by concrete sidewalks. A few slat fences were left, but these, too, were going. In their stead, chain-link fences were being raised.

There was a hospital, on the hill, which loomed over the rest of the neighborhood. Its psychiatric ward, on the top floor, was commonly referred to as the crazy house. Children used to line up on the street to stare at the top floor, waiting to see one of the patients. At the slightest sign of movement on any of the floors, they would run, screaming happily, home to safety and normalcy.

Safety and normalcy. This meant the smell of kishka or kielbasa reaching from kitchen to hall and all through the house. On Mondays, bleach and ammonia in every staircase welled up from some hundred white-washed cellars.

Beyond the hospital, enemy lines. Names like Carrozza, Damiano. Pizza houses, not ours, not our own.

Most of the people in our section spoke Polish, and all of the older children understood the language when they heard it, but they didn't speak it themselves. In the market on Saturday morning, over the smell of fruit and fresh-butchered meat, rose the steady and soothing chirrup of Polish.

The market was a favorite gathering place. It was the only store in the three-block shopping district that still covered its floors with sawdust. The older children would slide in it, and the little ones, hanging onto a coat sleeve or hem, would make tentative marks with their shoes. My own dream when I was small was to be free of my mother, free of all grownups, free to storm and slide up the aisles, a whirl of chips falling on every bottle, every jar, every tissue-wrapped lemon and apple and orange.

But secular pleasures, even those only imagined, were few. The real center of the neighborhood was the church. Everyone, even the drunkards like Diana Dogonka's father, went to church on Sunday mornings. The ones who went early were considered holiest, whereas the ones who went to noon Mass were virtual atheists. My parents went to 6 a.m. Mass with my grandmother and Aunt Clara, whereas I went to "children's" Mass at 8:30.

My classmates were there, unwilling, kneeling starch-straight because of the nuns who were stationed every third row.

Even though we went to church every week, few of us seemed to know when to sit, when to stand, when to kneel. We always had to look at each other or watch the nuns in the first pew. I always promised myself that I would learn the routine so thoroughly that the class would look at me before rising, before kneeling. And yet it was always the good girls, like Maryann Zbel, the girls who never talked in school and who never got their hands hit with the ruler by the nuns, who knew what to do. Despite my promises to myself, I was always off in a daydream.

May was the cruelest month, the month of Mary. It began with a procession through the neighborhood streets. The boys carried a large plaster statue of the Virgin and the girls followed, emptying baskets of rose petals along the way, all of us singing over and over again, a long, strangely sad Polish hymn. I hated the whole thing; I think that all of us did, the boys in crisp navy suits, the girls in starched white dresses and knee-length white socks.

Old tapestry banners recalling miracles at Lourdes, Fatima, and Guadalupe were held high, usually by the older men in the Sacred Heart Society. We grew dizzy from the incense—singing, casting the petals of flowers in the warm spring streets.

The neighborhood people would come down from their porches and stand at the curb. Some would lean out of upstairs windows. The old women would cry a little and try to sing with us, but always much too slowly.

In the evenings these old women would go to church in groups to say the rosary. Since few of the babkas had even attempted English, it was said in Polish. When the priest had hurried through his part of the prayer, the tired, soft, hiss-chirp would begin, all at once, dwindling slowly, with each of the women praying at a different pace. Wrinkled and sad, most of them fat and dressed in dark colors, they huddled over their beads down at the small side altar. My grandmother was one of these.

The only occasion in church that I enjoyed (although I managed to look every bit as put upon as my friends) fell on the Saturday before Easter. The girls would come in babushkas and light jackets, carrying baskets of food to be blessed for the Easter morning meal. We would kneel close to the center aisle, with the baskets placed on the floor beside the pews. Filled with the sweet smell of Polish sausage and home-baked raisin bread, the church seemed less forbidding; perhaps, too, because the agonies of Lent had passed and we no longer had to spend each Friday afternoon making Stations of the Cross, and because the purple shrouds that covered all of the statuary had at last been taken up. Absent, too, was the regiment of nuns, so that we could sit or slouch as we chose.

And then the priest would appear—heralded by two altar boys waving censors—filling the air with the familiar church incense, covering, temporarily, the warm and alien kitchen smells.

We would kneel as straight as if the nuns were yet behind us, and up the aisle the priest would walk, swinging a silver shaker, splashing the baskets and the company with tepid holy water. Afterwards we would shuffle out, complaining together in the churchyard, then swagger home to beg the now sanctified raisin bread, eggs, or sausage. Each family kept a store of unblessed food, too, although nothing could equal the share in the baskets. But never once would our parents permit us to touch, let alone eat, the food that had been blessed before Easter morning.

The younger women, a group that included our mothers, did not go to rosary, nor did they participate in our devotions. Instead, they played bingo in the church basement. I went only twice and, although I was bored by it, I was jealous of the girls who went regularly because they seemed so much more grown up than I. And so I always wheedled and whined to be able to go.

My mother never won anything except an Aunt Jemima cookie jar, but my Aunt Clara won almost every time she played: towels, doilies, and a salt and pepper set. Once, on one of the two nights I had been allowed to go, Aunt Clara won the fifty-dollar jackpot.

She told me to place the red see-through chips on her card, but I was slow, too slow, and eventually she took over. I was almost asleep, my head pressed against the narrow table, when she called out, "Biiiiiingo!" We danced the polka in the streets that night on the way home, and the next day my aunt bought a turkey and we had a huge family dinner at my grandmother's, just like Thanksgiving, to celebrate.

Aunt Clara told all of my aunts and uncles and cousins that I had brought her luck, and so I got to pull the wishbone with her, although, as usual, she won.

She always won. I had seen her pull the wishbone with my cousin Stash, and with my father. She always won at everything. She even won a toaster once in the church raffle. It wasn't first prize, but still a win. Each of us had to sell five books of tickets, which was pretty easy because relatives usually bought an entire book. But Aunt Clara won her toaster, and she was the only one in the entire family who had bought a single ticket. One!

It was she to whom the Blessed Virgin once miraculously appeared. It was, in fact, the Virgin's only appearance in Western Pennsylvania.

My Aunt Clara had never been my favorite. I remember her sitting on the front steps in the summertime drinking beer, setting the bottle on the steps beside her after every swig. I used to worry that my friends would see her, but if they did, they never told me, never teased me about it.

Aunt Clara. She was a very loud woman and her teeth were laced with gold. She laughed a lot, throwing her head back so that all of the fillings would show. When she hugged me, she squeezed too tight and her breath smelled of beer and her cheeks of powder. I would squirm to get away from her, but she always managed to get me, always hugged me more than she ever hugged anyone else.

Her rooms were next door to us, small, and cluttered with her winnings and her handiwork. She crocheted for people in the neighborhood, pillowcases, hankies, things like that. All of our sheets had been bordered by Aunt Clara, and she made my mother's finest tablecloth, reserved for Christmas and Easter dinners. Most of my aunts and uncles bought doilies from her to give as wedding presents and to use in their homes. My parents did not use doilies except for one long one across the dining room buffet, and so, in our house, all of the doilies that Aunt Clara had given us were upstairs in the third drawer of my parents' chest of drawers, wrapped in white tissue and smelling faintly of lavender sachet.

But Clara's rooms had a lot of doilies, and long crocheted strips with tasseled edges hanging from the window frames and on the door between her bedroom and sitting room. There were many religious statues—the Infant of Prague, the Virgin in her various guises, a small wooden statue of Saint Joseph—with sanctuary candles burning red and blue before them. And on the wall at the entrance, a white enamel holy water font. Her rooms were hot and the holy water was always lukewarm. I loved to dab it on my forehead when I came in, and so I never really minded having to make the Sign of the Cross when we went there, even though we didn't do it at home—only at church or at my grandmother's and Aunt Clara's.

On the day the Virgin appeared, my aunt had finished a blue tablecloth. Every year on that day, June 12, she used that cloth, and uses it today. "It was blue, and blue is her color," my aunt told everyone later. "I should have known, because I'd never made a blue one before."

When she called on my mother that night, she did not behave as if she knew the Virgin was coming. Instead, my aunt came an hour before the bingo was to start, as she always did, settled in the green armchair with a loud, deep sigh, as she always did, and, pulling off her shoes, began to rub her feet, which she did only when she had spent the day delivering her needlework.

"Please can I go?" I asked my mother.

"Not tonight, Kotka," my mother said, and before they left, they each kissed my cheek for luck.

May devotions ended, I had nothing to do that night. My father worked a crossword and listened to the radio and I went to bed early. In a fuzzy way, I remember hearing my nickname, Kotka, being called in my sleep. This had happened only once before, on a New Year's Eve four years back. I heard my name, and then, over bells and shrieks that sounded like the noon whistle at the mill down the street, I heard my mother say, "It's 1946!" She told me I said, "Oh," and rolled across the bed, never really waking. This time, though, she didn't allow me to fall asleep again. Instead, she stood me upright beside the bed and switched on the overhead light. I started to snivel and she handed me a pile of clothes.

"No, don't cry," she said as she sat on the bed and began unbuttoning my pajama top. "You must get dressed," she told me. "Your aunt has seen the Virgin." Then she shouted down the stairs, telling my father, in Polish, that he'd better hurry.

My mother always spoke to my grandmother only in Polish. To my father and to my aunt, she spoke English, except when she said something to them that I was not supposed to know.

Now she had had this relapse. She turned to me and said something still in the mother tongue.

"It's still night," I whined, gesturing at the blackness through the window, but she ignored me. She went into the bathroom and began running the water, and then came out with a washcloth and began rubbing it across my face.

My father opened the front door, and I was startled to see the street filled with people, all of them hurrying toward the hospital. I had never seen so many people, not even during the day. At night it was unthinkable. I could remember waking at night and going in the darkness to the window. It would be stone quiet and no one was ever out. Now, it looked as though church had just let out. No, more than that, even. As if the 6 o'clock, the 8:30, the 10 o'clock, and the noon Masses had all let out at once.

I saw many children I knew and I called to them as they were hurried along. Loretta Mozdien waved to me and her mother smacked her. Maryann Wrobleska walked as though she were about to take communion, her hands folded in prayer, eyes uplifted. I am reminded of that night now when I see movies involving the evacuation of villages—war movies, science fiction movies.

We walked now up the hill as quickly as we could without leaving my grandmother behind. She began to recite the rosary out loud—Matka boska, swieta boska—soft, chirping phrases. My parents joined in, and the people behind us joined in, and soon the street was a moving murmuring mass of people praying. Then someone began singing the May Day hymn, and the May procession was enacted there on the hill, but with no need now of the plaster statue and the banners.

"Aunt Clara saw her?" I asked my mother when we stopped to let my grandmother catch her breath.

My mother whispered, as if speech were forbidden. "I would have seen her, too, but I left before Clara did. I won a cookie jar. That was the Virgin's way of appearing to me."

"A cookie jar?" But we were on the move again and my skeptical question was lost in the singing, louder now as we neared the hospital.

There must have been a thousand people at the top of the hill. Some of the men wore sweaters over pajama tops and trousers. Women were there in housecoats and pincurls, and some of the children still wore their pajamas entire, with a shawl or coat thrown over them. Although it was June, it was cool and a wind had been lifting the dust in the streets all evening, as though it might storm. The wind had died down now, or perhaps it had been trampled in the crowd, and yet it was chill.

We sang and stared up into the night sky. Now and then a voice would break through and shout "I see her!" or "There she is!" in Polish, and all of the people would clap their hands and sing louder and faster and then make the Sign of the Cross. I looked for our priests, expecting to see one of them in the crowd, his trouser legs peeping out from under a hastily donned cassock.

Inside the hospital, people were silhouetted against the windows. We could see nurses in white, standing with the crowd for a time, but usually they would go back inside, I guess so that others could come out. The children who came to taunt the crazy people, they were there, but neither laughing nor afraid.

"Maybe," I said to my mother, "one of the crazy people got out up there." Suddenly my grandmother's arm darted out and grabbed my own. She shook me, shook me until my mother made her turn me loose. Even then, she gave me an evil look and spat upon the ground before crossing herself with great indignation and resuming her song.

"Well, maybe one of them did," I said, and my mother led me away from my grandmother, who was now beating on her breast and begging forgiveness for her errant grandchild.

I looked up beyond the building, trying to find my first star. I could find none to wish on.

I tried to focus on the building, but saw the building only, with people black against the light within—people on every floor, even the top.

Perhaps I was possessed by the devil. The nuns had told us of such people, and of others. Of those who turned to stone for eating meat on Friday, or those who swallowed their own tongues for taking communion in a state of mortal sin. Perhaps I was in a state of mortal sin. Perhaps the Virgin had come to all but me.

I sang louder and louder, raised my voice until it grew thick in my throat, but still did not see her.

A fire engine appeared. It came slowly, as fire trucks are driven in parades, but with its headlights on, the fire bell clanging. A man called through a megaphone, "Go home, go home. There is nothing here to see." And someone from among us shouted, "Protestant!"

The crowd laughed and cheered and applauded. But the singing had stopped. The fireman trained a huge light on the building and it ran up the side like a roach. The light hovered at the rooftop, then began to creep along the edge. The roof was indeed empty. "You see? There's nothing there," shouted the man with the megaphone. "There is nothing there!"

My Aunt Clara's voice came shrill through the crowd. I could not see her, but her voice was clear as she explained away what had happened. "It is a miracle," she shouted. "She would not let the Protestants see her. She would not let them shine their lights upon her. It is a miracle."

The Virgin was Catholic. The Virgin of Guadalupe, of Lourdes, of Fatima, was Polish, too. Of course the Protestants would not be able to see her. Nor would the Italians, nor the Irish. The Virgin was ours.

My grandmother translated all of this to two of her friends who spoke no English. They nodded, grave with knowledge. They, and then everyone, took up the cry again: "Miracle, miracle," in English, so that the firemen would know.

"Okay, folks," the man, whose voice had taken on the huskiness that my own had when I'd try to sing too loudly, tried again. "Take your miracle home with you. Go on home." The light still shone on the empty roof.

Then my mother's voice grew loud at my side. "I won a cookie jar!" she shouted, as if to say, "Explain that away if you can."

"That's right," my father hollered, shaking his fist. "That's right, she did."

"Okay, people." The fireman had not heard. "Okay. You can see she's gone now, so go on back. Go back home." The huge truck began to move, turtle-slow, down the street, and everyone began to back from it, from the man with the megaphone, from the building.

We backed away, too, like all the rest, not turning our eyes from the hospital, but shuffling backward, staring at the spot where She had been, trying not to trip or lose our balance, not to shove or be shoved, but trying, too, not to relinquish that which was especially ours: the Virgin of Polish Hill, my own Aunt Clara's Virgin.

Angelina

My grandmother used to buy
chickens for a quarter apiece
from the people on the hill;
she'd twist their scrawny necks
painlessly with leathery
quick olive hands
then whack off the head
with a thick-bladed hatchet
she sharpened weekly on her
grindstone in the dank,
dugout cave cellar where
we kept drainpipes stuffed
with paper and rags
so that rats from the creek
couldn't sneak in at night.
Saturdays we washed clothes
in the wringer in that
low-ceilinged stone-hole,
far from a child's paradise.
Upstairs noodles dried
on clean white sheets
draped over beds and chairs;
we blessed a huge tub of dough

with the sign of the cross,
then punched it down and
turned it into bread.
For supper she served
broiled knobbly chicken,
a few potatoes, dandelion greens,
and always, bread.
We sweated all day for Sunday,
a clean house and spaghetti.
She'd start the sauce before mass,
then made sure we ate it all:
"Mangia, mangia," she crooned,
"Tank God you don't got no TB."

My grandmother was always old.
I have a picture of her young,
maybe twenty, in the 1930s.
Already she'd started shrinking,
sitting outside on a footstool,
thin legs tightly pressed,
hands clasped, Mona Lisa lips,
eyes dipped with sadness.
Five babies too many,
not enough time to sew
the aprons she sold
door to door, saving pennies
to buy the house where
she spent the first month
picking roaches off the walls.

My father, she didn't want—
she punched her belly, like
dough, threw herself down steps,
still he stayed inside her;
she visited a doctor, with
Nicky, a small boy then, at
her skirts; the doctor said,
If I kill the one inside you,
I have to kill this one first.

Gramma never said that was sin;
but, "Don't let no boys
look under your dress."
That was sin as bad as stealing—
Gramma called thieves "Black hands,"
men who waited behind the house for men
on payday on their
way to the beer garden.
Booze was sin too, worse,
because her husband drank,
but yearly her kitchen filled
with wine air of boiled grapes
that she grew and picked—
gallons of dago red she jugged
and let go to vinegar
hidden in the dark cellar.

Her eyes went bad first,
suddenly, glasses, no good,
"I know your voice,"
then she knew everyone,
stopping people in the streets
to hear their voices, to hug
them and say, "I love you,"
to every stranger she met,
swearing it was 1944.
She quit planting gardens,
but the ground, so fertile,
sprang to life each year:
roses, poppies, garlic,
tomatoes, peppers grew side by side.
Still she knew which was the
flower to place in the vase
in front of the plaster Madonna.
The fig tree out back
quit blossoming, her grape vines
fell, she didn't notice,
TV did her no good, senseless voices.

She remembered her family's names,
Pearl Harbor, some broken Italian.
Daily she trekked miles,
to church, to town—
toward the end, sometimes
wearing only a slip, coat, boots.
People in church gasped,
called my father to come get her;
she smiled all the way.
My parents finally dressed
her in street clothes each night
never knowing when and where
she'd go, nothing stopped her.
Until the day they laid her
in a strict hospital bed.

The day I visited her
she asked if she was in church;
she looked like an angel misplaced:
her hair, long, undone, silver,
the sanitary hospital smock
floating over her thin body,
knowing somehow that I
knew, she ran her thin hands across
my face and felt the
tears she couldn't see.
Two days later, my father
walked into the room,
she was screaming,
the angel had flown—
and left the body,
small, calm, smiling.

I waited each night at the wake
for her thin hands to grab me,
hold me close to her, hugging.
But when I touched the fingers,
stiff, like tough roots
growing above ground, I

knew their movement done.
But even as my sisters and I
carried the casket, I thought
she'd jump out, demand to
walk that church aisle by herself
as she'd done for the last
fifty years, stopping
at each pew to tell
strangers, "I love you."

I bless my dough each time
I make bread—
four hands punch it down:
mine, young and strong,
and two old skinny ones.

Maureen Brady

Novena

1

All through the years that Aunt Mary Elizabeth sent me novenas I didn't fully understand them or her or who she was to
me. She was gaunt. She stood cooking on the coal stove with
her back to me, wearing a cardigan sweater. Her shoulder
blades were like the hooks on the kitchen wall, where the
coats hung—blunt prominences. I thought of the scarecrow
in the garden, the overseer. Large scapulae without the flesh
filled out. This is what I thought of when her Christmas card
came addressed to Mr. and Mrs. Brian Maguire and family.
Inside the card was a tiny envelope and inside this envelope
a small card inscribed with the message: Commencing December 20, 1950, and continuing for the next nine days, fifteen novenae will be said for you at the request of Miss Mary
Elizabeth Maguire. How had she decided on fifteen when
there were six of us?

2

Mother bought dish towels for our family to give to Aunt
Mary Elizabeth for Christmas. I wandered through the gift
shop after mass and imagined myself grown up, with my own

money, buying her a beautiful blue holy card with a radiant picture of Mary on it, or perhaps a scapular. A scapular was to be worn under your clothing, against your skin. The problem was to think of Aunt Mary Elizabeth with skin. She seemed to use her body only as a skeleton she traveled with—to church, to the factory, to the cemetery where she visited the dead.

3

All winter she wrote letters that started and ended with "The roads are so slippery." She described traveling the river road to the factory every day. "The curves are treacherous," she said, "and the snow gets plowed right over the river bank, and it seems like that's where I'll end, if the arthritis doesn't get me first."

4

"Are you scared of the dead?" she asked me once. "I mean, does the idea that their flesh has gone cold and heavy frighten you?"

"I guess so," I said, our white-gloved hands clasped together.

"You needn't be," she said. "Think of the lightness of the spirit without the body."

Was it walking in the cemetery that made me think her teeth had rattled as she spoke?

5

Spring was her time. In June she wrote, "It's not that I wouldn't like to see you, but the nerve of my brother to think I would go away on the long weekend when he knows perfectly well that I always visit the dead on Memorial Day."

Then: "Things grow up so bad in the summer. If you come to visit me you might pass right by this place and not know it's here."

I always think of her in spring—the ground still hard and barren, the snow in dribbles on the north side of the hill. I think of holding her hand, climbing between the gravestones toward Granny and the others—Aunt Mary Elizabeth's still-born sister and my great uncle Jack, who plunged over the river bank and required a good deal of prayer since he had been a drunk.

6

Once I sat on one of the stones. Mary Elizabeth had wandered over to visit the neighbors' graves, and I found a low stone and sat with my dress pulled down over my knees, my black missal in my lap. I wished that I had one with gold pages. I closed my eyes and tried to communicate to Aunt Mary Elizabeth with my will: Next year, for Easter, please notice that I don't have a missal with gold-edged pages. Mine had red edges. I opened my eyes again and stared at the sharp contrast of the black book and the white gloves, so pure. She came from behind and pinched my rear just below my waist. She had bumpy joints in her fingers from the arthritis, and so I couldn't believe she could pinch that hard. I started to yelp, but her teeth were in my ear, rattling. "Hush," she said in a whisper. "You were sitting on someone's spirit. How would you like someone to sit on yours?"

A large cloud moved in and I was shivering by the time we reached the car.

7

At home I had a section of my top drawer marked off for Aunt Mary Elizabeth's gifts: Granny's funeral card, a scapular, a white lace mantilla, my blue rosary, some holy cards I alternated regularly so that a different one was showing, my missal, my white gloves. I was a lover of baseball and carried my baseball cards with me. Each time I changed my underwear, I had a glance at my Easter gifts, and I knew they were mine, although I was not sure who I was that had them.

8

"Do you still have the rosary I gave you last Easter?"
"Yes, Aunt Mary Elizabeth, the blue one."
"You are a good child to hold onto your things."
She told me my cousin lost hers. "She puts it in her lap, and when she kneels it drops and her mind is so much on God that she doesn't hear." Aunt Mary Elizabeth said she told Coleen, "The rosary is a circle, never finished. You can always say another one." She is really telling this to me. "Still I see her rushing," she says of Coleen. "You would think she was going somewhere."

I always thought that Aunt Mary Elizabeth would will all of Granny's religious objects to this cousin, the first female heir in my generation, but then I saw that I might have a chance if I didn't lose my rosary, if I learned to keep going around the circle without boredom.

9

I lost my religion the year I went away to college, but continued to receive my novenas from Aunt Mary Elizabeth in with the family package at Christmas. By the time I was an adult with my own money and could have bought her holy cards, I had forgotten I ever intended to. I had my own apartment, my own dresser. In the top drawer, my missal sat under the last pair of white gloves she had given me. Never worn. She who refused to betray the dead for a Memorial Day weekend away could not be told that I no longer went to church, no longer wore my white gloves, carried my black missal.

But Christmas, a card addressed to me—Miss Irene Maguire—and inside the card, a tiny envelope, and inside that, fifteen novenas. For me, alone. Scarecrow. Overseer. She knew. A woman of vision.

10

"I wish I could travel to visit you but I don't know when," she wrote. "I go down the river road and back six days a week and the factory is always there. They own you in this life but they won't have me in the next."

"At last the roads are not so slippery so I hope you'll come for Easter."

11

Winter was hard here, much freezing rain and the pipes froze more than once, but now I have a warm sun on my back and cool brown earth at my feet. I rake the soil that has just been tilled for the garden. My hands are thin-skinned from winter. Blisters begin to form and the muscles of my back feel as if they are curling into a rope, but the evenness of the patch of ground I have finished draws me to go on.

12

Her brothers always say that Aunt Mary Elizabeth is a spinster because they did such a fine job of protecting her from their not-to-be-trusted contemporaries when she was young. I wonder what Granny told her. In my memory, Granny is an old woman with pure white hair, and wrinkles so deep they enfold my imagination. She rocks in a high-backed wicker rocker. She has false teeth, and as I hover around her chair she takes them out, covers their entire mass with her hands, and rattles them in my ears. I tell her this gives me goosebumps and she chuckles at my fears.

When Granny died, my mother and father decided I was too young to go to the funeral. How could I explain to them that I thought she meant to invite me?

13

The winter coats still hang in the hall, heavy gloves poking from their pockets. I must cover my hands to go on raking. I am over a decade past childhood and still, in my top drawer, I have a section for relics. And in all these years since Aunt Mary Elizabeth gave me my last pair of white gloves, they have never been worn.

14

The gloves are soft, inside and out, and soothing to my blisters. It is Easter Sunday. I rake my garden until the entire patch has constancy. The gloves are perfect. I am light-headed with the discovery of them. I furrow several rows for early planting, stoop and drop the seeds with careful spacing. I go back and cover the seeds with a small hill of dirt, tamp it with my gloved hands. I send a message to Aunt Mary Elizabeth: These rows are my novenas for you. I hope that the sun is shining in Pennsylvania, where, I know, Aunt Mary Elizabeth must be visiting Granny in the graveyard.

15

My gloves are still pure white on the back side but have turned brown on the palm side. I remember her pinch, so sudden, so firm. I go on tamping the earth, feeling the rope muscles of my back touched by the sun.

Kay Marie Porterfield

Spilled Milk

My grandmother has told me the story so often, I vividly recall the milk house although I have never been there. It is built of gray stone gathered from the fields and held together with chalky mortar. A patch of moss by the door looks like a velvet pincushion. Inside: a cream separator, the churn, gleaming tin pails, and butter paddles, their wood frayed from years of use. I see them through her eyes as she recites them like the rosary, like a charm.

Even though she died three years ago, she comes to me in dreams to add more detail—an inch-long tear in the screen patched with black darning thread, the speck of the man coming toward her on the road, framed by the door. So tiny is he that at first she mistakes him for a fly, as she lifts the pails of raw milk and pours them into the separator's mouth. Not a cloud mars the sky.

She whistles "The Prisoner's Lament" off-key to take her mind from the milky smell, faintly sour in the August heat. Uncle Mike and Aunt Rose have gone in the buggy to town to buy a part for the mowing machine. My grandmother's gingham dress is plastered to her back and a damp, red curl sticks to her flushed cheek. At thirteen she is gangly, still frail from her years in the orphanage.

"It wasn't so bad, living on Uncle Mike's farm," she tells

me long afterward when her pale hair is blue from a rinse bought at the five-and-dime. "Certainly not as bad as with the nuns." The beatings and long days spent mending buckets of stockings, the cruelties handed out by the children who had parents but nonetheless were boarded at the home, weren't the worst. Those were nothing compared to the man who rented the orphans to beg for him.

He wore a bowler hat and a scratchy black wool coat, and he always arrived right before Christmas. "You make more of a profit begging around the holidays," my grandmother lets me know. Her housedress pulls tight against her hips, as solidly plump as the flowered cushions on her brand-new Sears loveseat.

"He'd ask for about a dozen of us, and I'd hide because I didn't want to go," she says as she dusts. "But since I looked so pitiful, I was always picked. He'd take us on the ferry to Milwaukee, take our coats away from us, and dump us out in the street." She stops her work now to hug me, and my nose fills with the scent of Tabu bath powder. "He'd paid the nuns a certain amount, and we had to make that back for him plus a profit or else he wouldn't let us eat our supper. Stale bread."

Her face closes with remembering. "The snow was never white in Milwaukee, always dirty gray like pigeons." A shudder passes through her. "Dirty and cold, so cold. Sometimes he'd rip our clothes to make us more appealing to the fine folks with money, and when he'd return us, he'd tell the nuns we tore them playing. They'd slap us and send us to bed without eating." My grandmother and I spend the remainder of the afternoon playing bingo, and she teaches me to play cards.

The Christmases she produces are spectacular and always include a reading of "The Little Match Girl." Her lace-covered table is crammed with ham and turkey, mince and pumpkin and apple pies. A mountain of presents spills from beneath the tree to fill the living room. Each year I receive more dolls to make up for the ones she never had.

"You're spoiling her," my mother grouses annually.

"I have a right," is my grandmother's ritual reply, jaw set, eyes flashing blue fire as if gas jets burn behind them.

I am not afraid of her temper. She turns it against me only once, on Saint Patrick's Day, when she pinches me hard enough to bruise my arm for wearing the orange ribbon that my mother insisted on tying in my hair. Crying harder than I do, she then bakes me a custard with nutmeg and cinnamon. "All's fair in love and war," she warns me sadly as I eat the peace offering from her best china. "It's part of being Irish."

There are other parts to being Irish. We don't cry over spilled milk, not for long anyway. As proof, she instructs me to consider our wakes: whiskey- and tear-soaked celebrations of passage for a stiffening corpse laid out in a coffin on the dining-room table. We keen, wailing heart-wrenching sobs, and later tell jokes and stories, laughing ourselves silly with just as much enthusiasm. Some of us drink. "We know how to live," she teaches me, "and we know how to die. And we know how to tell about it, too."

On rainy afternoons I stay with her to keep her company while Grandpa works, and she fills me in on what she's learned of the Easter Rising, secondhand of course, because she, after all, was living with her Uncle Mike here in Michigan. While my grandfather reads meters for the water department, we take turns standing on the ottoman, waving our arms and raising our voices in impassioned speeches for home rule. Since neither of us will pretend to be the hated English, we Irish volunteers wedge ourselves behind the sofa, aiming our fingers at invisible troops.

A voracious reader, she glibly paints word pictures of Dublin Castle and Connolly Street, of De Valera and Pearse, but she lets me direct the scenes she sets. "I don't know how to play," she tells me. "All I learned to do was mend stockings and scrub floors, so you will have to teach me." I take delight in showing her how to barricade Connolly Street with a card table tipped on its side, how to make a Sinn Fein flag from a dish towel tied to a broomstick.

My mother is not pleased when she comes to pick me up.

"Your grandmother's time in the orphanage affected her," Mother warns in the car later. "She's never even been to Ireland, and we aren't *that* Irish." She grinds the gears. "Well, *she* may be, but I'm certainly not, and you're even less so." Her hands grip the De Soto's steering wheel. "She's always stretched the truth. Next thing she'll be telling you about the stone angel falling on her father. It was a load of stone blocks." Two bright spots of color appear on her cheeks. "With her, everything is high drama."

Afterward I am forbidden to be alone in my Grandmother's presence for two months because she is a bad influence on me. So for two months I shell peas and snap beans for canning. Standing on a tall chair, I iron my father's shirts, wondering all the time how Grandma will ever manage to play without me.

One afternoon when my work is done, my mother curls my hair, using sugar water for setting lotion. As she winds the curls in tight spirals, she holds the metal bobby pins between her teeth. I have never been quite so afraid of her. Then she sends me out with a quart jar of water to pick dandelions in the yard between our house and the barn. Standing in the kitchen window, she watches as bees swarm around my head like a buzzing brown cloud. I try to defend myself with the water, but even so, two of them sting me. When I run to the house, shrieking and crying, she orders me to my room to wait for my father to come home. "She deliberately poured water on herself," she says to him, and he spanks me to calm her. I believe that my grandmother was lucky to live in an orphanage.

When my grandmother and I are finally reunited, I ask her to tell me the story about her father and the stone angel. She pulls a tin of butter cookies from the cupboard and brews tea in the pot with the shamrocks on it. "Patrick was a dancer and a drinker," she tells me as we get cozy on the loveseat. The faint smell of Grandpa's cigars lingers in the room. "A boxer, too," Grandma continues. "A devilishly handsome man with blue eyes and black hair, a black Irishman with a black heart to match, Patrick was. He was a master stonemason."

She pours more milk into my tea and stirs it. "Before I was born, before Ma died, he helped to build the Catholic orphanage where I stayed."

"How did she die?" I would rather listen to my grandmother than listen to the radio or even go to the movies.

"I was two and she was thirty-six when she died," Grandma says. "She was big with a baby inside of her when she went out to the back yard to boil the wash and hang it. She took a chill and she died of pneumonia two days later, on Christmas day, coughing blood. They called the priest, who came in his black coat, smelling of whiskey, and gave her last rites. I don't remember much else—just my da crying and then lying on the floor later in his own vomit from drink. I was so young I couldn't figure out why we didn't open the presents." When she recounts this suffering, it is as though it had been inflicted on someone else.

My grandmother's mother was beautiful, the daughter of a lumberjack who farmed when the virgin timber in Michigan had all been cut. After marrying her off to the Irish stonemason, he moved to northern California to fell redwoods. There are no pictures of him or of his daughter, so I must take her at her word. "He ached to feel his saw blade bite into the soft wood of the biggest trees in the world, just like a knife going through butter," my grandmother recounts. "And he died when one of those very trees fell on him." She thinks for a moment and hints that this family history of having heavy objects fall upon us with crushing force may be a curse.

Then she goes on. "After Ma went to heaven, Da would be gone for days at a time, drinking and womanizing. Min, who was eleven, did her best to raise us. Frank had a paper route. Every night when he was finished, he'd bring me a cream puff wrapped in paper from the bakery since I was the baby and he liked me best. Sometimes when Da came back, he brought us money, so we got by."

By then the orphanage was long finished and Patrick was working on Saint Alphonsus Church. A statue he was carving toppled and smashed the bones in one of his legs, crippling him. She describes the angel to me, how it had her mother's face, how its gray wings arced toward heaven like a prayer, defying the weight of the stone they were carved from. "It was as if his heart was already flawed," she tells me. "When the angel fell on him, it broke wide open." We both nod wisely at the poetic justice in this.

She tells me that nobody cares to take the time to make such angels today. If I want to see good work like that I will need to visit a cemetery or the church. She herself will no longer set foot in a Catholic church, not after the nuns. When she must pass either church or nun, she hurries to the other side of the street. Even so, she teaches me to say the beads, to cross myself, and to recite at least one Hail Mary before I go to sleep each night, silently so my mother won't know.

If her father couldn't work, he still could drink, and that became his full-time occupation. He returned home only to move his children from tenement to boardinghouse—rough places as my grandmother remembers them. "Finally we were out in the street where it was even rougher," she says. "My grandparents couldn't afford to take us in and the other relatives only wanted Anna and Mabe, who were old enough to keep house. Min found a live-in job caring for an *Episcopal* priest's children." She frowns at this disgrace.

"Then, of course, neighbors told the nuns on Frank and me, who were the youngest, and they locked us in the home like prisoners." Abruptly she switches the subject. "Let's play Easter Rising." We do, making believe that the British have taken us captive in Dublin Castle and we must break out. While we plan our escape, my grandmother sings "The Prisoner's Lament." "If I had the wings of an angel," her voice strains and crackles. I join in. "Over these prison walls I would fly, I'd fly to the arms of my darling, and there I'd be willing to die." By the time Grandpa comes home from work, we have managed to break free and put supper on the table.

When I see her the next week, she has decided I will write her story and the story of the Irish race after I am grown. Someone must stand witness to what has occurred, even a distant witness. We have the gift of gab, she allows. It is in our blood from the famine time and well before. It comes from the pain of being misunderstood for centuries, and if we do not write about the pain or tell it in a story, it often gets us into trouble. Since she has only an eighth-grade education, she judges I might be the better grammarian, and therefore the task falls to me. "When you do it," she insists, "you must change our name to Kelley, so no one will recognize us."

For months, her storytelling escalates. I learn of bright spots in the orphanage, about how she wore out her shoes sliding down the hill in winter because there were no sleds. And when the nuns whipped her, she would look at them defiantly and say, "Thank you very much, Sister. Have you finished?"—which would set off another round of beatings. Once, on a bet, she pulled off a nun's habit to see if sisters shaved their heads as was rumored. They did, and that prank earned her yet another whipping. She teaches me to read tea leaves, and invariably tells me I am coming into money. She shows me how to twist the stems carefully from apples to discover the last initial of the man I will marry. She instructs me on the art of avoiding black cats and ladders.

In the home, her big brother Frank watched after her, holding her hand whenever he could, and when he couldn't, smiling a rakish smile at her from across the room like Patrick's ghost. Mostly the boys and girls were separated, though. Her eyes fill with tears when she talks about the morning she came down to breakfast, took her place on the bench, and looked across the room for Frank, who wasn't there. For days the nuns wouldn't tell her what happened to him; finally, one informed her that he'd died, to forget about him. Months later, she learned that some second cousins had taken him since he'd grown old enough and strong enough to help on their farm.

She teaches me to wear spotless white gloves when we go to town. She shows me where the fairies sleep in her garden and promises me I will one day see one because she knows in her heart I have the sight. Every year we celebrate our birthdays together, since they fall only a few days apart.

The worst part about the Irish is that they drink, my mother informs me repeatedly. They drink because their imaginations work overtime. There are other bad things that she won't detail because I am too young to hear them. My grandmother has never touched a drop of spirits and she forbids my grandfather to drink, because she has seen the power of whiskey. Lips that touch liquor will never touch hers. Her sisters are all slaves to drink, though, and even her beloved Frank has succumbed. "Sins of the fathers," my mother grumbles on our way to a meeting of the Women's Christian Temperance Union at the Methodist church, and she adds something about whores and barflies. I wonder if they are as black and ominous as the fly on the milk-house screen in my grandmother's best story.

In late summer, as my grandmother and I inspect the snapdragons and the phlox in her garden, she gets to the part about the fire in the orphanage. She had no place to go except with Uncle Mike and Aunt Rose, the latter a dreaded Protestant. "When they saw how bad off I was," she tells me, "Uncle Mike, a good Irishman, told the nuns they could go to hell before he'd send me back to that place. I couldn't even sit in a chair; I didn't know how to anymore from sitting on the benches. 'You'll take this poor girl back over my dead body,' Mike told them." Her voice is as brave and clear as when she gives her home-rule speeches. I feel like clapping and cheering.

"When the trustees from the orphanage came to get me, Uncle Mike held me on his lap and put his arms around me. He threatened to punch the man's lights out." She smiles. "And he would have, too, if the terrible fellow hadn't left right then. So they served us with papers and took us to court. I can still remember how the nuns said that because Uncle Mike hadn't married in the Church, he and Aunt Rose were living in sin and that I'd lose my mortal soul if I stayed there. I was born and baptized a Catholic so I belonged to the nuns lock, stock, and barrel. But the judge at the hearing just looked at those old nuns and said, 'I married this couple right in this very courtroom. If you keep saying they aren't legally married, I'll hold you in contempt. Case dismissed.'"

My grandmother's fist pounds the side of the toolshed like a judge's gavel. She smiles so broadly she shows her teeth, which she is ashamed of because they are crooked.

Her teeth may be less than perfect, but she has good legs, which she shows off to her advantage and my mother's chagrin. Like a racehorse's, they are *very* good legs. In fact, it was those very legs which attracted my grandfather's eye when she was eighteen and on her own, working in a candy store. Both of them ended their engagements to other people, she to a handsome boy named Frank. My grandparents married within the year, but that is another story.

Her best tale remains the one about the day in the milk house that faraway August. The black spot through the screen slowly spread like a stain, and she saw it was a man. Frozen, she was terrified it was the orphanage official who had lain in wait for her to be alone. Many a night she had stayed awake, rigid with fear she'd be kidnapped and returned to the sisters. Now, since there was only one door, she was cornered like an animal.

As the stranger came closer, she could tell he was just a raggedy hobo with matted hair. His shoes were tied together with twine and his pants were so dirty and old they fairly glistened in the sun. Her shoulders relaxed, and she heaved a sigh ... until she recognized the stranger as her long-lost da, and the pail of milk she'd been lifting flew crashing to the stone floor as if it had wings.

What could she do but hurl herself out the door with the fury of a banshee and start pounding her old man's chest with her fists? His yellowed teeth were rotting, his face was bearded, nose red-veined from years of drink. Oh, but she would have known those eyes anywhere. They haunted her dreams. She hated those eyes burning into her, wanted to put them out.

He was pitiful, she says, and stank to high heaven, but she was relentless. And when he wouldn't fight back like an honest Irishman, but whined, begging her to forgive him and take him in, could she do anything but refuse him? Mother of God, once she knew for certain he wouldn't kill her, she knew without doubt that she would kill him, finish the job the stone angel started. Someone seemed meant to die that day. Suddenly afraid of the consequences of that murderous rage on her mortal soul, she took off on her racehorse legs, running toward the farmhouse with him flapping and wheezing behind her. "I slammed the door in his face." Her voice rings with triumph. "I told him I hoped he rotted in hell; he'd have me back as a daughter over his dead body." Giddy with excitement, although I've heard the tale at least six times, I let out the breath I have been holding. "And that was the end of it," she concludes. Before I can fully recover, she directs me to find the cardboard bingo cards and goes off to look for her button box for markers.

Obviously it is *not* the end of it because she tells and retells the story for the rest of her life. During the Alzheimer's years, it blurs like a bad print of an old movie. The images are nearly unrecognizable, but since you know the story line by heart, you make allowances. After the fatal heart attack, she began invading my dreams, and the focus has become so painfully sharp, it hurts me to view it directly.

In the time between my childhood and my grandmother's death, I managed to escape the weight of my mother, but my lips did touch liquor and, nearly crushed by the bottle, I forgot to write Grandma's story. Instead I married a man from the South Bronx who, although he was not Irish, resembled my great-grandfather Patrick in more ways than I care to recount. Let's just say he was a boxer in his own right. Later, too long after I'd turned from drink, I ejected him from my life, cursing his dark heart and telling him I hoped he rotted in hell. In the days before my thirty-sixth Christmas, I let the dirty clothes pile up, afraid that if I did the wash it would seal my fate. I read my tea leaves that always foretold I would be coming into money which never arrived.

Finally, sick and tired of grieving over spilled milk—mine, my mother's, my grandmother's, which lay mingled in a clotted puddle—I decided to wipe up the mess by sending away to the orphanage, the county courthouse, and the department of health for the records that would substantiate or disprove my grandmother's history.

My great-grandmother did die on Christmas Day in 1902, exactly as I'd been told. Her husband deserted his children shortly afterward, and my grandmother was committed to the Grand Rapids Catholic Home for Orphans when she was seven, along with Frank, the brother she idolized. I have the papers to prove it, those and the court records from the custody battle the nuns waged against Mike and Rose five years later. There are newspaper clippings, too, about the orphanage fire. And Frank's boy, now an old man with a pacemaker, confirms the begging in Milwaukee.

As it turns out, though, Patrick lay cold and decomposing long before my grandmother's thirteenth summer. He was buried in a pauper's grave outside the churchyard, and since the drink finally caught up to him in winter when the frozen earth was difficult to spade, he shares his final resting place with two other derelicts, one of them nameless, none of them properly waked. And although that blackhearted, drunkard of an Irishman did lay the stones for the orphanage that would imprison his own daughter's mind and heart throughout her life, he was no stone-carver. Saint Alphonsus Church doesn't have any stone angels. It never did.

Cecilia Woloch

The Shock of Creation

Everywhere I float in my mother's eyes
watery, dark, she remembers
I was tiny and calm, I was *perfect*, she says
my new teeth and the shock of creation.

She is holding her chin in the palm of her hand
and I have turned to her
at the dining room table, at last
we believe one another.

And no one says *tenderly* or *redeeming* or
father forgive us.
Blurring, we know who we are,
how I've grown nervous and strong
and why she did not rush to save me.

Judith Ortiz Shushan

V-E Day

The church bells woke me, bells from all over town. From the misguided Protestants to the amorphous Unitarians, every denomination clamored for attention. But none were as loud, as clear as the Catholic bells, befitting the voice of the one true church, I thought. Actually, location explained the strength of the sound; our house crouched at the foot of a steep hill that rose five blocks to meet Sacred Heart Cathedral, so the Catholic bells cascaded down the hill and poured through my window.

Was it a holiday? I could think of none. My mother burst into our room and rushed to the bed we shared and gathered me into a rare hug. "The war is over!" she cried. "Daddy's coming home!"

Daddy's coming home. After so much time that I couldn't even remember him, this husband, whose photograph sat upon my mother's blond chiffonier, next to La Virgen de Guadalupe; this rather stout, round-faced father, who smiled out of his seriously starched uniform at the family he left alone; this soldier, who wrote letters from strange countries on tissue-thin blue paper with the most important parts blacked out by someone who kept the secrets; this warrior, who would display burn scars on his hands from heroics in a fiery tank; this liberator, who opened the gates of unmentionable places, where unspeakable things happened to people—to children, even—places that had become the locale of my midnight dreams, was coming home.

"Get up! Get up!" my mother sang as she fled the room. "Come to Gramma's when you're dressed!"

I knelt on our bed to look out of the window, to see what such a special day would look like.

Bells, sirens, car horns tangled in knots, and the sounds were wrong somehow; they did not, to me, sing of joy but of confusion.

I caught a sudden movement to my right, on the dirt road that began at the end of our street, the road that led into the barrio. My mother was so proud that our house was on the edge, wasn't actually *in* the barrio, where most houses had outside toilets. Another movement and I saw a skinny dog run up the dirt road between the barren brown sentinel hills that flanked the entrance to Chihuahuita, the colonia. The dog ran, turned abruptly and barked, howled, nose pointing to the barrio, tail between his legs; then he turned and ran toward our house, only to repeat his frantic antics once again. Was he running to warn me, or was he trying to escape while attempting a sad show of bravery? For following him was a grim parade of dozens of black shapes crawling, slowly crawling on their hands and knees, crawling through the dry New Mexican dust, crawling up the dirt road, turning the corner by my house to crawl up the hill to church. Old Mexican women in black gowns and black mantillas, oblivious to dog and dust, dusky ancient women in a black jumble, sluggish black moths with wings curled protectively around dry bodies, crawling.

Was this the beginning of the Three Days of Darkness the nuns told us about? ... when devils would roam the earth and the only light would come from blessed candles burning in good Catholic homes, and instant death and eternal hell would be the price of giving in to temptation to peek at the horror outside.... But no. "Daddy's coming home," she had said. This day would bring other meanings.

The bell-laden air grew thicker with the drone of Spanish

prayers—louder, louder as the viejas climbed the hill beside our window, empty mouths murmuring in deep faces swathed in jet. They climbed, crawled toward the Catholic bells, toward the Father, Son, and Holy Ghost, a nightmare on the loose in the streets.

As they crawled they kept dark promises to dark saints and to a god notorious for breaking promises. Sterile rituals: those crawling, praying women, giving obsequious thanks for the end of one hell and the beginning of another, grateful to God for the return of sons and grandsons; such innocent blasphemous piety, pleasing God with ritual humiliation. ✓ What sort of god would find this pleasing?

I looked up at the sky, which seemed so low, so cement-heavy, bleached, colorless. The very air was bruised with bells, that frenzied iron sound that left a taste of rust in my mouth, clanging, clanging. And where was the moon? The sky should hover darkly on such a midnight scene, but this was dream spilling into day, night things intruding as something dark sucked on the world.

"You were born old," my mother used to say. She still does. I caught my face reflected in the windowpane and imagined it framed by a black mantilla. I stared at that face, wondering whether I would become a real child now that daddy was coming home.

My father did not, certainly could not have returned that very day—V-E Day—yet I remember his return accompanied by those bells, the day of the black parade somehow confusing itself with the day I saw him again.

We did not know each other. We had expected so much more.

I slept alone now, my father having reclaimed his place beside my mother. The world had been transformed that crawling day, but now, instead of the bells, there were my father's midnight cries, my mother's murmuring comfort, my father's sobs and challenges to God as he relived the dark things he never described to anyone.

In time my father crawled back to ordinary problems. Perhaps they were even harder to take than the war, because they must have seemed so much more real.

My mother crawled back into marriage, to a feigned dependence that she could never make real. Too late: she had been too strong too long.

And I crawled away, always away, until I grew old enough and brave enough to look back and silence the bells.

Elizabeth Spires

Falling Away

Memory: I am sitting at my desk in sixth grade at St. Joseph's Elementary in Circleville, Ohio. It is a winter morning in 1964, and we are in the middle of catechism. The classroom is old-fashioned, with high ceilings and wood floors, the crucifix above the front blackboard in a face-off with the big round clock on the back wall. The room smells of chalk and soap and dust. There are six or seven tall windows that can be opened in the spring and fall but that are shut tightly now. The heating pipes knock. The room is uncomfortably warm, a little steamy. The early morning snowfall has put all of us in a dreamy, slow-motion mood, everyone, that is, except our teacher, a study in black and white, dressed in a heavy black habit and black veil, white wimple, collar, and bib. A crucifix hangs from a black rope belt knotted around her waist; she has told us that if she holds it and sincerely repents her sins at the moment of death, her soul will fly straight to heaven.

Sister M—— points outside with her long wooden pointer, the same pointer that often comes down with a *crack*! on the desks of unsuspecting daydreamers, bringing them back to this world with a start. Outside, each snowflake is lost in the indistinguishable downward spiral of the heavy snowfall. The voice that is not a voice comes back, her voice, imagined, reconstructed from memory: *How many souls are in hell?*

More than all the snowflakes that are falling today, yesterday, tomorrow. I try to imagine a number that large, an infinite number, and cannot. Then I try to follow the path of one individual snowflake in its slow, yet inevitable, drifting descent, but lose it in the swirling pattern of white against white.

The lesson continues: *How long will those lost souls pay for their sins? For all eternity.* Eternity. How can we, at eleven years old, she must be thinking, possibly be able to conceive of just how long eternity is? *Imagine the largest mountain in the world, made of solid rock. Once every hundred years, a bird flies past, the tip of its wing brushing lightly against the mountaintop. Eternity is as long as it would take for the bird's wing to wear the mountain down to nothing.*

Ever after, I connect hell and eternity not with fire and flames but with something cold and unchanging, a snowy tundra overshadowed by a huge granite mountain that casts a pall over the landscape. Like the North or South Pole in midsummer, the sun would circle overhead in a crazy loop, day passing into day without intervening night, each object nakedly illuminated, etched sharply in light and shadow, unable to retreat into night's invisibility. If I were unlucky, I'd be there one day, for *forever*, dressed in my white communion dress, white anklets, and black patent leather shoes. And there would be others, too, a field of stopped souls who couldn't move or speak, but who suffered the cold, suffered inaction, without sleep or forgetfulness. Like children playing freeze tag on a playground, the field of souls would stretch over the horizon past the vanishing-point. The only moving thing a small black spot in the sky, the bird that flew high over our heads once every hundred years when the century flipped over, like the odometer on a speeding car.

Clock-time and eternity. Darkness and light. A poem lies in the experience of that grimly metaphysical catechism class, one that I can't write, though I've tried many times. It comes to me in shards and fragments, frozen, like I am, when I enter the memory:

... and so I imagined the edge of the world,
a great domed space, black stones
and ice, where I'd stand forever
not dressed for the weather,
my heart beating fast as a metronome.
And the bird flying past
would come so close, I'd hear
its heart beat fast as my own.

  If the bird needed food,
  what did it do?
  Did it sing as it flew,
  a shining black syllable?

Now when I look in your eyes—
two tunnels running backward
to infinite light, infinite darkness—
I think what Time will do to those
who admit so freely what they have to lose.
White dress, black shoes,
what is a life anyhow?

Titled "A Lesson in Eternity," the poem remains unfinished, unresolved, the final question unanswered. I had a dream recently, a more benign version of a recurring nightmare. Usually, I am back in grade school or high school completing a requirement that I somehow missed or deliberately avoided. I am in my adult mind and body among children, carrying the burden of adult memory and consciousness. I am threatened with not passing, not graduating, and thus, not going on to the next "step," if I don't make up for childhood omissions. It is a dream that suggests, in its many different variations, that I have not finished "old business." In this dream, however, I am back at St. Joseph's not as a student but as a teacher. Teacher of what? I haven't been told. No one is there. I walk through the empty classrooms, a dream landscape of small wooden desks in neat rows, polished and shining, and freshly washed blackboards, all of it held in suspension, waiting for something to happen. A bell to ring.

The classrooms to be flooded with shouts and light. It doesn't matter that the school has been closed for years. Standing in the dark hallway, I'm thinking how I'll finally see through the keyhole into that polarized world of good and evil, guilt and absolution, that even a fallen-away Catholic can't escape. After all, I have all time. Have all eternity.

Cathleen Calbert

Fainting

Those steps, cooler than I could have believed,
and my face in absolute harmony. The collapse
of my body. Only my cheeks, toes, fingers remaining.
Then the voices of men or, more often, women
in tones of despairing angels, devoted solely to me,
calling from above. Each moment, a miracle,
and I suddenly wonderful, a child Hermione:
"Look! Her eye's opening. The color's returning."
When my skin awoke, drops of water blessed
the top of my head to the soles of my feet.
From other children, it's true, there was
some mean-spirited talk of ray-guns
and susceptibility. Well, we were all
trapped in church, and it wasn't their fault
if they couldn't stop breathing.
Not for them the drama, being lifted into the arms
of strange men and whisked away. Yes, the beauty
of it was not being guilty of anything. For I tried
to hold on, my uneven curls unraveling, and I
kneeling, big shoulders on either side of me, and I
watching my hands press together, the little gloves,
a white wicker purse dangling from one wrist.
Inside: a hanky and a dime. I tried waiting

until I could walk down the aisle and be given
a little something to suck on, always comforting,
the wafer dissolving on the roof of my mouth,
like Chinese paper candy, so mysterious and lingering.
Then I'd be happy, and it would be ending.
But sometimes, I'd have to leave early,
and a child doesn't leave easily.
I'd wait until it was too late—"Why didn't you
tell me?"—until my eyes were large and dark
as I looked up to find my mother's face. Then the rush
to lay me out, in the air, on the concrete,
ladies pulling down my dress, trying to press my knees
together (they could not stop dividing),
waking to promises from my repentant mother
of love and new Sunday mornings until everyone
gave up on my legs and talked softly to me.
So Emily was wrong to be afraid, wasn't she?
For I knew then, I knew I could be controlled
only until I let go.

Sharon Myers

The Forbidden List

When I was ten, my mother, who was divorced and had no marketable skills, clung precariously to filegirldom in the basement of a state bureaucracy in Boise, Idaho, on the strength of her knowledge of the alphabet. This allowed the three of us, my toddler brother, my mother, and myself, to live in three tiny rooms in the basement of an old house on a tree-lined street close to downtown and the capitol building. We could not afford a television or any form of entertainment that cost money, but we lived near the library.

As usual, I hauled books back and forth from the library. One day, my mother looked at one of the books and said, "That's on the Church's Forbidden list."

Forbidden list? There was a list of books you weren't supposed to read?

I had read so many books! It was possible I had already done something forbidden. Where was this list? I wanted to see it. Why hadn't anyone ever told me about this list? It had never occurred to me that books might be evil. I was eager to learn what the criteria were.

"Mom, where can I see the list?" Was it tacked up on the parish bulletin board? How could I have missed it?

Well ... she didn't know exactly, but she knew there was one and she didn't have a very high opinion of it. It was old-fashioned; she herself had read that book ...

I wasn't adult enough to share her ambivalence. Books were such an important part of my life, and so was the Church.

This was serious.

"Where is the List!"

She guessed the Bishop would know.

I put on my roller skates and went to the Bishop's.

His housekeeper answered the door. I had taken my roller skates off. I respectfully asked to see the Bishop. She asked my name. Sharon Myers. She said to wait a moment. Falling maple leaves combed the air. She returned. "He'll see you. Wait right here." She ushered me into his empty office.

His office was covered, floor to ceiling, with books. It was a beautiful alcove of polished hardwoods and carpeted hush.

He entered. I kissed his ring. I took my place on the interviewee side of the desk. I was dead serious.

"What can I do for you," he asked. He did not ask me smiling. He did not reveal any condescension toward me as a child.

"Father, I have been told there is a Forbidden list of books. Do you have the list? I would please like to see a copy of the list."

He didn't have a copy of the list.

Where was it?

He guessed it was in the Vatican.

How did anybody know what books were forbidden if nobody had a copy of the list?

And anyway, what was it in books that got them in so much trouble?

I had a book at home and my mother said it was on the Forbidden list. Would I be committing a sin to read it? How many sins had I already committed?

I wanted to get this straight. I pushed my pigtails back and waited, eager to know.

But he didn't answer. He called his housekeeper. "Please prepare hot chocolate for my guest," he requested.

"You like books, don't you?" he said.

That was how I met Bishop Kelly.

His housekeeper returned with a tray of crystal and silver with a silver pot of hot chocolate. Little bars of shortbread hid under silver canopies on real lace napkins.

We drank hot chocolate and Bishop Kelly talked about the Church and the Forbidden list. He talked about Galileo and the Inquisition and antiquated law and observed law and intentions and interpretations and what was and wasn't an evil influence—for that matter the very nature of evil and of truth—and he invited me to see his library.

Bishop Kelly had an excellent library.

I saw the book my mother had recognized. *Madame Bovary*. Had he read it? Yes. Could I read it? Yes.

I had permission to read a forbidden book.

I pulled down a few other titles and examined them. "Father, are all these forbidden books?"

"Yes."

Bishop Kelly had an entire library of forbidden books.

"Can I read this one?"

"Yes. You can read any of them you like."

I had permission from the Bishop to read all of the forbidden books.

I swelled with pride.

"Come back when you like. Borrow the books you will."

His gown whispered away over the carpets.

I roller-skated home, weighed down with forbidden books and self-esteem. My mother listened to my report with interest and wonder.

"So," she said. "So."

"I always liked Bishop Kelly," she said.

Over the months that followed, I returned books to the Bishop's library and often, though not always, he would sit with me over hot chocolate in his office and discuss them with me. Sometimes he would pull one down and say, "I think you'll like this one," but most of the time he let me graze, reading one book suggested by another, propelled into and out of different centuries and different minds, absorbing some concepts, indifferent to others. I understood as a child understands, and that understanding is remote to me now. I don't remember all of the books, but many of them were "classics" of literature, some of them expensively bound.

When we moved away at the end of the year, Bishop Kelly gave me his blessing, his head bowed over mine in the dark hardwood doorframe of his office.

I missed him. After two years we returned to visit relatives and I saw him again, arranged in gold brocade in his coffin among thick floral tributes amassed before the main altar of the cathedral. I was thirteen then, and had come to learn that what was truly forbidden was the intelligence he had acknowledged in a girl and the wisdom of seeking one's own vision.

Valerie Miner

Misty, Tiled Chambers

"Nine is old enough to learn to swim," Mom said, letting me have the window seat on the bus.

"But *you* don't know how to swim," I protested.

"Exactly!" she pronounced with the infallible logic she always used when refuting arguments with my own words.

Mom made me wear my heavy jacket and her own long, wool scarf. She wore the old red coat and her neck looked too long that morning. When I was mad at my mother, I found fault with her appearance—especially with her skinny face and bow legs. I was furious with her today because it was twenty degrees outside and she was dragging me all the way to Hackensack for swimming lessons.

"But, Mom, it's too *cold* for a bathing suit. Why don't we wait for summer?"

"It's crowded in the summer. This way you'll be able to swim at the pond when the hot weather starts; won't that be nice?"

"I'd rather learn piano."

She looked past me at snowmen guarding white lawns along Madison Avenue.

"Why can't I take piano? Jackie has lessons."

"Music lessons are expensive, dear. Besides, you'd have to practice. We could hardly afford a *piano*."

I stared at an icicle forming on a telephone wire. "I could practice on Jackie's." I looked back with expectation.

She was picking absentmindedly at a callus on her palm. It was about to bleed and I tapped her. "No, don't do that; it's bad for you."

She smiled, then peered out the window again. We were silent for the rest of the trip.

As we pulled into Hackensack, she took my hand. "You'll like swimming. Give it a chance."

The YMCA was an imposing building, but lacking the ornate drama of St. Mary's Catholic School. Here I noticed one crucifix, no statues, a lot of plain windows, and a big desk. A woman with kinky, blonde hair gave Mom a form and took some money. She nodded at me insincerely. Soon Mom was marching me down a dark corridor and I remembered a movie where ancient people sacrificed their children to the gods.

The locker room had a green smell. It was hot and humid, like July. I caught a glimpse of a fat woman without any clothes, but Mom hauled me over to a stall and handed me the regulation suit. The dark blue knit material was scratchy and stank of disinfectant. I thought about Mom taking me to the doctor, telling me to get undressed and lie on the table while she stood by, tall and invulnerable in that horrid red coat. How could she wear a heavy coat in this muggy room? This wasn't the first time I had doubted her sanity. Maybe I could run away to Jackie's and sleep under the piano.

"Hurry along, dear, we only have five minutes before we meet your teacher."

Mitch was waiting for us outside the ladies' dressing room. He was a tall man with red hair on his chest and head. At first glance, he reminded me of Buster Crabbe. Shyly, I stared at the locker-room door. The italicized *Ladies* was so much more adult than the block-lettered GIRLS marking the bathroom at school. *Ladies*. I tilted my head at the same angle as the white letters. I would tell Jackie about this.

"How do you do?" Mitch had a broad smile, but I didn't register the rest of his face because he reached down to shake my hand. And I noticed that he had several fingers missing. I watched the goosebumps rise along my arm.

Mom nudged me. Maybe she saw, too, and we could go home now. Instead, she said, "Say 'How-do-you-do?,' Gerry."

I knew it was rude to stare at people's handicaps. I knew I should be too adult to mention it. And yet I imagined his hand sticking in my throat, right above the "How-do-you-do?"

"Well, a lot of people are shy at first."

I noticed he was talking to me rather than to my mother.

"You'll be fine once we get in the water. Shall we test the temperature?"

He took my hand and I tried not to *feel*, just as I would try not to smell when I went to the bathroom at the movies. Instead, I concentrated on the high, winding echoes of the Hackensack pool. For the first time I noticed that there was a whole class of swimmers in the far end—the deep end—of the water. Mitch nodded toward the wading section.

He turned gently to Mom. "You'll want to sit up there," he said, pointing to the bleachers. "That way, you won't get wet."

Coward, I thought, as she found a seat and let the strange man lead me down the cold metal ladder. I soon forgot her when he showed me how to duck my head in and out of the water. Then I experienced the miracle of floating. I hardly thought about his hand until he led me back to my mother beneath the italicized *Ladies* sign.

"A natural." He patted my shoulder. "Regular mermaid. See you next week, Gerry?"

"Oh, yes, next week," I answered, surprised by my enthusiasm.

It was a very cold winter, but each week we took the bus to Hackensack. Once I had learned to dog-paddle, Mitch graduated me from the wading section. Every so often I would look up and see Mom watching closely and pretending to be brave. After the lesson she always took me to Woolworth's for an egg salad sandwich and a ginger ale. I had completely forgotten about the piano. I hardly saw Jackie any more because she spent so much time indoors, practicing.

One night I dreamt I was sitting on the edge of the pool, dangling my feet. The water had turned black and I was singing, trying to entice the missing fingers to surface from the bottom of the water.

During the day, I tried not to think about Mitch's hand. I never mentioned it to Mom. At first I thought it would be impolite to talk about his handicap—for surely she must have noticed it, too. Then I worried that she hadn't noticed and that if I told her about the missing fingers she would cancel the lessons. None of the reasons made sense, but it seemed important to remain silent. I succeeded in forgetting about Mitch's hand until the week we began diving lessons.

He took me to the deep end, dove in himself, cutting the water sharply, swimming underneath, graceful as a dolphin. He surfaced with a big smile. "See how easy it is?"

"Sure." I stood shivering, suddenly remembering this was late January and it was sleeting outside.

"Just try jumping first," he called. "I'll catch you."

I stood there, bolstered by his smile. Then I glanced over at Mom's encouraging face. The air was an endless expanse; the water, I knew, would be worse, for it went down fourteen feet. Suddenly I jumped. Down. Down. I couldn't decide between terror and exhilaration, and then I was safe. Mitch was holding my hands; we were looking at each other, sputtering and laughing.

"Brave girl," he said.

I laughed, pumped my feet up and down and held onto his hands. Suddenly I was conscious of the missing fingers and panicked about drowning.

"Don't worry." He caught my frown. "Just hold on and I'll swim us to shore."

Those four feet were interminable as I struggled to keep afloat, to hide my revulsion, to keep from throwing up.

"There," he said as we reached the safe metal ladder. "It's a little early to knock off, but you've done a lot for one day."

I nodded, not daring to meet his eyes, for he must have

known the cause of my distress. "Thank you, Mitch. See you
. . . next Saturday."

I couldn't eat the egg salad sandwich. When Mom asked
what was wrong, I broke down and sobbed, finally managing
to confess.

She regarded me carefully. She listened as all my fears
spilled out. Did he have a kind of leprosy? Was it catching?
Or polio? Sometimes the Salk vaccine didn't work and I knew
kids got polio from swimming. Were the missing fingers dangerous? Would he lose his grip and let me slip to the bottom
of the pool? Mom patted my perfectly formed hand and reassured me that I was safe. She speculated on how he might
have lost his fingers—in an industrial accident, in the war.

The war, I decided. That night, watching a World War II
movie on TV, I imagined Mitch on the front line, perhaps the
scout who went ahead of other soldiers to clear the way for
his buddies and in the process . . .

Sergeant Mitch taught me the crawl, the side-stroke, the
breast-stroke, the elementary back-stroke. I still had trouble
diving. But he was impressed with my progress and told Mom
I was his best student.

I liked the side-stroke because I could see all around me.
I would look up at the ceiling and consider the funny, yellow
light pouring through the high windows. I liked to peer
down the length of the pool and watch the fat lady doing
her laps and the toddlers splashing each other. Searching the
bleachers, I would wave to Mom, who smiled as I swam past
her fears. When I looked up at her nowadays, she seemed
more relaxed. Sometimes she even sat back in her seat with
her feet out on the bench in front of her.

The side-stroke made me feel like a graceful machine or
one of those scissor bugs at the pond. It always put me in a
quiet mood. I found the back-stroke too slow, just as I considered the crawl too fast. With the breast-stroke, I could fly,
clearing a path through the cool water with my strong arms.

Sometimes Mitch and I played tag and he would dare me to chase after his sleek shadow on the chlorine floor.

The locker room felt more comfortable now. I watched steam weaving around the dented gray lockers and I imagined this mist as angel hair breathing from the naked female forms. Mom made me get dressed in the cubicle, but many swimmers, particularly the older women, weren't at all shy. The different shapes were fascinating: tall, lean women with tiny breasts; others with chubby legs and big tummies. Everyone with that triangle of fur above the legs. I had a big curiosity because my mother was always very modest about her own body. Despite Mom's efficient method of whisking me in and out of the dressing room, I learned a lot. One woman always creamed her legs, slowly, as if she were putting on delicate silk stockings, her hands rising higher and higher until she almost touched the triangle. Everyone had a different system for attaching the bra—some would snap it in front and then ponderously turn the bra around before putting their arms through the straps. Others were astonishingly quick at hooking from behind. The bras came in all sorts—flimsy cheesecloth models like the one my friend Karen wore; lacy, black styles and large, white contraptions with metal supports, which made me think of the hairshirts Sister Martin talked about. Maybe women saints wore metal under their breasts. I loved the mingling scents of talcum powder, and deodorant and perfume. I eavesdropped on the ladies' quick conversations about gaining and losing weight, raising kids, and shopping. By late February I was a regular; several women began to greet me by name.

Sister told us we could write about anything we liked, so I was surprised when she asked me to stay after school to discuss my essay on Mitch's swimming lessons.

"Sit here," she said in that voice she reserved for serious talks. "Is it true, what you've written in your paper?" she asked slowly.

I looked into her long face, relieved that I could reassure

her it wasn't a lie, that I had, indeed, mastered four strokes, although my diving was still giving me trouble.

"Very nice, dear. But is it true that you're taking lessons at the YMCA?"

"Yes, Sister," I answered proudly. "All the way in Hackensack. Every Saturday."

She breathed deeply and looked at me with kindness. "But what can your mother be thinking about? The YMCA is a *Protestant* organization."

"Oh, I know that, Sister. There are no statues, anywhere. It's a very plain building. But the pool is pretty, with lots of blues and greens—" I stopped at her impassive face.

"Dear, remember what we learned in catechism class about the First Commandment. You shouldn't be participating in a Protestant organization."

"Oh, I see," I said, in that voice Mom used when she didn't want to make a decision right away and planned to talk with my father first.

She changed her tack. "And swimming in the middle of winter? Hackensack is a long way to travel. Have you considered piano? Mrs. Sullivan teaches piano in her home."

"No." I shrugged. "Swimming is more useful." The anger rose suddenly in my throat. "Music requires too many fingers."

Sister decided not to pursue this last point. She tapped my knee and said conclusively. "Gerry, I'm afraid that you'll just have to stop going there."

"I see." I wasn't sure how convincing my neutrality was because I was concentrating on holding back the tears.

The next week Mom and I were back on the bus to Hackensack. Mom explained that Sister was mistaken. She couldn't have understood that I was just learning how to swim, that it involved no religious instruction.

I stared out at the gray slush and the lawns peeking through the snow. This was a moral crisis for me because I didn't want to displease God. I didn't want my attendance at the YMCA to damn me to hell. What good would swimming do me there? On the other hand, I loved that old building and my new friends in the locker room. And Mitch.

"Don't worry," Mom repeated. "Trust me. Sister Martin means well, but sometimes the nuns are a little . . . innocent about the world. They could get lost in their rules and regulations."

I shrugged, but I felt very grown up. Although Mom complained about the nuns to Dad, this was the first time she had ever said anything to me. I tried to conceal my satisfaction.

"Trust me. Wasn't I right about swimming being fun?"

That was the day I did it. I wasn't sure what had got into me. I walked out to the fourteen-feet sign, put my head down, and dove straight into the green water.

"Perfect," Mitch called, treading gracefully, holding out his hands to congratulate me.

"Perfect," Mom called from the bleachers.

"Perfect," I surfaced, reaching eagerly for his hands.

All winter during my tenth year I took the long bus ride from Dumont to Hackensack. Through the snow I traveled to those misty, tiled chambers where I learned how not to drown.

Dorianne Laux

Augusta

For my mother
Frances Margarette Comeau

She is born in a white room
in winter, in the short
light to a shout of birds, the sky
locked in ice. Found on a convent
doorstep, nuns' black hoods dip
like coal scuttles to her cry.
Fed potato milk, she thins
into adolescence, grows beans up poles
in a patch behind the chapel.

Piano practice. The oldest nun
breaks a switch from a branch,
holds it over the keys, rings
the twig off her knuckles until
the right note sounds.

Summer cracks the dirt road.
She sits on the rotting end
of the porch, smokes cigarettes
stolen from a visitor's purse.

Draws nipples on the sculpted cherubs.
Is beaten for this.
Is beaten for most things.

Night rolls her body over, thin cot
smells of piss and moldy ticking, the moon
peeling as she leaves, elbows sharp,
her new heels spike through snow.

Italian, he says, her dark hair
wasted in his hands. *No*, she whispers,
Algonquin, works with him to make
a single shape.

This is where I begin, as a fist
pounds the wall for quiet. As snow
breaks loose from the eaves.

I am not old enough to remember
the broom handle in his hands, her teeth
skipping kitchen tiles, blood
that spattered the bassinet to dotted swiss.

Winter can't hold her in. Her tracks
leave blue chains on the snow, a path
from his open door of yellow light.

In California she speaks French, sips
amber tea, ice chipping in a sweaty glass.
She meets the sailor who will become
my new father. He holds me to his chest.
She smiles. Her hand covers her mouth.

Ana Castillo

Saturdays

c. 1968

Because she worked all week
away from home, gone from 5 to 5,
Saturdays she did the laundry,
pulled the wringer machine
to the kitchen sink, and hung
the clothes out on the line.
At night, we took it down and ironed.
Mine were his handkerchiefs and
boxer shorts. She did his work
pants (never worn on the street)
and shirts, pressed the collars
and cuffs, just so—
as he bathed,
donned the tailor-made silk suit
bought on her credit, had her
adjust the tie.

"How do I look?"
"Bien," went on ironing.
That's why he married her, a Mexican
woman, like his mother, not like
they were in Chicago, not like
the one he was going out to meet.

Pier J. Roberts

The Virgin Mary and the
Paso Robles Cliff

I don't remember the exact moment I stopped believing in God. I just remember that one day it hit me like a ton of bricks that the whole thing was a big hoax. Basically, I just couldn't figure out how, if there was this nice old guy in the sky with a long white beard, there could be crippled children and starving people. And really, I couldn't understand why he'd put me here in this situation. I mean, I hadn't done anything wrong, anything big, that is, like murder or sex or anything. I was only eleven years old. What could I have done? Okay, I'd told a few lies, some of them bigger than others, and sometimes, when no one was looking, I'd take my little brother Michael's head in my hands and bang it around, not real hard, just a little hard. I'd only done that like three or four times, and it was because everyone seemed to like him a lot better than me, and I didn't think that was fair.

The only person I told about my disbelief in God was my best friend, Margaret. She couldn't understand it.

"What do you mean there isn't a God?"

"Just what I said." I looked at her stern and hard like I was a teacher. "Think about it, Margaret. First Santa Claus, then the Tooth Fairy, the Easter Bunny. I mean, all these things people tell us to believe in and then later they laugh at you for ever believing. I'm going to beat them on this one, Margaret. Stop believing before they start laughing."

"I don't know, Rose. What about heaven and hell and all that stuff? It's pretty scary if you don't believe."

"Oh, Margaret, I just don't buy it, that's all. I mean, have you ever prayed to God really hard for something and gotten it?" I thought I had her here for sure.

"Well, yes, actually." Margaret looked real smug all of a sudden. "Remember when I wanted a baby brother or sister. I prayed to God for that. And look, about a year later I got baby Karen."

"That might have just been a fluke," I said, scrunching up my face real hard, thinking. "It sure doesn't work with me." Like last week. I'm outside playing with Michael, and I hear them arguing—fighting and screaming. So I start to pray, *Dear God, please don't let this be a bad one, please don't let it go on for a long time.* I'm scared, yeah, but I go inside anyway. Sometimes they stop fighting when they see me. So I go in and she's standing there against the wall, crying and kind of talking real soft to him. I don't remember what she's saying. And there's a bottle of ketchup on the counter, and I watch him pick it up. So I try again, *Please God, don't let him throw it at her, please God.* He just stands there, acts like he's a big league pitcher or something. Just winds it up and lets it go. Not at her exactly, more like to the wall next to her. The bottle just shatters all over the place. All this ketchup drips down the wall into a big heap on the floor.

A big pile of red ketchup mixed with all these sparkling pieces of broken glass. It looked really weird. Maybe that's when I stopped believing in God. I don't know. The whole thing stayed there for a couple days, too. Neither of them would clean it up.

I didn't think I was any different once I stopped believing in God. I felt exactly the same, and nothing really major happened after I made the decision. Then Sister Mary Helen asks me to stay after school one day. Okay, I admit I get a little nervous about the whole thing at first. But real quick-like I figure out what's going on.

"Rose, is everything okay?" she asks. "You seem a little distracted in class."

I look at her and think how pretty she is. She sure doesn't look like my mom. I want to touch her skin, to see if it's real. It looks like some sort of velvet or silk or something. I decide right then and there that I'm going to be a nun when I grow up. Then, just because I'd always wanted to know if they shave their heads or not, I just blurt it out, just like that, I couldn't help myself. "Sister Mary Helen, do you have hair under that veil?"

"Well yes, I do, Rose, I certainly do," she says, but she kind of sings it like, and I think, my mother sure doesn't sound like that. "Rose, is everything okay at home?" she asks.

"Oh yeah, fine." I try to sing it back like her, but I know it sounds kind of chokey and I think, *Please God, don't let me cry, please God.*

"You're sure?" she asks.

And I say it better this time, kind of like I'm happy. "Oh yeah, fine!"

She continues anyway, and now I just want her to shut up. "Rose, I've talked to Father Patrick about this. Now, we all know your family very well. Your mother's having a hard time right now, isn't she?"

"I don't know," I say, and now I really just want her to shut up.

"Rose, do you know what an alcoholic is?"

"Yeah," I say, even though I'm not totally sure. I mean, I know what alcohol is. I've even tried it before. I didn't really like it. It felt like a burning campfire inside my throat and then it smoldered out when it got to my stomach.

"Well, Rose." She looks out the window now, and all of a sudden I feel kind of sorry for her, 'cuz I can tell she's having a hard time with this. "Alcoholism is like a sickness, Rose. And sometimes, when people are sick, they act funny; they don't quite know what they're doing. And they don't always mean the things they say or do. Now, if your father acts funny sometimes, I don't want you to be angry at him, or to think he's done something wrong, or that he's mad at you. He's just sick right now, Rose, that's all. And he's trying very hard to get better."

She kind of starts to hug me, but all that material gets in the way, and I just want out of there, anyway. So I pull back quick-like and say, "I got to go, Sister, I'll see you tomorrow."

When I get home I look up *alcoholic* in the dictionary, just to make sure I got it right. "One who practices continued excessive or compulsive use of alcoholic drinks." Someone who drinks a lot. Well, yeah, that was just what I thought.

Then I go to my older sister, Anne, and I just say it straight out, "Anne, is Dad an alcoholic?"

"Who told you that?" she asks, putting down her *Sixteen* magazine.

"Sister Mary Helen," I say, looking at her real cold, like I'm feeling mean.

"Ah, shit," is all she says, and stares back at me for a long time. Then she reaches inside her nightstand, takes out a pack of Kools and says, "Come on, let's go smoke a cigarette out the bathroom window."

I don't really like to smoke, but I like to do the things that Anne does, so I go along with her. When she gives me a drag, I try and pretend like I've been doing this all my life, but I still cough, anyway.

She starts in with the same "It's a sickness thing," just like Sister Mary Helen, and I just turn it off. I mean, I remember last year when I was sick. I had the chicken pox and it was really awful. I had a very high fever and itchy spots all over my body. At least I got to stay home from school for a week. I mean, I was really sick. But that didn't make me start throwing ketchup bottles at people or anything.

Finally I decide I have to put this God thing to a test, so I come up with a great idea. I ask Margaret to come with me, but I don't tell her why until we're halfway there. We're on our way to the Paso Robles hillside, the biggest cliff anywhere near our house. It has this one steep, chalky side, where we go in the summer to slide down on big cardboard sheets. (I'm always just a little bit afraid to do it, but I don't tell anyone, and I just go ahead and do it anyway.) So I pull out from under my jacket this Virgin Mary statue with little birds at her feet that my Grandma gave me last year for Christmas.

"What's that for?" Margaret asks.

"I'm going to throw it off the Paso Robles Cliff," I say, holding my head real straight-like.

"Why?" Margaret just doesn't get things sometimes.

"Well," I say, "I figure that if there is a God, then there must be a Jesus, and if there's a Jesus, he sure won't want me throwing a statue of his mother off the cliff, and so, he should come down and stop me. If there isn't a God, and no Jesus, and I just throw this statue off the cliff and nothing happens, then we'll know for sure. At least we'll know for sure, Margaret," I repeat.

"I don't know if it's a good idea, Rose. Something really bad could happen."

"I have to try it, Margaret. That's it. Final. Are you coming with me or not?" I ask with determination and march ahead of her. She follows behind me, of course. I knew she would.

We go to the top of the cliff. There's no one around and I'm feeling pretty confident. So I say real loud, my face lifted up in the air, "God, or Jesus, if you're there, come down right now, and let me know. Otherwise, Jesus, I am just going to throw your mother off the Paso Robles Cliff." I'm actually kind of expecting, or maybe hoping, for something to happen. Lightning would be nice. We wait for what seems like forever. Nothing happens. The air is crisp and still, hardly moving at all. I hear a dog bark in the distance. So I try again, just in case. "This is your last chance, God, or here she goes." Nothing. Me and Margaret and the Virgin Mary, that's it. So I pull my arm way back, like I'm a major league pitcher, wind it up, and let the old Virgin go. We watch her sail out through the air over the cliff. Then we hear her hit the ground and shatter into a million pieces at the bottom of the cliff, down near where the creek is. I turn toward Margaret and she's almost crying, I can tell. "That settles it, Margaret, I guess there isn't a God."

"Let's get out of here." Her voice is shaky and I feel kind of bad I made her come with me. I probably could have done it by myself. "I was really scared, Rose, really scared. Come on, let's get away from here." We run all the way down the big hill, race across the park and down more streets until we get home, both of us panting and our cheeks burning red.

The next day at the dinner table I can tell that Dad's sort of sick again. He's acting kind of funny and barking things out at my mom. This week he hates Anne, I can just tell. It's been a long time since it was my turn and I feel pretty lucky about that.

So he starts asking Anne where she was after school, why she was late.

"In the library," she says. Even I wouldn't believe that.

"Where else?" he asks, but his words are starting to sound strange, like they're all smushed together.

"Just at the library, that's all." Each of her words sounds real clear, one right after the other. This goes on for a while until Anne starts getting kind of nervous and says, "Can I please leave the table? Please can I leave the table?"

"You're lying. Where the hell were you this afternoon?" Anne gets up, just like she's going to leave the table anyway. We never do that. That is like the one big rule in our house. You stay at the table until you're excused. "Don't you leave this table," he yells suddenly, standing up and grabbing the empty chair next to him like he's going to throw it at Anne.

Please don't let him throw it, God, please don't let him, I pray.

"Where the hell were you?" he repeats.

My mother jumps up and puts herself right in front of Anne. "John, if you throw that thing, I'm leaving. I mean it this time. I'll take the kids and go to my mother's. John, for God's sake, don't throw that chair."

My dad turns stiff-like, then lowers the chair slowly and sits back down at the table. We're all breathing real fast. I can hear my mom's and Anne's breath all coming real quick. There's no other sound in the room, except I hear my heart pounding real hard inside me. Then my Dad lays his head on the table and starts to cry. I'd never seen him cry before, never.

Nita Penfold

Our Lady of Perpetual Night Contemplates Her Lack of Faith

The legion of nuns possessed it.
Faces framed in stiff white, jowls accented,
sour eyes at attention, crossing themselves,
fingering heavy black rosary beads that clicked
and scraped the hard backs of pews where they knelt
like a line of zoo penguins waiting for their portion of fish.

The young priests had it. Firm smiles,
faces like half-baked bread, they talked glibly of Scripture,
preaching sermons while practicing "keeping custody"
of the eyes,
clean white hands rising and falling
to the rhythm of the Mass.
Bold men in black dresses with sweaty palms,
passing out the bingo cards as if they were holy relics.

Faith. She wished it could be like a smallpox vaccine:
innoculated at Baptism—sudden sting that bubbled
into a blister, irritating for a few days, then leaving

a pebbly scar she could show to prove she had it.
But she knew it never would have taken, anyway.
Even the sharp slap of the rheumy out-of-town bishop
at Confirmation failed to make her a soldier of Christ;
plastic-covered scapular sticky between her new breasts,
the protection of her dead brother's name
never halting the ache that, on bad days, still drags her
into the church's great spiraling vault: this questioning,
the need to know for certain,
what can only be taken on faith.

Dinty W. Moore

Redeemers

A woman as round as she was tall bobbed in the doorway of my seventh grade classroom, like a black-and-white balloon ready to pop. "Mary Louise," she said. "Come along now."

My classmates just looked away, as if they didn't know me. I stood from my cramped desk and followed Sister Useless into the dark lobby, where I saw my mother, staring into the center of a leaded-glass window. Her hair was tucked under a scarf, and she was wearing a soiled sweatshirt. Mom looked my way and said, "Mookie, honey. Come on."

We walked to the car as fast as possible, headed south on Cranberry, and drove past all these ugly townhouses that looked cheap and low class. I stared up the driveways, into the yards, to see how many people had dogs.

No one did.

Not only had she left my father and moved us five miles away, but I had to go to Holy Redeemers after that, and Holy Redeemers was a loser school. The first day, I met a kid named Eggs Benedict. His real name was Louie. He was small, with greasy hair and red pimples, fourteen and still trying to pass seventh grade. Exactly the kid I had expected to find.

We were outside at recess, at the edge of the parking lot, watching a game of dodgeball, when he asked, "You got a name?"

"Mookie," I answered.

Only the nuns called me Mary Louise. I was twelve and skinny, with hair that was still trying to decide what color it was.

"Know anything about sex?" Eggs asked.

Normally, I would have ignored him, but I said "What?" because at least he was talking to me. Up to that point, all the other Redeemer kids had acted like I was an orphan.

"Sex," he said again. "I saw my parents."

Before I could stop him, he described what he had seen. His description was disgusting, but what was interesting was that he started sweating and kept sweating all the way through his story. His eyes got big, and he began to smell bad.

When he was done, I said, "So what?"

"So what?" He spit on the side of the wall. "So if you get married, your husband's gonna do it, too."

I slapped him. "Don't be a jerk," I said. Then I walked away with my back to him, trusting that even a pimply, greaseball retard like Eggs Benedict wasn't going to hit a girl in front of everyone.

The new house was not much different from the old one. We had the same red sofa, the same dining room set with broken chairs, and the same faded gold drapes. My mother had to hem them because the new windows were tiny.

It didn't bother me as much as I thought it would that my father wasn't around, because he had never been around that much before. He was either selling car insurance or sitting in some bar watching baseball.

But two weeks after we moved, he visited and said, "I'm not boozing anymore." He sort of mumbled this, looking down at the scratched coffee table.

My mother nodded and just stared at his jacket pocket until he took out the checkbook.

Dad was sitting on the red sofa and began to sink, because

the springs were shot. He was tall, with curly brown hair, and was wearing his green suit. "How's school?" he asked.

"Okay." I could tell my mother was studying my reaction, and I didn't want her to get mad about something I said. I had to live with her.

"How's the new neighborhood?"

"Okay." I looked down at my geography homework. It was my favorite subject.

"Have you made new friends?"

"Some." I tried to say this so that neither of them heard me.

Dad looked at Mom. "It's better for her here," he said.

Mom nodded, and looked at the checkbook.

I hated that my parents were divorced, because I knew everyone in the world thought there was something wrong with me. And I didn't at all like having half a set of parents. It made me feel like half a kid.

Monday, at Redeemers, Eggs told someone that I had French kissed him. It was a ridiculous lie because no one would ever believe that anyone would ever want to French kiss Eggs Benedict. After school, I challenged him to a fight.

A few eighth-graders were standing around on the corner, watching three men feed tree limbs into this big orange chipper. "Why'd you lie," I asked Eggs, shouting over the noise. "Why'd you say I kissed you?"

"I didn't," he hollered back.

"Your brother squealed," I yelled. Eggs had a little brother, George. George had the biggest ears in the fourth grade.

I shoved Eggs hard enough to knock him back into a puddle, with people watching.

"Girls shouldn't fight," he hollered. "It's not ladylike." Then he just sat in the water making faces at me.

Eggs and I got to be friends after that. Partly because he just kept coming to me at recess and talking, whereas most of the other kids still acted like I had a disease. I also caught on that he was not as stupid as everyone thought. When I asked him a question, he always said something close to the right answer. But I watched him in Miss Dewberry's class, and whenever she would ask him anything at all he just sat there and grinned.

One day, after school, I asked, "How come you flunked out two times?"

"Aw," he said. "School is stupid."

"Yeah, right. But now you're going to go to school longer than everyone else, you dope."

"Like I care," he said.

"You should care."

"Like I care."

Then he told me that his father, Mr. Benedict, a man who fixed cars in his garage, made Eggs scrub oil off the driveway and haul broken parts to the dump every afternoon, while never making the brother with the big ears do a thing. Eggs thought his father hated him.

I told Eggs about how I never had a dog at the old house because my father thought they were dirty, and how I couldn't have a dog in the new house because our landlord wouldn't let us. My mother showed me right in the lease where it said that.

I told Eggs that I liked dogs a lot, especially Labrador retrievers because they look like they're smiling, and that I wouldn't even care if my dog drooled all the time.

Eggs said, "So? Let's steal one."

Sister Useless, the round one, had a dog. I don't understand how she managed this, because nuns weren't supposed to have stuff in those days, but she had a big chocolate lab named Jude, and when I told this to Eggs, he said Jude was the dog he wanted to steal. He didn't even know Sister Useless, but I told him enough about her to make him hate her guts. Her name was Sister Eustace, but we called her Useless because she never left her office except to punish someone. I told him how useless she was, and Eggs said, "Sure, all adults are useless."

That was the actual moment I finally decided I liked him.

*   *   *

We spent time at the Liberty Plaza, a bunch of stores that no one shopped at since the big mall went up on Peach Street. Eggs said he was going to teach me to steal things, as practice. "Some jerks steal because they need to," Eggs explained. "But it's better if you do it just for fun."

We went to the Drug Fair and looked at all kinds of stuff. My whole head felt warm and dizzy. Next thing I knew, I was staring at a yellow hairbrush and Eggs was hissing, "Just take it, Mookie. Just put it in your bookbag."

We stole a lot after that.

Mom found a job at a photo studio inside Sears. She had to dress and wear makeup, and she looked prettier than before. One night when she got home from work and was making us tuna and cheese sandwiches, I got up the nerve to ask her what had been on my mind. "Now that Dad stopped drinking so much, are we going to move back?"

She didn't answer and I began to wonder if she even heard me, but then she said, "Your dad and I just don't get along."

"Yeah, but you could work it out."

"I don't think so, honey." She sounded far away when she said this, as if I'd just asked her a question about how Chinese people live. Then she went upstairs to change.

I had to be careful. If she could leave my father, I wondered, did that mean she could leave me, too?

Soon after, Eggs and I made a deal: since he was helping me steal the dog, I'd help him pass seventh grade. He started coming home with me after school and we did homework and watched TV until my mother came in. And like I suspected, he wasn't stupid at all. Before long, his grades were all As and Bs.

A week later, he showed me this big, stiff, oversized baby bib and I knew right away what it was. What the old nuns wore.

"Where'd you get this?" I asked.

He grinned. His brown eyes were bright and jumping around. "Where do you think?"

"I don't know. Where?"

"I stole it, mosquito head." He could barely stand still, he was so pleased with himself. When Eggs was happy, he was easy to like.

"I know you stole it. But where?"

He whispered in my ear. "I was in there. The place where all the nuns live. *Is it ever weird!*"

He explained that, first, he found a kid who delivered newspapers to the nuns. Then he gave the kid a dirty magazine in exchange for letting him go along on the route. The convent seemed empty and he asked the paperboy kid about it, and the kid said the nuns all went into the chapel and said prayers together before dinner. So Eggs walked into one of the nuns' rooms and stole the bib. The paperboy kid was scared silly and would probably never recover.

The reason I even knew that Sister Useless had a dog was that she showed us a picture once. She brought a photo of Jude trying to eat a chair leg and made every kid in class write a letter to the bishop about why she should be allowed to keep the dog at the convent. Like we really cared. It was a ridiculous name for a dog, anyway. "After the apostle," Useless explained. "The patron saint of lost causes."

She should know.

But I looked at the picture long enough to see that Jude was one wonderful beast. Big, brown, with a red tongue. And after I told Eggs about the dog, I got more and more excited, thinking that Jude would soon be mine.

Meanwhile, Eggs and I hit the Drug Fair again. I got a *Seventeen* beauty tips book, some orange barrettes, and a red lipstick. Eggs got a magazine to replace the one he gave the paperboy kid, a can of sardines, and some rubbers. I knew about rubbers from what some boys had said to me at recess. They looked different than the ones you put on your feet.

*   *   *

It was after one of those shoplifting lessons that Eggs said
he wanted to have sex with me. I ignored him, figuring any
answer at all would just be encouragement. Then he told me,
"You know, you're lucky your parents are getting divorced."

"That's the dumbest thing you've ever said," I snapped
back. We were talking about this in his clubhouse, which I
never even knew he had until the day before. It was in the
woods behind the Plaza and it was just a hole in the side of
a hill with boards up against it, but he had stolen a rug and
some chairs.

"Hey," he said. "You're lucky your mom left your dad because otherwise she would have got mad one night and shot
him while he was asleep." Eggs got these ideas out of
magazines.

"That's impossible," I said.

"Yeah. How do you know?"

"Because my mother wouldn't shoot anyone."

He put his face close to mine and asked, "You never
thought she'd leave your father, did you?"

"No."

He moved even closer, scaring me a little. "Well then, you
don't know what she'd do, do you?"

I pushed him away while I tried to figure an answer, but
I couldn't, so finally I just changed the subject. "What about
Jude?" I challenged him. "When are we gonna do it?"

"Soon," Eggs said. "Very soon."

The next Monday, after school, when my mother was working late at Sears, Eggs grabbed my arm. "Today's the day."
The convent was on Eighth Street and took up a whole city
block because nuns from all the different Catholic schools
lived there. Eggs found out that there was a courtyard in the
middle, where they kept Jude. He told me if we got Jude out
he would keep him at the clubhouse for me, but only if I

agreed to have sex. He said rubbers would keep me from getting pregnant.

I figured the best thing was to ignore Eggs. It made him all the more nervous.

At 5:35 we snuck into the convent through the door the paperboy kid used, walked up this big hallway past all sorts of crucifixes and pictures of dead nuns, found the courtyard, fed Jude some dog biscuits Eggs had stolen, slipped the leash on, and started walking out. Simple as pie.

But when we were leaving, a tiny nun, who seemed about two hundred years old, stopped us. "Taking the dog for a walk?" she asked, trying hard to see us through her wire bifocals. I could tell it bothered her that she couldn't place our faces.

"Yes ma'am," Eggs answered cheerfully. "Jude is going for a walk. Yes he is."

"Are you from the Honor Society?" the old nun asked.

"Yes ma'am. This is our nature project."

The nun put her glasses away and touched my arm. Her skin was dry, like a snake. "That's nice of you children," she said. "God bless you." Then she wandered off.

We took Jude to the clubhouse in the woods and fed him four cans of Alpo, stolen. Eggs wanted to send Useless a note with letters clipped out of magazines saying he would kill Jude if she didn't quit being a nun and go to Alaska. But I talked him out of it.

We renamed the dog Otis.

He had big brown eyes, and he smiled, and he had little flaps of pink skin that hung down from either side of his mouth. I could tell looking at him that he liked us kids better than he liked the nuns.

Otis fell asleep on the rug right away, and Eggs started kissing me. I let him, because I was going to be thirteen soon and wanted to know what it felt like, but I made sure that Eggs understood I would literally kill him if he told a single soul. Then we stretched out on the piece of carpet Eggs swiped, holding on and kissing. It was like sex, I suppose, or good enough for the first time. But we didn't take our clothes off.

Eventually we took Otis to Eggs' house and told everyone that we had found him in the woods. Otis was really mostly my dog but just didn't live with me. Mrs. Benedict was nice about me being over there all the time; she was probably just glad to have someone around the house with clean hands.

Miss Dewberry, meanwhile, was so impressed by how many As and Bs Eggs was getting that she jumped him right from seventh grade to ninth so that he could go to school with kids his own age.

My mother kept taking pictures at Sears and met a boyfriend named Pete. She worried whether I liked the guy or not, but I told her to do what she wanted. She would have, anyway.

Dad started drinking again right away and didn't come over much at all.

I still steal things sometimes, but I don't need to.

Otis died within a year, but he died happy. I used to spend hour after hour petting the square bone of his forehead, soothing him.

"Somebody loves you," I would say over and over. "You lucky dog. Somebody finally loves you."

And in my memory, Otis looks up at me with those big wet eyes, drops his long tongue into my hand, and says the same thing right back.

The exact same thing.

Marilyn Murphy

Girls at the Altar

Sister Rose Edmond, of the Sisters of St. Joseph, was one of my favorite teachers. She taught seventh grade at St. Patrick's grammar school in Long Island City, New York. I loved her. All of her pupils loved her. She responded to our obvious adoration with blushes and smiles and a slight ducking motion of her head that caused her sheer black veil to flutter slightly. I used to touch her veil secretly whenever she walked past my desk. I thought she was beautiful, the most wonderful person I had ever known.

It was during my months with Sister Rose Edmond that I decided to become a nun when I grew up. I, too, would wear a pretty habit and live in a convent full of women. I would be the teacher of adoring children and, like Sister Rose Edmond, would let my pupils distract me into telling stories instead of finishing math lessons, or collecting homework, or giving a scheduled test. I would give all of the good jobs—washing the blackboard, cleaning the erasers, decorating the room for holidays, running errands to other rooms or to the convent—only to the girls, just like she did.

One day a note was sent to our classroom, requesting the immediate attendance of all of the boys at a special altar boy meeting in the church. The girls were at least as pleased by this break in routine as the boys. We loved our class time without the boys because Sister would stop whatever we were doing and regale us with stories of her childhood or her experiences in the various convents she had lived in. This time, however, she was just getting started when the boys returned. They didn't burst in and scramble noisily to their seats as they usually did. Instead, they marched in proudly and quietly. They were accompanied by Father Vallaci, who lined them up along the walls of the room. Father announced, unnecessarily, that the boys had come to show us their new altar boy outfits. We girls filled the room with gasps of pleasure at the sight of such magnificence. The boys had been transformed from those dirty beasts who persecuted us daily into visions of angelic beauty. They were dressed in floor-length, bright red cassocks with mandarin collars and self-covered buttons from collar to hem. Over the cassocks were snowy-white, knee-length surplices, abundantly trimmed in lace at cuff and hem. To complete the costume, large, satin bows, bright red and gorgeous, bloomed at their throats. They were something to see, standing with eyes downcast, still and quiet, like a row of medieval saints.

When Father was sufficiently satisfied with our admiring responses, he escorted the boys out of the classroom. Sister began telling us about the sacrifices our poor parish had endured in order to raise the money for new vestments for our priests and altar boys, worthy of use on the altar. I hardly heard a word. I was grappling with a new idea, one that was exciting and disturbing. I interrupted her flow of talk with a question.

"Sister, why aren't girls altar boys?"

The look on Sister's face reminded me of the times I asked my mother questions about something I did not realize was a taboo subject. I could tell that bad news was on its way. She said, "Girls are not altar boys, Marilyn, because only men and boys can serve on the altar." She gave me a sweet look, one intended to get me on her side, to let her answer suffice. I ignored it.

"Sister, why can only men and boys serve on the altar?"

"Because that is the way God wants it," was her weak reply.

"I don't understand," I persisted, noting that the other girls were paying close attention to the exchange. "It doesn't make sense to me."

Sister noticed the quiet intensity of the other girls, too, so she went on a while about how God called men to the priesthood and wanted women to be Sisters, and the different responsibilities they had. I was unimpressed. I thought a priest had a boring job and had no desire to be one. I already knew what sisters did, and was going to be one when I grew up. However, I had just developed a burning desire to be an altar boy in the meantime. I wanted to wear those beautiful clothes, to stand before the entire congregation and carry the mass book from one side of the altar to the other. I wanted to walk beside the priest during communion and hold the gold plate under communicants' chins. I wanted to ring the mass bells! Already I could see myself, kneeling, bent over and praying "mea culpa, mea culpa!" with the priest, wearing those spectacular red-and-white clothes.

Sister realized she had lost me and wasn't doing too well with the other girls either, so she took another tack. She began to speak about the way God had intended things to be, about God-ordained roles for women and men in the religious life and in the world. She told us that Church law forbade women to be in the area of the church around the altar except to clean it or change the altar linens or arrange the altar flowers. Only twice in our lives were we privileged to be invited into the altar space: once when receiving the sacrament of confirmation, and again when we were married at a nuptial mass or took our vows as nuns.

Most of us sat in stunned silence as the import of what Sister was saying sank in. She did not say that girls and women were unclean, that we could contaminate the sacred places, but the message that we were considered unworthy was shockingly clear. My mind began racing. Vinnie O'Rouke, who played with his little thing in class, was good enough to be an altar boy and stand at the altar, but none of us girls was good enough, and never, never, never would be! I was horrified.

"I don't believe it," I stated flatly. "I don't believe God meant things to be the way you say they are." Sister's voice took on a compassionate tone as she tried to convince and console me. "It is true," she said. "And you will understand and agree with this when you get older."

I was angry and adamant, as well as heartsick at Sister's betrayal of us. "I will never agree because you are wrong," I insisted. "If God made us both, then he made girls at least as worthy and important as boys."

"But the Church teaches . . ." she began.

"Then the Church is wrong," was my reply.

Now Sister was truly upset. She tried to explain why it was impossible for the infallible Church to be wrong, but I remained unconvinced. We had reached an impasse. I told her I would think it over, that I knew something was wrong and that sooner or later I would figure it out.

Several times after that day, Sister Rose Edmond tried to talk about the subject with me privately. I refused to discuss it. She made sweet overtures of friendship by frequently sending me on errands to the convent and praising my schoolwork out loud. I was unmoved. Sister had sided with the boys. She had betrayed us. How could I trust her after that. I assuaged my broken heart by transferring my affection to Sister William Agnes, but there was no relief for the injury done my girl-spirit or my girl-faith. Everytime I saw the boys at the altar in their splendid red cassocks, my prayers dissolved in a wash of anger, envy, and confusion. I went to communion with a troubled spirit, always aware that, beyond the rail, there were no girls at the altar.

Irene Zabytko

St. Sonya

We were taught at St. Nicholas that in order to become a real saint you have to have some extraordinary event happen to you; some miraculous phenomenon that cannot be refuted by the godless scientists. Then you have to be dead and wait a few hundred years before a pope remembers you and declares you a saint and pilgrims go around collecting relics made of your dried-out bones, expecting to be cured of cancer or leprosy. My ex-friend Sonya Machneiwska actually achieved one of the prerequisites to sainthood; that is, she managed to get some notoriety after experiencing a miracle. But that's as far as she got.

I hadn't thought about Sonya or her "miracle" for years until a few days ago when I was waiting in a long line at the supermarket. My eyes wandered over the strategically placed magazines, whose bizarre headlines always caught my attention: "Elvis Found Alive and Manages K-Mart in Texas"; "Diets from Mars—They Really Work!" I was about to pick up a fashion magazine when I glanced at another headline: "Mexican Girl Has Stigmatas—Hands and Feet Bleed Every Lent." And I remembered my old friend Sonya and her stigmatas and how it changed our friendship.

Before Sonya got holy, I used to spend a lot of time with her. We were school friends, although she was two years ahead of me at St. Nicholas. She lived down the block from me, on Rice Street in the Ukrainian neighborhood on Chicago's west side. Every morning, she stopped by my house so that we could walk to school together. There she sat in my kitchen, waiting for me to get ready for school, staring at me from behind her narrow eyeglasses with the cheap rhinestones barely blinking on the corners of the frames, her typical milk moustache caked into a thick white rim above her upper lip. She never understood my clever jokes or why I liked to read books without pictures. I was able to put up with Sonya's dullness because I was the one who chose which games we would play after school without any quarrels or objections from her. My favorite "let's pretend" game was playing "nuns" in the basement, for which my mother kindly donated two old black cotton housedresses for us to use as our nuns' habits. Sonya and I made black veils out of old pillowcases, which were really a deep navy blue, and we fastened them to our heads with white strips of gauze around our foreheads and faces. We tied several strands of black and silver rosaries around our waists and hung plastic crucifixes around our necks with string. After a good hour or so of dressing-up in the costumes, we installed our "classrooms" in separate parts of my basement, with our various dolls as our students. We actually taught our dolls from our own school books, and hit them mercilessly when they misbehaved or didn't do their homework, just as the nuns beat us in real life.

Sonya always came to my house. There was only one time when she asked me if I "would dine wid her" at her house. Just like that. She must have heard that on a television show, because Sonya never said classy things like "dine."

The first and only time I went to her house, I was greeted by her stout mother, Pani Machniewska, who was sitting in the kitchen, her great hairy legs supported by another chair. She wore a filthy print housedress smeared with cooking grease and held together with mismatched buttons and one huge safety pin, and she was intently looking at herself with a hand mirror that had a cheap gilt frame. With her other hand, she was delicately scraping between her perfectly black, rotted teeth with the edge of a blunt knife. Sonya introduced me as the kid who had the German shepherd. I suppose that her mother was an animal lover, because she immediately took an interest in my presence. "Is dog man or woman," she asked me in English, then proceeded to tell me in more fluent Ukrainian about the animals she used to have on her farm back in the old country. I stared at her black teeth and saw that they looked like bits of coal, like the last embers in an open campfire. She spoke in a high-pitched, whiny voice that might have been irritating if I hadn't been concentrating on her teeth. She said she had to go to work and that Tato, Sonya's father, would make us dinner. She worked in the evenings, cleaning floors at the Prudential building, which Sonya proudly referred to as "da biggest buildin' in Chee-ca-ga." I knew that other buildings had since surpassed it, but I was too polite to challenge her within earshot of her mother.

Pan Machniewski appeared in the kitchen wearing thick white socks, without any shoes. At first I thought he had been in a bad accident, and had to wear casts on his feet. Sonya didn't bother to introduce me to him, and he ignored me as he prepared our dinner—hot dogs and French fries. Before Sonya's mother left for work, she began to cry, and to blabber something in her whiny voice, stroking her husband's hair upward into little peaks on his head. Pan Machniewski simply stood with his back to the sizzling potatoes, looking straight ahead without any indication that he heard his wife or noticed what she was doing. He had that lockjaw look of Slavic peasant stoicness that hides any facial expression, any twitch of embarrassment or affection. I thought I shouldn't be there. It seemed a private moment, but Sonya had gone to the bathroom, and I didn't know where else to go because I hadn't been to the house before, so I stupidly stood by the table, watching.

Sonya's mother stopped blabbering, noticed me, smiled her black grin, and said goodbye as though nothing had happened. Then the Pan went back to his cooking, and I was relieved to see Sonya back in the kitchen, kissing her mother goodbye.

I first heard Sonya's father's deep voice when the food had been put on the table and he said, "comon youse kids." The food was surprisingly wonderful. He made the French fries as thin and crispy as if they had come from an American hot-dog stand; he even steamed the buns. But there was no point in complimenting him. Pan Machniewski ignored me and ate silently with a scowl on his forehead. The next day, Sonya came over, as usual, but she never invited me to her house again.

It wasn't long after my visit to Sonya's house that I heard her father had died. Then it occurred to me that his aloof, taciturn appearance must have been due to his illness, but I didn't feel especially sorry or unhappy over his death. Actually, my disappointment was aimed at Sonya. After her father's funeral, she rarely came over to pick me up for school. She came down with various flus and migraine headaches, followed by oversleeping in the mornings. Whenever I waited for her, I was late and in trouble with the nuns. Eventually, she missed school altogether for various amounts of time, but as it happened, I didn't miss her too much when I walked to school on my own.

Months later, when I did see her again, Sonya had become more taciturn and stoic, like her father, and was uninterested in playing our games. For one thing, she was obviously wearing a bra because her small chest suddenly swelled into two symmetrical cones. She had also bleached her hairy legs and underarms with lemon juice, because her mother wouldn't let her shave them, and bragged that she started having periods. She seemed older and different, and I felt oddly betrayed by her growing up without me.

Once, I came home from school and found my mother in the backyard, talking over the fence with Pani Nesterenko, better known in the neighborhood as Big Marya's mother. It wasn't unusual seeing Pani Nesterenko talking to my mother because the Pani would use our yard as a shortcut to Chicago Avenue, where the stores were. Big Marya was about Sonya's age, but could probably order a drink in a bar without any problem because she developed a very curvacious figure before her time. She wore tight sweaters with very pointy bosoms, and stretch pants that accentuated her derriere, and she was the first girl from my neighborhood to actually frost her brown hair into white streaks. I never had the courage to talk to Big Marya, but I used to watch with great interest when Pani Nesterenko led her daughter back home, yelling at her in the street.

On this particular day, though, Pani Nesterenko and my mother weren't talking about Big Marya. They were talking about my ex-friend Sonya.

"I tell you, Pani, I was there," said Big Marya's mother. "She called me at midnight to cry that her daughter was a saint. Oh, those Machniewskis! They're all crazy, and now that the father is gone, Sonya acts like she has something missing upstairs."

"But this isn't the first time this happened," coaxed my mother. "I heard she had this thing before."

"Oh, yes. The first time was about three weeks ago, when Sonya had a bad dream and woke up with these sores on her hands. Sonya waited for her mother to come home from work and said to her, 'Oy, mama, I got these cuts.' She was bleeding all over her nightgown. Pani Machniewska wanted to hit Sonya for messing up the floor and her nightgown, but she said that Sonya looked so strange and sick that she called me up. So I went, and I saw she had this hole, like the color of a plum, and it was bleeding, so I poured vodka and bound up her hands right away with some old cloth around the house. Then it seemed fine and she went back to sleep, so I went back to sleep. And what do you know, three weeks later, I got another crazy call from Pani Machniewska in the middle of the night again; this time her darling's feet are bleeding. *Isus Christos,*' says the Pani to me. 'It comes from God.' She showed me Sonya's new holes. Marya says Sonya does it to herself, for attention. I don't know. But I took off the old bandages on her hands, same thing—it didn't heal. Well, maybe this is from God. Who knows. It's crazy."

"So, what's happening?"

"Well, Pani Machniewska isn't going to let this go on. She's afraid Sonya's gonna wake up with a spear wound on her side, like Jesus Christ, and that would kill her for sure. I just left them a few minutes ago. I told her to take Sonya to a doctor. Maybe it's a skin problem or something. Pani Machniewska was so mad she told me I needed a doctor for *my* head and practically kicked me out of her house. Some friend, ay? Who else would wake up in the middle of the night if it wasn't me? When I was leaving her house, she yelled at me that she's taking Sonya to the priest."

"Ssh," my mother suddenly whispered. Sure enough, along came Pani Machniewska, tottering on thin-spiked high heels, her heavy body heaving and stretching the seams of her fancy black dress with angel-winged see-through sleeves, and a black lace mantilla on her hair. Sonya was behind her, wearing a black velvet dress that would have looked very nice on her except that the effect was spoiled by her bandaged feet and hands. She had a hard time keeping up with her mother and seemed to be in a lot of pain, judging by the scowl on her face. They walked past Pani Nesterenko and my mother and Pani Machniewska whispered, "*Slava i soosy Christy*— "Praise Jesus Christ." The two women stared after Sonya and her mother and Pani Nesterenko loudly whispered, "She's acting holier than the girl."

Without properly greeting my mother or Pani Nesterenko, I rushed past them, fibbing that I had forgotten something at the priest's rectory.

It was easy catching up with the Pani and Sonya because they were walking so slowly, as though in a procession. I said hello and that I had to see the priest and where were they going all dressed up. Pani Machniewska was wiping her eyes and begged Sonya to hurry. Sonya lingered, surprised that I had an appointment at the rectory. "Guess what," she mumbled. "I gotta go, too. On account of becuz of sumpin' weird." And the three of us walked to St. Nicholas in solemn silence.

When we got to the rectory, Pani Machniewska announced

to Monsignor Satchko's secretary that she and her daughter, "who was going to be a saint," had arrived. I looked at Sonya, who didn't appear to be embarrassed but, rather, in awe.

Father Satchko was new at St. Nicholas, and apparently had a hard time adjusting to his parishioners. During his church sermons, he carried on about issues that really didn't make one's throat too lumpy, such as why Ukrainians didn't have their own television shows on American TV. He had a smell of sweet liquor about him, and was seen around the neighborhood walking his St. Bernard in the early-morning hours. One of the babas, Pani Dydiak, happened to be awake one morning, and was about to go outside her house to sweep her sidewalk, when she saw Father Satchko's dog defecating on her lawn. Since then, there was an undertone of dissatisfaction about the priest's work at St. Nicholas, and it was remarked at more than one after-mass coffee gathering that he should be transferred to another place.

We waited for Father Satchko for what seemed an unusually long time. Pani Machniewska fidgeted with her handkerchief and kept slapping Sonya's hands whenever she picked at her bandages or her nose. Finally, we were ushered into his big office, where Father Satchko, looking totally bored, sat behind an enormous oak desk surrounded by pictures of the Pope, an icon of St. Nicholas the Miracle Worker, and other holy pictures on the walls behind his chair.

"*Slava i soosy Christy,* dear, dear Father," whined Pani Machniewska.

"*Slava na viki,*" said Father Satchko, twitching his bushy eyebrows. "Is this the little girl?" he asked, looking at me.

"No," Pani firmly said, pushing Sonya toward the desk. "This is my darling daughter Sonya. She's the one chosen by our Lord."

I was afraid that I would be asked to leave, but no one noticed me anymore.

"Now, let me understand this . . . this event," said Father Satchko. "Your little girl here . . . Sonya, right? Sonya has been waking up and finding sores on her hands and feet. Like, as they say, stigmatas?"

"Like our Lord!" cried the Pani, rocking back and forth on her little spikes.

"Please, Pani, sit down. Now ... Sonya? Sonya, would you let me see your sores?"

This was what I had been waiting for. The priest came up to her and beckoned her to sit on a chair next to the Pani, who was trembling quite a bit as she unwound the bandages from her daughter's hands. It was just as Pani Nesterenko described—holes the size of a nail and all purplish in the middle of each hand. Then Sonya took off her shoes and undid the bandages herself from her feet. The same type of sores showed.

"I see. Thank you." Father Satchko went back to his desk and began writing something. He didn't seem to be bored anymore, but, rather, excited, and I noticed perspiration rings beneath the arms of his black cassock. "Are you in any pain, Sonya?" he asked her in English.

"No, Fadder. It's juz messy," Sonya answered slowly, while looking at the gashes on her hands.

"Did you have dreams at night when this happened?"

"Well, Fadder, like I dreamed dat me and Big Marya had a date wid Ringo Starr."

"No, Father," interrupted the Pani in Ukrainian. "Sonya had a dream about Saint Theresa. Sonya, dear, remember, you told me."

"Well, dat was maybe before dese tings started happenin' I tink."

"Please continue," said Father Satchko.

"Yeah, I had a dream about Saint Terese. No, it wuz Saint Bernadette. I get dem confuse."

"Yes, tell me more," said Father Satchko.

"Well, see, me an' some kids saw dat movie about her in religion class, so I guess I remember some stuff. Like she didn' say nothin' to me or nothin'. Like, she was, you know, uhn, like da movie I seen."

"Oh," said Father Satchko, writing down something again. He asked a few more questions, such as how often she went to church and to confession and when she last received Holy

Communion. Then he said to the Pani that this sort of thing may mean nothing at all, so Sonya should see a doctor about those sores just to be on the safe side. Pani was visibly disappointed, I had hoped for something more miraculous, and Sonya seemed dazed by the entire procedure. Pani helped Sonya rewind her bandages as the priest said soothing things, such as how we are all special in the Lord's eyes, and finally he dismissed us with a blessing.

We walked back home via another street. Pani Machniewska rang Pani Dydiak's doorbell and started complaining about how blind and stupid Father Satchko was before we were even inside the house. "He calls himself a priest? A monsignor? He don't know a miracle when he sees one. Sonya, show Pani your sores."

I was feeling sorry for Sonya, who was being treated like a show animal commanded to do tricks, but she seemed not to mind. "Yoy," cried Pani Dydiak. She crossed herself a few times. "That Father Satchko. Yoy. He's a bad one! I've seen bad priests in Ukraine; I see them here. He's a bad one. Yoy, what his dog did to my grass!"

The two ladies talked and complained and it was so boring because Sonya didn't want to go outside or come back to my house to play as we used to. She sat there, her mouth open, watching her mother and not saying a word about anything. I wasn't so impressed with her sores the second time she showed them. They were only purplish scars on her hands and feet. I had seen worse when Mischa Lesnichisyn bashed his head on a swing in the schoolyard one recess.

Sonya's mother and Pani Dydiak were drinking tea in tall glasses, but when a bottle of vodka appeared on the kitchen table, I saw that this was going to be a very long visit. "C'mon, please . . . let's go out somewhere," I insisted. Sonya thought hard about it, as though I had asked her for the formula to the hydrogen bomb. Then she said okay. Her mother didn't mind that Sonya was leaving without her because she still had plenty to say about Father Satchko. I was glad to get out of there, and genuinely happy to have Sonya back to myself again. "I found another black dress we can use for a nun's costume," I said.

She didn't say anything until we reached my street. "Uh, look, I gotta go now," she said.

"Why? Aren't you coming over to play?"

"Uhm, I gotta see somebody." She hesitated and looked around. "Uh, like Marya and me got us some boyfriends."

"Oh." I didn't know that she and Big Marya were friends. I hadn't even suspected that Sonya would have a boy interested in her.

"Well, that's okay," I said, trying to hide my disappointment. "Can I come, too?"

She laughed. "Naw, youse too young. Youse a baby still. I gotta go." She turned down another street. "Hey," she yelled back. "Better not say nuthin' to my mudder. See ya!"

"I hope you bleed to death!" I yelled at her after she left my sight. I went home alone.

On Sundays, now, Pani Machniewska and Sonya walked to church with an entire crowd of people stalking behind them and singing hymns. Some of the babas carried lit candles when they walked. Even my mother took part in the procession. There were rumors that various people were healed after touching the sores, but I never saw any crutches hanging outside Sonya's gate.

Soon, outsiders took an interest in Sonya and she was written up in the Chicago newspapers, with pictures of her holding up her hands with the holes, and her mother standing behind her with a look of sheer adoration. Sonya looked totally bewildered with her ridiculous cat's eyeglasses sliding down her nose, unable to adjust the frames with her hands held up in the air. All that was missing was the halo around her head. When her story hit the newsstands, Sonya was interviewed by a local television news reporter. There was Pani Machniewska's jowls on the six o'clock news one evening, her hair done up like Zsa Zsa Gabor's. She was obviously very nervous because whatever the reporter asked, she kept repeating with tears in her eyes that "God call my baby. . . . Miracle! Is miracle for my Sonya." Sonya showed her hands

and started talking in her dull voice, as though she was recit-
ing a poem at school. "It's God's will, I tink. We all gotta be
nice and good wid each udder. No more wars an' stuff. Like,
I tink what dis miracle is about is like, uhn, a message for
peace on urd, and like love 'tween brudders."

I personally thought it was very embarrassing watching
Sonya trying to be saintly on television. My mother said that
Sonya's mother shouldn't say anything or at least should have
done something with her teeth. Then Father Satchko appeared on the screen. He kept stressing that "the Church
must be cautious in these matters," but you could see he
really enjoyed being on the air and acting as though he was
responsible for Sonya's miracle.

When Sonya came back to school on a more regular basis,
the same nuns who used to keep her after school because
she never had her homework were now fawning over her.
She was invited to eat with them at their special table in the
school cafeteria behind a big screen, which shielded them
from the din of the students. They must have eaten much
better food behind the screen. It made me ill to hold out my
plastic plate while the cafeteria ladies sloshed it full of white
bread cut in diagonals, covered with chipped beef beneath a
thin, brown flour sauce. I would have bet that the nuns and
lay teachers behind the screen were eating steak. And there
was stupid Sonya, saying inane things in her bad grammar
with a mouthful of porterhouse simply because she happened to have special holy sores.

It was as if she was already canonized. Several times, I
spotted her on the playground during recess, surrounded by
some kids and preaching to them. It was the same lecture
she gave to her dolls in my basement in the old days. I
wanted to smack her saintly face to death, and give her a
reason to go to heaven sooner.

The spring after her miracle occurred, she was unani-
mously appointed by the nuns in our school to be the May
Queen, which meant that Sonya was chosen to crown the
statue of the Virgin Mary with a laurel wreath. It was an honor
usually bestowed on the most academically advanced, devout,

and prissiest eighth-grade girl student. Everyone in the school knew that the honor rightfully belonged to Roxalena Holova, but then Roxalena didn't have the stigmatas blooming on her hands and feet.

On the big day, Sonya was in the front pew, with her mother in the crowded church. She wore a fancy floor-length dress with a train. It was hard from where I was to see her feet, but her hands were bandaged as usual with what looked like gauze interlaced with streams of ribbons that matched the blue tint of her satin dress. I was in the balcony, singing with the choir. I could clearly see Sonya slowly parading toward the altar, where the large statue of the Virgin was standing. As she was stepping onto a footstool, Sonya caught one of the heels of her shoe on the hem of her dress. She swayed a bit and almost fell backward, but managed to save herself by grasping the Virgin's shoulders. The wreath she was carrying dropped to the floor. Sonya was about to stoop down and pick it up when Father Satchko loudly whispered from the pulpit, "Just stay right where you are. Don't move, Sonya, or the statue will fall." Sonya looked up at him, smiled, and waved her arm. Then she patiently waited—we all patiently waited—for one of the altar boys to retrieve the wreath while she stood on the stool, twirling her hair with one of her bandaged hands, and softly humming to herself.

After the ceremony, I went for a walk instead of going home. It was a beautiful, warm Sunday. On Walton Street, which was outside the Ukrainian section of the neighborhood, a group of teens, some in black leather jackets, stood on the corner. A transistor radio was blaring out a rock station, and some boys were pitching pennies. I heard giggles and a girl's voice shouting, "youse better not." As I came closer, ready to cross the street so that I wouldn't have to pass them and maybe be harassed by the boys, I saw Big Marya hanging on the arm of one of the boys in leather jackets. They were laughing and pointing at another boy and at Sonya Machniewska. Sonya and her friend had their arms linked together, and rubbed their hips against one another like crickets. I think he was trying to kiss her lips, but I wasn't sure because Sonya had a lit cigarette in her mouth. I said hi.

Sonya smiled. "Hey, how waz I in dat ting?"

"Oh, just great, Sonya. Who's your friend?" I asked shyly. It was awkward to see Sonya, still in her May Queen dress and ribbony bandages, being pawed by a boy.

"Oh, him. He's jus' a friend. Ain't cha?" She blew a ring of smoke at him, and quickly kissed him when he closed his eyes from the smoke. Big Marya and the others laughed.

"See, like we gotta be nice to everybody. Right?" Sonya laughed.

"Hey, gimme a cigarette," Big Marya said to another boy. He tossed her one and then said to me, "Hey, you want one, too, squirt?" He had acne all over his face and neck.

Everybody laughed. I wasn't sure what to say and I looked to Sonya for help. "She don't want dat. She plays wid dolls," Sonya said.

"Yeah? You play with dolls?" the boy said, coming closer to me. He took Sonya's cigarette out of her mouth and thrust it in my face. "Try it."

"I have to go home, now," I said. I was afraid, so I made a point of carrying my prayerbook at chest level so that they could see I wasn't about to join them in their idea of fun. I said goodbye and turned my back to them as quickly as I could. I heard one of them say, "Go home to your dolls." I thought it sounded like Sonya, but maybe it wasn't.

When I came home, I found a group of women speaking to my mother out in the backyard. They were probably there to look over my mother's new garden, where her first tulips bloomed, and, of course, to gossip. Pani Nesterenko and Pani Dydiak were among them. They were all talking about the May Queen event.

"She looked so saintly," one Pani said. "She should go to a convent school."

"Oh, that's a good idea, Pani," Pani Dydiak said. "That's a child of God, all right. Not like some girls around here."

Pani Nesterenko took offense. "I know you're not talking

about my daughter! My Marya is a good girl. Not like your son, the car thief."

"Oh good, you're back," my mother hurriedly said to me before Pani Dydiak could reply. I came up to the ladies and said hello.

"Where were you?" my mother asked, pushing my bangs from my eyes, a nervous gesture she had.

"Oh, nowhere. Just with Sonya and Marya and some boys."

"Boys!" Pani Nesterenko shouted. "You tell me where she is!" Pani Dydiak nodded her head and said smugly to the others, "Just like I thought."

I felt wicked. I was going to show Sonya and her mean new friends what sort of games I could play. "Marya is with Sonya," I said innocently. "They're smoking cigarettes on Walton Street with some boys in leather jackets."

"Ah-ha!" Pani Nesterenko said. She was livid. She abruptly left my mother's yard. The other ladies also quickly said goodbye and left to follow Pani Nesterenko. Before my mother could stop me, I ran in another direction back to Walton Street.

"Oh, oh," yelled the greasy boy who wanted me to smoke. "Your old lady's here!" Pani Nesterenko's bulky frame stormed over to where the kids were. She carried an umbrella, waved it over her head, and shouted in Ukrainian, "Hey, you, Sonya! I knew you were no good! You're supposed to be a saint, and here you are leading my Marya to sin! Wait until I tell your mother!" She hit Sonya on the head and then started after the boys, who swore at her as they swaggered away from the scene. Pani pushed Sonya and Marya in front of her to make them march homeward. "I'm telling your mother right now," she shouted. "Pick up your dress; you're getting the hem dirty," Pani Dydiak shouted after Sonya.

The sun was in my eyes, but I know that Sonya looked at me. I remember so clearly her pained expression, her forlorn march to her mother's in the same gown that only that morning she wore for a more triumphant procession. I looked away and ran home.

As expected, Pani Nesterenko told not only Sonya's mother

about that afternoon but everyone she could find who would listen. After the May Queen day, it wasn't surprising that Sonya's popularity waned. It would have, anyway; just about everyone in the neighborhood had already seen her sores at least once.

Sonya and I avoided each other after her fall from sainthood. She graduated from St. Nicholas and went on to some girl's Catholic high school far away from the neighborhood. Once, I saw her waiting for a bus on Chicago Avenue. She was smoking a cigarette. Her hair was much redder than it had been, and teased up into a bouffant. I wondered about her sores, but because she was wearing gloves and black leather knee boots beneath her short school uniform, it was impossible to tell if she was still "holey."

The very last time I saw her was at the Europeska Bakery, where she worked. Her hair was a deep beet red, then—brittle with hair spray, and some of the teased ends were sticking out of a hairnet. Her eyes were still magnified behind the rhinestone glasses, but were now accentuated with thick, black eyeliner and greasy, heavy green eye shadow. Fake lines were drawn beneath her lower eyelashes, like Twiggy's. At first I didn't recognize her behind the counter, slicing bread for a Pani who wanted hers cut very, very thin. She was also slow and patient when another Pani rudely asked Sonya for a taste of the kolachy to see if it was fresh. While I waited for my turn, I watched her hands at the slicer, wondering if she had any scars, or at least if little halos, auras, or something still radiated around the places where the stigmatas had appeared. I got closer to the counter, and saw nothing at all.

She took my order, and hardly talked. She sliced my bread and handed it to me in a bag. "I guess you're back to normal," I said to her shyly.

"Oh, yeah. Dat's de end a dat."

"Are you sorry? I mean, about not having any more miracles happening to you?"

"I dunno. I didn't ask for it or nuthin'. The boys like me better bein' normal. Who wants to go out wid a saint? But my mom cries a lot now dat I lost dem sores. Like she really taut I was sumpin' dere for awhile. Say hello to your mom for me, okay?" She smiled at me before she turned her attention to the next customer. I went home with the bread, wishing, in spite of my past resentment, that the bread I took from her, Sonya's hands, was somehow symbolic and connected to something sacred like Holy Communion. It wasn't. It was ordinary bread from an ordinary bakery that my ex-friend Sonya Machniewska had sliced with her ordinary hands.

I suppose the real miracle is that Big Marya became a nun, much to Pani Nesterenko's pride. I wonder if Sister Marya ever tells her students about Sonya's stigmatas and how she might have been a saint if she wasn't so human. Probably not. No one ever talks about it anymore on Rice Street.

PART THREE

A Temple of the Holy Ghost

Fish used to taste like meat until God let Eve bathe in the ocean, my brother told me one day.
                                    —Josely Carvallo

Alison Stone

Starving for God

Twelve years old and always happy,
I am fortified
By the religion of control.
Although fat follows me
Like a retarded twin, I will remove
These hips and tempting breasts.
Already I am healed.
I have stopped the blood.

The others are jealous.
They fail to praise
The sculpture I have made.
They do not see
It is their way, not mine,
That leads to death.

I am stronger than that.
Hunger is a prayer
For the time when I will have no flesh
With which to sin.

I see perfection
And am almost thin enough
To slip through the door.

I run, I burn, I am blessed.
I will not stop
Until I touch
The pure ivory bones of my Temple.

Cheryl Marie Wade

Into the Light of Day

> *Pain—has an Element of Blank—*
> *It cannot recollect*
> *When it began—or if there were*
> *A time when it was not—*
>
> *—Emily Dickinson*

It is somewhere in that time between midnight and dawn when silence couches my parents' house, when the only sounds alive are the creaks and groans that hint of secrets. I am awake. I am awake because my inner voice has screamed me to be. I am awake because the air in my little pink room is thick with the heat of dread. I am awake because, somehow, I know he is awake.

I have to be awake. I have to be awake so that I can stop the world, make it spin backward, make myself stop thinking thoughts so evil that sweet Jesus himself would take joy in putting a stake through my heart to end them. I want to be awake so that the screaming voice inside will finally come out. I want to be awake so that I can say it. Say the truth. Say the truth I refuse to say, the truth I refuse to believe.

And I lie in my ruffled bed, sweating, adding my own stinking perfume to the air. I can see him looking over at his wife, making sure she is secure in sleep; then, lightly easing his big birdy legs over the edge of their bed, their satin-quilted queen-size rack. He puts his gimpy feet, always so sore, always so tired and bruised-looking, into his brown slippers—the ancient ones, properly broken-in to suit his properly broken feet. Perhaps he glances over his shoulder as he slips through their door. Perhaps he doesn't care if she sees him leave.

Then I hear it: their door. The cautious creak as he trespasses into the hallway. His footsteps: a muffled sliding. Shlp. Shlp. Care for silence in each step. Shlp. Shlp. . . .

Oh, God. It cantbecantbecantbe whispers my heart with each beat. My cheeks burn Mama; Gramma, my cheeks burn. Is there no air in here to breathe? Daddy, did you steal the air?

I stop breathing. I hear the silence as he stands before the water heater. To warm himself? To listen? To reconsider?

I decide to jump up, clang about, make noise to summon helpful spirits. No. I decide to tiptoe to the closet, pull all the clothes on top of me. Yes! There it will be cool and I will breathe. I will never be seen again. I silently chant pleasegod as my mind struggles to make my legs move.

But of course my legs don't move; they know that if they move it will be an admission. Pleasegodpleasegodpleasegod my breath whines with each shallow, labored effort. Ohgodplease. Ohgod. . . .

A sudden flash: his silhouette framed by the ever-shining light in the hall. Huge. Grotesque. His head like a buffalo. The light blinds with mercy. The scent of day's-end Old Spice—gentle, embracing. A footstep. Then, the element of blank. Like Emily's dear sweet pain: The Blank.

The electric guitars blare, the DJ razzes. It's morning. A school day. My handsome, affectionate, brown-eyed daddy, the holder of all keys to love and pain, pokes his head in the door, gives me a sweet, warm wink: "Up and at 'em, Sis."

I smile. I get up. I put on my fuzzy pink pullover, the one

that almost disguises my just-about-to-be small titties; the blue and gray plaid skirt; gray kneesocks (Mother loves me to be coordinated); and my white bucks. I pull the gold and seed pearl cross Gramma gave me, with the hope I'd be a good Catholic girl, from around the back and untangle it from my long, silky hair. I love my pretty pretty hair I think as I look into the mirror at my shadowed eyes.

I kiss Mom on the cheek, and when I feel my father's thick, sensuous lips on mine in good-bye and look into his dark, soft eyes, a rush of confusion shatters my spine.

But I am composed. I step out into the ordinary day, a good Catholic girl.

Tracey Bolin

St. Maria Goretti

(1890–1902) virgin and martyr
St. Maria Goretti was born at Corinaldo,
Italy, in 1890, into a family of poor farm
laborers. On July 5, 1902, Maria was at-
tacked in a bedroom of her home by eigh-
teen-year-old Alessandro Serenelli. She
resisted his advances and was stabbed repeat-
edly with a long dagger. She was canonized
on July 25, 1950.

from *The Book of Saints*
by Victor Hoagland

When Alessandro confessed,
he said it was like stabbing
wood, your body falling towards him
stiff and open like a branch.
You were eleven.
Below the farmhouse we
went on threshing beans, oxen
breaking casings on the stone road,
dust startling the air, drying
on my arms like a torn net.

In the web of roots they found
his knife. Men knelt beneath almond trees,
weeping as the mayor called you our martyr.
They spread your stained garments
on the church steps, and we tore at them like birds.
My mother pinned a piece by our crucifix,
pierced another with needle and thread
to tie around my neck.

All remembered the girl you were,
carrying water over the scarred earth,
your silver hands balancing the vase.
When I fainted near the well, you
poured water over my wrists, the cup
of your hands above me like a dove.

On your last day we circled your bed,
praying with the priest as we waited for miracles.
How white everything was—
the silver monstrance, the ivory
rosary tying your hands,
your face against the linen,
blessing us. When the priest held the chalice
to your lips, wine spilled from your mouth.

In moonlight the path to your grave
is a luminous scarf drifting through
the ruined orchard. I follow it
to the hills above our village,
pressing your relic against my throat,
touching tree bark with my tongue.

Jane Kremsreiter

Confirmation

The first time I saw Maria Sanchez, sitting on a swing in the school playground, I knew she wasn't like the other eighth grade girls. It wasn't just that she had pushed her knee socks down around her ankles and draped a fine silver chain over her left sock. She had also let out the hem of her uniform skirt so that it grazed her calves, even though the rest of the girls rolled their skirts at the waistband to make them shorter. Worst of all, she had wrapped a yellow chiffon scarf around her hair—turban style—and only her bangs were visible from the front. They spilled onto her forehead in a dark wave.

I didn't talk to Maria that day in the playground. I was the new kid and had a strong intuitive feeling that Maria was an outsider. I knew from experience that talking with an outsider in the first few weeks of school could banish me forever from the insiders. I needed girlfriends—the kind I read about in library books. Quiet, respectable girls to share secrets with while we combed each other's hair. But then, on Friday afternoon, my religion teacher had us push our desks together in long, horizontal rows and sit alphabetically across. No one in my religion class had a last name that started with a Q or an R, and that's how I ended up next to Maria Sanchez.

When Maria slumped into the chair beside me, I smelled the fragrance of sandalwood soap. She pulled a paperback

Bible from her silver, vinyl tote bag and drew concentric circles on its cover. Maria must have felt me staring at her hands because she twisted the ring on her third finger and looked up at me.

"You like it?" she asked. "My mom brought it back from Arizona. She bought it from an Indian."

Maria offered me her hand. I held it lightly to admire the ring.

"That looks like real turquoise," I said.

Maria smiled and slipped off the ring. "Here," she said. "Try it on."

I pushed the ring over the knuckle of my second finger— it was too big for my third finger—and turned my hand so that the light reflected off the silver.

"It looks nice on you," Maria said.

Just then, Sister Margaret Mary instructed us to turn to Paul's first letter to the Corinthians and Maria put out her hand for the ring. I pulled frantically, twisting my skin until it turned red and puffy.

"Just leave it, will you?" Maria whispered. "You're never going to get it off, now. You'll be able to get it off later, when the swelling goes down. Just don't forget to bring it back Monday."

All through class I tugged at the ring, stopping only to turn the pages of my Bible. I didn't want to wear it home. When the bell rang I balled my hand into a fist, covered the ring with my thumb, and watched Maria walk out alone, swinging her tote bag, oblivious to the cluster of girls who whispered behind her. I put my fist in the pocket of my sweater and hurried past them all, pressing my thumb against the turquoise stone as if the ring could send out a beam of light to ward off the group of girls I so desperately wanted to join. Should one of them see that ring, my fate would be sealed. I would be paired forever with Maria.

The fall I turned thirteen, "forever" meant the long, slow unfolding of days leading up to my graduation. My mother promised we would not move in the middle of the year this time, that I would graduate from Saint Helen's. I needed some stability, she said, what with my father running off to Atlanta and all. My mother didn't understand that losing my father wasn't the problem.

The problem was Creep. A week before school started, we had moved into Creep's one-bedroom apartment and I had to sleep on the scratchy green couch. After a few weeks, my mother got a job as a cocktail waitress, and with her earnings bought a white velour slipcover for the couch. During the day, Creep sprawled there in nothing but black socks and boxer shorts, watching TV. Each night I would brush his curly black chest hairs from the white velour before I'd sit there to do my homework. I couldn't do anything about the faint stains left from his greasy hair, so I took to throwing a sheet over the couch and hiding my pillow behind the laundry basket when I left for school in the morning.

Often when I came home from school the bedroom door was closed and I could hear the rustle of sheets under the radio's blare. Sometimes hours would pass before my mother would emerge, flushed and buoyant, to make a pot of blueberry tea and pat my hand before again closing the bedroom door between us.

On Monday I brought Maria's ring to religion class wrapped in a piece of pink tissue paper. Maria was already in her seat when I arrived, her Bible open and her nose almost touching the page. She ran her finger across the lines, stopping now and then to write something in letters so tiny I couldn't read them. I tapped her upper arm. It felt muscular, solid as a boy's.

"I brought your ring back," I said, and pulled my chair out. Its metal feet screeched on the green tile floor.

"Mm hmmm," Maria mumbled.

I held the tissue-wrapped ring out for her and when she didn't react, dropped it onto her Bible.

"Did we have an assignment?" I asked.

Maria shook her head. "I don't think so."

"Then what are you working on?"

Maria pushed the Bible so that its spine rested on the crack between her desk and mine. Each place the words *Him* and *He* appeared in reference to God, Maria had scratched out and written in Him/Her or He/She. I think my jaw must have dropped because Maria laughed and said, "You're not shocked by that are you?"

I shook my head. "Of course not," I lied. I was shocked, all right. She had changed the Bible. How could she do that?

"If we're going to read fairy tales about some all-powerful being, we might as well make it a little more honest. You don't believe God has a sex, do you?"

"No?" I said like a question. Up until that instant, I'd never thought of God as anything but the Father.

"It's *so* primitive." Maria flipped through the Old Testament. Red markings darted across the pages like ants. "I'm up to the psalms," she said, and slammed the book shut.

Maria unfolded the pink tissue and stuck the ring on her third finger. "Hey, what's that?" she said, examining the tissue. "Is that a pubic hair?"

I glanced over at her desk and, sure enough, a black curly hair sat in one of the valleys Maria had made in the pink tissue. I felt a warm embarrassment creep up my neck, horror at the implied connection between that little hair and my most private parts. Usually I didn't quite believe that other people knew I had a triangle of hair hidden beneath my red plaid skirt. I looked again at Maria. She had the hair on the tip of her finger. I searched for a way to explain it, unwilling to let her see my embarrassment.

"That's just Creep's chest hair," I finally said with a casualness that sounded false.

"Creep?" Maria narrowed her eyes. "How could you let someone named Creep get his chest anywhere near you?"

"Believe me," I said, feigning boredom. "I wouldn't if I had the choice."

Maria looked at me with interest. Just then, Sister Margaret Mary clapped her hands and told us to open to Acts I. Maria flipped open her Bible and shoved it onto the crack between our desks.

"Hold the place," she whispered.

I started to protest, but Maria was already digging through her silver tote bag. I reluctantly followed the text with my finger and hoped none of the other girls would see me sharing a Bible with Maria.

Maria pulled a small yellow notebook from her bag, held it on her knee, and wrote something. Then she slipped the notebook onto my lap. She put her finger on the Bible to hold the place as I read her question.

Who is Creep, and why don't you have a choice?

I took a pen from the pocket of my sweater and wrote my answer, short and to the point.

Creep is my mother's lazy, ugly boyfriend. We live with him. He takes naps on the couch, where I sleep at night.

Maria smiled as she read my answer. Then she wrote back: *I thought you meant he forced you to do IT.*

I felt diminished in Maria's eyes. I suddenly wished Creep—well, not Creep, but someone much younger and more attractive than Creep—had forced me to do IT. I sensed this would impress her. Despite my lack of interest in developing a friendship with Maria, I would have welcomed her admiration.

I once Frenched with a boy, I wrote.

Maria would not be outdone.

I've done IT. A hundred times with my Soulmate. His name is Cliff.

I could have stopped the whole thing right there, and a big part of me wanted to. I held the yellow notebook in my lap, not sure what I would do. Before I could decide, Maria slipped the notebook off my lap and started writing.

Maybe not a hundred times. Anyway, that's not important. Cliff says what matters is our place in the universe and finding out what's true.

Cliff was fifteen and went to an undetermined high school not far from Saint Helen's. I can still picture the way he flipped his head back to shake the hair from his eyes, his cheeks a mottled red, his dark eyes feverish and passionate. He traveled the country by sneaking into passenger trains and hiding in the bathroom, much to the dismay of his simple and often abusive parents. Twice he was suspended from school to punish him for his long, unapproved absences, an irony that amused Maria. Like us, Cliff had attended a Catholic grade school, but because of his disdain for the Church's hypocrisy (a phrase Maria was fond of), he insisted on attending a public high school.

Over the next few weeks, Maria wrote every day in religion class. She described the casement window in the basement that Cliff would escape through when he was grounded, the smoked oysters and rye crackers he often ate for lunch, the green socks he wore as a kind of signature. She wrote about his cold, passionless mother, with her gray eyes and sensible shoes, and his angry, vindictive father, who punished him for things he didn't do.

I found myself daydreaming about Cliff in other classes and anticipating religion class with an urgency that surprised me. Cliff was brave, fearless, whole. I was confused, cowardly, disjointed. I wanted some of his spirit.

Sister Margaret Mary was the most feared and hated teacher at Saint Helen's; that was clear to me even as a newcomer. She was tall and lean, with a narrow face and eyes that glowed like blue flames in her pallid skin. Her hair was curled tight and sprayed into stiff waves that stood out around her ears like a helmet. She wore sallow shirtdresses, heavy stockings, and flesh-colored booties that stuck out at the back of her shoes.

In the fifth week of school, Sister Margaret Mary announced that starting next week we would divide our religion class into two parts. The first half of the period would be devoted to Bible study, as usual, and in the second half we would begin our preparation for Confirmation.

By this time my desire to hear about Cliff had blossomed

into a notebook relationship with Maria. I hadn't yet had much success getting in with the other girls, but I wasn't ready to give up yet, and so I quietly turned down Maria's invitations to meet after class and she finally stopped asking. Maria must have sensed that Cliff was my interest, not her, and so she wrote little about herself.

For the week following Sister Margaret Mary's announcement, Confirmation was our topic. Maria gleefully condemned the practice and what she called the myth of the Holy Spirit. *Cliff says they must think we're really stupid if they expect us to buy all this stuff about flames descending and these guys speaking in languages they've never even heard before,* Maria wrote. *Where's their proof?*

I wrote my agreement in the yellow notebook. No one had to know how irreverent I'd become. My rebellion was safe between two pieces of cardboard. And so, when Maria wrote a long, detailed account of Cliff's handling of Confirmation, I supported him without pause. After all, he did the right thing. He stood up in his eighth grade religion class and said he didn't want to be confirmed, he didn't believe in the myth of the Holy Spirit. He was beaten by his parents, suspended from school, and taunted by his classmates, but he held fast. He stood by his beliefs. I wrote my applause at the end of the story. Brave, fearless, righteous Cliff.

On the first day of our split religion class, everything started out as usual. Sister Margaret Mary walked the long rows of desks, her crepe soles silent on the tile floor. Maria wrote furtively in the yellow notebook and I followed the text with my finger as a boy in the first row read a monotonous section of Acts II. I have been in car accidents since that time, and nearly died once when a truck ran me off the road on my bicycle, but I have never felt as utterly terrified as I did when I saw Sister Margaret Mary's eyes land on that yellow notebook.

I hit Maria on the thigh and she flipped the notebook shut. Just as she was about to shove it under her uniform skirt,

Sister Margaret Mary, her face hardened into a fist, reached over Maria's Bible and plucked the notebook out of her hand.

It lay on a pile of books and papers for the remainder of Bible study as Sister Margaret Mary continued her patrol. I didn't dare look at Maria. I kept going over in my head the things I had written about Confirmation. How could I explain any of this? If she would just leave the room for a minute, I could grab the notebook and tear it to shreds. Surely the punishment for that would be less severe than the torture I would sustain when she read the notebook.

At the end of Bible study, Sister Margaret Mary stood rigid at the green chalkboard and wrote CONFIRMATION in heavy block letters. I glanced over at Maria. She had this strange, serene look about her. Only her bitten lower lip gave away her tension. Sister Margaret Mary looked back at the class.

"When we are confirmed," she said. "We choose to be adult members of the church. As infants, our parents made the decision for us. But as young adults we make our own decision. This is a grave and sacred time for all of you. Now, everyone stand. Repeat after me: I choose to be an adult member of the church. All together now."

We all stood and a strange medley of voices said blandly, "I choose to be an adult member of the church." I heard my own voice, vacant and quiet, and felt a hollowness beside me.

Maria was not standing.

She was sitting, rigid and serene, still biting her lower lip, her hands folded piously in her lap. Sister Margaret Mary pointed a long finger at her. The room fell silent.

"Stand up, Miss Sanchez."

Maria stood and dropped her hands at her sides.

"Do you choose to become an adult member of the church?"

Maria shuffled her feet.

"Speak up, young lady, I can't hear you." The finger wavered in the air, still pointing at Maria.

Maria took a deep breath, then said simply, clearly, resoundingly, "No."

Sister Margaret Mary's pointed finger dropped to her side. The whole room turned and stared at Maria.

"Do you understand the gravity of what you just said?" Sister Margaret Mary's voice quivered in a solemn whisper. "Let me ask you again. Do you choose to become an adult member of the church?"

"I already said no, Sister."

"Come here, Miss Sanchez." Sister Margaret Mary stood rigid at the chalkboard as Maria walked toward her. The silence was so profound that I could hear an irregular click from her heel, as though a tiny stone had wedged itself in the rubber. When Maria reached the front of the room, Sister Margaret Mary shoved her toward the door and then turned back to face the class. "I don't want to hear a sound out of you." She said this with such menace that the room stayed silent even when we knew she was out of earshot.

I slept little that night. With the yellow notebook still in Sister Margaret Mary's possession, I was certain my fate would be the same as Maria's. I wondered if I'd ever see her again. Rumors had quickly spread about Maria. I heard that Sister Margaret Mary beat her with a leather strap until she screamed her apology. I heard that she was kicked out of school, that her father threatened to kill her. I heard that she was seen standing in the ticket line at the Greyhound station. I heard her name whispered in the corridors and on the playground, even among the fifth and sixth graders in the cafeteria line.

When I walked into religion class the next day, Maria was not there. In the front of the room stood Sister Margaret Mary, writing a prayer on the chalkboard. I wanted to run, my fear was so great, but instead I sat at my desk, opened my Bible, and pretended to read.

When the rest of the class had filed in, Sister Margaret Mary leaned forward on her lectern and looked hard at me. The room swam in a white haze. She pulled the yellow notebook from the pocket of her sweater.

"Olivia," she said. "Do you know who this notebook belongs to?"

I felt a swell of tears push at the brims of my lower lids, and bit my tongue to keep from crying.

"It's Maria's," I said in a muffled voice.

"Have you ever written in this notebook?"

"No," I said. I could feel my hands shaking and I sat on them to make them stop.

"I didn't think so." Sister Margaret Mary slipped the notebook back into her pocket.

I saw Maria a week later. I was walking the long way home from school when I spotted the yellow chiffon scarf tied to her silver tote bag. She was crouched at the edge of the sidewalk, picking up bits of green glass from the curb. The glass shown like emeralds in the sunlight. I would have walked quickly by and pretended not to see her, but she looked up just as I was passing. I stopped dead.

"Olivia," she said. I noticed there were dark circles under her eyes.

"Hi, Maria. Where have you been?" I felt this sudden desire to hear the full story; partly because I was curious, and partly because I missed Maria, much as I wanted to deny it. I crouched beside her to help with the glass.

"I spend religion class with Father Garfield. He's explaining to me about Catholicism. He thinks I'll give in and get confirmed, but I won't. I can't be a hypocrite." She sighed. "Nobody understands. Except Cliff."

And suddenly I remembered Cliff doing the right and noble thing, always, despite opposition. I remembered my written applause in the yellow notebook when Cliff stood up and said he wouldn't be confirmed. I looked at Maria and saw Cliff. I don't know what came over me, but all of a sudden I was screaming.

"Cliff is a lie. He doesn't exist. You lied to me all that time and I'll never forgive you for it. Liar! Liar!"

Maria didn't answer. She held my eyes for a brief moment

and I was filled with shame. Then she went back to picking up the bits of glass. I watched her for a moment, but could think of nothing to say.

I closed my fingers around the shards of green glass in my palm and started home. Even when I felt the sting, even when I felt the wetness seep between my fingers, I kept walking. I stopped in the alley next to my apartment building and spilled the blood-stained glass beside the curb. Sharp pains shot from my hand up to my shoulder. I sat on the curb and moved the fingers of my wounded hand until I could do it without wincing.

Barbara Hoffman

The Blessed Mother, Momma, and Me

Momma snapped the sheet taut across her bed and threw the other end to me. It was then she must have noticed my breasts budding out through the white blouse. Her head bowed, eyes cast down, she started to talk. Mumbled something about the husband's penis going inside the wife's vagina; said sex was holy and then said something about the purity of the Blessed Mother. I snapped the sheet back. What the hell could I say to that? The only question in my mind was, Where did this sex stuff take place? Of course, I didn't ask my mother. I knew it had to be the bathroom. Anything private took place in the bathroom. I tried to picture it: my mother and father standing next to the gleaming white toilet bowl, she lifting the skirt of her cotton plaid housedress; he fumbling with the buttons on his paint-covered overalls. My mind wouldn't go any further.

Smoothing the sheet at the top of the bed, folding it over, she finally looked at me, said, "Never let a boy put his tongue in your mouth." *Yuck,* I thought, *why would I ever want to do that, all that spit.* I just didn't understand the purpose of this conversation.

Soon, we bought my first bra. Could there be anything on earth smaller than a white cotton double A Maidenform bra lying on the counter at May's Department Store. Then Billy, the tall, skinny boy on the next block started hanging around; his coal black eyes were always drifting to the two spots where my bra pushed my shirt out.

That early summer day we all decided to walk to Alley Pond Park—Billy, me, Ann, Malcolm, Marene, Tony, and Debbie. Billy stayed near me the entire time. He had this funny look on his face, sort of a half smile, but nervous. This was just another trip to our special hangout, but something in Billy's coal black eyes . . .

The bottle, the empty glass soda bottle lying in the leaves: Billy picked it up, spun it on the bare wooden picnic table; it pointed at me. Suddenly, I was behind the big oak tree with Billy. I don't remember putting one foot in front of the other to get there. His head bent; his lips brushed mine. I drew back. Again, his lips, oh, on mine. His tongue— wet, warm—snuck out, touched my lips, singed my lips. I drew back. His tongue snuck out; my lips on fire; tongue touched tongue; oh no, the Blessed Mother, tongue touched tongue; oh no, Momma, tongue touched tongue, oh boy, Billy.

Linda Nemec Foster

Learning About Sin:
The French Kiss

Sister Immaculata said
it was disgusting:
letting a boy put his wet
tongue in your mouth
and liking it. Her own mouth
opened in disbelief and words
caught in her throat
like confused starlings.

Nothing was heard but the beating
of glossy black wings as her
voice fluttered and struggled—
as if to defy gravity,
as if to be assumed into heaven,
as if to be rid of us
and our bodies, our bodies.

Maura Stanton

Nijinsky

I pushed open the red door of my new high school. I still
thought of it as my new school, although I had been enrolled
since September and now it was almost the end of Novem-
ber. The low, modern hall was brightly lit. I was late. The
doors were already shut on the soundproofed classrooms,
and I could hear the hum of the fluorescent tubes hidden
behind the translucent glass squares of the ceiling. I stopped
at my locker and slowly changed into my heavy uniform saddle oxfords. I had nothing to fear. I had merely to go to the
office, explain that my bus had broken down, and take an
approved tardy slip to my first-hour teacher. My new school
was so different from the old school I had transferred from
after three years that sometimes I felt light and thin, as if I
were a person in a dream. I half expected the hands of the
other girls to slide right through my body, especially when
I stepped into the bright, noisy cafeteria with its small tables
for four and its huge, abstract mural, or watched one of the
softly veiled sisters, her head thrown back, laughing with a
group of girls in the lounge.

My old school had been celebrating its Centennial when
my family moved to Minnesota. Its high, sooty walls, its dim
hallways and enormous flights of stairs had made me dread
waking up on school mornings. The sisters were bitter and

grim-faced; they were always collecting money for charity. There were even placards on the candy bar machine down in the sour-smelling basement cafeteria, where we ate our bag lunches in silence at long green tables.

I liked to think that I had changed since starting my senior year at the new school. But I was still nervous. I remembered the pinched-lipped Latin teacher, who used to humiliate me at the blackboard, with great vividness. Even though I had so far, in this new school, been able to recite my Spanish dialogues by heart, my throat clenched painfully when I rose to speak. But the black, kindly eyebrows of Sister Rosa reassured me.

I felt cheerful as I entered the main office. Waxy plants in straw baskets hung from the ceiling. Some oddly shaped leather chairs were grouped around a chrome coffee table. The secretary, typing at her blond wood desk, nodded routinely when I muttered my excuse, and handed me a slip of paper to fill in. She was young, and her nails were polished a frosty rose. She buzzed the principal's office, and in a minute Sister Olga swished out in her black-and-white habit, her rosary clicking against the metal door frame.

Sister Olga had a freckled, moon-shaped face. She smiled, and glanced at my excuse when I handed it to her. Then she bent over the desk and signed it with a felt-tipped pen.

"You're a senior, aren't you?" she asked.

"Yes, Sister."

"The seniors are meeting in the Little Theater this morning—and every Friday at this hour from now on."

"Yes, Sister."

She handed me the tardy slip. "One of our older sisters, from the Mother House in Wisconsin, is visiting us for a few months. She'll be giving lectures on music."

"Yes, Sister." I folded the paper in my hand. "Thank you, Sister."

I felt dismayed as I walked back down the hall to the Little Theater. It was one thing to appear late in my small religion class, which met first hour, and was taught by a friendly, overweight sister who liked to interrupt her theology with personal stories about her girlhood in Kansas City. But it was quite another thing to open the door of the Little Theater, where the whole senior class was assembled, and face a stranger. Still, the sisters who taught at this school were pleasant, and modern in their views. I expected that I could slip unnoticed into a back row seat. A few months ago, in my old school, I could not have done it. I would have hidden in the lavatory. But I felt I had changed. I was much less timid now, and could even talk animatedly to the other girls in my classes—I was not always pretending to read in homeroom.

The back of the Little Theater was dim when I opened the door. The aisle slanted steeply down past bolted rows of red and yellow and blue chairs. I heard the rustle of the other girls craning around to see who I was. I kept my eyes lowered, but managed to spot an empty seat down on the left. I moved toward it, trying to appear casual.

"Young lady? Young lady, stop right where you are!"

The voice calling up to me was so sharp and querulous that a great wave of heat washed across my face. I was stunned. I could hear the girls around me holding in their breath.

"What do you think you are doing?"

I looked in the direction of the voice. The stage lights fell in a circle, illuminating a tall sister who stood at the podium, just below the rim of the stage itself. She wore the huge, old-fashioned headdress, which all the other sisters of this order had abandoned.

"I asked you a question, young lady!"

I felt betrayed. I held out my slip of paper and struggled for words. "I have a tardy slip, please, Sister."

"You have what?"

"A tardy slip," I repeated.

"And do you think that excuses you? I was talking, and you interrupted me. You opened that door. I was talking about one of the most beautiful pieces of music in the world, and you came in late!" Her voice rose. She raised her right hand and shook her index finger wildly in the air.

"Sister, I'm sorry." The skin around my lips began to tingle. I had always expected this kind of attack in my old school, but I suddenly realized how much I had lowered my guard in the last few months. I felt faint with humiliation, but at the same time I knew that the salty lump in my throat was caused as much by anger as by tears.

"Sit down!"

"Yes, Sister."

"And if you ever interrupt me again—if any of you girls ever interrupt me again when I'm talking about art and beauty—I will deal with you personally, after school."

I sat down as quickly as possible. The girl beside me, who had long, straight hair that she must have ironed carefully every morning, raised her pale eyebrows discreetly and shook her head in the direction of the podium. I felt immediately comforted. I reached up to wipe the sweat off my forehead, but the same girl leaned toward me warningly.

"Don't touch your face," she hissed.

"What?"

She was unable to answer, for the sister at the podium was staring in our direction. I dropped my hands to my lap.

"Now I want you girls to listen to this music with pure souls," the tall sister said, her voice lower and calmer. At first I thought her white face was fuzzy, but looking at her more closely, I realized that her skin was only heavily wrinkled—her face, in the frame of her pleated wimple, looked like a drawing by Picasso. She extended her arms on either side of her body. "I don't want you to have any erotic thoughts when you listen to this music. It's beautiful music. Nijinsky was sorry afterwards for the evil way he danced. He was a pure man, a good man, but sometimes he was tormented. He always asked for forgiveness. We were close friends. Perhaps I'll tell you more about him sometime. But now I want you to listen to this beautiful music by Debussy."

She turned to a record player with fold-out speakers on the edge of the stage behind her, and touched the switch very quickly, as if she were afraid of it. A record dropped to the turntable and in a minute the haunting notes filled the Little Theater. The sister kept her back to us, and watched the record spin around as attentively as if it were a whole orchestra of musicians.

I took advantage of the music: "Are we going to be tested on this?"

The girl next to me shrugged. She shifted in her chair so that her mouth was close to my ear. "Her name's Sister Ursula. She says if you touch your face, you'll touch anything."

"What do you mean, touch your face?"

"Sex." The girl stifled a giggle. "She means sex."

Next Friday, we seniors were reminded over the P.A. system that we were to assemble in the Little Theater for another music lecture. It had begun to snow outside, and I was reluctant to leave my desk by the window. I could have sat there watching the flakes all day.

Sister Ursula was waiting for us at the podium, her arms folded. She watched us file silently to our seats. The room was chilly and damp, as if the registers, which were beginning to blow dry heat from the ceiling, had only just now been turned on. I rubbed my cold hands together, then tried to stick them up the sleeves of my brown uniform jacket. I thought I could see the shadow of the snow on the skylight above my head.

For a long time Sister Ursula only stared at us—she seemed to be looking us over row by row and face by face. I heard embarrassed coughs and nervous stirrings all around me. I kept my eyes focused at a point above Sister Ursula's headdress, hoping she did not remember me from last week. I had deliberately changed the part in my hair this morning.

My friend, Andrea, who sat beside me, scrunched down in her chair. Behind her hand she whispered, "I wish she'd get started."

"Me, too."

"She's spooky, isn't she?"

I nodded. Sister Ursula reminded me of the sisters who had terrified me in my old school—the Latin teacher, of course, and Sister Mary St. David, who measured our skirt lengths and rummaged through our purses, and the principal, Sister Vincent de Paul, who had once pinched my arm for breaking line to get a drink of water. I felt annoyed that I should be confronted with a specter from my gloomy, depressing past just as I was feeling comfortable in this brighter and more modern world.

"What man," Sister Ursula asked in a loud voice, "is the greatest dancer in the world?"

We looked uneasily at each other. Finally a thin girl with blond, greasy bangs raised her hand.

Sister Ursula nodded at her. "Stand when you answer."

The girl stood up. "Nijinsky was the greatest dancer, Sister."

"What do you mean—was?" Sister Ursula gripped the podium with both hands. She began to rock it back and forth.

The girl swallowed. "I mean—I think he's dead."

"Dead!" Sister Ursula shouted. "Of course he's not dead. Where did you get such an idea?"

"I don't know," the girl whispered, her neck and face coloring brightly. "I thought I read it somewhere."

"Sit down. Don't you ever answer a question with misinformation."

The girl sat down. I realized that the muscles in my stomach were clenched as tightly as if I myself had been Sister Ursula's victim.

"Now, Nijinsky, of course, loved Stravinsky's music. One day he tried to explain how the 'Firebird' reminded him of God—we were walking together in Paris. I remember it was raining, and his hair was soaked." Sister Ursula shook her head. "But he was so happy—he didn't notice. He looked like an angel. Later we went to mass together."

Sister Ursula went on to talk about bassoons and oboes and descending chords, gesturing with her claw-like hands. I knew nothing about music. I had never heard of Nijinsky or Stravinsky or the other people that Sister Ursula kept talking about. I looked up at the skylight, hoping that the snow was still falling. I had no boots with me, but if it continued to fall all day it would nevertheless be a pleasure to feel the cold lumps in the arch of my shoe as I walked through the drifts. I began to hum Christmas carols in my head. I think I almost fell asleep, for I was startled by the first notes of the strange music Sister Ursula suddenly began to play. But she switched the record off abruptly after a minute. She came a few steps up the center aisle and stood looming over the red-haired girl who sat at the end of my row, resting her chin on her hands.

"What are you doing?" she hissed.

The girl gasped. "Sister?"

"What are you doing with your hands?"

"Nothing, Sister."

"Nothing? What do you mean, nothing? Take your hands away from your face, do you hear?"

"Sister, I wasn't doing—I was just leaning—" The girl's voice shook. She pressed both her freckled hands against her chest.

"You don't understand yet, do you?" Sister Ursula softened her voice. She let out a sigh. She looked around at the rest of us. "Never touch your faces, girls. Never. It's a terrible habit. If you touch your face, if you play with your bangs, rub your nose, if you even rest your chin on your fist no matter how innocently—someone watching you knows what it means."

We stared at her blankly and uneasily. Andrea was pinching the hem of her plaid skirt convulsively between her thumb and index finger, and the girl on the other side of me had splayed her fingers rigidly across both knees.

The snow fell slowly but steadily for the rest of the day. Hour to hour and class to class I watched it stick and finally thicken on the brown grass. Then it began to cover the sidewalks, and during Art, my last class, I could hear the clank of the janitor's shovel around the corner of the building. I kept looking up from the piece of wood I was sanding to check on the flakes: they kept coming down in eddying but satisfactory gusts. The Art teacher, a young sister with strong hands and a bad complexion, kept breaking out into bits of song as she went from table to table checking on our work. In my old school we had done nothing in Art except drawing exercises and still lifes, but in this class we were always working with power tools, pouring cement into molds, folding paper, breaking colored glass with hammers and twisting copper wire into shapes.

"You can go ahead with your first coat of stain," Sister Melissa said, bending over my shoulders.

But by the time I got my newspapers spread, my brush cleaned, and waited my turn for the can, the bell had rung.

"Shall I wait until Monday?" I asked.

"It shouldn't take you more than ten minutes," Sister Melissa laughed. "Artists don't work by the hour, you know."

I spread the reddish stain rather hastily across my piece of wood. The other girls in the class were rolling up their newspapers and gathering their books. My strokes were uneven and a hair from the brush stuck to the wood. I picked it off with my finger and left an ugly streak. I brushed over the wood again, trying to keep my strokes smooth. But I was impatient to get out in the snow.

At last I finished staining the edges and propped my piece of wood against the wall to dry. I was all alone in the Art room. Even Sister Melissa had disappeared. I pressed the lid back onto the can of stain, but as I gathered up my newspapers I knocked over the plastic cup holding the camel's hair brushes, scattering them across the floor. I got down on my hands and knees.

"What are you doing!" a familiar voice shouted at me. "Get up at once!"

I looked back over my shoulder. Sister Ursula stood in the middle of the Art room, her hands on her hips. She seemed very tall from my position on the floor. Her brown eyes shone under her heavily drooping lids. Her skin had the texture of a boiled potato.

"I'm picking up these brushes, Sister," I said, trying to keep my voice steady.

"Get up! You look like a dog down on all fours like that—what a shameful way to use your body."

I got slowly to my feet.

"Clumsy," she said, watching me. "Why are you so clumsy? And what terrible posture."

I stood facing Sister Ursula, my face burning. The windows behind her were steamed up now, and I couldn't tell whether it was snowing or not.

"Touch your toes!"

"What, Sister?"

I stared at her headdress, with its elaborate pleats. Up close the linen seemed yellow—or it may have been the light. All day the story about Nijinsky's madness and death had been passed from senior to senior, for the girl Sister Ursula had humiliated had looked him up in the encyclopedia.

"Why are you standing there? Touch your toes," she repeated. "And don't crook your knees."

I leaned over and let my arms dangle. I felt frightened and light-headed. The muscles behind my knees strained sharply.

"Go on!"

I straightened up. "I can't, Sister. I'm too stiff."

"Stiff! You're a child."

"I can't do it, Sister."

She must have caught the note of hysteria in my voice, for she cocked her head and moved back a step. Suddenly she leaned over and with heavy, panting breaths began to touch the floor with the palms of her hands. She did it over and over. I stood watching her in horror. Her veil flew up over her headdress so that I saw its stiff underpinning. Each time she rose up, her face was redder and more congested than before. Finally she stopped and leaned against the blue cinder block wall, gasping for air.

"Are you all right, Sister?"

"Of course," she sputtered. She rearranged the front panel of her habit. "Just remember—" she began.

"Yes, Sister?"

"Just remember—" She took one final, deep breath, then seemed to recover, although her face was still a deep pink.

"Just remember that when you dance, when you walk, when you move even a finger—you are praising God."

"Yes, Sister."

"When Nijinsky danced, he danced for God." She lowered her voice almost to a whisper. "He used to come to my room and dance. That was before I took my vows, you understand?"

I nodded. My whole face felt numb. I wanted to run past her but my books and folders were on the radiator across the room, and I needed them to do my homework that weekend.

"Right before my boat sailed," Sister Ursula went on, "he came to see me at the hotel. He begged me not to leave. I had to throw myself on the ground in front of my crucifix— I couldn't bear to look at him. He wanted to dance for me one more time but I was afraid to watch—I had dedicated myself to God, you see, just as he had dedicated himself—" She broke off with a sigh. Then her eyes seemed to focus on me more sharply. "Why are you so fidgety?"

"I have to catch a bus," I said quickly.

She looked at me sternly. "Then go. And keep your hair clean—you should be ashamed to let it get so oily."

I gathered up my books, my eyes stinging with unshed tears. Sister Ursula's last remark—since I had washed my hair only yesterday—caused me to mutter and blink my eyes in anger all the way home on the bus. I hardly noticed the snow. I kept going over the scene in my head—refusing, in many bitter phrases, to touch my toes. I told her over and over that Nijinsky was dead.

On Saturday I went tobogganing with Andrea. The sky was a deep and perfect blue; the snow seemed whiter than any snow I remembered. The sharp, cold air filling my lungs as we sped down the hill in the park was exhilarating; but each time, as Andrea steered us away from Minnehaha Creek, and we slid to a halt under the spruce trees where the ground was bumpy, I felt depressed. I could not keep the thought of Sister Ursula out of my mind, no matter how I tried. I was especially perplexed by the contrast between my dark uneasiness and the cheerfulness of everything around me—the glowing faces, the red and blue knit scarves, the laughter, and the flying mist of snow that rose up from under the speeding toboggans.

My fingers moved stiffly inside my mittens by the time we began to pull the toboggan home. We took the shortcut around Lake Nokomis, kicking up smooth, untrodden snow. My toes felt swollen in my boots, even though I was wearing two pairs of socks. Nothing remained of the sun but a cold pink glow in the west.

"Why are they letting her do this to us?" I asked Andrea.

"Are you talking about that crazy nun again?" Her voice was muffled in her scarf. "If you're afraid she'll recognize you next Friday, cut class."

"And what about the Friday after? Anyway," I said, looking out at the gray lake, which was beginning to thicken and freeze around the edges. "It's not just me. It's all of us. Do we have to sit there and be humiliated? Do we have to put up with all her weird ideas—next she'll tell us that Lincoln is still alive!"

"Ignore her, then." Andrea pointed to a shed which two men in red earmuffs were hammering together on the shore of the lake opposite the bridge. "Look! They're putting up the warming house—we'll be able to skate pretty soon."

"That's right where the woman drowned last summer, isn't it?"

"You have a morbid mind," Andrea said, jerking the rope on the toboggan so that it bumped across the sidewalk, which circled the lake.

A wind was blowing across the snow. Andrea's words depressed me even more. I had been part of the crowd which watched the divers dredge the lake. I had seen the woman—who had committed suicide—brought up, and although she was wrapped immediately in plastic, I had glimpsed her heel, shriveled and gray as my own when I stayed too long in the bathtub.

I decided to speak to the principal about Sister Ursula Monday morning. I knew it was partly cowardice—I wanted to cover myself in the event that Sister Ursula singled me out again—but it was also partly benevolence, I told myself. The other seniors had never experienced these erratic and unpredictable outbursts from a teacher. There was no reason they should have to put up with the ugly and terrifying behavior that had finally given me—in Andrea's words—"a morbid mind." It also occurred to me that the other sisters on the staff had no way of knowing what was going on in the Little Theater on Friday mornings.

I was given an appointment to see Sister Olga during my afternoon study hour. I was tormented by the delay, for I knew from experience that my power to act diminished with reflection. I imagined the cold stare that would replace Sister Olga's friendly glance when I dared to criticize another sister. She would hate me for the rest of the year.

I could hardly swallow my bologna sandwich in the cafeteria. I sat by myself at a table by the window. The temperature had risen, and the dead grass was beginning to show in patches through the melting snow, which was by now heavily trodden and gray. I tried to invent another reason for wanting to see Sister Olga, but only half-heartedly. I knew I was doomed to go through with my idea. I had been deformed by the sisters at my old school—there was no other way of viewing it. I knew I hadn't been born with this morbid and gloomy vision. But years of submission to ridiculous whims had turned me into an unsmiling outcast—I looked at the groups of relaxed and normal girls at the tables around me with envy and despair.

At two o'clock I presented myself to the secretary. My face was already flaming with embarrassment, and my mouth felt dry. I was told to go into Sister Olga's office. She sat in a swivel chair behind her large, uncluttered desk. A metal crucifix with a burnished silver Christ hung behind her on the yellow cinder block wall. The wall behind the canvas Captain's chair, where Sister Olga gestured for me to sit, was covered with a huge pastel painting of indeterminate shapes—clouds or flower petals or waves.

"You're new this year, aren't you?" Sister Olga said. She nodded at me encouragingly. "What can I do for you?"

I swallowed. "I want to talk about—" My voice cracked. My lips felt so numb I could hardly move them.

Sister Olga stopped smiling. She leaned forward across her desk. Her eyes were intensely blue. "Don't be nervous," she said. "Anything you say to me will be held in the strictest confidence."

"Yes, Sister," I said.

"Are you having trouble with one of your classes, is that it?"

"No, Sister—not exactly, Sister. It's about Sister Ursula," I blurted out.

"Ah!" She blinked. She leaned back in her chair, folding her arms. "Go on. I think I know what you're going to say."

"She says if we touch our faces, it means we're evil—we're thinking about sex. She frightens people—she yells at us for no reason." I felt my voice warming, for the expression on Sister Olga's face was one of concern, not anger. "She thinks that Nijinsky—he was a famous ballet dancer—is still alive. But he died in 1950. She says she used to know him."

Sister Olga sighed. "Let me explain to you about Sister Ursula. I'd rather you didn't repeat this to any of the other girls, but since you've come to see me, I think it's only fair that I explain." She looked at me shrewdly. "You think Sister Ursula's crazy, don't you—because she thinks Nijinsky is alive?"

"I don't know, Sister," I murmured.

She shook her head. Her heavy nylon veil rustled against her round collar. "A very small part of our order has always been cloistered, you see. But we've agreed—in consultation with the Bishop—that the cloister is not a valid response to the modern world. Anyway, no one entering our order has made that choice for years. Mother Superior has decided that we should bring our few cloistered sisters back into the world. We plan to put their secular abilities to use—Sister Ursula, we knew, had been composing hymns for years—so we brought her here to lecture to you girls on music." Sister

Olga picked up a pencil from her desk and began to roll it absently between her fingers. "You *are* learning about music, aren't you?"

"Oh, yes, Sister," I said quickly.

"Sister Ursula has not seen a newspaper or magazine since she took her vows—she's not uninformed about history, of course—the wars, the presidents, the new Pope, that sort of thing—but she only knows what she's been told. And since no one ever guessed that she was interested in Nijinsky—" Sister Olga coughed discreetly. "We've just told her. She seemed to take it calmly. We showed her the article in the encyclopedia."

I leaned back in my chair, beginning to feel relaxed. "Was she a dancer? Did she used to live in Paris?"

Sister Olga shrugged. "We know nothing about her except what she herself tells us. There weren't any files kept on girls who entered the convent before the First World War. We don't even know her exact age—she seems to have forgotten. Now, as for the other part of your complaint—" Sister Olga laughed. "When I was a girl we were warned about patent leather shoes."

"My mother told me about that," I said.

"Sister Ursula has very old-fashioned notions about decency." Sister Olga stood up, her rosary clicking. "But you get the Church's modern view in your Family and Marriage class, don't you?"

I nodded vigorously.

"Just relax and be a little understanding. Sister Ursula doesn't have advanced views about the behavior of young women—but you shouldn't let her upset you." Sister Olga moved across to the door, and stood holding the knob.

I rose to go. "Thank you, Sister. I feel much better."

"Good. I'm glad to get those cobwebs out of your head. I'd rather you didn't gossip about poor Sister Ursula, however—we're trying to make her adjustment to the modern world as easy as possible."

"I won't say a word to anyone," I promised.

Sister Olga opened the door for me. I heard the clatter of

the typewriter as I passed the secretary's desk, but I was suddenly so light-headed and buoyant that I could hardly see ahead of me. The bell rang for the change of classes. I was caught up in the stream of brown-uniformed girls moving down the main hallway.

The Little Theater was empty on Friday when we filed in for our music lecture. Andrea found a seat beside me. She blew her nose into a pink tissue, then rolled the tissue into a ball. "Are you scared?" she asked.

"Not any more."

"Good." She stuffed her tissue into her torn jacket pocket. "She's just a crazy old nun."

"I don't think she's crazy," I said carefully. "She's just old. I feel sorry for her."

The side door near the stage opened, and Sister Ursula entered. We all quieted and coughed and cleared our throats. The movie screen had been rolled down, and Sister Ursula's headdress made a fantastic shadow against the white as she passed in front of it.

She stopped at the podium. She stretched out her arms and gripped it tightly. Her face once again seemed fuzzy to me—I decided that the eerie paleness of her skin was due to her many years in the cloister.

"She doesn't have any eyebrows," Andrea whispered.

"They're white. You just can't see them," I whispered back.

"Girls," Sister Ursula said sharply, "I have an apology to make to one of you." She turned her head slowly from side to side. "Where is the girl who told me that Nijinsky was dead?"

We looked around at each other. Finally someone said, "She's not here today, Sister."

Sister Ursula bowed her head. Her chin seemed to fold into the stiff cloth of her wimple. When she looked up again, she was squinting. The skin beneath her eyes appeared swollen.

"Then let me," she said, her voice cracking, "apologize to

the rest of you instead. That girl was right. Nijinsky is dead. Nijinsky is dead," she repeated. "It's written down, so it must be true." She paused and looked blankly around as if she did not know where she was. "And he was mad—all those years he was mad."

I saw the curly head of the girl in the row ahead of me nodding in agreement.

"Let me tell you something," Sister Ursula went on, her voice stronger than before but still hollow and directed more at herself than at us. "I never had a vocation."

Again she paused. She seemed to be shivering and I leaned forward nervously. I was afraid she might have a stroke. Sister Olga had said that she took the news of Nijinsky's death calmly, but she did not look calm now. Beside me, Andrea reached down for her Spanish book. Out of the corner of my eye I saw her surreptitiously open it on her lap.

"I didn't go into the convent because I wanted to serve God. I went into the convent because I thought I was going mad myself. You see, I was never happy, girls. Never! Never in my whole life—I was born with an iron band around my heart, I think. There are weights in the tips of my fingers."

Sister Ursula extended her arm in front of her, trying to spread out her fingers, which curled inward toward her palm. I could not take my eyes away from her face. It no longer seemed fuzzy to me. I could see every line in her skin and below it the pulsations of her muscles.

She brought her arm slowly back to her side. "And what about the wings on my shoulders?" she asked. "Can you see them?"

I heard someone snickering behind me, but most of the girls whose faces I could see had their eyes rigidly downcast.

"Can any one of you see my black wings?" she asked again. "Of course not. That's why I went into the convent—to hide them under my habit. At night, when I'm sleeping, the wings close over my body. I have the most evil dreams about Nijinsky. I've tried to live a holy life, but it's no use—when I'm writing my hymns, the evil wings brush the paper—I write horrible things."

I found I was gripping the metal armrests until my fingers ached. I glanced desperately at Andrea, but she was hunched over her book, mouthing Spanish words to herself. No one in the whole room seemed to be looking directly at Sister Ursula. Every girl I saw when I turned my head was slumped down in her seat as far as possible, horrified or embarrassed. I was the only one up on the edge of my chair. I tried to shut my eyes, but they opened of their own accord. I fought hard against the idea that was growing in the back of my mind: I had more in common with Sister Ursula than with anyone else in my new school.

Sister Ursula groaned loudly. "What have I done? I've frightened all of you, haven't I? But I only meant to apologize, I only meant to make you understand—oh, I'm wretched, wretched!"

She buried her face in her hands.

Louise Erdrich

Saint Marie

Marie Lazarre, 1934

So when I went there, I knew the dark fish must rise. Plumes
of radiance had soldered on me. No reservation girl had ever
prayed so hard. There was no use in trying to ignore me any
longer. I was going up there on the hill with the black robe
women. They were not any lighter than me. I was going up
there to pray as good as they could. Because I don't have
that much Indian blood. And they never thought they'd have
a girl from this reservation as a saint they'd have to kneel to.
But they'd have me. And I'd be carved in pure gold. With
ruby lips. And my toenails would be little pink ocean shells,
which they would have to stoop down off their high horse
to kiss.

I was ignorant. I was near age fourteen. The length of sky
is just about the size of my ignorance. Pure and wide. And it
was just that—the pure and wideness of my ignorance—that
got me up the hill to Sacred Heart Convent and brought me
back down alive. For maybe Jesus did not take my bait, but
them Sisters tried to cram me right down whole.

You ever see a walleye strike so bad the lure is practically
out its back end before you reel it in? That is what they done
with me. I don't like to make that low comparison, but I have

243

seen a walleye do that once. And it's the same attempt as Sister Leopolda made to get me in her clutch.

I had the mail-order Catholic soul you get in a girl raised out in the bush, whose only thought is getting into town. For Sunday Mass is the only time my father brought his children in except for school, when we were harnessed. Our soul went cheap. We were so anxious to get there we would have walked in on our hands and knees. We just craved going to the store, slinging bottle caps in the dust, making fool eyes at each other. And of course we went to church.

Where they have the convent is on top of the highest hill, so that from its windows the Sisters can be looking into the marrow of the town. Recently a windbreak was planted before the bar "for the purposes of tornado insurance." Don't tell me that. That poplar stand was put up to hide the drinkers as they get the transformation. As they are served into the beast of their burden. While they're drinking, that body comes upon them, and then they stagger or crawl out the bar door, pulling a weight they can't move past the poplars. They don't want no holy witness to their fall.

Anyway, I climbed. That was a long-ago day. There was a road then for wagons that wound in ruts to the top of the hill where they had their buildings of painted brick. Gleaming white. So white the sun glanced off in dazzling display to set forms whirling behind your eyelids. The face of God you could hardly look at. But that day it drizzled, so I could look all I wanted. I saw the homelier side. The cracked whitewash and swallows nesting in the busted ends of eaves. I saw the boards sawed the size of broken windowpanes and the fruit trees, stripped. Only the tough wild rhubarb flourished. Goldenrod rubbed up their walls. It was a poor convent. I didn't see that then but I know that now. Compared to others it was humble, ragtag, out in the middle of no place. It was the end of the world to some. Where the maps stopped. Where God had only half a hand in the creation. Where the Dark One had put in thick bush, liquor, wild dogs, and Indians.

I heard later that the Sacred Heart Convent was a catchall

place for nuns that don't get along elsewhere. Nuns that complain too much or lose their mind. I'll always wonder now, after hearing that, where they picked up Sister Leopolda. Perhaps she had scarred someone else, the way she left a mark on me. Perhaps she was just sent around to test her Sisters' faith, here and there, like the spot-checker in a factory. For she was the definite most-hard trial to anyone's endurance, even when they started out with veils of wretched love upon their eyes.

I was that girl who thought the black hem of her garment would help me rise. Veils of love, which was only hate petrified by longing—that was me. I was like those bush Indians who stole the holy black hat of a Jesuit and swallowed little scraps of it to cure their fevers. But the hat itself carried smallpox and was killing them with belief. Veils of faith! I had this confidence in Leopolda. She was different. The other Sisters had long ago gone blank and given up on Satan. He slept for them. They never noticed his comings and goings. But Leopolda kept track of him and knew his habits, minds he burrowed in, deep spaces where he hid. She knew as much about him as my grandma, who called him by other names and was not afraid.

In her class, Sister Leopolda carried a long oak pole for opening high windows. It had a hook made of iron on one end that could jerk a patch of your hair out or throttle you by the collar—all from a distance. She used this deadly hook-pole for catching Satan by surprise. He could have entered without your knowing it—through your lips or your nose or any one of your seven openings—and gained your mind. But she would see him. That pole would brain you from behind. And he would gasp, dazzled, and take the first thing she offered, which was pain.

She had a stringer of children who could only breathe if she said the word. I was the worst of them. She always said the Dark One wanted me most of all, and I believed this. I stood out. Evil was a common thing I trusted. Before sleep sometimes he came and whispered conversation in the old language of the bush. I listened. He told me things he never told anyone but Indians. I was privy to both worlds of his knowledge. I listened to him, but I had confidence in Leopolda. She was the only one of the bunch he even noticed.

There came a day, though, when Leopolda turned the tide with her hook-pole.

It was a quiet day with everyone working at their desks, when I heard him. He had sneaked into the closets in the back of the room. He was scratching around, tasting crumbs in our pockets, stealing buttons, squirting his dark juice in the linings and the boots. I was the only one who heard him, and I got bold. I smiled. I glanced back and smiled and looked up at her sly to see if she had noticed. My heart jumped. For she was looking straight at me. And she sniffed. She had a big stark bony nose stuck to the front of her face for smelling out brimstone and evil thoughts. She had smelled him on me. She stood up. Tall, pale, a blackness leading into the deeper blackness of the slate wall behind her. Her oak pole had flown into her grip. She had seen me glance at the closet. Oh, she knew. She knew just where he was. I watched her watch him in her mind's eye. The whole class was watching now. She was staring, sizing, following his scuffle. And all of a sudden she tensed down, posed on her bent kneesprings, cocked her arm back. She threw the oak pole singing over my head, through my braincloud. It cracked through the thin wood door of the back closet, and the heavy pointed hook drove through his heart. I turned. She'd speared her own black rubber overboot where he'd taken refuge in the tip of her darkest toe.

Something howled in my mind. Loss and darkness. I understood. I was to suffer for my smile.

He rose up hard in my heart. I didn't blink when the pole cracked. My skull was tough. I didn't flinch when she shrieked in my ear. I only shrugged at the flowers of hell. He wanted me. More than anything he craved me. But then she did the worst. She did what broke my mind to her. She grabbed me by the collar and dragged me, feet flying, through the room and threw me in the closet with her dead black overboot. And I was there. The only light was a crack beneath the door. I asked the Dark One to enter into me and boost my mind. I asked him to restrain my tears, for they was pushing behind my eyes. But he was afraid to come back there. He was afraid of her sharp pole. And I was afraid of Leopolda's pole for the first time, too. I felt the cold hook in my heart. How it could crack through the door at any minute and drag me out, like a dead fish on a gaff, drop me on the floor like a gutshot squirrel.

I was nothing. I edged back to the wall as far as I could. I breathed the chalk dust. The hem of her full black cloak cut against my cheek. He had left me. Her spear could find me any time. Her keen ears would aim the hook into the beat of my heart.

What was that sound?

It filled the closet, filled it up until it spilled over, but I did not recognize the crying wailing voice as mine until the door cracked open, brightness, and she hoisted me to her camphor-smelling lips.

"He *wants* you," she said. "That's the difference. I give you love."

Love. The black hook. The spear singing through the mind. I saw that she had tracked the Dark One to my heart and flushed him out into the open. So now my heart was an empty nest where she could lurk.

Well, I was weak. I was weak when I let her in, but she got a foothold there. Hard to dislodge as the year passed. Sometimes I felt him—the brush of dim wings—but only rarely did his voice compel. It was between Marie and Leopolda now, and the struggle changed. I began to realize I had been on the wrong track with the fruits of hell. The real way to overcome Leopolda was this: I'd get to heaven first. And then, when I saw her coming, I'd shut the gate. She'd be out! That is why, besides the bowing and the scraping I'd be dealt, I wanted to sit on the altar as a saint.

To this end, I went up on the hill. Sister Leopolda was the consecrated nun who had sponsored me to come there.

"You're not vain," she said. "You're too honest, looking into the mirror, for that. You're not smart. You don't have the ambition to get clear. You have two choices. One, you can marry a no-good Indian, bear his brats, die like a dog. Or two, you can give yourself to God."

"I'll come up there," I said, "but not because of what you think."

I could have had any damn man on the reservation at the time. And I could have made him treat me like his own life. I looked good. And I looked white. But I wanted Sister Leopolda's heart. And here was the thing: sometimes I wanted her heart in love and admiration. Sometimes. And sometimes I wanted her heart to roast on a black stick.

She answered the back door where they had instructed me to call. I stood there with my bundle. She looked me up and down.

"All right," she said finally. "Come in."

She took my hand. Her fingers were like a bundle of broom straws, so thin and dry, but the strength of them was unnatural. I couldn't have tugged loose if she was leading me into rooms of white-hot coal. Her strength was a kind of perverse miracle, for she got it from fasting herself thin. Because of this hunger practice her lips were a wounded brown and her skin deadly pale. Her eye sockets were two deep lashless hollows in a taut skull. I told you about the nose already. It stuck out far and made the place her eyes moved even deeper, as if she stared out the wrong end of a gun barrel. She took the bundle from my hands and threw it in the corner.

"You'll be sleeping behind the stove, child."

It was immense, like a great furnace. There was a small cot close behind it.

"Looks like it could get warm there," I said.

"Hot. It does."

"Do I get a habit?"

I wanted something like the thing she wore. Flowing black cotton. Her face was strapped in white bandages, and a sharp crest of starched white cardboard hung over her forehead like a glaring beak. If possible, I wanted a bigger, longer, whiter beak than hers.

"No," she said, grinning her great skull grin. "You don't get one yet. Who knows, you might not like us. Or we might not like you."

But she had loved me, or offered me love. And she had tried to hunt the Dark One down. So I had this confidence.

"I'll inherit your keys from you," I said.

She looked at me sharply, and her grin turned strange. She hissed, taking in her breath. Then she turned to the door and took a key from her belt. It was a giant key, and it unlocked the larder where the food was stored.

Inside there was all kinds of good stuff. Things I'd tasted only once or twice in my life. I saw sticks of dried fruit, jars of orange peel, spice like cinnamon. I saw tins of crackers with ships painted on the side. I saw pickles. Jars of herring and the rind of pigs. There was cheese, a big brown block of it from the thick milk of goats. And besides that there was the everyday stuff, in great quantities, the flour and the coffee.

It was the cheese that got to me. When I saw it my stomach hollowed. My tongue dripped. I loved that goat-milk cheese better than anything I'd ever ate. I stared at it. The rich curve in the buttery cloth.

"When you inherit my keys," she said sourly, slamming the door in my face, "you can eat all you want of the priest's cheese."

Then she seemed to consider what she'd done. She looked at me. She took the key from her belt and went back, sliced a hunk off, and put it in my hand.

"If you're good you'll taste this cheese again. When I'm dead and gone," she said.

Then she dragged out the big sack of flour. When I finished that heaven stuff she told me to roll my sleeves up and begin doing God's labor. For a while we worked in silence, mixing up the dough and pounding it out on stone slabs.

"God's work," I said after a while. "If this is God's work, then I've done it all my life."

"Well, you've done it with the Devil in your heart then," she said. "Not God."

"How do you know?" I asked. But I knew she did. And I wished I had not brought up the subject.

"I see right into you like a clear glass," she said. "I always did."

"You don't know it," she continued after a while, "but he's come around here sulking. He's come around here brooding. You brought him in. He knows the smell of me, and he's going to make a last ditch try to get you back. Don't let him." She glared over at me. Her eyes were cold and lighted. "Don't let him touch you. We'll be a long time getting rid of him."

So I was careful. I was careful not to give him an inch. I said a rosary, two rosaries, three, underneath my breath. I said the Creed. I said every scrap of Latin I knew while we punched the dough with our fists. And still, I dropped the cup. It rolled under that monstrous iron stove, which was getting fired up for baking.

And she was on me. She saw he'd entered my distraction.

"Our good cup," she said. "Get it out of there, Marie."

I reached for the poker to snag it out from beneath the stove. But I had a sinking feel in my stomach as I did this. Sure enough, her long arm darted past me like a whip. The poker lighted in her hand.

"Reach," she said. "Reach with your arm for that cup. And when your flesh is hot, remember that the flames you feel are only one fraction of the heat you will feel in his hellish embrace."

She always did things this way, to teach you lessons. So I wasn't surprised. It was playacting, anyway, because a stove isn't very hot underneath right along the floor. They aren't made that way. Otherwise a wood floor would burn. So I said yes and got down on my stomach and reached under. I meant to grab it quick and jump up again, before she could think up another lesson, but here it happened. Although I groped for the cup, my hand closed on nothing. That cup was nowhere to be found. I heard her step toward me, a

slow step. I heard the creak of thick shoe leather, the little
plat as the folds of her heavy skirts met, a trickle of fine sand
sifting, somewhere, perhaps in the bowels of her, and I was
afraid. I tried to scramble up, but her foot came down lightly
behind my ear, and I was lowered. The foot came down
more firmly at the base of my neck, and I was held.

"You're like I was," she said. "He wants you very much."

"He doesn't want me no more," I said. "He had his fill. I
got the cup!"

I heard the valve opening, the hissed intake of breath, and
knew that I should not have spoke.

"You lie," she said. "You're cold. There is a wicked ice
forming in your blood. You don't have a shred of devotion
for God. Only wild cold dark lust. I know it. I know how
you feel. I see the beast . . . the beast watches me out of your
eyes sometimes. Cold."

The urgent scrape of metal. It took a moment to know
from where. Top of the stove. Kettle. Lessons. She was steadying herself with the iron poker. I could feel it like pure
certainty, driving into the wood floor. I would not remind
her of pokers. I heard the water as it came, tipped from the
spout, cooling as it fell but still scalding as it struck. I must
have twitched beneath her foot, because she steadied me,
and then the poker nudged up beside my arm as if to guide.
"To warm your cold ash heart," she said. I felt how patient
she would be. The water came. My mind went dead blank.
Again. I could only think the kettle would be cooling slowly
in her hand. I could not stand it. I bit my lip so as not to
satisfy her with a sound. She gave me more reason to keep
still.

"I will boil him from your mind if you make a peep," she
said, "by filling up your ear."

Any sensible fool would have run back down the hill the
minute Leopolda let them up from under her heel. But I was
snared in her black intelligence by then. I could not think
straight. I had prayed so hard I think I broke a cog in my

mind. I prayed while her foot squeezed my throat. While my skin burst. I prayed even when I heard the wind come through, shrieking in the busted bird nests. I didn't stop when pure light fell, turning slowly behind my eyelids. God's face. Even that did not disrupt my continued praise. Words came. Words came from nowhere and flooded my mind.

Now I could pray much better than any one of them. Than all of them full force. This was proved. I turned to her in a daze when she let me up. My thoughts were gone, and yet I remember how surprised I was. Tears glittered in her eyes, deep down, like the sinking reflection in a well.

"It was so hard, Marie," she gasped. Her hands were shaking. The kettle clattered against the stove. "But I have used all the water up now. I think he is gone."

"I prayed," I said foolishly. "I prayed very hard."

"Yes," she said. "My dear one, I know."

We sat together quietly because we had no more words. We let the dough rise and punched it down once. She gave me a bowl of mush, unlocked the sausage from a special cupboard, and took that in to the Sisters. They sat down the hall, chewing their sausage, and I could hear them. I could hear their teeth bite through their bread and meat. I couldn't move. My shirt was dry but the cloth stuck to my back, and I couldn't think straight. I was losing the sense to understand how her mind worked. She'd gotten past me with her poker and I would never be a saint. I despaired. I felt I had no inside voice, nothing to direct me, no darkness, no Marie. I was about to throw that cornmeal mush out to the birds and make a run for it, when the vision rose up blazing in my mind.

I was rippling gold. My breasts were bare and my nipples flashed and winked. Diamonds tipped them. I could walk through panes of glass. I could walk through windows. She was at my feet, swallowing the glass after each step I took. I broke through another and another. The glass she swallowed ground and cut until her starved insides were only a subtle dust. She coughed. She coughed a cloud of dust. And then she was only a black rag that flapped off, snagged in bob wire, hung there for an age, and finally rotted into the breeze.

I saw this, mouth hanging open, gazing off into the flagged boughs of trees.

"Get up!" she cried. "Stop dreaming. It is time to bake."

Two other Sisters had come in with her, wide women with hands like paddles. They were evening and smoothing out the firebox beneath the great jaws of the oven.

"Who is this one?" they asked Leopolda. "Is she yours?"

"She is mine," said Leopolda. "A very good girl."

"What is your name?" one asked me.

"Marie."

"Marie. Star of the Sea."

"She will shine," said Leopolda, "when we have burned off the dark corrosion."

The others laughed, but uncertainly. They were mild and sturdy French, who did not understand Leopolda's twisted jokes, although they muttered respectfully at things she said. I knew they wouldn't believe what she had done with the kettle. There was no question. So I kept quiet.

"*Elle est docile*," they said approvingly as they left to starch the linens.

"Does it pain?" Leopolda asked me as soon as they were out the door.

I did not answer. I felt sick with the hurt.

"Come along," she said.

The building was wholly quiet now. I followed her up the narrow staircase into a hall of little rooms, many doors. Her cell was the quietest, at the very end. Inside, the air smelled stale, as if the door had not been opened for years. There was a crude straw mattress, a tiny bookcase with a picture of Saint Francis hanging over it, a ragged palm, a stool for sitting on, a crucifix. She told me to remove my blouse and sit on the stool. I did so. She took a pot of salve from the bookcase and began to smooth it upon my burns. Her hands made slow, wide circles, stopping the pain. I closed my eyes. I expected to see blackness. Peace. But instead the vision reared up again. My chest was still tipped with diamonds. I was walking through windows. She was chewing up the broken litter I left behind.

"I am going," I said. "Let me go."

But she held me down.

"Don't go," she said quickly. "Don't. We have just begun."

I was weakening. My thoughts were whirling pitifully. The pain had kept me strong, and as it left me I began to forget it; I couldn't hold on. I began to wonder if she'd really scalded me with the kettle. I could not remember. To remember this seemed the most important thing in the world. But I was losing the memory. The scalding. The pouring. It began to vanish. I felt like my mind was coming off its hinge, flapping in the breeze, hanging by the hair of my own pain. I wrenched out of her grip.

"He was always in you," I said. "Even more than in me. He wanted you even more. And now he's got you. Get thee behind me!"

I shouted that, grabbed my shirt, and ran through the door throwing it on my body. I got down the stairs and into the kitchen, even, but no matter what I told myself, I couldn't get out the door. It wasn't finished. And she knew I would not leave. Her quiet step was immediately behind me.

"We must take the bread from the oven now," she said.

She was pretending nothing happened. But for the first time I had gotten through some chink she'd left in her darkness. Touched some doubt. Her voice was so low and brittle it cracked off at the end of her sentence.

"Help me, Marie," she said slowly.

But I was not going to help her, even though she had calmly buttoned the back of my shirt up and put the big cloth mittens in my hands for taking out the loaves. I could have bolted for it then. But I didn't. I knew that something was nearing completion. Something was about to happen. My back was a wall of singing flame. I was turning. I watched her take the long fork in one hand, to tap the loaves. In the other hand she gripped the black poker to hook the pans.

"Help me," she said again, and I thought, Yes, this is part

of it. I put the mittens on my hands and swung the door open on its hinges. The oven gaped. She stood back a moment, letting the first blast of heat rush by. I moved behind her. I could feel the heat at my front and at my back. Before, behind. My skin was turning to beaten gold. It was coming quicker than I thought. The oven was like the gate of a personal hell. Just big enough and hot enough for one person, and that was her. One kick and Leopolda would fly in headfirst. And that would be one-millionth of the heat she would feel when she finally collapsed in his hellish embrace.

Saints know these numbers.

She bent forward with her fork held out. I kicked her with all my might. She flew in. But the outstretched poker hit the back wall first, so she rebounded. The oven was not so deep as I had thought.

There was a moment when I felt a sort of thin, hot disappointment, as when a fish slips off the line. Only I was the one going to be lost. She was fearfully silent. She whirled. Her veil had cutting edges. She had the poker in one hand. In the other she held that long sharp fork she used to tap the delicate crusts of loaves. Her face turned upside down on her shoulders. Her face turned blue. But saints are used to miracles. I felt no trace of fear.

If I was going to be lost, let the diamonds cut! Let her eat ground glass!

"Bitch of Jesus Christ!" I shouted. "Kneel and beg! Lick the floor!"

That was when she stabbed me through the hand with the fork, then took the poker up alongside my head, and knocked me out.

It must have been a half an hour later when I came around. Things were so strange. So strange I can hardly tell it for delight at the remembrance. For when I came around this was actually taking place. I was being worshiped. I had somehow gained the altar of a saint.

I was laying back on the stiff couch in the Mother Superior's office. I looked around me. It was as though my deepest dream had come to life. The Sisters of the convent were kneeling to me. Sister Bonaventure. Sister Dympna. Sister Cecilia Saint-Claire. The two French with hands like paddles. They were down on their knees. Black capes were slung over some of their heads. My name was buzzing up and down the room, like a fat autumn fly lighting on the tips of their tongues between Latin, humming up the heavy blood-dark curtains, circling their little cosseted heads. Marie! Marie! A girl thrown in a closet. Who was afraid of a rubber overboot. Who was half overcome. A girl who came in the back door where they threw their garbage. Marie! Who never found the cup. Who had to eat their cold mush. Marie! Leopolda had her face buried in her knuckles. Saint Marie of the Holy Slops! Saint Marie of the Bread Fork! Saint Marie of the Burnt Back and Scalded Butt!

I broke out and laughed.

They looked up. All holy hell burst loose when they saw I'd woke. I still did not understand what was happening. They were watching, talking, but not to me.

"The marks . . ."

"She has her hand closed."

"Je ne peux pas voir."

I was not stupid enough to ask what they were talking about. I couldn't tell why I was lying in white sheets. I couldn't tell why they were praying to me. But I'll tell you this: it seemed entirely natural. It was me. I lifted up my hand as in my dream. It was completely limp with sacredness.

"Peace be with you."

My arm was dried blood from the wrist down to the elbow. And it hurt. Their faces turned like flat flowers of adoration to follow that hand's movements. I let it swing through the air, imparting a saint's blessing. I had practiced. I knew exactly how to act.

They murmured. I heaved a sigh, and a golden beam of light suddenly broke through the clouded window and flooded down directly on my face. A stroke of perfect luck! They had to be convinced.

Leopolda still knelt in the back of the room. Her knuckles were crammed halfway down her throat. Let me tell you, a saint has senses honed keen as a wolf. I knew that she was over my barrel now. How it happened did not matter. The last thing I remembered was how she flew from the oven and stabbed me. That one thing was most certainly true.

"Come forward, Sister Leopolda." I gestured with my heavenly wound. Oh, it hurt. It bled when I reopened the slight heal. "Kneel beside me," I said.

She kneeled, but her voice box evidently did not work, for her mouth opened, shut, opened, but no sound came out. My throat clenched in noble delight I had read of as befitting a saint. She could not speak. But she was beaten. It was in her eyes. She stared at me now with all the deep hate of the wheel of devilish dust that rolled wild within her emptiness.

"What is it you want to tell me?" I asked. And at last she spoke.

"I have told my Sisters of your passion," she managed to choke out. "How the stigmata ... the marks of the nails ... appeared in your palm and you swooned at the holy vision...."

"Yes," I said curiously.

And then, after a moment, I understood.

Leopolda had saved herself with her quick brain. She had witnessed a miracle. She had hid the fork and told this to the others. And of course they believed her, because they never knew how Satan came and went or where he took refuge.

"I saw it from the first," said the large one who put the bread in the oven. "Humility of the spirit. So rare in these girls."

"I saw it too," said the other one with great satisfaction. She sighed quietly. "If only it was me."

Leopolda was kneeling bolt upright, face blazing and twitching, a barely held fountain of blasting poison.

"Christ has marked me," I agreed.

I smiled the saint's smirk into her face. And then I looked at her. That was my mistake.

For I saw her kneeling there. Leopolda with her soul like

a rubber overboot. With her face of a starved rat. With the desperate eyes drowning in the deep wells of her wrongness. There would be no one else after me. And I would leave. I saw Leopolda kneeling within the shambles of her love.

My heart had been about to surge from my chest with the blackness of my joyous heat. Now it dropped. I pitied her. I pitied her. Pity twisted in my stomach like that hook-pole was driven through me. I was caught. It was a feeling more terrible than any amount of boiling water and worse than being forked. Still, still, I could not help what I did. I had already smiled in a saint's mealy forgiveness. I heard myself speaking gently.

"Receive the dispensation of my sacred blood," I whispered.

But there was no heart in it. No joy when she bent to touch the floor. No dark leaping. I fell back into the white pillows. Blank dust was whirling through the light shafts. My skin was dust. Dust my lips. Dust the dirty spoons on the ends of my feet.

Rise up! I thought. Rise up and walk! There is no limit to this dust!

Catherine Shaw

Wild Women of Borneo

... was what a red-faced, stamping
nun called the eighth grade girls
who bleached and teased their hair
into moonlit jungles,
whose ripe mango breasts
pressed against
their uniform jumpers,
whose pierced ears glittered
with bright primeval hoops.
Wild Women of Borneo:
barefoot at the Christmas mixer,
rocking and rolling
in shameless ecstasy.
Wild Women of Borneo:
smearing their cheeks with rouge!
Hidden behind my books,
I watched them smoking
in the schoolyard,
their private rite.
Singing of the Virgin's power,
I saw them primp at holy mass,
their minds on
no immaculate conceptions.

They favored white lipstick,
black slips,
a perfume called *Tabu*—
I tell you, I studied those girls
the way I studied my catechism,
reading them for questions,
memorizing their answers
and never quite solving
their glorious mysteries.
O Wild Women of Borneo,
that red-faced, stamping nun
who gave me As and praises
never guessed
with what transfixion
my heart attended you—
or with what unrest.

Lin Florinda Colavin

The Calling

The only sound was the scratch of pencils on paper. Lupe's fingers slipped the note into my cupped hand. I brought it slowly back to my desk. A quick glance to the front of the room told me Sister Euphricine's head was buried in the math book propped up on her desk. Positioning my own book so that it made a screen, I carefully began to unfold the note.

Lupe and I were seniors at Sacred Heart; four years of experience with Sister Euphricine had taught us all that extreme caution was needed in this class.

"Dear Ginny," Lupe had printed in big clear letters, "can you stay after school? We can clean Sister Euphricine's blackboards—see if she's got any candy stashed away. What do you say?" She had ended it with a huge question mark.

In Sister Euphricine's room you couldn't even cough without her giving a ferocious look. No one dared make a sound. No one, that is, but Lupe. She'd cough, clear her throat, fuss around. When Sister would look up furiously, Lupe would smile this great big smile, and offer to clean the blackboards; Sister wouldn't say a word. Maybe that was one of the reasons I liked Lupe so much. She had guts.

Sister Euphricine was the strictest nun in the entire school. She must have been at least eighty years old. Her face was all crinkled up; she walked with a cane. She was pudgy and her white habit, which all the other nuns kept immaculately clean, was full of spots and always off kilter. Everyone knew she had diabetes. All of the other nuns watched her to make sure she stayed on her diet.

Sister's room was in the corner of the second floor of the plain brick building that had replaced the original school building built in 1890. We were juniors when Lupe had discovered Sister E's candy stash the first time she offered to clean the classroom. Sister left the top drawer of her desk slightly ajar. Lupe told me she just couldn't help but see the box of chocolates sitting there. She ate three. Sister never said anything. From then on Lupe always offered to clean the room. All of the other girls thought she was crazy.

Lupe lived in East Los Angeles with her grandmother and her mother. She took the bus to school every morning. Her mother had been sick for a really long time and it was during high school that Lupe had actually lived with her. Before that she had lived in a place for kids run by the nuns. I lived with my mother and father and younger sister about a mile and a half from school in another part of L.A. called Lincoln Heights. The gangs in our area painted their insignias on the buildings. My mother did not believe it was safe for us to take the bus, so almost every day she picked us up after school.

Whenever I could, I stayed to help Lupe so that we could spend extra time together. It meant walking home, but it was worth it. Sister Euphricine would totter back to the convent leaving the two of us alone in the empty classroom.

"I can stay—lets do it." I wrote on Lupe's note. Carefully I began my slow swing backward to Lupe's waiting hand. At that moment Sister Euphricine looked up from her book directly at us. Heart pounding, I quickly bent over my notebook and began to write furiously.

Suddenly there was a crash. Sister Euphricine's trig book pitched onto the desk, exposing the paperback she had clutched in her hand. A half-naked woman sprawled across the cover of a murder mystery. There was a moment of stunned silence.

"Get back to work!" Sister thundered. No one dared laugh out loud. We bent our heads over our books as the room began to shake with smothered giggles. As soon as the bell rang, we grabbed our books and bolted out of the door. In the hall we exploded in shrieks of laughter. Everyone, that is, but Lupe; Lupe stayed behind to ask if we could clean the room.

"It's all set." Lupe patted me on the back out in the hall. "I'll see you here after eighth period."

Lupe and I had met as freshmen. It seemed as if we had always known each other. It was hard to believe that in a few months we'd graduate. I didn't like to think about it.

There were 400 girls at our school. Boys were not allowed on campus—not even inside the gate. The only males at the school were the janitor, Mr. Davis, and Father Malloy. I liked it, though. I didn't even mind the gray pleated skirts and white blouses we wore every day.

The nuns who taught us at Sacred Heart were Dominicans. I tried to imagine what they'd look like without the white coif and black veil around their faces. Some of the old ones like Sister E had bits of hair sticking out, so I knew they didn't shave their heads. I liked the way their white habits swayed when they walked, but it was hard to imagine they had real bodies under all of that material.

After eighth period Sister Euphricine hobbled off, sternly reminding us to make sure the door was shut and locked when we finished. Left alone we happily began cleaning the room.

"Do you think she left that book in her desk?" I asked.

"Are you kidding?" Lupe laughed. "She's got that thing tucked away in her habit." She opened the top drawer of Sister's desk. There was the candy. Even though I'd done this with Lupe lots of times, I still felt we were committing a sacrilege.

"See, I told you. No book." Lupe beamed. "Would you like

a chocolate, my dear?" She whisked the lid off the box and with one hand behind her back, offered me the chocolate.

"Don't mind if I do." I never could bring myself to take more than one. Lupe and I sat side by side on the desk top and savored the candy, taking small bites to make it last.

"Do you think Tony is picking up Ruthie today?" I asked, licking the last of the chocolate from my fingers. Ruthie was lucky enough to have a boyfriend.

"I don't know—she didn't say anything to me." She pointed to the street below. A riot of gleaming chrome on low-slung cars sat double parked along the narrow street between the school and the church. Every day after school boys waited to pick up girls. Once a month or so one of the nuns would go out and shoo them away. The next day an announcement would come over the PA reminding everyone that boys were not allowed to pick students up after school. For a few days they waited around the corner, but nothing kept the congestion of boys away for long.

They were handsome boys, dark with slicked-back hair. Some wore their white tee shirts with the sleeves rolled up, a pack of cigarettes tucked in the cuff. They eyed every girl who walked by. If a girl walked too close, they'd lean out the window and call in a low voice, "Hey, honey, you want a ride?"

When this happened to me, I'd keep walking, my heart pounding in my chest—my eyes straight ahead. My body felt penetrated by the open stares of their dark eyes, although there was a part of me that wanted to roar away with one of them, cuddled up close, his arm around my shoulders. But I was terrified I'd never get back.

"Do you think Tony's cute?" I asked Lupe as I watched Ruthie get into his 1952 blue-and-white Chevy.

"Yeah, I guess. Why else would she go with him? She says she likes his car, anyway."

Lupe didn't seem to care about boys one way or the other anymore. If they asked her if she wanted to ride, she gave them the same big smile she gave Sister Euphricine and said, "No, thank you." She used to go to the school dances, but lately she always seemed preoccupied. When I asked her if she was going or not, she'd say, "They're just a waste of time." Something was changing about Lupe, but there seemed to be no way to ask her what it was.

I went to the dances, every one of them. I hated them, but I went. The guys who drove the hot cars never asked me to dance. The only boys who asked were the ones who wore glasses and had crew cuts. They didn't know how to dance and always stepped on my toes. I could never think of anything to say and they all seemed to expect to dance close. It was a relief each time the music stopped. But then I'd be left standing along the wall trying to pretend that I didn't mind waiting for someone else to ask me to dance.

It was at a dance that Lupe and I actually became friends. We were freshmen and we knew each other, but we weren't good friends. We had both been dropped off at the same time. There were a lot of guys waiting around outside like they always did. I paid my money and went in by myself. The auditorium was dark and a three-piece band was playing a slow Elvis song. It was packed and hot in there, but only a few couples were dancing. Everyone else was just standing around.

I didn't see anyone I knew. I couldn't really see without my glasses, and I never wore glasses to a dance. Somehow I tripped right over Lupe's foot.

She grabbed me and I grabbed for the wall. We both missed and ended up in a heap on the floor, with a circle of people around us. I was too embarrassed to notice who helped me up. A Sister came over and asked us if we were all right. I escaped to the bathroom.

Lupe was already there. One look at each other and we burst into fits of laughter. We couldn't stop. Someone came in and asked what we were laughing about. We laughed harder. We had to lean on each other to keep from falling down.

When we finally stopped, it took us ten minutes to get our mascara and lipstick back on straight. As we came out of the bathroom, two guys with slicked-back hair came in our

direction. The band was playing "Rock Around the Clock."
They were going to ask us to dance. My heart started pounding. Suddenly Lupe and I started talking real fast to each
other. Even when the guys came right up to us, we didn't
stop talking or look their way. Finally they went away.

Nobody else tried to ask us after that. We discovered that
the room next to the auditorium was open. From inside this
room we could still hear the band. We danced every fast
dance together. After a while we were hot and sweaty so we
sat down on the floor in our best dresses and talked. When
we heard the band leader say that it was the last dance, Lupe
stood up and held out her hand. "Can I have this dance?"

"Certainly." We danced cheek to cheek with our arms
around each other, just the way the boys always wanted to
dance. I could feel my breasts rubbing against Lupe. I started
to giggle.

"What is the problem?" Lupe demanded, sounding like Sister Euphricine. We both burst into giggles, but we didn't stop
dancing close. I could feel myself close against Lupe's breasts
and stomach, her eyelashes on my cheek until the song
ended.

Since that night, Lupe's been my best friend. We always
take a long time cleaning Sister Euphricine's room. This time
it was after four when we finished.

"Lupe, I've got to get home. I've got trig to do and piano
practice and Latin homework besides."

"Boy, I'm glad I don't have to take a language. I hate languages." Lupe sighed as we walked outside.

"But you're going to need a language if you go to college."

"Yeah, but I don't know if I'm going to college, anyway."
Lupe shrugged her shoulders. Only a few of us seniors were
planning to go to college. Most of the others were getting
married or looking for jobs. Lupe never said anything about
what she was going to do after high school.

Three of the seniors had applied to be Dominican Sisters.
Our homeroom teacher explained that being a nun was the
highest calling God could give a woman; getting married was
next, and last was to be single. I didn't think I wanted to be

a nun—I hoped that wasn't my calling—but I didn't want to end up on the bottom of the list, either.

Once one of the sisters had taken me to her chapel. It was very small, decorated in blue and gold. Double rows of pews faced each other, and a simple altar with a white linen cloth stood in front of a round stained-glass window. The afternoon sun coming through the window illuminated the entire space. One of the sisters knelt in the first row of pews nearest the altar, praying. It was so holy and quiet and she seemed to be bathed in a golden light; in that moment I wished with all my heart that I could be one of them.

When Lupe called me at 7:30 that night I had just finished my trig.

"Ginny, guess what?" Lupe's voice had a strange thin pitch to it I'd never heard before. "I've been accepted to the convent!"

"You what?"

"I've been accepted to the convent!"

"But you didn't even tell me you'd applied." I was in shock. "How come you never told me anything? I thought we were best friends?"

"We are best friends. Silly; I didn't want to say anything until I knew for sure. I didn't want everybody talking about it."

"But I wouldn't have told anyone."

"I know, but I couldn't say anything until I had been accepted. They sent me a list telling me everything I'm supposed to bring. Listen to this:

5 pairs of muslin sheets
10 pairs of wool undershirts
10 cotton underpants."

I couldn't concentrate on what Lupe was saying. I didn't want her to go away. Maybe I had a vocation, too. I could apply and Lupe and I would be dressed in long white habits, praying side by side every morning in the chapel. We'd teach sweet little kids all day, and in the late afternoon we'd walk arm in arm in the convent garden and relax. After dinner, when the sisters have recreation, we'd sit laughing and talking quietly as we embroidered altar linens. At night we'd sleep next to each other, curtains drawn around our separate beds.

Lupe broke into my daydream; her voice had dropped to almost a whisper. "We even have to bring twenty boxes of Kotex; no tampons allowed."

"Lupe. I didn't know you wanted to teach school."

"I don't."

"But if you become a Dominican you'll have to teach."

"I'm not going to be a Dominican. I've been accepted by the Poor Clares."

"The Poor Clares? The Poor Clares are cloistered nuns." My throat felt like it was closing up. The Poor Clares never set foot outside the convent grounds. They prayed day and night every day of the year. They didn't wear shoes; they couldn't talk. Only their families could visit them and then they had to talk to them through iron bars as if they were in prison. Going into the cloister was about the same as dying.

"Lupe, how could you? You're crazy. What will you do there for the rest of your life?"

"Pray." She laughed. "What else. Ginny, I really think that this is what God wants me to do."

I wanted to scream at her, What about me? How can you do this to me? But if God wanted her to do this, there was nothing for me to say.

"I'm glad for you, Lupe," I managed to say. My heart felt wedged in my throat. "I've got to do my Latin. I'll see you tomorrow."

That night I pulled the covers over my head and curled down into chilly sheets, feeling colder than I remembered feeling ever before. When I finally fell asleep, I dreamed that Lupe and I had gone into the cloister.

When I awakened, I dressed quickly as I could, and got my mother to take us to school early. I found Lupe in the school office. I dragged her out into the hall. "I had this terrible dream. I dreamt I was a cloistered nun. I thought you were praying next to me, but when you turned in my direction, there was no one inside the habit. It was a nightmare. It was so horrible."

"Oh, Ginny, you're so silly." She laughed. It was the second time in two days she'd called me silly. She didn't understand. How could she decide to go away? We were best friends. Tears choked my throat.

"Did you get all those trig problems done?" she asked, as if this wasn't the worst day of my life. "You want to go over them?"

"Lupe, I've got to go to my locker. I'll see you first period." I rushed up the stairs, blinking back tears.

I didn't see Sister Euphricine until I smacked into her. I fell forward; she clung fiercely to the banister, steadying herself as best she could.

"What are you doing! Can't you look where you are going!"

I couldn't say anything. I was crying too hard.

"Well, are you hurt?"

"No." I buried my face in my hands. "I'm sorry. I'm really sorry."

"You need to look where you are going. I could have been hurt. What's the matter with you, anyway?" she demanded sternly.

"Nothing, nothing. I'm all right."

"Well, if there's nothing wrong, why are you crying?"

I couldn't speak.

"Get up and give me a hand." She leaned heavily on my arm. "Now, walk me to my room."

I did as I was told. Once inside she shut and locked the door. She sat in silence at her desk until I stopped crying.

"All right, now you can tell me why you are so upset."

"Lupe is going into the cloister. I'll never see her again." The words rushed out of my mouth.

"Oh." She paused. "Lupe. I see." Sister's voice was surprisingly quiet. The old nun looked out the window. "I remember when I was a girl, I had a best friend, Bertha. We spent all our time together; we even studied for the University together.

"One day she told me she was getting married. Her fiancé was from another town. After she left, I never saw her again."

I was shocked. This crumpled-up old woman had once been a young girl. Had she giggled and talked far into the night, the way Lupe and I did?

"Didn't you feel terrible when she left?"

"Yes." She nodded slowly. "I can still remember how I cried. My mother didn't know what to do with me. I didn't think I'd ever get over being sad."

"I'll never get over this. It's never going to be all right with Lupe gone. No one can ever take her place."

"That's true. No one will take Lupe's place." Sister Euphricine's voice was solemn.

I was surprised. I had expected her to contradict me. Quiet filled up the corners of the empty room.

It no longer mattered where I was or who I was with. I began to sob harsh racking sobs.

The bell rang for the first period. Out in the hallway girls bustled into classrooms. Sister Euphricine reached over and touched my shoulder.

"I don't have class until second period, Ginny. You may stay here. I'll tell Sister in the office that you are not well." She limped to the door and then turned. "Ginny, it takes time to heal." She closed the door softly behind her.

After my sobbing stopped I laid my head on the cold slick desk top and watched the clouds. A brisk wind scurried them along, speeding them to unknown destinies. I watched them drift away until they disappeared into the vast blue sky.

Jeanne Schinto

Before Sewing
One Must Cut

It was 1968, and I hadn't been paying a bit of attention. I was fifteen years old.

Then suddenly Mr. Perrotti, the chief groundskeeper for the church, who lived on church property with his family—whose two daughters actually *swam* with the nuns, regularly saw nuns in *bathing suits*, in bathing *caps* (with chin straps, they reported), and, God knows, so might have he—walked out.

It was a Saturday afternoon lecture in the high-school gymnasium, and he did not leave quietly.

Father Daniel DeCicco was speaking about the Vietnam War in his youthful singsong that made me realize he was really just an altar boy who had grown up. The gym was filled with Sister Corita banners, someone's private collection of colors, lent to the school for the occasion, flying high above our heads. My eye had been caught by them. I wasn't listening to the small, dark, lean Father DeCicco any more closely than I listened to him in church—that is, for the voice rather than the actual words, except when he threw in some Beatles or Monkees lyrics ("I'm a Believer . . ."), which he did none too adroitly: it always sounded so adultishly forced. Then, the next thing I knew, Mr. Perrotti was out in the aisle yelling and shaking his fist at him.

Mr. Perrotti was related, though only by marriage, to a famous football player, but he himself was big. He looked as if he were wearing shoulder pads underneath his clothing, though his pants drooped in the seat. He was the bus driver I'd had from kindergarten through the eighth grade. He, in addition to the groundswork, general maintenance, caretaking, gravedigging, etc., drove us children to school; drove the old nuns to the dentist in their gray station wagon (when a younger nun wasn't free to do it); drove the priests' gray Cadillac to the shop for a tune-up.

He also seemed to me to be my second father (even before my first one passed away). It had nothing to do with my mother. It had only to do with me. As a child, I had admired him. He seemed always to make it a point to tell the truth, or at least to tell whatever he was thinking. He had been in the Service with my real father and had shown me a snapshot of my father and himself at the Air Force barracks, bath towels wrapped around their middles, nothing else, both of them eating dripping ice-cream cones in the North Carolina heat.

He'd shown me this to tell me something about my father, something a father wouldn't necessarily have told his daughter, himself. This was when my father was ill and looking about a hundred years old.

Mr. Perrotti, whose first name was Lester (anglicized from Leonardo), had taken a special liking to me when I was a playmate of his daughters. Of all their friends I knew he liked me the best. I could tell that he liked the way I acted. He definitely liked the way I got his jokes. He probably felt sorry for me, too, now that my father was dead. I also knew he expected no less of me. He would say to his girls, one a year younger than I, one a year older: "Hey, why can't you two do like Maria?" He still called me Maria, even though Juliet Leeuwen had been given the lead in our eighth-grade production of *The Sound of Music*. Two years later he was still trying to tell me I should have had it. (I'd stopped reminding him that I'd been too shy even to audition.) This was mostly when I saw him at the church or somewhere else uptown, not at his house, because I didn't go over there to hang around with his daughters much anymore. We were starting to have different friends. Overweight ("good eaters"), in the "B" track, and one of them with a bad case of psoriasis, Paula and Joanie Perrotti now tried to make up for their shortcomings with loudness, and I'd grown embarrassed for them.

Mr. Perrotti was wearing a suit on the day of his outburst. Strange sight, him in a suit? Not so strange: he wore one every Sunday to the ten o'clock Mass. The anger wasn't unfamiliar to him, either, but his target was a new one. The young Father DeCicco stopped talking and lowered his prematurely bald head.

Sonny Perrotti, the chief lifeguard at the beach for three summers running, stood in the aisle with his father, looking solemn and proud, hands behind his back. He was the Perrottis' beloved only son. Every summer in his orange bathing suit he boxed boys' ears and made them eat their beach cards. Girls liked him, but not dozens of them—only one at a time. On his breaks, he did not show off for a crowd with the rescue surfboard; he merely mooned (or argued) in the shade of the pavilion with his latest. Then, back up into the chair to blow his whistle every five minutes.

Sonny did not look at all surprised by his father's rage. He wore the same self-satisfied expression as the ushers in church, who stood along the side walls during Mass, waiting to rush up the aisles with their long-handled collection baskets and sweep them under everybody's nose.

Mr. Perrotti kept shouting, walking backward and forward down the center aisle made by rows of metal folding chairs. He looked like a very large bird, upset. That is, he looked as if at any moment he'd sprout wings and fly around the place. Or else slap someone right across the face. He had a strange, mottled skin, like camouflage, on his own face. He claimed it was a tropical skin problem he'd picked up during his years in the Service. I had no reason to believe that he was lying, though I remember once my father had belittled that line. It was also my father who had told me Mr. Perrotti had never quite got over the fact that he hadn't seen action.

"Action," "Missing in Action," "POWs," "this country," Mr. Perrotti was saying now. I had an aisle seat and looked up at him, into one of his armpits, as he flailed his arms, and I caught a scent of after-shave lotion. Sitting on the aisle in class, when a nun walked by, you could look up and see underneath her cardboard bib: her neck, the outline of her breasts covered by minutely layered folds of coarse black cloth (nuns were braless, it was plain), and catch a smell of her, of nuns, of harsh soap, of scrubbing, of trying to be scentless and failing. There were both opened and unopened bottles of after-shave in our medicine cabinet at home. Would my mother eventually throw them into the trash can, or would I?

"Anytime, day or night," Mr. Perrotti said. He had a pointy chin and seemed to be pointing with it as well as with his finger at Father DeCicco. "Right now, go over there," "me and my only son," "we're ready," "our country, God bless it!" Sonny stood tall, legs apart, hands still locked behind him.

When the old Father Brumley, our pastor, tried to calm Mr. Perrotti, with his wrinkled, reasoning hands, he only managed to fan Mr. Perrotti's ire all the more. Now he was talking about "faggots," "free lovers," "Greenwich Village," and "mixed marriage."

Father DeCicco listened with his head bowed. Or else he might have been praying.

He was a handsome priest. We girls, including Mr. Perrotti's own two daughters, called him, gigglingly, "cute." Actually, he looked exactly like an Italian-American movie actor, but with less hair—one of the young, tragic-eyed ones, like Al Pacino in *The Godfather, Part I*, only we wouldn't know that for another few years.

At my father's funeral (it had been earlier that same fall), I was offered a job after school and on weekends by one of the other priests in the parish, the fastidious Father Gerard. When he asked me, I was standing at the muddy gravesite, a red carnation in my hand. Caroline Castiglione's father, the undertaker, had handed it to me, wearing a rubbery smile, surprisingly sincere. I had on an old black skirt and runs in both stockings from having caught them on fallen twigs I'd stepped over on the cemetery path. As we spoke, others were talking, too, and I had to ask him to repeat what he had said to me. For one, my Aunt Janey was complaining loudly about how the cemetery was kept up. And why shouldn't artificial flowers be allowed? Why not? She wanted to know. She wanted an answer from somebody and she wanted it now.

The Knights of Columbus paid the bulk of our funeral bills. Money was a problem. My mother also needed time alone; with a job I'd be out of her way. So, one day shortly after Mr. Perrotti's demonstration, I finally took Father Gerard up on his offer, and walked up the stone steps of the rectory to pay him a visit.

The church, the rectory (where the priests lived), and the elementary school I had attended were all on a choice piece of property in town, on the main avenue. The high school, the convent, and the Perrottis' house were all out in the back country, on a former estate complete with the pool where the nuns swam, stables (empty), and a rose garden with sculpture, where the Perrotti daughters and I had liked to play hide-and-seek when we were younger. The Bishop of Bridgeport, an egg-shaped man, had consecrated it all, including the Perrottis' house, garage, truck, and two cars—one of them a Mustang convertible that Sonny sometimes drove.

The kitchen of the rectory was a clean, orderly place of no raised voices, just like the rest of the house. The back door opened out onto a walled, well-tended garden of green and gold and flickering black shadows. I could see only a corner of it from where I stood in the doorway leading into the kitchen from the long front hallway.

Father Gerard stood beside me, knotting and unknotting his arms. He made me think of pure intelligence, a bolt of it, like the angels, only much less calm. The hair of the slim, perpetually nervous priest was white, ethereally, though he probably was no older than my father would have been. His legs were long and thin and seemed to be always in motion, bending like straps, and the black priest-pants he wore were surprisingly tight. I stood self-consciously in my blue-gray school uniform, and he did the talking for both of us.

"There's a way to a successful interview, for a job, or for school, or for anything, don't you think? When you go to your college interviews, the admissions officer will ask you, 'Well, are you a good student or a bad student?' And if you say, 'I'm a good student, Father!' won't *you* sound conceited. By the same token, I *don't* believe you'll be wanting to say, 'Oh, I'm a bad student!' So what do you do?"

A Hispanic woman was down on her knees, scrubbing the kitchen floor with a brush. Father Gerard introduced me to her: "Maria Cristina," rolling his r's and moving his hands as if he were conducting a choir.

Maria Cristina stood—a small, erect young woman, very calm. Her face was smooth and brown, her smile simple and relaxed. She dried her hands on her apron, looking as contented as a businessman's wife. Immediately I envied her.

Rocking back and forth on his heels, Father Gerard remarked that Maria Cristina had worked for them six years. Smiling and coloring with embarrassment, the little woman rubbed the counter with a cloth, looking almost saintly, actually dignified in her menial work. I thought: she must be beyond any sinful passions of her own. I also thought: I should take my cues from her.

Father Gerard must have been asking me for a second time if I wanted some tea, and finally I heard him and said yes.

He spoke to Maria Cristina in a histrionic Spanish, and they laughed together about his inability to put a tea tray together. I looked at his long white fingers, the fingers of a pampered man. At last she got things down from the cupboards for him, using a step-stool to get the extra sugar from the cannister to refill the bowl.

I saw that Maria Cristina was wearing little pink Capezio flats, the kind that everybody, including myself, was wearing lately—when I wasn't in my school uniform, that is. They made her feet look attractive and feminine. Her fingernails were painted, too, I noticed as I watched her put two fragile-looking cups and saucers on a tray.

Everything is going to be all right, I thought.

I was given the job of answering the door and the phone after Father Brumley's secretaries had gone home—that is, on weekdays from five to nine—and also on both weekend days, from one to nine. The main reason for my being there was in case the hospital called to ask for a priest to give a patient the Sacrament of Extreme Unction. There was always a priest in the house, on call, and I was to buzz that priest's bedroom on the telephone intercom and tell him what room in the hospital to go to.

This sounds exciting, maybe, but most of the hours I spent there were extremely boring, endlessly long, and fraught with temptations, despite my pile of homework. People seemed hardly ever to die, or if they did, they did not call for a priest.

On Saturdays, the priest on call also would tell me his confessional number so I could run and get him out of there, if necessary. That only happened once, and it was Father DeCicco on whose cubicle door I had to knock. For a small man he moved quickly, taking long, powerful strides. His black cassock swept the dusty sidewalks between the church and the rectory's front door. I had to run to keep up with him.

He unzipped his cassock right there in the rectory's front hallway and stepped out of it before running with it over his arm upstairs to his room. "Thanks, hon'," he threw back over his shoulder.

Underneath the cassock he was wearing the regulation black priest-pants and a white V-necked undershirt, and he had scuffed black loafers on his feet.

He sped away in his electric-blue Volkswagen Beetle.

I sat at a desk in a bay window in a room at the front of the rectory. It was filled with exotic knickknacks that Father

Gerard, Father Brumley, and others had brought back from
their travels all over the world. Out the window was my
world—by that I mean Main Street.

Sometimes people came to the rectory door, looking for
a handout. I was to keep them waiting outside on the doorstep and buzz the priest on call. He would give the person
the prescribed amount of money in a manila envelope. People, women mostly, sometimes came with suitcases, requesting Father DeCicco. I tried so hard to hear what they
were saying (and, alternately, tried to ignore the temptation
to listen). They would sit together in one of the parlors off
the main hallway with the door closed. Afterwards, Father
DeCicco would walk the woman to her car, his arm around
her waist. I watched the arm of Father DeCicco encircling
the waist of Teresa Masters for fifteen minutes one day. She
leaned into his shoulder, crying. Her husband was the police-
man who crossed people at the corner by the bank with the
clock.

On the wall directly across from my desk there was a modern painting of Christ on the cross: an aerial view; the paint-
er's eye had been only about three feet above the crown of
thorns. I liked this painting a lot, not only because it was as
soothingly familiar as my bedroom wallpaper by now, but
also because I knew it meant something I did not quite understand—that particular angle of vision meant something
special, I mean. And I caught myself wondering if even the
priests knew exactly what it meant. One day I was idly studying the painting once again, when Father Gerard flew into
the room, saying with his arm thrust out toward me: "Now,
that's 'demure.' "

He had Sonny Perrotti in tow. Sonny, who'd shaved his
head for a swim meet with Precious Blood, who'd shaved *all*
his body hair—*everywhere*, according to his sisters—was
being prepped for the College Boards by Father Gerard on
weekends, as a special favor to the whole Perrotti family.

Sonny rubbed his nose with both hands, abruptly, like a
fly. He looked particularly insect-like without any hair.

" 'Demure!' " Father Gerard intoned. " 'Sedate in manner

or behavior; reserved; feigning modesty or shyness. See synonyms at *shy.*' " Then he turned on his heel, and Sonny followed, still scratching himself, and giving the impression that he was being led by the ear, although Father Gerard had not touched him.

Later that same day, after Sonny had gone home, I could hear Father DeCicco and the old Father Brumley in the dining room, chatting over a late Saturday lunch. They exchanged witty stories, using many voices, and asked each other demonstratively for seconds on the food that Maria Cristina had so lovingly prepared.

I liked these two priests, liked them far better than Father Gerard, even though he was the one who had hired me. I couldn't ever imagine telling my troubles to him. I might have told them to Father Brumley, but would he understand? He might even fall asleep. It could be only Father DeCicco, if that time ever came.

Father DeCicco not only had many who sought his counselling; he had many personal friends, too. He got by far the most phone calls of anyone, often long-distance. There was no time he considered the phone an intrusion. He never said, "Hold my calls for the rest of the afternoon," the way Father Gerard did, pressing on his temples. Unlike Father Gerard in another instance, he never made sure that I had hung up my extension before he started speaking.

I had the feeling that Father DeCicco and Father Gerard did not like each other. I had the feeling that Father Gerard had taken Mr. Perrotti's side on the afternoon of the anti-war lecture. Father Gerard hated Communists. Once, he told me a long story of how one single Communist Party member at an American high school had convinced nearly his entire class to join his subversive efforts. (I couldn't help being impressed by such a persuasive young person.) Perhaps Father Gerard actually hated Father DeCicco. I thought: I will have to protect him.

While Fathers DeCicco and Brumley lunched, Father Gerard, who'd retired upstairs, suddenly ran downstairs and

flung himself around in the hallway. He was crying and bearing news that he'd heard on his radio:

"An electric fan! An electrocution!" He put his face in his
hands.

"He said it would kill him if he ever had to leave the
monastery, and so it has," Father Brumley said in quiet
wonder.

"Did he really say that?" Father DeCicco asked in his boyish
voice.

"He did." Father Brumley coughed respectfully.

December, 1968, and Thomas Merton was dead, only it
would be over a decade before I would truly learn who he
was, reading about his dissolution, conversion, subsequent faith,
subsequent doubts in books from a secondhand bookstore.

Because I spent so much time at the rectory, next door to
the church, I stopped going to Mass, as if the long hours and
close proximity made up for my absence. Because all of the
priests heard my voice on the telephone intercom, disembod-
ied, and (I felt sure) could recognize it as me sight unseen,
I stopped going to confession. I planned to have a lengthy
one somewhere else—in Rowayton or Milford—someday. As
soon as I learned to drive and got my license I would go. (I
walked to the rectory; it wasn't very far from my house.)

Maria Cristina lived close by, too, and though we never
saw each other except at the rectory, we became friends. We
devised a little language we both could understand, and she
fed me things. When I learned that Maria Cristina had three
children at home, her being at the rectory made less sense
to me. Who was taking care of them? They took care of each
other, she told me.

Maria Cristina and I sat around the kitchen table and
smoked. Supplying myself with cigarettes was an endless
problem, due to the expense. I gave my mother the money
I made here, and I certainly couldn't bring myself to bum
endlessly from the hardworking Maria Cristina.

I took to sneaking upstairs and searching the rooms of the

priests who smoked. (Father Gerard actually was the only one: I used the forays as an excuse to snoop in the non-smokers' rooms as well.) I knew who was home and who wasn't: they all told me, so I'd know whether to buzz their rooms or just take messages. Sometimes, especially on Saturday nights after Maria Cristina had gone home, I was the only one in the whole place. Even the priest on call would be out, though he would have given me the number where he might be reached.

I crept up the red-carpeted stairway one Saturday evening. And be assured, there was no reason for me to be up on the second floor of this place: the ladies' room which Maria Cristina and I used was off the kitchen. If caught, I had no excuse whatsoever. None except that I might have heard voices (preferably celestial) or smelled smoke, I suppose. Even so, I regularly took my chances, as on this night, when, with pounding heart, I pushed open the unlatched door of Father DeCicco's room.

I found, quite simply, the usual mess: pajamas on the unmade bed, underwear in a circle on the Oriental rug, packets of Carnation Slender (later, I would learn he was so thin because he fasted for peace on liquids-only for three out of the five weekdays), and other signs of life. The unusual item was on his desk: a bonus—an unfinished letter written in his own scribbly hand. Did I try to resist reading it? I wish I had; the words shocked me:

I pray you will trust your instincts and lean into this. That you will permit it to cut you, heal you, and cut you again. That you will stare at it into its own center. And that you will accept the faith that you will find there. Accept it because there won't be anything else, and because you will know that the absence of anything else is no more a void than death is an ending. You must accept who you are and what has happened to you.

I put the letter down and closed the door, and went downstairs. I hadn't recognized the name on the letter. Why did I feel that the words should have been written to me? I sat for a long time without moving before I lit the cigarette I'd taken from Father Gerard's room. It was a very expensive cigarette wrapped in pink paper from a box of multicolored ones: a brand called Nat Sherman. A few years later, I would pass that tobacco store on a stifling hot day in New York, but by then I would have already quit smoking.

When Sonny arrived the next Saturday afternoon (for his coaching, I thought), he wasn't alone. There was Mr. Perrotti, with a sad-eyed wink for me, and Mrs. Perrotti, too. She was softly crying, dabbing her eyes with a well-used Kleenex, and would not look at me. Nor would Sonny, who kept his hands locked in front of his genitals, like a prisoner in handcuffs.

Mr. Perrotti, like a man with his hat in his hand, asked for Father Gerard. I buzzed the priest's room and led the Perrottis into one of the parlors. Then, before I sat down at my desk, the doorbell rang once more. It was Sandra Czezanski, with her parents, and her face blotchy from crying. She was a short girl with large breasts, in my class at the high school. When Father Gerard came swiftly down the hallway, he herded them into the same parlor with the Perrotti family.

I listened hard and learned that Sandra was pregnant. It seemed very important to everyone that the conception had taken place on the darkened steps behind the backdrop at the last C.Y.O. dance. Father DeCicco was in charge of those dances and asked only that couples refrain from lying down, whatever else they were doing. But it seemed that though Sandra had not lain down, still she had got "knocked up," to use the words of her own father. "That's what happens when you let a guy in a black dress give your kids sex education," Sandra's father said.

Sandra was leaving for Puerto Rico the next day for an abortion. What her parents wanted to know was if she would be able to confess immediately after the procedure and still be forgiven. Her father was a doctor and knew someone down there who would perform the abortion. Her mother

was going down with her. And if Sonny ever went near Sandra again, after her return, he would have his two legs broken, Mr. Perrotti offered.

Father Gerard hedged. He said he'd think about it and would
provide an answer for them when Sandra and her mother got
back. But Dr. Czezanski told the priest he didn't quite understand. They were offering to pay his way down there, to accom-
pany the women, to give absolution to Sandra right there on
the spot. A lengthy silence followed. Then Dr. Czezanski spoke:
"Aw, Christmas! Will you give the girl a break?"

"I'm trying to think of a way, Doctor, believe me," Father
Gerard said evenly.

"Well, try harder. Isn't there some Supreme Court to go
to?"

"Well, there's the Vatican, but I wouldn't get them involved
if I were you. They aren't known for their lightning dispatch.
Besides, they aren't likely to be as 'intrigued' as I am by your
sheer audacity."

It was finally decided by Dr. Czezanski that "some Puerto
Rican" would be found on the island to absolve the girl.

The Perrottis stayed on after the Czezanskis left. After a
while, there was even some laughter, but the voices all were
low; I couldn't make out any of the words. Then the phone
rang and I had to tell Father Brumley that his reservation for
four at Sherwood's had been confirmed, and when I looked
again, the parlor door was open and the Perrottis were gone.

The next Sunday, Mr. Perrotti and Sonny walked out on
Father DeCicco for the second time. But this was a different
item entirely from the walkout on the lecture in the gymnasium. First, this was during his sermon in church; and second,
a few other men followed. They all stood outside, having a
loud discussion as the Mass continued on inside. Father Gerard went out the rectory door to go over to speak with
them, his black dress whipping in the wind. He wore no coat,
and he was smiling.

At school, Sonny Perrotti started saying hello to me. "You

gonna be my friend now?" he asked. "Sure," I said, walking backward to my locker, a ridiculous grin on my face. He was holding a clutch purse—Sandra's; she was in a nearby classroom locked in conversation with the somber Sister Bonaventure. I suddenly hated myself.

When Sonny came in for his next appointment with Father Gerard, he slouched down in a chair in my office and asked me how it was going. I told him that I knew about Sandra's abortion. "Oh, that, yeah," he said, momentarily confused, rubbing his jaw, like a prizefighter. "Who told you?" he asked cautiously.

"I heard through the parlor door."

"Figures," he said, satisfied. He hummed awhile, then asked: "You like working here?"

"I like some of the priests. I like Father DeCicco."

"He's a pansy," Sonny laughed.

"No, he's not."

"He's a faggot."

"He's not."

"He's a Commie."

"He isn't."

Sonny stood up and came very close to me, his belt buckle to my nose. Then he pushed his face into mine. I tried to push him away. He caught my arm, but I didn't let up until he did.

The following day, after Mass, Mr. Perrotti knocked out Father DeCicco. One punch was thrown, on the front steps of the church. You're no father of mine, Lester Perrotti, I thought; I called the police. As luck would have it, it was Teresa Masters' husband who responded to the call. No charges were filed. Father DeCicco rested in his room, and Maria Cristina and I took turns bringing him traysful of things that might tempt him to eat.

When, a short time later, Father DeCicco was asked to leave the parish, he did one better: left the priesthood altogether. A black mark on his soul for all eternity; the blackest, in fact, for ex-priests. A few weeks after that, I heard (from the Perrotti sisters, all the louder and larger) that he was living with a woman outside Boston, but the rumor was never confirmed.

Before I left my job at the rectory, the hospital called only one more time to say that someone was dying and wanted last rites. The trouble was, I couldn't locate the priest on call—nor any other priest for that matter. It was on a Saturday night. Who was supposed to be on call? Who? Who? Which one? When the phone began to ring again, I started running all around, upstairs and down, trying to find somebody. Then I stopped, walked slowly back to my little office, smoothed the back of my black skirt, and sat. I folded my hands on the desk, but not to pray. The phone just kept ringing.

Gaël Rozière

El Regresar

Back in Mexico City, where she grew up,
a young girl invites her to a Christmas party,
a procession where Joseph and Mary seek shelter,
girls and boys under a familial roof,
music, chicken mole, chaperoned dancing.
She wonders why they've invited her.
She no longer remembers how to get there.
The taxicab driver is unable to help
so she asks directions from an Indian man
who seems to know where she is going.
In the cab he puts his hand on her thigh
and lets it rest there.
It feels comfortable, even natural
as his hands slide over her white dress,
cover her breasts, his fingers
at the top of her stockings.
The taxicab driver stares straight ahead;
the stranger still gives directions
while she lays back, closes her eyes
and gives way to pleasure
as she never would have done
when she was younger—

lest the girls in white repudiate her,
the familiar streets turn to ice
not like the fire of her flesh
under his hands.

Francine Prose

Excerpt from
Household Saints

One afternoon they met by previous arrangement at Borough Hall. By now, Leonard had persuaded Theresa that the retreats were a waste of her time; he had promised her a tour of Brooklyn Heights. As they walked along the promenade, Leonard recounted the history of the construction of the Brooklyn Bridge. Suddenly he stopped in mid-sentence and said,

"Would you do me a favor?"

"Sure."

"It's these curtains.... My mother sent them to me for my room. For days now, I've been trying to figure out ... Being a male, I'm not exactly an expert at hanging—"

"I'll put them up for you," said Theresa. "I'd be glad to."

It was so simple, Leonard couldn't believe it had worked, not even when Theresa was actually sitting beside him on the living room couch, with "Bitch's Brew" playing on the stereo. Although he knew that such scenes took place every day, it didn't seem possible that he would be personally involved in one. Other men, maybe, but not Leonard—who never had luck with girls beyond a few uncomfortable college coffee dates. And now that it was really happening, now that he was clinking the ice cubes in his Chivas Regal (which, he discovered, he didn't much like), he felt a peculiar detachment, as if he were somewhere else, far away, looking at a Chivas Regal ad in a magazine.

He reached out and took Theresa's hand. As he ran his fingers over her palm, his detachment gave way to anxiety. What in the name of God was he supposed to do next?

Leonard knew, from his reading how other girls reacted at this critical juncture: They swished across the room to check out the view from your terrace. They asked you to freshen their drink. They pointed out that the record on the turntable had run out. But Theresa did none of these things.

She said, "The curtains?"

"Right," said Leonard. "The curtains."

He recognized this as the crucial point in a seduction—certainly no time to give up or get discouraged. Yet still he could not get it through his head that seduction was humanly possible.

"Come on," he said. "They're in the bedroom."

Astonishingly, Theresa followed him into his room. After much searching, he found the dark blue fiberglass drapes in a box at the back of the closet. It was obvious that they were not the urgent problem he'd claimed to be facing, but Theresa didn't seem to care.

"Anything to hang them on?" she said.

Leonard located a neatly stapled package of collapsible rods and pins. He pictured his mother buying them at A&S, barraging the salesgirls with nervous questions.... The last thing he wanted to be thinking about now was his mother.

Theresa sat on a chair by the bed and began slipping the hooks beneath the presewn pleats, her fingers working so nimbly that Leonard was moved, and felt that he was witnessing some age-old—even primal—female activity. She stood on the chair to hang them, and Leonard was so stirred by the way her blouse tightened over her back that he was ready to risk anything for a look at the flesh beneath that white schoolgirl's shirt.

And yet when he said, "Take off your clothes" (the words came out so garbled that he had to clear his throat and repeat himself), it was less out of lust than curiosity to see if such a thing could happen.

Acting as if she hadn't heard, Theresa drew the curtains, got down off the chair, and stepped back to admire her work. The afternoon light shone blue into the room. She had heard him, but it hadn't sounded like Leonard. For the voice that had ordered her to take off her clothes was so commanding, its authority so plainly derived from some secret knowledge of her own destiny, that it never occurred to her to disobey.

Theresa turned to face Leonard. Then very slowly, looking straight at him, she undressed and lay on top of the bed, staring up at the ceiling.

In the blue light, she looked like a drowned woman, floating, pale and lovely, miraculously uncorrupted by the water. It was a sight so beautiful—so wondrous, so unexpected in his room—that Leonard began to pray.

"Blessed Lord Jesus," he whispered. "Get me through this and I promise you, I'll never do it again."

But it couldn't have been Jesus who showed him how to undress and lie down beside Theresa so quietly that she wasn't even startled. How would Jesus have known how to hold her and kiss her, how to enter a virgin so slowly that it didn't hurt? It couldn't have been Jesus who told him to wait and let Theresa catch her breath, then give him the go-ahead to move—slowly at first, then faster, like the expert Leonard knew in his soul he wasn't.

And so, because it was not Jesus who had gotten him through, Leonard felt no obligation to keep the solemn vow he had made Him, and he and Theresa did it again and again and again.

As Leonard and Theresa piled sin upon sin, Theresa wasn't thinking of anything so abstract as sinning. At the time, her mind was empty, but later, while Leonard slept and Theresa lay watching the light change from blue to black, she had plenty of time to think. And what she thought was: Her mind had not been empty so much as absent altogether.

Someone else had done those things in bed with Leonard.

The possibility of winding up in Leonard Villanova's bed had honestly never occurred to her. Over the past months, she had come to think of him as a brother, a friend. And if he sometimes held her hand and kissed her ... She knew boys liked such things. She herself had felt nothing impure. What was the harm?

Even as she undressed and lay naked on the blankets, she had felt an overwhelming sense of freedom. The saints spoke of floating out of your body, and that was how it was for her. She was not in bed with Leonard of her own free will. She was following someone else's orders.

Now she wondered: Whose?

Obviously, Leonard was the one who'd told her to take off her clothes—but she'd never felt as if she were obeying Leonard. Traditionally, it was the devil who tempted and wheedled and dragged you into sin—but she hadn't felt the devil's presence in the room.

That left God. But why would God lead her into bed with Leonard Villanova?

Suddenly she remembered all of the saints who had fornicated, lied and stolen, all the pickpockets and con men and whores. Augustine, Magdalene, Mary of Egypt—Theresa made a mental list. She thought of the robber crucified with Jesus and saved, the great sinners plucked from the midst of their evil lives and sanctified. For a moment, she thought: Maybe St. Therese's Little Way wasn't the only one; maybe that was why God had brought her to Leonard Villanova's dark bedroom.

She put her hand on Leonard's bare chest, felt his measured breathing and experienced a rush of tenderness and awe. It was as if she were touching God there, in Leonard Villanova's skinny chest.

Amber Coverdale Sumrall

Last Confession

We stand in the vestibule of St. Andrew's Church, digging into our purses for white lace handkerchiefs and bobby pins.

"Shit," Karen mutters. "I can't find it."

"Here, use a Kleenex. My mother does."

"This looks really stupid," Karen says, laying the tissue on top of her teased and sprayed-until-stiff hair. "I'm glad Tony can't see me."

We start to giggle, remember where we are. We've driven twenty miles to make our confessions in a strange church so that the priest won't recognize our voices. Last month I went to Father O'Connor, our parish pastor, and confessed to "touching myself in an impure manner about twenty times."

"Oh, and how's your mother, dear?" he asked. "Is she still getting those terrible headaches?" It was all I could do to finish my Act of Contrition.

This church has a new priest from Czechoslovakia, who, we've been told, doesn't speak English very well. We're counting on his not being able to understand it either.

Karen picked me up in her sister's powder blue '57 T-Bird. As soon as we left my house we put mascara and white lipstick on, rolled our skirts up, and lit cigarettes.

"Mary went to St. Andrew's last week," I told Karen. "All she got for her penance were three Hail Mary's."

Mary and Bob have been going steady for three years, ever since eighth grade. She wears his pale blue St. Christopher medal on a silver chain around her neck. All the Sacred Heart girls envy her because she's so sophisticated and her boyfriend's captain of the St. Francis football team. Mary was the only girl from Sacred Heart to be chosen as one of the St. Francis cheerleaders. Mary, Karen, and I hide in the chemistry lab during gym and talk about our boyfriends. Mary drops hints about going all the way in Bob's candy-apple red Chevy.

"Never take your panties off," she cautions. "You won't be able to get them back on in time if the cops come. And don't ever kiss his thing, no matter how much he begs you, because he'll stick it down your throat and make you throw up."

We hang on her words like flies on flypaper.

Once she took off her white uniform blouse and showed us her bra. It was sheer pink and beige with lace and fancy stitching. You could see her cleavage with just one button undone. Mary called it French-cut; she said our bras looked like the tail lights on Studebakers.

The Catholic Church has a problem with anything French: kissing, underwear, movie stars. French films are automatically added to the Legion of Decency Condemned List. It's a mortal sin to watch them. If you get hit by a truck and die after seeing Irma La Douce you'll go straight to hell.

St. Andrew's is cool and dark inside. It takes awhile for our eyes to adjust and find the Holy Water font. Karen and I daub the blessed water on our foreheads and throats as if it were cologne. We genuflect and slide into the last pew. Votive candles flicker in red and cobalt blue glass. An old woman, draped in a black lace mantilla, feeds quarters into the slot in front of the statue of St. Anthony, patron saint of the lost and found. She lights candle after candle, lips moving in constant prayer.

"I hope she finds what she's searching for," I whisper. "Maybe we should light a candle to be on the safe side."

"Forget it. Let's save our money for hamburgers afterwards. This confession will be a cinch."

We kneel, cover our faces with the palms of our hands, pretending to examine our consciences for sins. But we're just going through the motions; we already know what we have to confess. Sins of impurity in thought, word, and deed. Mortal sins committed with full consent of the will. I search for a way out of the mortal sin category, but the case against me is airtight.

I could have gone to Father Flanagan, our assistant pastor, but he sighs and moans so much that you feel each sin is a thorn in his side. He is very pale and sickly for such a young priest, and always carries a scarf-size handkerchief clutched in his hand; I don't think he has the constitution for hearing mortal sins against the sixth commandment.

I feel as if I'm in a trance, watching the candles flicker in the dark church. It's like being in a subterranean cave, a retreat from the drone of the world. I stare at the statue of St. Anthony and pray for a sign, some incentive to continue believing, like the blinking of his holy hooded eyes. Something small, easy; not the stigmata that my mother wants. She's longed for it all of her life, as proof of her holiness. I'm sure glad she didn't get it and bleed from her hands and feet every month. She has enough problems with her period.

The old woman appears to have fallen asleep at St. Anthony's feet, rosary beads in hand. I wonder if she prays to him every day, if her faith is unshakeable. Mine seems to be going to the same place where my faith in the tooth fairy went.

The red light above the confessional flashes off and a gangly red-haired boy about fourteen emerges and dashes out of the church.

"He didn't say his penance," Karen whispers.

"Maybe he didn't get any."

"He sure was in a hurry to get out. Do you want to go first?"

I shrug my shoulders and leave the pew. "Good luck," Karen whispers. My heart is racing like it does before finals. I hold my breath, enter the pitch-black cubicle, and kneel on the padded riser. The air is musty and hot. I hear loud sobs coming from the opposite booth. I try not to listen to the woman's confession, and rehearse what I'm going to say.

Suddenly, her window slams shut and mine slides open. I can see the priest's shadow; he leans close to the grille, waiting for me to speak.

"Well, confess," he hisses. His breath smells like whiskey. I want to bolt but my knees are riveted to the kneeler. I must warn Karen. She's just started her period and there's no telling how she'll react.

"Confess!" he commands.

"Bless me Father, for I have sinned." He inches closer; I know he can understand me perfectly. I cling to my anonymity like a life raft.

"I French-kissed with my boyfriend twenty times."

His silence fills the confessional. I imagine him leaving his chamber and dragging me out, demanding my phone number, calling my mother.

Then his words, like spit in my face. "Filthy girl. Do you know where this disgusting practice originated? Well, do you? Do you?"

"Answer me!" he thunders.

"I don't know, Father." My voice is shaking.

"In the sewers of France. By prostitutes and their negro pimps in the sewers of France. You must vow never to engage in this filthy habit again. Do you hear me? Never again."

He sounds as if he's foaming at the mouth. "Beg the Blessed Virgin for forgiveness and say five rosaries for your penance. Remember Sodom and Gomorrah. God has no mercy for sins of the flesh. Now make a sincere Act of Contrition."

I am in shock. Why would anyone want to kiss in a sewer? My faith has been strained to the breaking point. I can't remember the prayer. He slams the door on my silence.

Poor Karen. I wait for her in front of St. Anthony's altar. The old woman has moved on to the statue of the Blessed Virgin, lighting candles and striking her breast as she prays. Tears are streaming down Karen's face when she leaves the confessional. "He called me a whore of Babylon," she whispers. "In perfect English! God, we got the wrong one."

"You can say *that* again."

"He gave me five rosaries."

"Me, too. Jesus, we'll be here all night."

"Forget it. I'm not going to do my penance. Let's just get out of here."

I look once more at St. Anthony. Last chance, I tell him. If only he'd blink or raise his uplifted fingers a fraction of an inch. Then I'd stay and make amends. But he is rigid, unyielding.

Karen rips the tissue off her head and runs out of the church. I follow without a backward glance. Too bad for you, St. Anthony.

"You drive," Karen says, drying her eyes with the shredded Kleenex. "I can't see straight. Let's go to Bob's. Did you get a whiff of him?"

"Yeah. He must know plenty about sewers."

"Sewers?"

"He said French kissing started in the sewers of France. And that prostitutes did it with negroes."

"He said that! He told me that whores were burned at the stake with witches. That they were used as kindling."

"God, Karen, I bet he'd like to toss us both into the fires of hell."

"Well," she says, "now we can do whatever we want. Since we're going anyway."

We pull into Bob's Big Boy, order burgers, fries, onion rings, a side of thousand island dressing, and cherry cokes. The carhops, hips swinging in tight brown pants, rush from car to car, leaning into windows, removing trays, and flirting with the guys. They all look like cheerleaders.

"Too bad all those prostitutes couldn't have managed to cart buckets of sewage and put out the fires underneath all those witches and whores," Karen says.

"Wait till Mary hears about this. Do you think she tricked us?"

Karen rolls her eyes. "You never know about Mary. She

acts like a goddamned queen most of the time. Let's cruise Colorado. Are you tired of driving?"

"Are you kidding! It's the only chance I get. I can't drive my dad's car until I get As in Deportment and Achievement Based on Ability."

"Fat chance," Karen says.

I put on the headlights and our carhop, whose nametag says Bunny, comes to remove our tray. Her long blonde hair is pulled back into a perfect French twist. The regulation brown cap perches on top. It would look totally ridiculous on anyone else. But these carhops manage to carry it off. They're sophisticated and beautiful like Mary, light-years ahead of Karen and me. "Nice car," she comments. "You girls stay out of trouble now, you hear." She winks as if we were guys. "Bye now."

"I bet Bunny doesn't worry about mortal sins," Karen says. "She looks like she's having a great time."

"None of them are Catholics, that's why. It must be such a relief."

We drive around Pasadena, but as usual there's nothing happening and it's too late to go to Hollywood. We are heading back down Colorado Boulevard when Karen lets out a deep-bellied yelp and rolls down her window.

"Watch this," she says, sliding her underpants over her shoes.

"Karen, what are you doing? Never take your underpants off in a car, remember?" She laughs, half-kneeling, half-squatting on the seat and hoists her bare bottom out the window.

"This is what I think of that fucking priest and the so-called Mother Church," she screams. "All of it."

"Karen, you're crazy. Get your ass out of the window."

"Behold the Whore of Babylon. Behold her great white ass."

A carload of black teenage boys pull alongside the T-Bird. They are hooping and hollering as if in a parade. "Hey, baby, I ain't never seen nothing sooo white before," one of them yells. "Yeah," another chimes in, "like a bar of Ivory soap, ninety-nine percent pure. Gotta watch out for that one per-cent though. Here, baby, lookee what I got for you."

Karen drops like a swatted fly. I step on the gas, look over to see a small, black ass hanging out the window of a maroon '54 Ford. "You girls like chocolate? Hey, mama, eat your heart out."

"Jesus," Karen wails. "Let's get out of here, fast."

I make an abrupt left turn; the boys continue straight ahead. They are yelling and honking their horn.

"You scared the shit out of me, Karen." She is laughing uncontrollably, now that we're safe. After awhile she leans back against the seat and closes her eyes.

"Would you ever go out with someone who's black?" she asks.

"I'd never get the chance; my mother would kill me before I left the house."

"Helen Rizzo's father nearly killed her. She used to live down the street from me. Someone broke all the windows in her car and wrote 'nigger lover' in white paint on the hood. She got obscene phone calls and death threats. None of her friends would speak to her anymore. When her father found out he beat her so bad she had to go to the hospital. Father Luppi said she deserved it. That she was a tramp."

"Jesus, that's awful. Is she alright?"

"I don't know, she took off with her boyfriend. Her dad's fit to be tied. I hope the bastard never finds her."

"Karen, would you?" I ask.

"Would I what?"

"You know, date someone who's not white?"

"We're not even supposed to date non-Catholics, let alone someone of a different race." She takes out her comb and teases her hair until she resembles a porcupine. "But, yeah, I would. Why not? Forbidden fruit is sweeter, they say."

In a few weeks Karen and I will be suspended from Sacred Heart for smoking cigarettes in the grotto of Our Lady of Perpetual Help. Her parents are heavy smokers and semi-lapsed Catholics to boot, so it's no big deal. She'll transfer to John Muir High. I'll have to scrub the grotto walls every week

until school's out, as punishment. My mother will forbid me
to see Karen, because she's a "bad influence." Rumors will
circulate that she's drinking whiskey and smoking marijuana,
that she dyed her hair blonde, that she's pregnant, that she
had an abortion in Tijuana. I'll sneak out and meet her for
burgers and cherry cokes once in awhile; we'll talk about her
new boyfriend, who happens to be black, and her plans to
move to New York after she graduates. She wants to live in
the Village and study sociology. She'll tell me that never will
she set foot in St. Andrew's or any other church as long as
she lives. I still have a ways to go before I catch up with
Karen. I'll never go to Confession again, but sometimes, when
I pass a Catholic church, I'll look inside for St. Anthony, light
a candle, and give him one more chance.

Patti Sirens

Holy Water

How God gets inside
those molecules
of H_2O
I'll never know

Must be the same way
the Spirit
slipped between
Mary's thighs
when she wasn't looking

Kathleen de Azevedo

The Fall Baby

I was named after Saint Veronica, the one who went up to Jesus and wiped *up* his bloody face while he hauled that big old cross. This really happened; she really did wipe *up* his face. And Jesus H. Christ, to show his appreciation, left a big imprint of his face right there on her towel. A miracle, and just for her. But my ungodly face, my long stringy hair and mushroomed nose, wasn't no miracle. And I wanted a miracle that fall. Real bad.

I phoned my boyfriend, Andy. "Come over here right now, Mr. A." I was sixteen and Andy was twenty.

"Why?" he shouted. Someone was welding up a storm at the gas station. He worked at the Spirit of '76, where he fixed motorcycles, his real passion.

"I'm on my way to sainthood. You just get over here."

Then I waited for him on the front porch steps. Thick smoke poured out of Troy's Auto Wrecking Yard across the street. I could hear the fire popping as it burned scrapped-up cars and piles of leaves neighbors had dumped over Troy's fence. Through the smoke, Andy rode on his Yamaha, branding the asphalt with tire tracks, and clamping onto the engine with his bony knees so he wouldn't blow away. He made the turn into the driveway and was off before the thing came to a complete stop. He tossed his gloves on the vinyl seat. "What's up, Ron?"

Oh, Mr. A, wearing a leather jacket with Moto Guzzi wings sewn on the back—I'm afraid to tell you, Mr. Captain America.

I laid my head on my knees, and played with some rocks on the ground. "I'm pregnant."

"You're?—" Cold air must have dried up his tongue. He blew a long cloud of breath and stared off toward Mt. Hough like he had just discovered our little mountain by accident.

But the miner's cabin on Mt. Hough was no *accident*. Andy had found an abandoned miner's cabin up in the woods while testing out one of his dirt bikes. He brought me up to the cabin several times, and we did it on the floor. Then I told him he should at least bring us a blanket to lie on. Next time, he did. For once, it felt good.

"How soon?" he said.

"Eight months. Something like that."

"Sorry."

"The hell you are."

He tossed up his hands and leaped on his motorcycle; the throttle snorted, and the Moto Guzzi wings flapped—and he was gone.

I wanted to shoot him outa the sky. "I'm gonna trash your 'cycle, fucker!" I flung myself back on the steps. Was I gonna tell my parents, who were swimming in a sea of whiskey, "Come out and dry off for a sec, Dad. Hey, Mom, I got some news!" I grabbed my belly with both hands—fleshy blob of dough—and dug in my fingernails.

I called up my girlfriends Gerri and Stacy. I lied and told them Andy and I had broken up. My girlfriends understood. The three of us met that night under the orange '76 ball, swinging baseball bats under a yellow moon.

I unlocked the side door to the garage with a key Andy had lent me a long while back. A sliver of ghost white shone on a small dirt bike. It wasn't the Yamaha, but it would have to do. We snuck inside and stood around that filthy thing. I swung my bat and let loose with a whack-attack and bashed in the gas tank. Stacy hammered new form to the handle bars and Gerri snatched tools from the walls and undid the motor.

I dug into my jeans pocket, flicked out a pocketknife, and cut a long slash in the seat; then, slowly, I knelt down in front of the bike, jabbed my knife into the tire, and cut him a lovely smile in the rubber. We backed away, gulped, and giggled at the chunk of metal-mess.

Gasoline from the gas tank dripped onto the floor like it was bleeding. Seemed like a waste of time, to smash up an already crapped up bike like that. Andy wouldn't even cry about it; he would just rebuild it. Gerri and Stacy kept jabbering and it got on my nerves, so I told them I wasn't coming over to watch TV that night. They left. I never told them the truth.

I decided to get an abortion. At sixteen I was supposed to know all about these things. Ha!

I laid in bed that night, vowing I wouldn't tell a soul. Downstairs, I heard my yell-drunk father crash into chairs and yell-blame my mother for throwing them in his way. My eight-year-old sister, Liz, who slept in the lower bunk, climbed the ladder into my bed, curled up, and pulled the covers over her head. I turned and faced the wall. I should've joined the convent like my Aunt Julie and stayed there until I outgrew my craving for juvenile delinquents on motorbikes.

Julie was my mother's sister. But they didn't look alike. My mother stood tall and elegant, but Julie was built like a small boy, packed in and short, with small breasts. Julie, family criminal and saint, went AWOL at her convent, joined peace marches, became a vegetarian, took drugs, and appeared one day at our doorstep, wild-eyed and fried. When the blizzard in her brain had settled, she bought a little house out among the pine trees and married a bald-headed older man who worked for the U.S. Forest Service.

I imagined Julie stretched out at the foot of my bed, wearing her large hiking boots and dangling her feet over the edge, smiling gently. "What's your trouble, Ron?"

"I'm pregnant. I don't wanna have a baby."

Then I imagined her reaching over and squeezing my toes, whispering, "It's okay."

"Don't tell Mom."

The next day after school, I rode my bike over to Julie's house. She was sitting on a tree stump in the middle of her garden, cutting a large sheet of plastic to protect her plants from frost. Good thing, too, 'cause winter was coming. I'd have to go easy on her; she was trying to keep her plants alive and I was barging in. She rose and brushed off her hands, and I ran over and clung to her waist. Like Siamese twins we walked into the house—me clutching, she confused. Me not letting go.

She made tea and I told her everything. I told her about Andy (she smiled), my parents drinking (she nodded), and finally, about how I was pregnant and wanted an abortion (she splashed boiling water everywhere, trying to fill the mugs, then gave up and slammed the kettle back on the stove with a "Shit!").

She snatched a tea bag, which ripped apart in her hand, tossed the spoiled bag into the sink, threw another tea bag into the mug, and grabbed the kettle again, swallowing hard.

I could tell she hated me now. "C'mon, Julie! I can't keep this baby!"

"What did Andy say?"

"Nothing, he hates me."

Julie sighed and poured the water. She handed me the tea and moved past me out the door and sat under the pine tree in her yard.

I followed her. "I can take care of the whole mess myself, you know." I jerked up my hand holding the tea. Tea splattered on my arm, burning like hell. "Oww!" I hurled down the mug.

"Good heavens, Veronica—"

"Just go with me to the doctor's. Huh?"

Julie looked wearily at the ground. "I can't."

My insides were boiling hot lava. "Well, you're lucky *you* lived in a convent. You're just lucky we let you live with us! 'Cause Mom said you were a freako hippie back then. And you weren't even punished! You even got married and got a little house in the goddam woods!" I had to catch my breath. "No convent will want me now, either."

I yanked up my bike and gave the kickstand a powie-kick. That's okay. I'll just ride headlong into a logging truck on my way home. The Catholic Church ditches you after holy communion, anyway. You'd have to be five years old to obey all the rules. God! Julie used to be so cool.

I heard her get up and walk over to me. She smoothed out the collar of my jacket. "Did you make an appointment?" she said.

"Thursday."

"Alright then."

So Thursday, I snuck out of the house and rode my bike over to Julie's. I just didn't want anyone to see her pull into our driveway. I wore a pair of baggy men's jeans and cinched it tight with a robe belt. I stole one of my father's old shirts and tucked my stringy hair under a fishing cap. I wasn't "showing" yet, but a glow inside—a nauseating glow—made me feel like I could erupt. I arrived at her house and hung out by the doorway, just in case.

Julie put on her ski jacket and glared at me as she fumbled with the front zipper. "Why'd you dress like a boy for? Why don't you admit you're a woman now, huh."

I'd never seen Julie in such a mood! She was tearing up closets and slamming doors, hunting for her purse. I felt pukey and vicious, and I ran to the nearest tree and pulled off slabs of bark until I could see the bare tree-bone under-neath. Grubs. White wormy grubs underneath the bark made me sick. I felt sick. Andy was probably riding away on his Yamaha in some hosanna-in-the-highest hill, drinking and smokin' grass with his friends—free, disgustingly free.

Julie came out and pressed a wet towel against my face. I must have looked pretty green.

As she drove me to the doctor's, Julie transformed back into a nun. Her eyelids looked like half moons as she checked out the red leaves floating down from the oaks. She pointed to Mt. Hough. "In a few weeks, the snow will cover that mountain."

Uh-huh. I slid down on the car seat and rested my feet up

on the dashboard. I glanced over at her and damned if she wasn't making the sign of the cross.

I sat up. "What in the hell did you do that for?"

"What are you talking about?"

"You crossed yourself."

"No, I didn't."

"Man, I saw you."

The car screeched to a halt on the roadside. She clicked off her seat belt and swiped the fishing cap from my head. My stringy hair fell to my shoulders. She started to say something, but shook her head and rapped her fingers on the steering wheel.

"C'mon," I said, "we'll be late."

"No we won't."

Great.

She spoke quietly and right at me. "I've always been put to the test, Ron. Sometimes I think the only reason I was ever in a convent was to be able to break away. Then I broke away only to run into you."

I turned away from her and folded my hands over my belly. My belly felt full, open, and alive. "You think it's a human being?"

She drew me to her side and drove with one hand on the steering wheel and one hand on my shoulder all the way to the doctor's office.

I laid on top of an examining table and they gave me a shot that sent me swimming through the white machines that were in the room. Counting backwards from fifty, I thought I fell asleep, but overhead, I saw Andy on his motorcycle. The Moto Guzzi wings on his jacket shimmered like a giant moth. He kept trying to start his motorcycle, but it kept dying down. Each time he tried to start it, the motor became softer and softer until its sound was no louder than a baby's cooing. Then, silently, the motorcycle sped away—out of my life—finally.

I woke up babbling "Andy-Andy-Andy" over and over again until I realized I was counting the white tiles on the ceiling and calling each one Andy.

The next day I told my mom I didn't feel so good, so she let me stay home. The house seemed unusually cramped that morning, so I sprawled on the front steps. Then all at once a cold north breeze bit into my ribs, and Andy rode pop-wheelie-happy into the driveway. I pulled in my legs and looked toward the wrecking yard. Get outa here, I thought; but I spied him from the corner of my eye.

Andy rolled into the driveway. This time he waited for the bike to stop before getting off. Then he slipped the ignition key out with both hands, trying to hush the motor. He swung his leg carefully over the seat and smoothed out his jeans at the thighs. Bits of his hair fell out of his knit cap. He stood in front of me and teased my foot with the tip of his boot.

I turned away. "What do you want, huh?"

"I wanna marry you."

"What?"

"I wanna marry you."

I sprung up from the steps and slammed my foot into his motorcycle, crashing it to the ground. That didn't even faze him. He glanced at the fallen 'cycle, then back to me. "Huh? Wanna get m?—"

"There is no baby, Andy."

Andy took a deep breath; then his face got puffy and soft, searching me with his eyes, trying to take 'n what I said.

"I got rid of it. I mean—yesterday, I—" Damn, he wasn't that dumb.

His eyes got large and watery, then he seemed to double over as he yanked at his cap. His face was crying-red.

I twisted my hair and pulled it across my mouth, chewing it and shivering. Andy still stood there. I couldn't cry in peace. Finally I flung my hair back. "I didn't think you wanted it!"

"Oh, yeah, I did!"

"It's too late for everything now, Mr. A."

He hoisted up the motorcycle and stared at the seat. Then, like a Moto-bird with its wings on fire, he jumped on the machine and flew along the surface of the road.

I ran out to the road and called his name, over and over, knowing that he wouldn't answer because he was gone. I stood by the mailbox, a flimsy tin box on a bug-eaten post. I could have kicked the box down; I could have stamped and crushed the metal and sent pieces of wood flying. But I didn't. Walking back to the driveway, I put one foot in front of the other, tracing his motorcycle tracks. I couldn't believe it. He wanted me; he wanted me so bad. I wanted to stuff him inside my belly, keep him there and hug myself, he wanted me so bad.

Kim Addonizio

Visit

We lay in your mother's bed
which you had taken down off its casters,
next to her dresser with its hidden contents,
her bras and nylon underwear and slips
tangled together, the round fan on the sill
turning toward us like a drugged woman's face
and then slowly turning aside.
Your mother was lying in a hospital room,
we had her apartment to ourselves—
table pushed to the corner, magazines
sliding from a chair,
my suitcase spread open on the couch.
When we made love
we shoved the covers in a heap to the floor
and you pulled me over you
the way a nurse would soon pull the white sheet
over her, you lowered me onto your cock
the way a man would lower the satin-lined lid of the casket
until it clicked shut.
I lifted myself above you, moaning,
my breasts grazing your face,
the Christ on the wall was gazing down,
blood on His hands and feet

where they'd hammered the nails deep
into His flesh—
finally I collapsed against your chest
and felt you coming, shuddering,
letting your grief wash into me cell by cell.
As we lay there, breathing hard,
I listened to your heart gradually slowing
and when you wanted to rise I held you
    down,
with my smaller body
I kept you from danger a few minutes
longer.

Joan McMillan

Nasturtiums

"... the past is a great darkness, and filled with echoes."
—Margaret Atwood, *The Handmaid's Tale*

1

I watch her carefully,
that young woman I was at 21.
No one is looking out for her.
Hundreds of miles from home,
she lives at a college
with white buildings
and a church whose bellchimes
announce Mass twice a day.
She wears a thin crucifix of silver,
sweaters of earth-toned wool,
skirts in soft folds
below her knees.
She has a pair of pink stockings
embroidered with blossoms,
notebooks overflowing with words
in radiant blue ink.

2

When her lover's hands travel her
skin,
she thinks of the way she once
touched a spiderweb's intricate silk,
leaving its threads unbroken.

Late in spring,
she opens her body to this man
whose dark hair captures light
like the sheen over quiet water.
She will not flinch when her blood at first
stains the thin cotton sheets.
Next morning, the sun
shines through a screen of leaves
beyond his window,
makes a quilt of shadows above their sleep.

3

Another man
follows her for months.
He is her professor, married, a former monk
who reads her the poetry of Gerard Manley Hopkins.
He praises every report she writes,
the knowledge she gleans for his lectures.
His shelves are cluttered with paper.
He is reluctant to throw anything away.
She avoids secluded classrooms, deserted hallways,
and sometimes feels puzzled about the way he stares.

4

At his office desk, he writes her name
again and again until the pen runs dry,
sees her as a maze through which
his slick paleness has the right to run.
While his family is away,
he plans the lure to his house, the net
of rage and hatred he will weave,
how he will threaten, destroy objects,
raise his hand to her face.
He wants her forced down,
torn into, made to repeat

the lines he loves to hear women say.
At the flow of her tears, his laughter:
This is what you are.
This is what you have always been.

5

She walks through the days afterward
as if caught on an endless chain.
She attends classes, keeps books
pressed to her chest,
abandons her lover without explanation.
If someone had beaten this woman into silence,
or held a gun to her head,
she would have known where to turn later,
but she cannot find the language for this:
something which left no visible wounds,
only her walled-up voice.

6

Years later, her secret
still wedges inside
like scars from a fire hidden
beneath the new cell layers of a tree.
She looks back at me from the mirror,
reminds me there is work to be done.
Though heat parches the ground
to a fine gray powder
this summer of drought,
I start a bed of nasturtiums
at the yard's edge,
their showy reds and yellows the color
of everything shattered which begins to mend,
reach to the earth
in the most simple belief,
that each seed planted must take root, lift
its small bright banner through the upturned soil.

Kristina McGrath

Housework

The world would come to an end, she thought, and she'd be here hand-washing his linen handkerchiefs.

She loved the dangerous rush of water, the small white sink near brimful. There were at least ten things left to do before he got home, but she stood at the sink and listened, scrubbing the linen thin, taking pleasure in the way light fell through the cloth when she held each handkerchief to the fluorescent. She loved fluorescent light. Fluorescent never lies, she thought, and scrubbed the linen thin.

She loved to feed him. She honestly loved to clean his clothes. And when she picked up what he let fall to the floor, mended his underwear or just plain splurged and bought him new ones, she felt that she healed him, partook in him, and in life. What she touched, he ate, he wore, was where he sat or crossed space. The peeled peach (he insisted) was so ripe, so intimate, had been touched nearly everywhere, had changed shape even, that it almost embarrassed her to see him eating it with absolute faith. She pictured him, and he sat there, spotless, eating a peach. It was 1948. She was the secret of his magnificence, and the handkerchiefs rose higher with the water.

Not that she ever thought of it that way. It just made her feel good to have everything done for him. He was somebody. And, he could be so appreciative. Not that that was everything, or anything, really. The doing was everything and the thanks was just a little something extra. Well, yes, she decided almost guiltily, she liked to be thanked, it made it nice. She loved it when he knew exactly who he had married. Three years ago, come June.

You're so good for me, we'll give it a whirl, he said, get married, and she nearly keeled right over. As if God himself had come down from heaven just to tell her: What you are doing for me is fine. She had said no to marriage more than once or twice. His was her fifth proposal. It seemed that every man and his brother from the North Side of Pittsburgh, who was just a little too nice or too shy or too something, had wanted to marry her; but he was somebody. He did drink just a little too much. But she would make him a life so good, he would have no reason for running from things as they are. The regatta of his handkerchiefs floated in the sink.

Life is either pleasant or my responsibility to make it so, she thought. Another clean Monday. She shut the taps and slapped the sink. One hundred percent linen, she said. He would be home soon.

With the car door slam, the songs began. He loved to make up little stories about his day at The Radiant Oven Company by stringing together various song titles and phrases. After roaring up to the curb, skidding on the cobblestone of Franklin Way, shutting off the motor and the radio songs, he boomed. Right then and there in front of the neighbors. Waving from their porches, they seemed to appreciate it, so she didn't mind enjoying it herself. He climbed the twenty-four steps of the rented house at 432 Franklin Way, a narrow alleyway cut from the backs of East Side streets near Trenton Avenue and the trolley line. The high house suited him. He waved back at the neighbors from the landing, and the door swung open.

Finding her there with everything dropped perfectly into place, including herself at the door, he'd widen his eyes and grin but keep on singing, and without the loss of one beat, hurl himself onto the sofa in time to The Gal (he sat) from

Kalamazoo (he crossed his legs with a flourish). She knew that that was Miss Glenny Hayes, Shoo Shoo Baby, who had been fired, My Darlin, My Darlin, In Tulip Time (it was spring). Then suddenly remembering her, he'd say, Whoops, well, so how are you? and then they'd laugh. He was the first person in the world who had ever really spoken to her in full sentences.

And so, with an old bent butter knife, she crawled to some far-off corner (he would be home soon) and began scraping the floorboards, unimportant, invisible, really, because of the monstrous furniture, except to her, she knew it was there. Dirt should be taken care of like the first small sign of sadness or flu. Otherwise, catching his eye, it would spread under the feet of their company, gad about like sugar, unfurl into the yards of lazy neighbors—the entire city a shambles before you knew it—if each one in it did not take it on under their own roof. Besides, he noticed everything.

It made him happy to see her doing things and she was happy to be of use while listening to the radio news. The world interested her, but there was that problem with the newspaper, a year or yes it was two ago (it was his, he said, snatching it back), so she never touched it again. "She's Funny That Way," he sang.

Things made such an impression, she thought, as she scraped behind the china closet, remembering that time as a schoolgirl in that convent she loved so much in the best of times. She had accidentally stepped on a white chrysanthemum in the convent yard. It had fallen from some poor excuse for a bush, which Sister What-was-her-name-anyway cared for. Every day of her life, it seemed, she was out there, digging. She liked talking to nuns. Well, not really talking, just listening to them pass in the halls, mouse mouse mouse and holy holy holy (she counted them) was enough. She was one of the chosen, sent regularly on errands, who got to see nuns actually do things like stir soup or crouch digging by a bush. She felt it under her foot. The old nun scowled and lifted, with thumb and forefinger, as if it were a repulsive thing, the farthest tip of her old brown shoe that was always dancing in a place beyond itself. That, child, the old nun snarled, could have been the heart of Jesus. Even now, eleven years later, she felt mortified. It could have been the old nun's heart itself, with all it had to live for other than that old bush. It could have been her own, or his. She promised to be more careful.

On those quick bird feet on her small feet she tiptoed on a Wednesday through the house when no one was there but her and her girl. She knew she was tiptoeing when the girl started it, too. She stopped dead center on the cellar stairs on her way to the kitchen, and set down her heels. Perhaps she had made a mistake, she thought; he was not the marrying kind. There was one child already; he loved her like the dickens, capable of it. But what were these sudden outbursts; what had she done? Everything around here has my name on it, he said; first comes me. Perhaps it was the eggs this morning that made him a stranger. She went to an empty room, shut the door, and gave him time. She had broken the yolks. She had done something. She would sit there at the edge of the bed, half the morning if she had to, and find it out.

With a confident dash of salt, she seasoned a pot of water in the late afternoon light that filled the yellow kitchen. She had the cookbooks memorized like a Shakespearean play. It was a common form of magic, pulling suppers from midair and boiling water on a low budget. Rattling something silver, at her business of which she was fond, of feeding who was hers and scooting them into a design around the table, she built with pots and pans the idyll of her mind and this was daily life: around it with a rag, picking up after it, rowing with the oar of it to the Mother of God, placing it next to itself, where it huddled warm and clean in a bunch.

Two at a time, she ran up the stairs to the small upstairs closet, with an armful of sheets. So this was life and this was life. The days were like rows of her bargain shoes that shone in the closet next to his. And here was the sound of the nineteenth century in a long dress brushing against the cold plaster as she pushed through the closet. And there was the cat on the stairs, climbing toward some higher realm, where things would work out. Things would work out because she was in love with the everlasting furniture, with the restfulness of plates stacked in painted cupboards, with the raising of husbands and children all the way down the alley, because she knew she was a part of something that keeps so many alive. She can please you, knowing the pleasure of safe mason jars and the calm of wooden spoons, the thud of good wood (her mother would have made that sound had she lived). Something sure as a cake could be done, and all of this was great and kind, small hellos to God. She would take care of hers, her corner of it would be a place to live.

Downstairs the cut carrots ran through the water rolling in its pot. The silverware lay ordered in blue shoeboxes with cardboard partitions in the deep drawers with which they were blessed. He had painted flowers and she had painted leaves on the face of the drawers and the cupboards, the two of them conspiring in some small but complicated plot against the larger tides of tornados and gunshots, of derelicts, senators and failed lovers, to be here, be counted, she said, in this strange world.

Good people, she reminded herself, are recorded in books. Everyone had at least one thing to be recorded. Any sadness you might have is often recorded as a good work. This is the way it is, she said to herself, in love with the beautiful ordeal of packing in the sheets in the small upstairs closet, and with the arabesques he sawed into tables and shelves. A good house, she thought, and slapped the sheets. Love, she said, this would sustain, and the feeling went with her into the supermarkets, into the streets, God bless us all. The feeling could go as far as The Radiant Oven Company, into the world; he would carry it there to Penn Avenue. And so she went on with it, this knowledge of where everything absolutely is, all the designs of which she was capable, as she built, to the last detail, the house from the inside.

And he had helped. His heart was to the wheel. He had given her a floor to match her Sunday dress. He painted it yellow with black polka dots, each dot a monument to something they could not understand. He loved doing and doing, yet how he sweat when he did it, sprawled there like a little boy or folded all upon himself, bug-eyed in the corner, goggling at his own perfection for days afterward, visiting it like a relative; and they said it couldn't be done. But everything was possible, she thought; what a talent. And told him so. You are a talented man. Everything he did, floor arabesque or drawer, he ran to have her see, and she would say, how lovely, you are a talented man. Tasks like this made him kind; and when he wasn't, well, she had enough love to change ten people let alone just one. He showed promise, able to love a floor like that. She had the power. She was in the house.

She had joined history. She was in the house. I love how you touch things, he told her; I know where to find them afterward. He took it personally when she reordered the drawers or dusted the wooden hands of the sofa, where he burrowed or sprawled, depending on his mood. It seemed to calm him. But everything needed so much, like the banisters. He slid down them just to rile her.

Sometimes it seemed he was beyond her—like the congressmen and the senators, only a little nearer—when he screamed like that, questioning where she'd been, who she'd been with. Everything was converging in their own bedroom, as if they were in an auto accident with history. My husband, right or wrong, she said, wishing there was someone to talk to about birth, about Hollywood and the Attorney General, about Hoover, about hiccups. The child still preferred crying over any other form of human expression. She was expecting again and the house seemed to run under her feet. Two months pregnant, he screamed; where were you two months ago? Mouse mouse mouse, she sang to the child. She would take care of everything. She knew how.

Housework made her dizzy sometimes, the way the seasons did when she thought of them too much—how they kept reoccurring, like stacks of dirty dishes. She stood at the sink, washing the dishes, feeling at peace with the whiteness of the appliances. Eventually it was her youngest daughter, their third, their last and not yet born, who would replace the seasons and the dishes as an image of time where she saw herself lost, important, found, small, and going on from there in a spin, but now it was the dishes that made her feel eager, indebted, and a part of some great wheel.

Why some of the best things in the world, she thought, happen like housework, in circles. Birth and death, for example, not that you could call that best. Funny, but it wasn't anything, really, just everything, whole kit and caboodle, one of the few facts (people get born and they die) that was neither good nor bad, though secretly she was convinced: birth was good, death was bad; and she was here and so she swept, on the fifth day, the floor for the fifth time that week. (They hated sugar under their shoes and he was always leaving it there.) And so she swept (the broom was new and bristly) as she said her secret prayer for her father never to die.

Her actions, she felt for a moment, were like those of God. He repeated himself, too, heaping snow and flowers, tornados and children down onto earth, taking them away, then heaping it all back down again. God was like one huge housewife, she thought, then blessed herself for the blasphemy. And please, she whispered into the towels, let it be a son.

Anyways, she thought, God was one huge housewife and everything big was patterned after something small, even though they told her it was the other way around. She stuffed the towels into the washer, considering the idea. Neighborhood pride, for example. Why, all he had to do was put in one new step, let alone the whole set that he did, and there were new steps all the way down the block, a whole way of life born from a single pair of steps. Enough good alleys like this and you'd have a city. I bring you, she said, this handkerchief, this man; this birdsong, symphony; this washed-down wall, this whole shebang. She was brimful with the idea of babies. This woman, she thought, and stopped.

This was silliness and, skittery, she said, liking the word better than what it meant. The insides of the washing machine twisted back and forth like the shoulders of someone at the scene of an accident. Her daughter made a sound, and suddenly she remembered the head of that lovely African insect she saw in *Life* last night. It resembled the monkey, and the monkey, man; though little girls, she thought, wiping her daughter's chin, resembled nothing and nobody but maybe other women. Your Mummy's a real rumdum, a real odd bird, she said to her girl, making her laugh.

She was afraid to be such an odd brown bird. This was how she thought of herself when she thought too much. When she was in company, some party he was always dragging her to and then he never wanted to leave, she sat in a corner, seeking out other people (usually other women, and only with her eyes; she didn't want to start up anything like a conversation) who could possibly be odd brown birds. Actually, it wasn't odd at all. Brown birds are very common, she thought, except when you felt like one.

Just last night her husband screamed that there was something wrong with her. She felt (whenever he swore like that) picked up and thrown into herself. It just took a while to get back out again, that's all. Anyways, tip tip, she said to her girl, taking her hand and climbing from the bottoms of the house (that's what her daughter called it, the bottoms), and thinking there was probably some truth to what he said because she did think too much.

She knew she thought too much when she found herself disagreeing with the Bible. Suddenly, at the top of the cellar stairs, she believed in evolution and hoped no one would ever find out. Who was she to disagree? Well, she must be somebody (she laughed and snapped the cellar light) because she did disagree, even with Darwin just a little, even if it was as a little joke. Man, she agreed, descended from the monkey—already her son, not yet born or of any shape much beyond light inside her, scrambled like one and tasted sweet as mud, while her daughter, born, sat there, like an unborn, like a piece of silk—and women (she went on) descended from space itself (outer space), resembling more a swirl of air than anything with a nose on it.

She meant no disrespect. Women were strangers, unfamiliar in their babushkas, their getups, odd and poking in their heads with apology, waiting on their pins and needles to say hello. They apologized for a lack of salt in things they brought, for unrisen cakes, the rain, a husband's lack of social grace. They apologized for being happy (they were never happy, just a little flushed), sad (they were never sad, only slightly under the weather or a little light-headed), or there at all. Champing at the bit, skirting the furniture, or wringing their hands in front of movie houses, they waited to be invited in and seated. Even in their own houses they were visitors, choosing wooden chairs. And when something buzzed, thudded, was still, they sprang into place, which was nowhere. Wherever they were, it was only temporary (they sat on window ledges; they stood on ladders). And finally, they weren't even sure about being pedestrians in public spaces. She watched from windows their feet brimming over curbs or onto them (they raced on their toes), letting automobiles or businessmen pass. They looked funny through the glass, distorted somehow (and pity-full, she said), like large girls.

Men were such a relief. And she was here, surefooted, taking care of one. She enjoyed it. Being inside the house was a comfort. She felt sorry he couldn't get to be a woman, too, sometimes. Large spaces made her anxious lately, especially when she thought of how she used to cross them, on horseback no less, at a gallop. Even now it made her giddy. Silenced at the moment of the jump, she soared (or rather the old moment did) inside her body, and from this great height she looked down on it (her body)), a stranger with whom she no longer liked to dance. Lately she never got far into conversation or Lake Erie, except a toe. The shell was water enough for her and she'd let him do the talking. She rocked her girl.

He was on this talking jag. All a lot of me me me or about people's rumps; everything flowered with parts of the body. You may as well listen to nothing as to that. He was drinking too much, flirting with anything in a skirt, and what was

worse, he spit on people's porches. (Like some large space
that would outlive her, he was getting out of hand; then he
bought her flowers.) It was just another of his many jokes as
they stood there marooned on the porch. Thank God, the
nice people (relatives) hadn't answered the door yet. Giving
him one of her famous looks (at his feet), she bent down
and with her new white handkerchief (the one with her initial stitched on it; she loved her own name) wiped at the
bleached porch boards, and with the opening door, rose up
and smiled.

Housework, she thought, was an act of forgiveness for what
you read in the newspapers. (He no longer minded that she
read it; he was always off somewhere she didn't name.) By
having supper always on time, whether he showed up or not,
she felt she forgave some great evil, or death itself, by the
fact she went on with it.

The girl in her lap was laughing now and talking of ponies,
ready to play alone again. She always invited her everywhere
through the house, if she cared to come, though lately she
did not. The child shook her head to the outstretched hand,
preferring not to go into the kitchen (she dropped greens
into water, flooded a pot in a rush of metal at the sink), into
the cellar (she swept with a sawed-off broom the last of black
water into the bubbling holes of the floor drain), into the
upstairs room (she set out his evening clothes; he appreci-
ated it). The girl was forever plopping herself down and having to jump back up again this time of day, late late afternoon
(her mother tempted her along with songs) until she gave it
up and sat, smack down on the floor, in the middle of the
hallway. Little white ponies, baby ones, she said to her girl,
and racing by, tickled her on the stomach with her mouth,
then was off again on her toes in the staccato of last-minute
tasks.

What was mean or ugly was not going to stop her, she
swore it, from finding something to look forward to. Her son
was born. She could hardly bear to look at him she loved
him so much. Real corn, she thought, but that's the way I am.

She felt accomplished as she climbed down the cellar stairs with her son in a basket. It was 1949.

She felt so clear and sad about the world when she did laundry. She liked this feeling of melancholy. It made her feel like she was telling the truth. It made her feel large, and above her head (she saw it), her soul seemed to drift like a paper boat out the cellar window into the gray sea of all Pittsburgh.

Cellar light was like a trapped thing and the same in every house. She studied it on walks. Windows half above, half below ground interested her, and the tops of ladies' heads bobbing in an element like water at twilight. It was always twilight in cellars, even in summer, even at noon. Down there the day was always ending like someone good who was dying. It made her want to stop and talk on her walks to the store. She imagined herself kneeling at cellar windows, Hey, and tapping on the glass, Hello, all the way down the block. The ladies would be shocked. What a novelty. Seeing someone there full in the face. Not the usual detachments: sawed-off ankles and shoes, the eerie crawl of living hoses and grass overhead, all things plain, misunderstood into wonderment or fear, or found there as they truly were, a wonderment, a fear: the earth was there, it was watered, it was soft, though sliced, suspended over your head, a lid; the living ones walked there in their shoes, their feet ran to meet each other. But here, a sudden human face, flesh, eyes. From sheer surprise, the ladies' heads would rise like balloons into daylight, followed shortly after by their bodies, one by one, ascending into Wilkensburg (their skin and dresses would be damp, smelling of soap, storage and earth, the twilight smell of warm leftover water, of green things kept out of light, also the sweetness of their tied-back hair) and, bursting into view, bumping into one another, all twenty-three of them at once, they would chat, the women of Franklin Way, East Side of Pittsburgh.

Dazzling, she thought. And in a rare backward look: I would have been a poet were it not for Sister What-was-her-name. She kissed six of her son's ten perfect fingers in time to the beat of Sister What-was-her-name, six kisses springing from the invisible rhythms of her invisible thought. She should have been a poet, she thought, because she felt aware of things that other people forgot. Not many took pride in what they did. But what she did made her sing, high and slow, this melancholy (as long as it didn't go on about itself more than it had to; she hated anybody brooding) made her feel like she loved her own heart. Always she had this slightest inkling she was somebody.

She held his head for hours and listened. He was so easily upset. Last night President Truman had finally told her that the Russians had set off an atomic explosion and she wished he wouldn't find out. And not about this morning sickness either. He was still upset about that Alger Hiss and his communist spy ring, so they said. Gospel truth, sons a bitches, he said, we'll be on their plates in the end. He sat on the sofa, his legs crossed, flipping his ankle. Helen Keller was on the radio last night, she said, ironing. Helen Keller listens to the radio, donya know. So how does she do it? Well, it seems she can just feel it. Sound has vibrations, you know, and all she has to do is touch the radio and there it is, the song. He nodded—let her believe what she needs to—and slept.

It would be such a joy, she thought, gliding the iron across the deep green of his workshirt, to see Helen Keller actually listening to music. A true and happy Christian, Helen sways lightly by the radio. It was an act of grace to find something lovely. Helen waves a hand to the rhythms of Tuxedo Junction, and with the other, listens. In Helen's house, everything has to be just so, they said, otherwise, walking across the room would be a terrible danger, from the stairs to her study, a terrible risk. It's like you're in the right church, but which pew do you go into? Was it like stepping through her own mind? she wondered. "Miss Keller rises early and answers all her own letters." The announcer's voice sounded almost merry.

No one was ungrateful for Helen's sorrow. Everyone seemed to believe in it so, as if Jesus himself lay across her eyes and ears. After all, exactly who would Helen be without her sorrow? To what do you attribute the reasons for your success? asked no one. Our little agonies, your gifts, she answered the same no one and stared at his body, slumped and snoring.

Any day now she would have to tell him about the morning sickness. She was pregnant with their third child. He was still in the middle of his fuss about the boy, and she couldn't scrape up the nerve, he'd lose his head. The doctor told her she was in no condition to have two children in two years, what with the miscarriages she had had so far. Her head reeled but the start of the child pulled her to earth with its own slight gravity. She had told her sister months ago. You're thin as a rail, sick as a dog, her sister said, and hit the roof. We will all come out of this better people, she thought; it was a sin to be unhappy.

It was that old public high school feeling. It was a standing joke there—Doncha get it, she's Catholic—and the iron shimmied in small tight strokes on the collar of his Richmond Brothers shirt. She stood off in the distance again; it was 1941 in the public schoolyard by a wire fence. She shuffled her feet, burrowing into the dirt her own slight place. She watched the others run shouting across the yard, their sound lost now, but their bodies still twisting with laughter eight years later, as if poked with invisible sticks. She stared at the crowd of young men and women. They could all be sent off to war or marriage, packed into houses or trenches, with bad grammar and (she gave them the benefit of the doubt) the tenderness of their pincushion hearts. She wished they would all stop having such a good time. It was 1941 by a wire fence in America and she wanted a cookie and rubbed her eye. You're nothing, she thought, without your sorrow. But still, it was a sin to be unhappy. For lack of money she had to be sent here—and there went peace and quiet, the convent, the singing lessons. (Not that she ever wanted to be a nun, she didn't—she loved horses, children, tennis, men.) That was the only thing she ever pleaded for, those singing lessons, and now, without them, she saw all the little 0 mouths of the people, empty and soundless, and his, opening and closing.

Without your little sorrows, she knew it, you saw nothing beyond your own nose. She made an 0 in the dirt with the tip of her black shoe. She looked at it and it made her like everyone a little more.

Housework had a rhythm like prayer. During a Hail Mary, God help him, the iron wobbled over the difficult cloth of his work pants, burnishing and polishing at the slightest touch. He hated that. God help him to be happy and nice, she said. Her stomach felt wooden but it made her real. Her legs felt flimsy, as if they were scribbled there in chalk beneath her, somewhere over the flowered carpet. Imagine, she thought, something nice.

Imagine a tree in full blossom, she thought, a sunrise, a saint at your front door, begonias or the snow on the sill outside your window—and you refused to look. You missed out on something brief that would boost you and your husband and your children up forever. The sunrise, to her way of thinking, was a saint. She would have made a good pagan. There would be so many things to adore. I should have been a pagan, she said to herself, a few years later, and began a rosary then for Senator McCarthy to remain silent, to please shut his trap, as she caught her hand in the wringer and screamed.

Contributors

Kim Addonizio has received fellowships from Yaddo, the Djerassi Foundation, and the NEA. Her recently completed manuscript of poems will be published in 1992 by BOA Editions. She is a widely published poet and a staunch ex-Catholic.

Carolyn Banks has published numerous short stories and essays in publications as diverse as *Family, Redbook, The Washington Post*, and *Penthouse* Forum. She is the author of four suspense novels and is currently at work on a collection of short fiction.

Tracey Bolin grew up in Ohio and Virginia and now lives in Los Angeles, where she teaches English at Crossroads School. Her poems have appeared in various British and American journals, books, and magazines.

Maureen Brady is the author of *Give Me Your Good Ear, Folly* and *The Question She Put to Herself.* Her book *Daybreak: Daily Meditations for Women Survivors of Sexual Abuse* was published by Hazeldine/Harper in 1991. She teaches writing workshops and is completing a novel, *Rocking Bone Hollow.*

Cathleen Calbert was raised in Southern California and is currently Assistant Professor at Rhode Island College. Her poems have appeared in *The New Republic, Poetry Northwest*, and *Shenandoah*, among other publications. She was a 1991 winner in Discovery, *The Nation*'s poetry competition.

Ana Castillo is the author of four books of poetry; the most recent is *My Father Was a Toltec* (West End Press, 1988). She won a Women of Words Award in 1988 and has received grants from the NEA and the California Arts Council. Her novel *The Mixquiahuala Letters* won an American Book Awards prize.

Lin Florinda Colavin was born and raised in Los Angeles in an Italian-American Catholic family. Since then she has fled both Los Angeles and the Church, and now lives along the Central Coast of California, where she is raising two children, working as a marriage and family counselor, and writing. Her work has appeared in *Touching Fire: Erotic Writings by Women* and *Ariadne's Thread*.

Kathleen de Azevedo grew up in small-town California as a half-Brazilian, full-blooded Catholic. Her confirmation name was Mary Magdalene. Her work has appeared in *Sojourner, Other Voices, A Fine Madness*, and *Dreams in a Minor Key*, an anthology of women's magic realism published by The Crossing Press.

Louise Erdrich, of Chippewa and German descent, is the author of the novels *Love Medicine, The Beet Queen*, and *Tracks*. Her two collections of poetry are *Jacknife* and *Baptism of Desire*. She lives in New Hampshire with her husband, Michael Dorris, and their six children.

Linda Nemec Foster is the author of *A History of the Body*, a collection of prose poems published by Coffee House Press. Her poems have been published in *Nimrod, Mid-American*

Review, Negative Capability, and *Poetry Now*. She lives in Grand Rapids, Michigan.

Joyce Goldenstern has been an active member of the Feminist Writers Guild in Chicago since 1982. Her work has been published in many literary journals, including *Other Voices, Whetstone*, and *Exquisite Corpse*. Her novella *Keeping Promise* was published by Quarterly West in June of 1991.

Mary Gordon is the author of several novels, including *Final Payments* and *The Other Side*. Her most recent book is *Good Boys and Dead Girls and Other Essays*. She is a Professor of English at Barnard College.

Kathleen L. Guillaume was born in Newfoundland in 1943, carrying her grandmother's uncritical love as well as her name, Louise, into this world. Influenced by a place known as the "Land of Cain," she considers herself a "Newf" at heart in spite of a California heritage.

Barbara Hoffman is a divorced Catholic girl, with three grown children, who teaches high school English. Her articles have appeared in *The New York Times* and *Newsday*, and her poetry has been widely published.

Kay Hogan is working on a full-length play and teaches creative writing in Saratoga Springs, New York. Her genre is the Irish Short Story and her work has appeared in *Descant* and the *Anthology of North Country Writers*. She lives with her husband and five children.

Jane Kremsreiter attended Catholic school in Chicago, where she grew up. She is a writer and graphic designer now living in Milwaukee. Her fiction has appeared in several literary magazines.

Dorianne Laux is the author of *Awake* (BOA Editions). She is a contributing editor for *Poetry Flash* and co-editor of

Americas Review. A 1990 NEA recipient and Bread Loaf Fellow, she has work forthcoming in the *New England Review.*

Audre Lorde is the daughter of Grenadian immigrants. Her writings include *The Cancer Journals*; a book of poetry, *Our Dead Behind Us*; two collections of essays, *A Burst of Light* and *Sister Outsider*; and the novel *Zami: A New Spelling of My Name.*

Melissa Anderson Lowry is a writer and technical editor whose work has appeared in the book *Northwest Originals: Oregon Women and Their Art.* A former magazine editor and television producer, she lives in Portland and is currently at work on a novel, *The Angels' Share.*

Gigi Marino is a poet and writer. She has also been a housekeeper, a shelf stocker, a Tupperware Lady, and a seaman. She currently teaches nonfiction writing at Penn State and at Rockview State Prison, and is working on a collection of autobiographical essays.

Mary McCarthy was awarded the National Medal for Literature. Her books include *Memories of a Catholic Girlhood, The Group,* and *How I Grew.* She died in 1989.

Kristina McGrath recently moved from San Francisco to Kentucky. Her fiction and poetry has appeared in *The American Voice, Harper's,* and *The Iowa Review.* She received a Pushcart Prize in fiction and New York State grants for fiction and poetry.

Joan McMillan grew up in the San Fernando Valley and attended Catholic elementary school, high school, and college. The events described in "Nasturtiums" remained as a particularly difficult silence for many years, until writing and the persistence of memory helped to unfold her process of healing. Her poetry has appeared in *Plainswoman* and *Touching Fire: Erotic Writings by Women.*

Valerie Miner teaches creative writing in the MFA program at Arizona State University in Tempe. Her five novels include *Blood Sisters, All Good Women*, and *Winter's Edge*. She is also the author of *Trespassing and Other Stories* and *Rumors from the Cauldron: Two Decades of Feminist Essays, Reviews and Reportage*.

Dinty W. Moore is the product of twelve years of Catholic education. She is an assistant professor at Pennsylvania State University's Altoona Campus and has published stories in *The Iowa Review, Southern Review*, and *Cimarron Review*.

Marilyn Murphy is an Irish-Italian, middle-aged feminist. She lives with her "particular friend" in a women's community, not unlike a convent, on the beach in Florida. A collection of her essays, *Are You Girls Traveling Alone?*, was published in 1991 by Clothespin Fever Press in Los Angeles.

Sharon Myers is a hysterical mother, a doctoral candidate in language education at Florida State University, a journalist, a court interpreter (Spanish-English), a teacher of English to international students, and a lover of swamps.

Nita Penfold is a director of religious education at the Unitarian Universalist Church in Milton, Massachusetts. Her work has appeared in *Cries of the Spirit: A Celebration of Women's Spirituality*, from Beacon Press, and in *Moving Out, Sojourner*, and *Earth's Daughters*.

Kay Marie Porterfield has been a writer ever since she discovered pencil and paper at the age of three. She is the author of four books on addictions and two on domestic violence, including *What's a Nice Girl Like You Doing in a Relationship Like This?*

Francine Prose is the author of several novels, including *Judah the Pious, Household Saints*, and *Bigfoot Dreams*, and a collection of short stories, *Women and Children First*. She lives with her husband and two children in New York.

Trudy Riley lives in Los Angeles. She has been a social worker for thirty years. She began writing five years ago after attending a workshop for women writers. Her work appears in *Women of the 14th Moon: Writings on Menopause* (The Crossing Press, 1991).

Anita Roberts lives in Vancouver and teaches assault prevention programs to children, teenagers, and women internationally. Her life and art are dedicated to the healing and empowerment of women. She has been published in *Other Voices* and *Prism International* and is presently working on a novel.

Pier Roberts has taught English in Madrid, Spain, and Oakland, California. She is working on a collection of related stories that take place in East Los Angeles. The Virgin Mary appears in much of her work.

Gael Roziere is a Rosen Method bodyworker and the author of *Witness to a Landscape* and *Artist's Alphabet*. Family, poetry, and healing are her primary interests. How her childhood Catholicism fits into this she does not quite know.

Jeanne Schinto is editor of *The Literary Dog: Great Contemporary Dog Stories* (Atlantic Monthly Press, 1990). Her first collection of stories, *Shadow Bands*, was published by Ontario Review Press in 1988. Persea Books published her novel *Children of Men* in 1991.

Gretchen Sentry outgrew most of her Catholic tendencies at an early age, except the urge to write and light candles. She has published work in *Coydog Review* and *Women of the 14th Moon: Writings on Menopause* (The Crossing Press, 1991).

Catherine Shaw has published poems in *Kalliope, Poets On*, and *Rhino*, among other literary magazines. She has worked as an editor for major book publishers. "Wild Women of Borneo" draws on her experience at Holy Family School in the Bronx in the early sixties.

Beverly Sheresh was born in Portland, Maine, and attended St. Joseph's for many years. Her work has appeared in *Yankee, Down East*, and *St. Anthony's Messenger*, among other publications. She lives in California with her husband and daughter.

Judith Ortiz Shushan completed five years of doctoral work in Composition at the University of California, San Diego. She teaches English at Cabrillo College in Aptos, California. "V-E Day" is an excerpt from a work in progress, *Beaner Blue*.

Rita Signorelli-Pappas was born in New York in 1945. She received her Master's degree in Italian literature from Rutgers University. She has taught courses in writing and literature at Valparaiso University and Purdue University. Her poems have appeared in *Poetry, Kansas Quarterly*, and *Southern Poetry Review*.

Patti Sirens went through twelve years of Catholic school, played guitar at the folk masses, then joined a New York punk-rock gospel band. She now lives in Santa Cruz, California, where she is a Kabbalist and boogie-boarder. She performs rituals, with her three cats as familiars. Her poetry has been published locally.

Elizabeth Spires is the author of three books of poetry: *Globe* (Wesleyan, 1981), *Swan's Island* (Holt, 1985) and *Annonciade* (Viking-Penguin, 1989). She lives in Baltimore, Maryland, where she is writer-in-residence at Goucher College and an adjunct visiting associate professor in the Writing Seminars at Johns Hopkins.

Maura Stanton teaches at Indiana University. Her novel *Molly Companion* was published by Avon in 1979 and reprinted in Spanish as *Rio Abajo*. She has published a book of stories, *The Country I Come From* (Milkweed Editions, 1988), and three books of poetry.

Alison Stone received degrees in creative writing from Brandeis University and NYU. Her poems have appeared in *Poetry, The Paris Review,* and *Ploughshares,* among other publications. She has exhibited her paintings in New York and Boston and is currently working as an English teacher and a Reiki healer.

Amber Coverdale Sumrall is a lapsed Catholic, wife, and teacher. She is co-editor of *Women of the 14th Moon: Writings on Menopause* (The Crossing Press, 1991), *Touching Fire: Erotic Writings by Women* (Carroll & Graf, 1989), and *Sexual Harassment: Women Speak Out* (The Crossing Press, 1992), and editor of *Lovers* (The Crossing Press, 1992).

Ellen Treen is an ex-wife, ex-mother, ex-smoker, and ex-Catholic (in practice, if not always in habits of the mind). Writing helps in the exorcism of religion, ritual, and patriarchy. Her stories have appeared in *Kalliope, Coydog Review,* and *Women of the 14th Moon: Writings on Menopause* (The Crossing Press, 1991).

Patrice Vecchione is the editor of three books, including *Fault Lines: Children's Earthquake Poetry.* She teaches poetry to children in Monterey Bay Area schools and teaches writing workshops for women. Her work has appeared in many publications, including *Quarry West, Puerto del Sol, Touching Fire: Erotic Writings by Women,* and *Women of the 14th Moon: Writings on Menopause* (The Crossing Press, 1991).

Cheryl Marie Wade is a forty-three-year-old crip who writes, performs, and edits books. Saving graces in her life are her partner of thirteen years, their three cats and German shepherd, a few supremely wonderful friends and relatives, work, and laughter, laughter, and more laughter.

Rita Williams is a freelance writer who has been published in the *LA Weekly* and *Venice Magazine*. Originally from Colorado, she presently lives in the San Fernando Valley and is the cofounder of a women's theater and a children's theater group.

Cecilia Woloch is the Los Angeles Coordinator for California Poets-in-the-Schools and a five-time recipient of artist-in-residence grants from the California Arts Council. Her poems have been published in numerous anthologies and literary magazines, including *Zyzzyva, Poetry/LA*, and *On the Bus*.

Yvonne is a poet, independent filmmaker, and essayist. For thirteen years she was poetry editor for *Ms.* magazine. She has received two NEA awards for her two books *Iwilla/Soil* and *Iwilla/Scourge* (Chameleon Productions, 1986). She believes that Catholic women (whether lapsed or practicing) have a major (but surprisingly submerged) artistic voice within the feminist movement.

Irene Zabytko is a past winner of the PEN Syndicated Fiction Project and the founder and publisher of OdessaPressa in Vermont, which recently produced *Don't Call Me Fluffy: Radical Feline Poetry*, poems written by her cat, Mimi Mimieux.

Permissions